Enter the fascinating world
of the privileged, whose facades conceal
their very private lives.
Until they are exposed by a ruthless woman...
a woman determined to get
what she wants—even if she has to
destroy the reputations of those she loves.

With consummate insight
and shameless candor, Barney Leason,
author of the
international bestseller, *Rodeo Drive*,
weaves yet another shocking,
sensuous tale of money, power and greed
in a glamorous milieu rife with

From the seductive shores
of the Isle of Capri to the hopscotch
bedrooms of Beverly Hills,
London, and New York, Leason lays bare
the lives and the lusts of
the rich and the depraved, their sins
and shame, their secrets and

Also by Barney Leason:

RODEO DRIVE

Scandals

a novel by
BARNEY LEASON

PINNACLE BOOKS NEW YORK

SCANDALS

An original Pinnacle Books edition, published for the first time anywhere.

First printing, October 1981

ISBN: 0-523-41596-6

Cover photo by Cosimo

Location: Palace Hotel
Gown by Ernest Reiko
Fur by the Tepper Collection
Jewels: Grosse Jewels by Christian Dior

Printed in the United States of America

PINNACLE BOOKS, INC.
1430 Broadway
New York, New York 10018

Scandals

One

That face. Sally Jones had her mother's face, those features that looked custom made, as if each of the parts had been individually selected to merge perfectly with the whole: the fine, fragile skin, very light blue eyes, a strong but not overly aggressive chin and, above it all, a thick crop of blonde hair, now in the last stages of a frizzy permanent.

Hamilton had never seen her before. But he recognized her instantly. She stood poised on the step above the Ma Maison dining terrace and coolly surveyed the crowd below. He got up and waved. Sally nodded and slowly moved toward him. For twenty-two, or whatever, he thought, she was certainly not lacking in self-confidence. That was like her mother too. The difference was in Sally's long, slim body. Her breasts, he saw, moved fluidly, free of a bra, under a denim shirt, the latter tucked into a pair of those designer jeans.

"Hi," she said. "How did you know me?"

"Easy," Hamilton said, grinning. "You look just like Virginia."

She seemed not so happy with his answer. "Yes . . . Virginia. I got my phone call too. She and Felix James are due here the end of next week—at last report."

"They're still in New York today, though."

Sally sat down, glancing at her watch. "Yeah. Right about now, in a couple of hours, New York time, they'll be at a cocktail party at Earl Blackwell's."

"Yes," Hamilton said, "for the book tour sendoff. Today New York; tomorrow the world."

Somewhat snippily, she said, "All-conquering authors. But they are hard-working little characters, aren't they?" Barely pausing, she continued, "Look, let's order right away. I'm in a hurry. That guy Jack Logan is a tough boss."

Hamilton chuckled. "I never heard that. He may be other things, but he's supposed to be the easiest guy in Hollywood to work for. What about a drink?"

She eyed him frankly. "Maybe he's extra rough on me. You know he's my former stepfather? Of course you do. But how come I've never met you before?"

"I don't know," he said, trying to slow her down. "When I worked in New York, you were always away at school. And how long have you been out here?"

"Just about a year. She never told me to look you up. Well, that figures. Now that she wants something . . ."

Hamilton was surprised, not shocked. It wasn't a new story, sibling suspicion of mother, mother's accomplishments, mother's exploits.

"Well," he said mildly, "that's not so bad. I'm happy to do whatever I can for Felix and Virginia. They were always extra nice to me."

Sally nodded reluctantly. "I suppose."

Shifting ground like the social quarterback that he wasn't, he asked, "Have you seen the book yet? I just finished reading it."

"I had to buy the goddamn thing," she complained. "Waste of money. Twelve-ninety-five. I should have waited for the paperback."

"Well, I assumed you'd buy it—of all people."

"Very dirty, they say," she rushed ahead. "I looked at it. It's got all the words. Fuck, shit, even the *C* word. I *am* astonished. I know about Virginia, but Felix? He always seemed so straight-laced."

"Exactly," Hamilton said. He leaned back, motioning for their waiter. "I'm going to have another drink

2

before we eat, so you might as well too." He ordered a bullshot. "Breakfast."

"Well, okay. A glass of wine with some ice. I don't drink much. I'm more into dope."

She watched for his reaction.

"Terrific," Hamilton drawled, "nothing like having lunch with a doper."

That set her back a little. Sally pulled a pack of cigarettes out of the little purse she wore on a long chain over her shoulder. Her brand was one of those in green paper, signifying mentholated mountain streams. She tapped out a cigarette and offered him one.

"Gave it up."

"How noble," she muttered. She lit the cigarette, inhaled, and seemed to relax a little. She smiled at him knowingly, bunching her lips, much as Virginia would have done. "My mother told me you're on your way to being the most important documentary filmmaker in the country."

"Virginia said that? Nice of her. But I wouldn't necessarily say it was true."

Sally thought for a moment, then said, "More necessary than the truth is the requirement of truth. . . ."

"Come again?"

"Confucious," she said smugly. "It's a Chinese saying I just made up."

Hamilton shushed a laugh. "That'll come in handy. I'm working on a China project right now—you needn't tell Logan. He might steal the idea."

Sally's eyes widened. "Is it true what they say? That he's the master of the rip-off?"

He did laugh this time. "I've heard it said, yes."

Abruptly, she changed the subject. "How well did you know Virginia in New York? She's a lot older than you are."

He had to be very careful, he warned himself. Surely this young thing couldn't have any inkling that he, Pe-

3

ter Hamilton, had oh-so-briefly, and then in not-infrequent recapitulation, been one of Virginia Preston's lovers.

"Older? I never thought of Virginia as older. I'm thirty-five."

"You don't look it," Sally said quickly. "You could get away with twenty-eight, easy. Hell, Virginia is forty-five if she's a day. Naturally, she wouldn't admit it. She claims she had me when she was seventeen. But that's a total lie."

"Let her lie," he said quietly. "Remember one thing about your mother. She's ageless. She'll be the same when she's sixty-five."

"I suppose." Sally managed to look sullen. "And chasing anything with pants on." Her eyes jerked up, fixing defiantly on him. "Did you recognize yourself in the novel? Everybody says it's a roman à clef that'll never need much deciphering. Joycean they ain't."

"What do you know about Joyce?"

"Jesus," she cried disgustedly, "I did go to school. I'm not such a dumkopf as I might look."

Sternly, Hamilton said, "Listen, my child, I never said you were a dumkopf. I just never expected to have a pretty girl dump Joyce on a table at Ma Maison."

"Well, dear sir of the older generation, that's a *very* male chauvinistic remark," she said stiffly.

Hamilton let himself slide to the side. There was no real good reason to be annoyed with her.

"I apologize. I should not want to be a male chauvinist piggy."

Curtly, she pursued him. "Well, *are* you in the book? I'd like to know so I can keep my eyes peeled."

"No." He said it convincingly. "Why should Virginia put me in her book? I'm sure . . ."

"Sure, *what*? That she's got enough scalps without yours?" Sally smiled doggedly. "You seem moderately interesting. I'm sure *I'd* use you." Her mouth twisted in

4

a half-frown, half-grin. "Well, at least you won't be suing them."

"Suing?" Hamilton laughed. "They're not going to get sued. Virginia has been writing her column for years, and she's never been sued—as far as I know. Virginia knows all the tricks."

"And then some," Sally added drolly.

Hamilton was aware of a soothing smugness. He was tickled by the knowledge—his alone—that he *was* in the book, along with a lot of other people. Little Virginia had used him unmercifully and verbatim. Her memory for words and people and situations was legendary. Virginia might attend the grandest, biggest social function and never take a note. But the next day, it would all be there in her column, *Bites from the Big Apple*, by Eve: the total guest list, an exhaustive examination of the clothes the women had worn, the dinner menu from soup to nuts, scraps of conversation heard across the room, who'd danced with whom and who'd left first and in what state of mind. Virginia possessed a built-in tape recorder not yet conceived by the Japanese, and she never needed fresh batteries. Once, in a sailboat, uncomfortably within binocular range of the Long Island coastline, he'd pleased Virginia by saying she screwed like a Titan—it was in the book. He smiled to himself.

"What makes you think your mother actually lived all that stuff? Virginia has a very vivid imagination, young lady. Sorry, I mean *Sally*."

Nonetheless, she smirked. "I'll be watching for you."

"Watch away," he said carelessly. "Now to business. What is it exactly that we're supposed to do for the famous writing team of Preston and James, for those authors of that madcap sexual tour de force called *Powerhouse*?"

"For one thing, as you very well know, you're elect-

5

ed to throw a small but elegant party for them at your house."

"Yes," he said slowly, "so I believe. And you are going to help me with the guest list, since I don't know anybody."

"Oh, come now," she objected busily, "that can't be true. Jack Logan says you know everybody in show business. We start with Jack's mistress, the great Mona Prissian. Mona, we hear, is going to get the female lead in the movie of *Powerhouse*, presuming Jack goes ahead with the movie."

"Presuming he gets the money together," Hamilton commented dryly.

"Meaning?" Sally asked sharply.

"Meaning nothing," he dodged. "Does it astonish you too that Miss Prissian is slated for number one?"

"Ha! Not very much. Mona, they say, is humping her way to the stars."

"God, how you shock and disillusion me."

"I'm sure. But Mona's problem is time. She's bordering on forty and hasn't really made it yet."

"She'd better carry on humpin' then. Hump around the clock."

"Yes, indeed."

"I get the impression," Hamilton said judiciously, "that you don't like her very much."

"I like Jack. Therefore, I can't like Mona much."

"I know, Sally, little dear, but there's nothing much very new about women like that. They're what you call career oriented."

"Good," she said sardonically. "So very good that you understand the phenomenon. I'm not trying to shock you, by the way, with all this Hollywood-type talk."

Hamilton shook his head grimly and pulled on the bullshot. "I think you are, though. But I'm not shockable. Maybe I am in the short range, but óver the long haul there's no way you could shock me."

"Great."

"Furthermore," he said, "I think you do it for effect. You can't convince me you're as tough as your mouth is."

"Well!" She downed some wine and then pretended to study the menu. Avoiding his eyes, she said, "It may interest you to know that I'm living with a man who's even older than you are. He's a man . . . on the legal staff of Jack's company."

"So?" Why should he care? "So what? I favor young girls living with older men, particularly lawyers. He'll be smart enough not to marry you and ruin your life."

"Christ," Sally said grumpily, "you sound like somebody's father. Besides, he's married already."

"Terrific! That must make you very happy—like running into a cul de sac in the Hollywood Hills."

"Fuck you," she growled. "I'm having a hamburger and a salad."

"Fine," he barked. Christ, he'd had it already with Virginia's darling daughter Sally. Who needed this kind of mental push and shove, particularly on a prematurely hot day in May? "Listen, if I distress you, you don't have to eat anything. As far as I'm concerned, you can *fuck off*. See, I know the words too. I didn't ask you to tell me you were living with some creep. The truth is, I really don't care."

He couldn't have made it any clearer that the only reason he had interrupted his day was because she was Virginia's daughter.

Sally's reaction was immediate and startling. She dissolved. Her eyes filled with tears, and she sighed contritely. "I'm sorry. I'm a pig."

Hamilton frowned. Suddenly, not comfortably, he was angry with himself and sorry for her. It wasn't easy for a girl in Sally's position. Then he remembered

7

that she functioned just like Virginia. Virginia, too, had been ever ready with a tear.

"Forget it," he said. "It's too warm for a scene. Let's be nice to each other. Okay?"

"Okay," she said humbly.

How funny. How strange. How reminiscent. They'd already been up the hill and down the hill again. He felt as though he'd known her longer than twenty minutes. Hamilton watched her as she took a handkerchief out of her pocketbook and shoved her nose into it, then wiped around her eyes. Fortunately, she was not wearing makeup. Virginia's daughter had no need for makeup.

Solemnly, they ordered lunch, another glass of wine for Sally and a bottle of beer for him. In the course of the meal, Hamilton agreed that it was up to him personally to call Mona Prissian and invite her to his house for the party. Logan would escort her, of course, but Sally explained that Mona, being so properly English, would require a formal invitation of her own.

Again, sarcastically, she said, "I think she did her toilet training at Buckingham Palace. You do know how she got her start—she was singing in the *Pirates of Penzance* in London, and one of her tits fell out of her dress. A director from Pinewood Studios saw, and liked."

Hamilton laughed freely this time, genuinely amused. "Jack will come to the party, won't he?" He wanted to be sure of that.

"Why not? There's no hard feelings. Besides, he's buying the book. So he'd better come."

There would be fifty people or so, in all. Sally said Logan Productions would pay for the whole thing. No, no, Hamilton insisted, he'd furnish the booze at least and make sure there were parking attendants because cars were always a problem up in the hills. Logan Productions would assign somebody to the door to keep

8

out the crashers. And what about catering? Easy. Jack had a good deal with the firm that usually did studio functions. Flowers? That would be Sally's job. What they wanted at the party were the most influential movie people, the book critics, social writers, and a smattering of those Angeleno butterflies who crossed the lines between show biz, banking, wealth, and what they called out here Etcetera. No points had to be made regarding the movie sale of *Powerhouse* since Jack already had that in his pocket. But Hamilton was realistic enough to know that one of the purposes of the party would be for Felix, Virginia, and the rest of the intimate entourage to help charm investment money out of the rich and mighty.

"And," Sally added in afterthought, "Felix wants us to be sure to ask his good friend Nora Sacks and husband. She's of the blue blood and blue book, and she's throwing them a dinner party too."

"How jolly," he said. "Yes, Felix would want that. And as for the media? He said they're already booked on the Morris Scarlatti radio show. Local TV?"

"Virginia told *me* that Felix has lined up a couple of morning shows. They're also doing some of those tacky cable talk shows. . . . We don't have to concern ourselves about that."

Hamilton smiled. "Felix is a P.R. mastermind."

Sally nodded. "I could've gone to work for Felix if I'd wanted."

"Social P.R.?" Hamilton made a face, then squelched it. "No, I shouldn't be snotty. Felix is good at what he does."

"I know, but you're right," she agreed. "That's not for me. I can't keep my mouth shut—you may have noticed."

"Yes," he said. "I can just picture you shocking the hell out of Mrs. Worthington and her deb daughter."

Gleefully, Sally hummed the Noel Coward tune:

please, please, Mrs. Worthington, promise not to put your daughter on the stage.

He held up his hand to stop her, leaning foward. "What I want to know is how are Virginia and Felix getting along? Is it romance—finally?"

Sally shook her head. "Hardly. At least I don't think so. That would really be a surprise."

"I guess so."

Sally looked archly at him. "I'm sure there's never been a sex thing between them. Do you think there has? No, not possible. Felix is happily married."

"So far as we know," he pointed out.

"No, no, cynical man," she said breezily. "It's always been a professional friendship, and now it's a money association. Even if the book is a critical bomb, they'll make a ton of money. Everybody wants to know what Virginia *really* thinks and what she's got in her files. And why not. They've worked hard."

"Virginia is a work demon," he concurred, "and so's Felix."

Sally nodded absently, lit another of her cigarettes, paused a second and then, once again, came at him directly. "I know all about your wife getting murdered."

Hamilton retreated. "That was a while ago," he muttered.

"They never caught the guy," she stated.

"Or guys." This was not something he liked to be reminded of. "You know," he said slowly, "it wasn't as if there was anything left between us. We were separated. She'd already moved to Malibu."

"With Jeff Scanlon."

"You've researched this?" he asked harshly. The guy, or guys, had caught Naomi and Scanlon upstairs in the beach house and killed both of them with knives.

"It wasn't pleasant for you."

"Pleasant?" he retorted. "No, it was not pleasant, not at all. . . . And I can tell you it was a damn good thing I had an alibi."

"Did they really think you did it?" Her eyes paced his face, hitting hard. "God!"

The memory made him weary. "Look . . ." He started to tell her to drop it. Tragedy was not fascinating—was she so young that she thought so? Flatly, he went on. "It wouldn't be the first time aggrieved husband goes after errant wife and no-good son of a bitch interloper. I *could* have done it." He stared at her fiercely, making his eyes say that he did have the killer instinct.

"You wouldn't," she exclaimed softly, "couldn't . . ."

"Oh, yeah? How in the hell do *you* know?"

"I know."

"Bullshit," he said roughly.

She didn't flinch. "What about now?"

"What *about* now? I've recovered, if that's what you mean. I'm not hung up or sterile from grief. I survived."

Sally nodded soberly, still searching his eyes for a clue. "I'm glad," she said simply. "She was Naomi, wasn't she? Perfidia Sinclair's daughter? Perfidia used to be one of Virginia's best friends."

"And still is," Hamilton murmured. "That's how I met Naomi in the first place—through Virginia and Felix and the aptly named Perfidia."

"Whom," Sally said quietly, "you don't particularly care for."

He smiled fleetingly. "I feel about Perfidia, my ex-mother-in-law, like you feel about Mona, except in spades."

"Did Perfidia think you did it?"

"Jesus . . ." He chuckled faintly. "I think so. Listen, child, why are you grilling me like this?"

11

Sally shrugged. "I'm . . . I don't know. Fascinated, I guess."

"If you're fascinated, then you've got to read the book. I'm sure the part for Mona Prissian is based on Perfidia Sinclair, her life and times, as they relate to Nathan Sinclair. In the book, he's called Marcel Power, ergo *Powerhouse*, cosmetics empire, and Perfidia is Pauline Power, the third and last Mrs. Marcel Power."

"I get it."

"Yeah, a turgid tale of sex, romance, and decadence in the skyscrapers of New York and aboard luxurious ocean-going yachts."

"Super!"

"Super slush. A not-so-Gothic romance."

Sally giggled. "You're funny. Not so funny as amusing. I'm glad we had lunch. Thanks for your time."

"Time? What's time?"

She laughed and put her hand over his, an impulsive gesture perhaps, but he was startled by her touch. Her hand was warm, yet cool.

"Time," Sally said, "is the face of the clock. It's what's behind the face that ticks."

He glanced at her eyes. They were shining, challenging him. He had to decide about her now. Sally was a flighty and moody creature, but there was something far back in the clear blue eyes, almost hidden, that impressed him greatly—a lucidity that signified deep understanding, but at the same time a determination of purpose.

"Would you mind running that past me again?"

Sally lifted her shoulders and grunted. "Forget it. It's too deep." She lit another cigarette, and he wanted to tell her to cut out the smoking. By now, they were drinking coffee, and Hamilton was toying with the idea of ordering a brandy. But lunchtime brandy was bad for you too. For the second time, she placed her hand

12

on his, now not impulsively. "I should tell you," she murmured, "that you're right about the cul de sac, smart guy. If the truth be known . . . my chum, well, he doesn't spend much time with me, so cul de sac'ed is about right. Maybe I'm lucky."

"You'll live," Hamilton said sympathetically. "Are you . . . in love with this character?"

She didn't reply directly. "Right now, it's kind of painful, maybe embarrassing."

"From close to my seat in senility, I can tell you it'll pass."

"No doubt," Sally said, then smiled forlornly. "I hope I can see you again sometime."

"We're giving a party together—remember?"

"I mean," she mused, fiddling with the top button of her shirt, "sometime. I suppose you don't have a job for me. Are you really going to China?"

Cautiously, he said, "Well . . . we're working on it. What are you doing for Jack?"

She was cautious too. "Go-fer," she said briefly. "I'm supposed to be learning from the ground up."

"Good. Stick with Jack. He's good at what he does. You'll learn a lot."

"Yes, I suppose so. What if I dropped up to see you in the afternoon once in a while?"

He knew what she wanted, needed—talk, discussion, the opportunity to bat her emotions around. He handled the proposition carefully. "Before or after my nap?"

"I'd always call you first." She was very serious.

Hamilton smiled. "You mean in case I had a broad up there with me?"

She frowned. "No, not that. But . . . yes, I suppose you might. I suppose, somebody like you, Mr. Good-Looking, you'd have a lot of them." The frown turned to a scowl. "Bastard!"

13

She made him laugh. "Call me whenever you feel like it, and whoever's there, I'll throw them out."

"Yeah, I'll bet," Sally said, almost morosely. "Look, I'm not kidding around, you know. I don't know what you think of me. Probably that I'm some kind of fucked-up kid. I *am*, a little," she admitted, her eyes intense. "But I think I'm more than that too. Talking to you once in a while might do me some good. And talking to me might do you some good, sailor," she added hopefully.

"Maybe," he said. "For sure, it would confuse my life. . . ."

"Confusion is the first mile in the cross-country race to serenity. . . ."

Thoughtfully, Hamilton stared at her. "That's exactly what I was going to say. I'm not a wise man, you know, and I'm not a child psychologist."

"I know that, for Christ's sake," she said impatiently.

"Okay, okay, I surrender," he said, lifting his hands. "Give me a call, anytime. "We'll have lunch . . . whatever you want."

"Whatever? What do you mean by whatever?" She chuckled happily. "Don't answer that." She hesitated. "You could call me too, you know, if you feel like talking, Pete."

"Don't call me Pete."

"Peter."

"Yes."

Sally. That face. Virginia. Virginia had a lot to answer for.

14

Two

Virginia and Felix were applauded cordially enough when they walked into the miniature ballroom in Earl Blackwell's penthouse apartment. Almost everybody, Felix James noted, clapped his or her hands in peer-group approval, except for his wife, Evelyn, and Wade French, their old-time friend and family attorney.

Virginia had Felix tightly by the arm. Her head, blonde hair unruffled, came scarcely to his shoulder.

"My, my," Virginia murmured, "isn't this wonderful, Felix?" She drew a breath, then whispered, "Why, there's little Evelyn."

Why was it that Virginia always referred to Evelyn as little? Evelyn seemed twice the size of Virginia, who wasn't much more than an inch or two over five feet. Although it was a warm day, Evelyn was wearing her mink stole over a suburban silk print dress. On her head was one of the veiled pillboxes she favored. A small, acid smile scoured Evelyn's pale, powdered face. On that of Wade French, there was a look of more studious concern.

Earl Blackwell, Felix's friend and sometimes collaborator on P.R. projects, crossed the room to take their hands in his. "Congratulations . . . Welcome . . . Bon Voyage," he said in a hushed voice. A waiter passed Virginia and Felix champagne. Earl held his glass to them and said, "Here's to the book!" Then he turned to the two dozen or so who had gathered in the ballroom and said more loudly, "I drink to Virginia Preston and Felix James, my friends, and to their marvelous new book, *Powerhouse*. Everyone," he smiled, "is talking about it."

There was a touch more applause, and Felix understood that they expected him to say something.

"Thank you, thank you all . . ." His voice did not carry.

Virginia's did. Within that compact little body of hers there was a deep and husky voice, almost a mezzo-soprano. Virginia lisped slightly. "Thank you ever so much, dear Earl, and dear, dear friends, for being here. I'm sorry we're running a little late. We were delayed at the studio. But what a beautiful going-away party this is!"

Earlier, their first post-publication talk show had been taped with Dick Cavett.

"How did it go?" Blackwell asked.

"Very well, I think," Felix said.

"We talked about everything *but* the book," Virginia elaborated.

"Oh, the book," Blackwell said nonchalantly. "That's secondary. He had you on because you are who you are."

"Whatever," Virginia said.

Thank God, the publisher had seen to delivering a heap of the books to the Blackwell residence. They were piled, gaudy and mint-new, on a table next to the open terrace door.

"But," Blackwell said, "the book is a great accomplishment. Now, enjoy yourselves. You'll have to sign some of them, of course. Nothing onerous. You're among true friends. When you hit the trail, it'll be a bit different. Tomorrow?"

"We leave for Washington in the morning," Virginia said.

"You'll see." Blackwell smiled. "It can be murder, but Eugenia and I loved it. You see, we have a good

16

crowd here for you. You know most of the faces. . . ."

Now that they were among friends, Virginia removed her white gloves and tucked them in her purse. She was wearing a dark blue linen suit. It enclosed her body neatly and was, amazingly, uncreased, even after the hours in the studio and the rush-hour cab ride. Virginia's hair was smooth, cut to pageboy length, as sleek and sophisticated as the rest of her.

Blackwell moved away, and before they merged with the crowd, Virginia returned to the matter of the interview. "Felix, what do you think about that little son of a bitch asking me if I was still a virgin when I first came to New York? Didn't he know I'd already had a child?"

Felix chuckled benignly. "I suppose not, dear. But you handled it very well." She was not convinced and stood beside him frowning. "Virginia, your image is that of the very proper lady. You handled it well," he repeated.

"By saying I was still chaste when I came to New York?" She smiled coyly. "I still could have been a virgin without being chaste."

Felix clucked again, less comfortably. Sometimes it did not do to take Virginia seriously. He made an inconsequential remark. "That was a long time ago, dear, and don't forget you were from another state."

But Virginia could be unrelenting when she hooked into her particular—or was it peculiar—logic. "You know, Felix, my love, a girl could blow the whole Sigma Theta Pudenda fraternity house and still be a virgin. But nobody could say she was very chaste."

Felix passed the back of his right hand across his forehead, feeling a slick of perspiration. He was aware that Evelyn's eyes were upon them. "Virginia," he murmured, "I'm glad you didn't say that on the show."

17

"Just hypothetically, Felix, just purely hypothetically."

"Virginia, you know I hate it when you talk like that."

"Oh, bother, Felix, there's much worse in the book."

"I know," he said, "and it's beginning to worry me just a little. Maybe I never believed it'd really be published. But there it is." He pointed at the arrangement of books.

Virginia smacked her hands together. "Beautiful!" she cried. "Well, Felix, it's too late now."

Smiling regally, she began the business of mixing. Virginia had an eye, ear, and nose for public relations, even though not she but he, Felix James, was the practitioner of the art. Felix, like Earl Blackwell, had always made his living, and a good one, alongside the media, although neither had ever been of the media. Virginia *was* Queen Media. At the time she had first come to New York, that moment to which Cavett had so slyly referred, she'd been twenty years younger, a dynamic and ambitious reporter fresh from Ohio. Her career had developed rapidly, then flourished, and at this point Virginia was one of the most widely read columnists in the world. Her formal beat was fashion, but by now *she* had defined fashion for herself as lifestyle and the people who created lifestyle. Over the past few years, Virginia had reached for more and more, and today her editors and publishers did not dare deny her free rein. The world, as they said, was her oyster. Virginia did whatever she wanted to do, whatever she thought was worth doing. She was reporter *and* commentator; so being, she was witty and incisive. She was a debunker, yet a conservator of society and social mores. Whatever she wrote, however, Virginia was never vicious. Even her "blind items," those disguised bits of gossip so lethal in the hands of others, were kindly—sharp little pinpricks in the jet-set blimp.

Virginia could be trusted with the worst kind of dirt. In her column, the dirt came out smelling of orange blossoms. Everybody loved her.

Felix followed Virginia for a moment, admiring her, and then turned toward Evelyn and Wade French. Fervently, he hoped Virginia's magic would hold up. For, in his heart, he feared for them. *Powerhouse* was awash with scandals, both current and those old and buried, acrid vignettes gleaned from Virginia's memory bank, those stories she had always chosen before not to use.

It would be all right, Virginia said, it would be fine. Nobody was going to admit to being in the book. To raise any sort of ruckus, legal or otherwise, would be to own up: yes, that's me, disgusting and in obscene costume, but me.

Virginia zeroed in on a West Coast literary critic, in town for some book function or other. Felix heard her say, "I know you! You're Lenny Thoreau. I read absolutely everything you write. Tell me, is it as mellow as ever out on the Coast?"

"Evelyn," Felix said, kissing his wife lightly on the right cheek. "How long have you been here? Sorry I didn't have time to pick you up."

Evelyn's mouth hooked down at the corner. She was not handsome when she frowned. Her eyes were unwavering and hot with imagined insult. "Think nothing of it, Felix. Wade came to my rescue."

Felix shook hands with French, a big man, solid and stolid. He wore his gray pinstriped Brooks Brothers suit as though it was armor. He was about the size of Henry VIII, but his grip was vapid.

"Hello, Felix—our literary giant."

"Not quite," Felix said uneasily.

French's head wobbled, as if he could not quite believe it. "Well, sport," he said, "you've certainly taken my breath away. I never thought I'd live to see you author of a steamy roman à clef." French glanced briefly at Evelyn. "We're all very recognizable, you know."

Felix drew back haughtily. "You? You're not in the book, Wade. Neither is Evelyn."

"Aren't we?" If French had not been Felix's friend, the expression on his face would have been a hostile scowl. "I don't know about me, Felix, but I didn't have any trouble recognizing Nathan Sinclair—or the House of Sinclair, or Perfidia. No trouble at all."

"Not so! It's fiction, Wade. No one should assume otherwise."

Evelyn didn't help. "Of course it's Nathan and Perfidia, Felix. Don't bother to cover up," she said severely.

"Felix," French went on heavily, "everybody remembers you worked for the old man. It's not going to take any expensive detective work to identify that repulsive old cosmetics tycoon. . . . Felix, this does not do good things for my peace of mind." Gloomily, French rubbed his fingers on his champagne glass and stared past Felix at the heap of books by the terrace.

"Maybe I should have let you read the proofs," Felix grunted.

French put up one hand. "No thanks. I'm glad you didn't. I don't want to know. As it is, if it comes to trouble, I'll have to disqualify myself. I couldn't take on a lawsuit against a friend."

"Lawsuit? What the hell are you talking about, Wade?"

"You haven't forgotten we still handle the House of Sinclair, have you? The legal department over there is all a-twitter. They take it for granted you and Virginia have done a deliberate hatchet-job on old Nathan."

Evelyn's face fairly jerked with recrimination. "It's all there, Felix dear, warts and all."

"Don't jump to such conclusions," he said coldly. As

an attorney, Wade, you know everything in life is a composite."

French moved his hands impatiently. His square face was like a rock, founded in the inertia of the courtroom. "Whatever you may say to deny it, old sport, people will assume it's the House of Sinclair—*yes*, warts and all. How can you write a book about an old man who's been married about a dozen times, walks with a limp, and have anybody think it's not about Nathan Sinclair?"

Felix felt like a man about to go over a cliff. "Wade, for God's sake, nobody has even seen Sinclair for the last five years. For all we know, he's dead."

French's heavy eyelids flickered with amusement. "Would that he were, Felix. But he's not. He's still going very strong. I don't see him, but I have the duty now and then to talk to him."

This was something Felix had not known. "You don't see him but you talk to him? How's that?"

French tensed, as if he were being goosed by his ethics. Reluctantly, he growled, "I go up to the apartment sometimes. We talk. *He* bellows. Over an intercom system."

"That's asinine," Felix said bluntly. "You put up with that? You might be talking to anybody. Maybe he *is* dead."

"No," French said grimly. "Nobody sees him, that's all, except for . . . those assistants of his."

Evelyn interrupted. "Don't badger Wade. It's a *very* dirty book, Felix. I've read it."

He tried to laugh, but all he could accomplish was an embarrassed stutter. Sweat trickled down the inside sleeves of his Turnbull & Asser shirt. "You weren't required to read it," he muttered.

"Felix, dearest," Evelyn said distantly, "I had no idea."

21

Lamely, he replied, "The sex scenes are all Virginia's imagination."

Evelyn wasn't smiling at all. "Then Virginia is even more active than I've always suspected. I had *no* idea."

"She has a very wild imagination, Evelyn," he said curtly.

"No doubt. That too." Evelyn glared at him. "My problem is to assure the starchy ladies of Maine that my Felix James is no relation to *that* Felix James who writes dirty books and goes on book tours with sex-bomb Virginia Preston. You are leaving tomorrow, aren't you?" Naturally, she knew that. They'd already talked about it. "Tomorrow," Evelyn announced stiffly, "I'm going home to Maine. You'll find me there—maybe—when you get back. I'm sure," she continued frigidly, "that you and Virginia will have a good time. I hope you'll keep *notes*. You are going to write a sequel, aren't you?"

"Not necessarily." He was aware of muscular contractions in his face and the pit of his stomach. She was being unfair. "Surely this isn't something you're taking *that* seriously. No," he said, realizing they were taking it far too seriously, "I see you are. You won't grant me the right to do something I've always wanted to do."

Felix was not a little boy, but Wade French pressed on, as if he'd been some sort of delinquent. "If you wanted to write a book, sport, why on earth did you have to take on Sinclair? I'm just praying the old man isn't told about it."

"Why," Evelyn supported French icily, "didn't you write a little historical romance? You have all those histories of Maine and the War of 1812."

"Why?" Felix realized he might fly out of control. They thought he was so reserved and malleable. "For God's sake, we have to write about what we know. What we know is about life in the big city. Are you

22

setting yourselves up as censors?" Jesus, he told himself self-righteously, it was not fair. It was not constitutional. And it was not friendly. If they'd had any sort of sense of humor, they'd be having a big laugh. He might have some doubts about *Powerhouse*, but he would defend to the death his right to write it.

"Felix," Evelyn decreed, "if it's your choice and duty to write a dirty book with Virginia Preston, whom I always considered a good friend, and then to go trotting around the country with her, so be it. My choice and duty is to go back to Maine."

"And you're going to meet up with us in Los Angeles," he reminded her.

"No," she said sternly, "that plan is cancelled. I am not going to be part of your smutty caravan. Besides which, dearest, you are, as they say, in the *shits* at the House of Sinclair, and I don't want to be dragged into that."

"I don't believe I'm hearing this," Felix said desperately.

"*Believe*," Evelyn said. "The fact is, you've done a rotten thing to a man who's always considered you his protègé, and friend. It's mightily disloyal, Felix, and I feel sick about it. But then," she sneered, "I suppose you never were that loyal to Nathan Sinclair."

Her accusation caused him physical pain. "You're referring to what?" he asked wanly. "What happened between Nathan and Perfidia? My dear," he sighed, "you were as responsible as I, or more, for getting her involved in Capri. Good God! You're bringing that up? It happened eighteen years ago, Evelyn. Jesus Christ!" he almost bawled, truly angry. "Goddamn it, Evelyn, and you too, Wade, there's plenty of muck to be dragged into the marketplace, if it comes to that!"

French's face became lardy. "Fire with fire? Is that a threat, Felix?"

"Of course not! I don't throw threats around." The fact they misunderstood annoyed him even more.

Evelyn's face was tight with righteousness. "Felix, the fact remains that it was you who let her go ashore that morning."

"And you went with her, Evelyn, for God's sake." He wanted to screech bloody murder. Calming himself, he said, "I'm not discussing this any further. I've said the book is *not* about the House of Sinclair and that's that."

Implacably, French shrugged. "The fact also remains that I'm on a permanent House of Sinclair retainer."

"What's this about 'the fact'?" Felix demanded. "The fact is the book is published and to hell with it. Damn the torpedoes!"

"Very nice, Felix," Evelyn said. "The word is, you've dumped yourself in a big mess."

Numbly Felix shook his head. He didn't know what to say. He knew what Virginia would have done. She would have snarled "So what?" and whirled away. But he was not of the same stuff as Virginia. Often he wished he were. The truth, let alone fact, was that Evelyn had never been supportive. She had done her duty in the ways that had been least trying for her. She had not wanted children—very well. She preferred Maine to New York—also very well. She attended some of his parties but never put herself out. *All right.* If his business had been a success, it was because of Felix, *his* hard work and glad-handing. Evelyn had never supplied more than a frozen presence. She was mocking and often derisive of what he did. She did not like his *sort* of people, and, to her, his career had always been shady and without foundation.

When Felix had been vice-president for public relations at the House of Sinclair, that had been just fine. But when he'd struck out on his own, one might have thought he'd become a race track tout. In Evelyn's view, his career was not a career at all, this talent for putting people together, making friends, and sharing friends with other friends. Evelyn's father had been a country doctor, a man with a "profession," a man like Wade French, who might have become a candidate for a seat in the Cabinet or board of directors or trustees. That was real for Evelyn. Whenever Felix had pointed out to her that public relations was as old as the Bible, she'd always retorted that so was whoring.

Felix removed himself several steps. "Lately," he said bitterly, looking her in the eye, "it's been a great comfort for me to know that you've been sitting happily in Maine, in your little stone house. I think you're right, Evelyn. I think that's where you belong."

Her eyebrows waggled stubbornly. "I'm glad you see it that way!"

Wade French coughed behind his hand. "Look, take it easy, sport. I don't want to see it come to this. Two old friends . . ."

"Sport, my ass," Felix exclaimed softly.

But Evelyn hooted so loudly that, across the room, Virginia turned her head. She understood something dire was happening. She flashed a smile at Felix.

"It's come to *this*, whether you like it or not, Wade. Come on! It's time to leave," Evelyn cried.

Felix laughed mockingly. "I'm sure *sport* will see you home."

French drew himself up angrily. "You're damn right I will, Felix."

"Good," Felix said. He felt like death, but he managed a chuckle. "Wait, don't you want me to autograph your book, darling?"

"No," French spouted.

"Not *you*, darling, I mean Evelyn."

Evelyn's face was quivering with rage. She tried to

25

skewer him with her eyes. "Felix, you can just go to hell!"

Felix grinned as best he could. "I'm on my way, darling."

Three

"Heavens," Virginia said, "does it smell of pot in here? No? But I guess you'd know, Lenny, being from California."

Thoreau chuckled. His lips were moist and red, buried as they were, vaginal-like, Virginia thought, between silky moustache and carefully trimmed beard.

"As a matter of fact," he said, "I've been known . . ."

"Good," Virginia said warmly. "Since you were kind enough to buy me dinner, it's only right that I offer you a small *toke* of appreciation."

Thoreau laughed at her quip and, without being bidden, lowered himself to sit loosely on the edge of her couch, his hands dangling at the sides of his corduroy-clad legs.

"Welcome to my home," Virginia said.

"It's great! I love it!"

The big living room was glass-fronted and faced the river from its situation near the top of the United Nations Plaza apartment building.

Virginia softened the lights and went into the kitchen to fetch the makings—cigarette papers and the remnants of some Tijuana Gold a friend had brought in from Mexico. She kept it in a clean sardine can in the refrigerator.

"Would you care for some wine, Lenny?" she called.

"Oh, yes, please."

"I've got some California stuff, in your honor," she sang out. She hoped it was still okay. Virginia didn't drink much, particularly when she was alone, and she didn't care for men who did either. Excessive alcohol seemed to lower their sexuality. That was the good thing about Felix, not that it mattered when it came to Felix. She washed out two wine glasses and dried them, then put everything on a tray and carried it into the living room.

"If you'll roll the joint, I'll put on some conducive music," Virginia said softly.

"Wonderful."

For a moment, Virginia tried to decide whether she really liked Thoreau all that much, and then what would be the best kind of music. Finally, she chose a tape of soft, old Sinatra and shoved it into the stereo slot, arranging the volume so the sound would be there but very much in the background.

When this was done, she poured two glasses of cold Chablis and sat down on the other side of the coffee table.

"You see," she said, "I never close the drapes. Isn't this a marvelous view of the river?"

On the opposite verge of the black water, yellow tracks of streetlights traced routes through the night, eastward toward the end of Long Island, the end of the world. Below, the river gave back blurred reflections of the city. Virginia had always felt that New York belonged to her, even when she'd just arrived from Ohio, having fled Orville Jones, her first husband.

She watched as Thoreau, his fingers soft and supple, meticulously built the cigarette. Virginia was not much into grass either, but she thought it would please Lenny. He was from California and, judging from what people said, Californians did little else but suck on marijuana cigarettes or snuffle cocaine.

"I always like to come to the Coast," Lenny said, glancing up mischievously.

Virginia tittered. "Lenny, this isn't the Coast. This is Back East. You're from the Coast."

He chuckled and coughed. "I know. But I always like to think of this as the Coast and where I come from Back West."

Well, she told herself, he was a little labored and not very fast with his wits. It took him forever to make the cigarette. Lenny was about forty, she supposed, perhaps only thirty-five, which would be good, maybe even younger, which would be even better. It was difficult to tell about Californians, that other race. The beard was deceptive. Relaxing in her chair, Virginia crossed her legs, then kicked off her shoes and tucked her legs under her. She wondered if the beard concealed a weak chin.

Thoreau murmured, "I know you have to leave early. I shouldn't keep you."

"No, I feel fine. No problem." At least he was considerate.

She was not tired. She was more unsettled and impatient with Felix James than she was weary of the day. They were in trouble, Felix had told her before they'd left Blackwell's. Nathan Sinclair was going to be difficult about the book. But so what, she asked herself now. What was he going to do? Was he going to claim that Marcel Power of *Powerhouse* was indeed Nathan Sinclair of the House of Sinclair? He'd look the fool but, of course, in more than one way, Nathan *was* a fool, and he didn't care who knew it. Virginia had never loved or liked him, even though she did appreciate that Nathan had once been Felix's sponsor and mentor. And what else had Nathan been to Felix? Perhaps there had been something else there, and it was the "something else" that made Felix sweat. Virginia suddenly realized that Felix had perhaps not come completely clean with her while constructing the book. She allowed this speculation, like a watch spring, to unroll in her head. Shreds of fact, linked by tendrils of guesswork—the stuff of gossip.

29

And Evelyn James. Yes, heavens, there had been something of a scene at Blackwell's, cut short by Evelyn's departure with Wade French, that hearty buffalo. Evelyn behaved like a jealous wife, and that was very stupid of her. Because, God knows, Felix and Virginia had never been anything to each other except very good chums. Virginia had known them forever, and Felix, in fact, had been her initial good contact when she'd come to the big city. Was Evelyn such a fool that she thought Virginia would play around with the couple who had afforded her summer solace in Maine, social entree in New York, invitations to weekend junkets to the Hamptons, Florida, and the Bahamas, as well as those sweet trips to Europe? Even, she recalled, thinking how ironic it was, those ten-day cruises in the old days aboard the Sinclair yacht in the Mediterranean? Virginia smiled, remembering. She had been one of the few who'd been able to abide Sinclair for a full ten days—but then, she loved caviar and French wine and butlers and footmen better than anything in the world. Most of Sinclair's other guests tired of his piggish behavior after three days and jumped ship at the first available port. Virginia had put up with the caviar and with Sinclair's pawing, and more. She remembered it frankly, for she was very honest with herself—one night when they'd been anchored that memorable time off Capri and the others had gone ashore, she'd even forced herself to go down on the old goat. The expression "old goat" fitted him perfectly too.

It was in the book, that little incident, and Sinclair would be telling the truth if he swore it was he and not the fictional Marcel Power who couldn't get it up. Ha! Virginia laughed to herself. Let him make the most of it, the old goat.

It was really humorous. Felix, naturally, assumed the incident had been yet another wild figment of her imagination, even though he knew the parts dealing with Perfidia Sinclair—Pauline Power—were based on hard fact. If the truth be known, almost every one of the sex episodes in *Powerhouse* had actually happened, if not to Virginia personally, then surely to one or another of her confidantes. Women were basically so wicked. They loved to tell all, particularly to a person like Virginia, who savored such stories but never passed them along in recognizable form.

Felix was a lump in many ways. So what if Evelyn was angry and ashamed? What about Evelyn anyway? Evelyn had never been one to confide in Virginia, but all the same, Virginia harbored definite suspicions about her. Evelyn and Nathan Sinclair? Virginia was certain there had been something there—she didn't know precisely what—even when Nathan had been married to Perfidia. Felix, of course, was blind to that. Or was he? Perhaps that was what bothered him.

Lenny had finally finished with the cigarette. He licked it shut with the tip of his tongue, put it between his red lips, and lit it. He drew in the heavy smoke and leaned back. "Heavenly," he sighed. "Your turn."

Virginia came forward on her knees beside the coffee table to take the cigarette from his hand. She put it awkwardly in her mouth and tasted. Smoke ballooned in her throat and chest, then swept upward into her sinuses and the frontal area of her head. Almost at once, or so it seemed, the lights and the river sharpened focus. Thoreau's beard began to shimmer. "Beautiful! Now, just a sip of wine."

"And to think," Lenny gurgled, "here I am with Eve."

"That's me," Virginia said faintly. She was a little dizzy, not being accustomed to the stuff.

Lenny chuckled, and his spittle glistened on the beard. During dinner he had been making much of her column, *Bites from the Big Apple*. And why not? Everybody in the world knew Eve was Virginia Preston;

they had to know, and she wouldn't have wanted it any other way. "I haven't read the book yet," Thoreau now confessed, "but I'm looking forward to it. Word gets around the industry. You may have a bestseller on your hands. It's supposed to be the hot book of the year."

Virginia smiled. "In every way."

Lenny grinned like a little boy, lifted his hand to his beard and stroked it. "Still . . . Eve . . . people say you and Felix James do know every story that ever happened here in your Big Apple."

"Yes," Virginia said, "the Big Apple and all the little worms. Should I say that? They've been very kind to me. But it is our business to know, Lenny. I've listened to the stories for twenty years."

Languidly, he nodded. "Since you got here from Ohio," Thoreau acknowledged. "You were married in Ohio, weren't you?" She nodded. "See," he went on, "I know all about you."

"Orville Jones," she giggled. "Can you imagine such a name?"

"Middle west to a fare-thee-well," he said, nodding. He was still nodding with complacent comfort as she moved again to sit on the other side of the coffee table, facing him, and put one hand on his knee. "Another little snort of that, if you please," he said. He took the cigarette and put it to his lips, inhaled, and exhaled luxuriously. "You're a fascinating woman." His words seemed to melt around the edges. "I've heard so much about you."

"Oh?" The remark jolted her benumbed senses. "What is it you've heard?"

"I dunno. I can't remember now. Just that you're one hell of a woman and also a first-class gossip-monger, than which there is, as they say, nothing lower."

He did not mean it as an insult, rather as a compliment. It pleased her in a professional way to be known as a "gossip-monger" for, after all, it was her trade and her craft. "The things people say," she responded. "Don't think I'm bothered by what people say."

"No." About this he was intelligent enough to be emphatic. "I believe, Eve, that you don't give a rat's ass what people say."

Virginia winced slightly but said, "Right on, Lenny! And I'll tell you something else. I've been too kind to all the worms for too long. I've kept their secrets—but I've kept files too."

"And now you're opening them to the unsuspecting world," he helped. "I love it!"

Virginia forgot her doubts about him. He *was* smart. His intuition came at her like a pot-powered juggernaut. He was handsome too, in that crazy California way, sun-soaked and therefore vague. Lenny was clearly a hedonist and slightly ruined. Virginia liked people who were just a little ruined. She thought fleetingly of her second husband Jack Logan. By now, Jack was probably wearing silk shirts open to the navel and gold chains tangled in his black chest hair. And her former lover, Peter Hamilton, another East Coast transplant to the State of Collapse. Hell, and a couple of dozen other boys and young men, their identities by now all run together, whom she'd either ogled or slept with at the Beverly Hills Hotel.

"Lenny," she whispered confidentially, "they're all going to be looking for a place to hide. But *remember*, it's fiction, and not one of them is going to point and scream: 'That's me!' "

Except maybe Nathan Sinclair, that old goat.

Thoreau nodded and took another long drag off the joint, pulling the ash past mid-point. He spoke even more generously than before. "I'm not one who sees anything wrong with the roman à clef as art form, you know. I honor Capote. Somebody has got to chronicle our life and times. History books are not nearly precise enough. You'll never get the feel for a historical period out of a history book. I don't care who writes it." His eyes widened professorially. "Where would we be without Samuel Pepys's record of the Great London Fire? Or De Toqueville? Or . . ."

Virginia rubbed her hand on his knee. "Please, don't mention the name Proust, Lenny. Felix keeps saying Proust. That's *his* rationalization for what we've done. I love Felix, of course, but he's merely a gentleman. Me, on the other hand, Lenny, all I wanted to do was to write a very dirty book with enough signposts in it so people would know that I know and that, as it turns out, they didn't get away with it."

"I love it!"

"Will you be in Los Angeles when we get there?"

"Sure," he said enthusiastically.

"Where do you live?"

"In a run-down apartment house in Venice, on the beach. Nothing like this, Eve."

Virginia exclaimed, "Well, Lenny, of course! This is it! Nothing in the world is better than this. Come on! Let me show you."

Virginia stood up and tugged him off the couch. She led him to the wide window. The lights beneath them glimmered and leaped, peaked and receded in the East River currents and across the river in Brooklyn. Virginia hooked an arm companionably around his waist. Lenny was bigger than she had thought. He was taller than Felix, and there was no pouchy fat under his arms. She hugged him. His body tensed.

"Beautiful, I love it," he muttered. He did not look at her.

Virginia shifted her body so that she was in front of him, but she was short enough that she did not hinder his view. Her head fit snugly under his bearded chin. Virginia pressed her linen skirt against the corduroy of his pants, her silk-covered breasts against his shirt, feeling the hard outlines of a handful of ballpoint pens tucked in the pocket. She lifted her head away and smiled up at him. The invitation was obvious enough for a dazed Californian, and Lenny tipped his face down to kiss her, soft-lipped, on the mouth.

"Eve welcomes you to the Big Apple," Virginia whispered teasingly. "Want a bite?"

Thoreau pressed a quivering chuckle into her cheek. "That's how it all got started, Eve. What's good enough for Adam is good enough for me."

Virginia folded her hands over the small of his back and stroked her belly against his thighs—and the hardening bulge in his corduroys. Thoreau kissed her again, less politely, not attempting to cover his desire with another comment. Virginia ran her hands from his hips to the front and felt his place. Good show, she congratulated herself, he wasn't a fag like so many Californians, at least so you'd notice. She found the zipper tab, pulled it down, and reached inside. "Mr. Thoreau! You're not wearing undies!"

"California beach bums never do," he said modestly, his lips trembling. "Undies can make you sterile."

It gave Virginia a big kick to play around like this, right in front of the picture window with the lights silhouetting her from behind. Some day, a barge or tugboat captain was going to put his telescope on the building and catch her at it. She was enough of an exhibitionist to get a thrill out of the possibility. The risk factor did a better job of heightening her excitement than Tijuana Gold or Russian vodka.

Virginia was too short to go down on her knees on the floor. She kept a little footstool with a petitpoint cover for that purpose, and she knelt on it in front of him. The corduroy pants dropped to his ankles, and he could not move, even if he'd wanted to. The tip of his thing was soft, like his lips, but hard as granite underneath. Virginia stared at it for a moment—these miraculous things always fascinated her; they were all the same, but every one of them was different too. It quivered and jerked when she touched her fingernail to it, and surged as she caressed it with her lips.

Lenny was still gazing, transfixed, at the cityscape. He groaned and muttered, "What about hopping in bed?"

"I thought Californians liked it every which way but in bed," Virginia murmured. "Besides, I don't have a water bed, Lenny."

"Oh," he said vacantly.

The lad's threshold was not far from the surface. He came almost immediately, disappointing her a little, filling her mouth with a creamy, sticky ejaculation much like a House of Sinclair hand lotion in consistency. Virginia indulged herself with hormone intake. She'd always figured it was probably rather good for muscle tone.

"Do I give good head, Mr. California?"

"Yes, yes, wonderful. I love it."

The bare words elicited an urgent request from between her legs. It had not always been that way, no, not always by any means. Again she remembered Sinclair. Had that night off Capri, on the Sinclair yacht, *Moisturizer II*, been the genesis of *Powerhouse*?

Virginia rose from the stool and slipped out of her clothes, tossing them carelessly toward the couch. She presented her body proudly to Thoreau, running her hands across her breasts—small, yes, but firm even in this forty-censored year of her life, down her belly and around to her smooth behind. He could not take his eyes off her. He disengaged himself from his corduroys, undid his wool knit tie, and slipped out of his shirt, spilling ballpoints across the carpet.

"Well?" Virginia demanded another assessment.

Respectfully, Lenny put his warm fingers to her breasts and thighs. Virginia dropped back down on the stool, and he knelt before her, in the posture of traditional adulation.

"You're all woman and two-hundred-percent Eve," he prayed.

Virginia spread her hands gently through his hair and pulled him forward. Thoreau kissed her nipples and lowered his face to her belly. Now she wanted to feel the soft beard on her legs, at her place.

But like Lenny, she could dissemble. "My name is Virginia," she gasped. "When I was in college, they called me Virgin for short—but that didn't last long."

"I love it!" he chortled.

Then Lenny was upon her.

Four

"Virginia is a lovable little vamp," said Jack Logan, who had been her second husband. "She's a shrimp physically, but she's got an ego the size of a boxcar—I suppose one should say the size of a whale."

"Yes," Peter Hamilton agreed, "if you don't want to mix your metaphors."

Logan lifted his feet to the side of his desk. He was wearing dirty tennis shoes, wrinkled khaki slacks, and a safari jacket unbuttoned halfway down his chest. Logan was the very model of a modern motion picture producer.

"You remember, Pete, we were only married about five minutes."

Hamilton did remember. They'd all been in New York in those days and a tightly knit little group: Virginia and Felix and Jack and himself. Logan had been working at Paramount's New York office and, even then, Virginia was near the apex of her career. Felix, from his social-P.R. vantage point, had fed them all information, invited them to his parties, arranged dates and, in general, used them to the hilt for his purposes. Hamilton had come to know the crowd through his job writing television reviews for the same newspaper that was Virginia's New York outlet.

Logan referred now to Hamilton's new life. "Still doing documentaries about disappearing pigmy tribes at the Congo headwaters, Pete?"

He laughed. "Not at this minute, Jack." Why should he let Logan in on his projects? "Working now on the state of marriage in modern America."

"Jesus," Logan sighed cynically, "fucking among the ruins."

They were sitting in Logan's big office at Twentieth Century-Fox. Logan too had progressed from his grimy start in New York. He was now head of his own production company, specializing, as he himself explained it, in trashy TV movies or tacky series based on the cheapest material that came over the transom.

Whimsically, he suggested, "You better talk to Virginia. From what my people tell me, that novel of hers is one long sex adventure."

Hamilton nodded. "Actually, as you know, it's the fictionalized story of Nathan Sinclair, ageless cosmetics czar."

"Yeah, shit." Logan's tanned, round face became creased with a frown that reached to pluck at his widow-peaked black hairline. Logan was a man of middle height, handsome in weary West Coast style, with a body that reflected careful dieting. In full scowl, he looked like an anxious con man. When he smiled, there was about him the air of a clever Jesuit. "But there ain't going to be any trouble about it, is there, Pete? No, nobody is going to make trouble for Virginia. They wouldn't dare." Logan's eyes sharpened shrewdly. "But what about Perfidia Sinclair? Is she still alive? Your former . . ."

"Mother-in-law?" Hamilton completed the equation. "Yes, she's alive. Her husband died last year—you remember Baron Putzi?"

"Sure—that asshole." So nonchalantly did Logan dismiss the deceased Baron Putzi von Thurnsteil, Perfidia's last great love. "Jesus, Pete, time fleets. . . . Virginia. Great, she was. We went wrong when I started traveling so much. I couldn't keep her down on the farm. It hurt, Pete—but I can handle it now. Jesus! Remember that old one-liner?" Logan's eyes crinkled, almost painfully. "If Virginia had as many cocks stick-

40

ing out of her as she's had stuck in her, she'd look like a porcupine."

"Jack, that's awful!"

But it was not far from the truth, and Logan should know, even if he didn't suspect how many—the sheer volume of cocks involved. Logan and Virginia had been married, despite his crack about five minutes, for the best part of two years. Never once, either before or after Logan began "traveling," had Virginia ceased screwing around. Did Logan realize he was possibly the most cockolded man in this century? Then, somewhat guiltily, he wondered if Logan had any idea that one of the cocks belonged to Peter Hamilton. Had that been before, during, or after Virginia's Logan interlude? All three, most likely. Whew! Mentally, he wiped his brow. Thank God he'd had the sense not to follow Jack Logan into Virginia's legalized boudoir. Yes, thank God, although maybe thank you not *quite* so much, God. For it was during this hectic period, six or seven years ago, that he'd met Naomi, madwoman Perfidia Sinclair's daughter by a marriage before the Sinclair debacle.

Hamilton laughed and stood up, shaking himself free of the memories. He stretched and ambled around Logan's executive office. The producer took a long brown cigar out of a leather box at the edge of his desk.

"Do I count more pictures in here, Jack?"

"A few."

Framed eight-by-twelves of Jack Logan in almost every conceivable Hollywood situation and in the company of most of Hollywood's reigning big names covered one wall of the office. If Jack survived another five years or so, Hamilton thought, the ceiling, too, would be covered with the black-framed memorabilia.

"Speaking of Virginia . . ."

"Which we were," Hamilton put in.

"Yes," Logan drawled. "One forgives Virginia most

anything, doesn't one? Did you ever consider that she was a verifiable nymphomaniac?"

"Jack—I don't know anything about that." With something of a shock, Hamilton realized Logan was still half in love with her. "What I *have* been wondering about," he added, "is why they've written the book, spilled all the beans."

Logan shifted his feet and blew a cirrus of smoke toward Hamilton. "Good question. I wonder why too. I also wonder if I'm in there."

Hamilton raised his eyebrows. "You haven't read it yet? Sally said you were buying the property."

Logan shook his head negligently and grunted, "I got somebody reading it for me. I don't have time to read all the shit that comes in here."

"But Virginia's book? I can't believe that, Jack."

"You better believe it, Pete. I don't make any distinctions. Shit is shit."

"Jack," Hamilton protested. "I read it, and it's not shit. It's not a bad book at all, and the guessing game is good. I do think it should be fireproofed and kept away from kids and old ladies. But it's not bad, considering the current popular taste."

Loftily, Logan said, "I suppose you're referring to its *genre*? Bullshit. I read biographies in my spare time. I want to start doing some serious drama, like all that Masterpiece Theatre crap."

Hamilton nodded and smiled to himself. Logan was one of a kind. "Let me know when you do," he said. "I wouldn't mind a crack at that myself."

Logan frowned. "From documentaries to serious drama? I don't know, Pete."

"Jack, you'll be going from garbage to the classics. If you can make the change, so can I."

Logan grinned waggishly, waving his cigar. "Don't call us, Pete. We'll call you."

"Turd," Hamilton said.

Logan continued to grin insolently. "You know, there could be a very important meeting here today."

"What might that be? Is Shakespeare coming in with a treatment?"

"No, the meeting of my foot with your ass," Logan guffawed. Then his eyes turned inward. "What the hell do you mean by making a play for my stepdaughter?"

"Former stepdaughter," Hamilton corrected him.

"No. Still stepdaughter. Just because Virginia and I called it finito doesn't mean I unload Sally too. I happen to think a lot of Sally. . . . Unfortunately, she thinks a lot of you," Logan sneered, "and how do I know you're not really a murderer?"

"Jack, go . . ." He stopped. They'd been over this ground before, but Logan seemed to take some particular joy in believing, or pretending to believe, that Hamilton might be an undetected Jack the Ripper. Over the past year, Logan had tried more than once to talk him into writing the story of Naomi's *coitus interruptus* by reason of sudden death. Logan was intrigued by the knives and the blood and, naturally, the dark presence of Perfidia Sinclair von Thurnsteil in the background. He maintained that Perfidia had to be some sort of sorceress. "Jack," Hamilton said finally, very seriously, "goddamn you, you don't know that I'm not a murderer, and if you don't stop saying that, I might take care of you too."

Logan wavered. "Sorry. I guess it's a bad joke, Pete."

Hamilton shrugged and turned to the pictures again, deliberately moving to the far end of the office. Over his shoulder, he said, "Sally and I are having lunch today. We're finalizing arrangements for the party I've volunteered to give for your ex-wife and Felix. I trust you *are* coming."

"You think I might be embarrassed?"

"No. I can't imagine Jack Logan being embarrassed

by anything. You *are* bringing the renowned Mona Prissian?"

"Jesus Christ," Logan exclaimed, "didn't you call her yet? She'll bust my balls if you don't call her."

Sardonically, Hamilton said, "I find it hard to imagine Jack Logan having his balls busted."

Logan looked gloomy. "Oh yeah? Mona is just that, buddy, a ball buster." He muttered to himself and looked under his desk. "Normally, that's where my dog sleeps. His name is Duke and he's a hairless Chinese schnauser. . . ."

"No!"

"Yes, Pete. I bought him to protect me from Mona," Logan said. "The son of a bitch is at the vet. I think she bit *him*. You ask why Jack Logan puts up with it?"

"I didn't ask—but tell me."

"She wants me," Logan said expansively. "More than wants. She is bugging me to marry her. I might have to do it just to get rid of her."

"That's a little . . . dense, Jack."

"Well, you might want to use the phenomenon for your docu-drama. Once I married her, then I'd be free to go my own way. Do you get it?" Logan pouted. Again, he flicked ash on the carpet. "Never mind. Mona's going to play Perfidia in *Powerhouse*. Yes, your ex-mother-in-law. No questions about it. She's already mangled my balls over it." Another expression took possession of his mobile face, a monkish slyness. "You know, Pete, it's not such a bad story, taking apart a guy like Sinclair—I mean Marcel Power. Cosmetics is one of the country's biggest industries. In the mind of middle America, it's more important than aerospace or computers. Beauty! Shit!"

"Face lifts, yes, body contouring," Hamilton fed him. "I met a plastic surgeon who's a body-sculptor. . . ."

"Yeah," Logan laughed. "Tit tightening. Pussy

44

reconstruction. Mona had that done—for me, she said. They even do toes nowadays."

"Not for us, though."

"No, we're too realistic about ourselves, aren't we?" Logan lifted his chin and patted it with the back of his hand.

"I don't know, Jack. I've been a little worried about the bags under my eyes."

"C'mon, Pete, you're too young for that," Logan jeered. "What are you now? Thirty-five? I'm five years older than you."

"You're ten years older than me, Jack."

"Fuck I am!" Logan ran his fingertips across his fleshy cheekbones and felt his nose. "How long's it been since you've seen Virginia?"

Christ, he thought, Logan could not keep off the subject. "About two years, I guess. I saw her in New York."

"Shit, I haven't seen her since we said good-bye," Logan said morosely. "I wonder how she looks."

"Marvelous, I'm sure. Virginia never changes."

"Yeah—ain't that something?"

"Sally looks just like her," Hamilton observed, curious for Logan's reaction.

"Tell me," Logan groaned. "Every time I look at Sally, I see that mother of hers. Except, of course, Sally is giant sized." Logan sighed and tried to blow a smoke ring. "Remember the time she went down to Norfolk to do that TV special about women in the navy? They say she screwed the admiral on his own poopdeck."

Hamilton shook his head tolerantly. "I don't believe that one, Jack, and you don't either. You could have used it in the divorce."

"Buddy-boy! Nothing came up in that divorce. We agreed. There are. certain things one didn't bring up." He halted abruptly. "I had to give her a little money,

45

that's all. I still have to give her a little money every year, believe it or not. An allowance, we call it. But if we go ahead and do buy this property, that's over."

"What? Tell me—has Virginia got something on you? Is that why you're still paying off a woman who probably makes more money than you do?"

"Naw." For a second, the hard black eyes became anxious. "It's Hollywood. The ways of Hollywood are ever mysterious."

"I wouldn't have thought any judge would give Virginia alimony," Hamilton said.

"Alimony, smalimony," Logan said irritably. "Forget it." He put his feet down on the floor. "Say, do you think Virginia and old Felix . . ."

Hamilton laughed. "No, Jack, I don't. Felix would be too scared, and that wife of his would never let him get away with it."

"Yeah," Logan agreed. "I always liked Felix, but essentially he's a very boring son of a bitch. I can't see how Virginia and he got together."

"For the book."

"Yes, the book. Imagine Felix James writing a filthy book." He contemplated his cigar for a moment. "What about you, Pete?"

Hamilton was startled. "What about me, what?"

"Have you got the hots for Sally?"

"Me? Of course not. I haven't even thought about her that way. We're party planners. And she wants to talk—she's trying to slide out of a love affair."

"What!" Logan exclaimed. "Shit! Who with?"

"I don't know who with," Hamilton lied. He was not going to tell Logan that Sally was entangled with one of his own men.

"Is she . . . very unhappy?"

"Right now, I'd say she ain't terrifically happy."

Logan stared at cigar ash. "I suppose I should bust his ass, whoever he is."

46

"You're kind of possessive, aren't you, Jack?" It occured to Hamilton that this would not be the first time a stepfather had become unusually attached to a stepdaughter, particularly one who looked and acted so much like her mother.

"You're goddamn right I'm possessive, and you better remember that, buddy." Logan's eyes narrowed, and he laughed with difficulty. "Listen, don't get any idea *I've* got designs on the kid. Right now, I've got all I can do to hang on Mona Prissian's tail."

"She, who will play Mrs. Sinclair number three."

"Correct," Logan said, "and the sexiest of Sinclair's eighteen wives and girlfriends. Also the most rotten, right? Funny about Sinclair though, Pete. You know, he's turned into the Howard Hughes of the perfume industry. Surrounds himself, à la Hughes, with protectors—except in Sinclair's case, they're some kind of religious fanatics with shaved heads and piss-yellow robes. Nobody gets past them to the master." Logan winked. "There's talk Sinclair is founding a new religion based on celibacy and Grape Nuts."

Logan knew all this? "You *have* read the book, Jack."

"Shit, a lot of that's in the book all right, but, frankly, we've also been doing a little investigating. All Sinclair's bolts have come loose."

"*Are* you in it?"

Logan merely frowned. "I didn't finish telling you about my dog. He's hairless, and I'm going to have him tattooed with my racing stripes."

"I didn't know you owned a horse, Jack."

"I may buy one."

"Jack, *are* you in the book?"

Logan's brown face lengthened. "Naw. The little shit! She didn't even think enough of me to put me in the goddamn book."

Five

Sally slammed her cranky little Fiat into low gear and entered the garage under her apartment building. Peter Hamilton: she repeated the name to herself. Peter Hamilton, neutral observer. They'd gone to lunch at the Bistro Garden this time and tarried so long that she didn't bother to go back to work. Jack would be looking for her, and he would be furious. Let him, she thought nonchalantly. Let him fire her if he wanted to.

Sally parked the car, turned off the motor, and took the key out of the ignition. She sat there for a moment, brooding. It was not anything she could establish as fact, but she suspected very strongly that Hamilton had been one of her mother's lovers. When they'd come to the point, again, of discussing Virginia, something opaque had fallen over his eyes. She hadn't wanted to ask him point blank if it was true. As much as she wanted to know, she did not want to know the truth. And Hamilton would have been a very bad liar.

Sally scratched her knee and then her thigh under her tight-fitting jeans. Glancing up at the rearview mirror, she examined her reflection. A mess. No, not exactly a mess, but she was not the manicured daughter of a perfect mother. Her hair was blown wild by the wind, and her lipstick was smudged. Sally looked herself in the eye. Yes, a truth: she did like Peter Hamilton, she liked him very much, more than was comfortable, since his attitude toward her was exceedingly cautious. He'd kept his eye on the cleft in her shirt, and she knew that when she slid out of her chair

49

to go to the ladies room, he'd been watching her like a hawk.

When they had parted, he had kissed her, yes, chastely, on the cheek. Hamilton was so reserved, almost enigmatic, she told herself, to use a term so popular in college English composition class. He thought half the time that she was an idiot. Whenever she popped one of her epigrams or made-up aphorisms, he came close to falling out of his seat.

Sally was not an idiot, and she was very sure of that. She had graduated *magna cum everything*, although she hadn't dared tell him so. It might have been too much. Maybe not. He was lively and very brilliant. His work was fascinating, and she liked the look of him, too—sandy-haired with rueful greenish eyes on the verge of a twinkle, and mouth curled to laugh. She wondered why they had never called him Sandy. He was a Scotsman there somewhere, and he was something she had not seen before.

Fuck Jack Logan, Sally said to herself.

Impatiently now, she opened the car door, maneuvered her long legs under the steering column, and jumped out. Her feet hit the concrete, she slammed the door behind her, and she marched, heels clattering, toward the elevator.

Hamilton had not referred again to her misalliance in Westwood. It was kind of him not to, but she was worried that he didn't care enough to ask.

Oh Christ! Her thoughts caught up. Why should Peter Hamilton be interested in her? No reason, no reason at all. All the starlets in town would be willing to pave his way to the Congo, or Brazil, or China . . . and if it were true that he'd had an adventure with Virginia, then all the more reason he wouldn't be interested in daughter Sally, a pale and too-tall replica of her mother.

Merde, Sally groused, as she got out of the elevator

50

and walked down the carpeted hallway to her apartment. It was almost five o'clock when she opened the door and stepped inside.

Jack Logan was sitting in the leather wing chair, staring down at the Wilshire Boulevard traffic. He didn't even bother to turn around. "Where have you been?"

Good that he wasn't looking in her direction. "Out to lunch with Peter Hamilton. He said you knew about it. We were talking about the party."

"Bullshit," Logan snarled. "He's crazy about you."

Sally stopped in the middle of the room to stare at the back of his head. It was too much to hope for, but she said, "I hope so."

At that, Logan swung around. His tanned face was drawn. A dead cigar was stuck in his mouth. "Sally, why did you tell him?"

"Tell him what?"

"That you were having an unhappy love affair."

"Well, isn't it? It's not hugely happy to be having a half-assed love affair with your own former stepfather. That's next door to incest, Jack," she said disgustedly.

Logan wailed and put a well-padded hand to his forehead. "Jesus, Sally, we're *not* having a love affair—because *you* won't. And anyway, how many times do I have to tell you that incest is in the bloodline? I'm not your natural father. He's Orville Jones. Therefore, no incest. Besides which, I was married to your mother only a couple of months."

"Twenty-four months and four days."

"Goddamn it, Sally, so who's counting?"

Now, Sally advised herself, she had to tell him they were through. "Jack," she said, trying to sound like Humphrey Bogart, "you and me, we're through."

"Sally!"

"Listen, Jack," she said, hard-voiced, "I don't know

51

what you think. Christ, man, you've got a mistress, that big sow Mona . . ."

"You're jealous!"

"Shit, no. I'm *not* your mistress. 1 never was. I let you . . ." She didn't finish the sentence. "Jack, how many mistresses do you want?"

He stared blackly at her. "Sally, you know Mona is strictly politics. I don't like old women."

Sally tilted her head. Yes, as far as Jack was concerned, the younger, the better.

"You're for real, Sally. Christ," he puffed, "this is a many-mistressed town anyway. You know that."

"Why should I know that? I've only been here a year."

"Sixteen months and five days," he corrected her smugly.

"Whatever . . . You're using me, just like you use Mona Prissian. But anyway, I've said it—we're through, Jack."

Finally, he took the smelly cigar out of his mouth. "Sally! Have I ever harmed you? Do I beat you? God-damn it, Sally!" His voice bawled, filling the living room. "Sally, I'm harmless, aren't I? What do I ask for? Too much?"

"No," she admitted, "but you don't give either. Let's just cut it now and think nicely of each other."

"You mean *wrap it*?" he asked blankly.

"Yes, like you do in the movies."

"Son of a bitch," he yelled, "is it because I'm a Scorpio? I remember—you said you didn't get along with Scorpios."

"You're secretive and selfish bastards," she acknowledged, smiling to herself.

He slapped himself on the forehead, shaking cold ash all over his safari suit. "Shit, honey, I'm only on the cusp! Sally, don't you know I worship your little body?"

"And Mona's," she reminded him again, "and God knows who else's. I've heard somebody caught you with a secretary under your desk, giving you the kiss of life," she added crudely.

His eyes jumped, and the distinctive widow's peak leaped like an arrow toward the bridge of his nose. "What! That's a goddamn lie, Sally!"

She walked the rest of the way across the room now and tossed her shoulder bag on the couch by the window. Then she picked it up again and took out her cigarettes. "Jack," she said softly, "I thank you for everything. I thank you for the apartment and the job. I came out here like a little moron, looking for adventure. I've grown up a little now, Jack, and you've got to stop depending on me."

"Depending on you?" he demanded fiercely. "I'll fire your ass."

"Go ahead." She shrugged. "But it might look bad."

"Shit, *you* had to tell Hamilton you were having an affair."

"Sure. But I covered up. He doesn't know. I said you were a married man. I think I said you were a married man with children. Nobody's going to make the connection—unless you do."

"Sally . . . Sally." His black eyes blinked tearfully.

Bother, she thought, he could be boring. But she wouldn't tell on him, not if he removed himself quietly. "Jack, I have to tell you something. I am honest, aren't I?"

"Yeah, too goddamned honest to suit me."

"Well then, let me tell you this—you're still in love with Virginia. I am *not* Virginia."

Logan slipped off his chair and wobbled toward her on his knees. He held out his hands imploringly. "And now you're going to leave me, like Virginia did. . . . You're taking up with one of Virginia's old lovers, you know."

53

That would hurt and he knew it. So it was true. But she still didn't want to believe it. "That's crazy, Jack," she said calmly. "Is that why you divorced?"

"Sally, goddamn it, it's true."

She regarded him solemnly, her tongue dry on her teeth. Peculiar, she told herself, very peculiar this tangle of lives and personalities. "I refuse to believe that," she said flatly.

Logan's knees thumped on the floor as he came closer. "Sally, ain't I harmless?"

She nodded, for that was more or less the way it was. She couldn't for the life of her understand why she had given in to him, even in small ways. "Jack! Get up! Come . . . *on*! Just forget about it. It didn't amount to anything anyway. How many times did we . . . did I . . . Oh shit!" The truth was bitter. She had let him touch her and she regretted it now, because of Hamilton.

"Jack," she exclaimed irritably, "it hasn't amounted to a hill of beans."

"Sally, you are cruel and inhuman. But worse! I can't stand the thought of you and Hamilton fucking."

"Goddamn it!" She tried to get up, but he grabbed her knees. "Jack, that's insulting, a really shitty thing for you to say. He doesn't even know I'm here. Now stop it, once and for all, or I'm going to squeal on you to Mona Prissian."

His tan turned a sick gray. "You wouldn't."

"Yes, I would."

"Son of a bitch," Logan whispered, continuing his self-induced agony, "you're a cock-teaser, just like your mother."

Sternly, Sally said, "I don't like that either. You're a shit, Jack."

"I ought to set my dog on you!"

"What? That goddamn mutt?" She chortled. "He's scared of his own shadow."

54

"He is *not*," Logan said weakly. "He's a hero, that goddamn dog. You'll see. I'm going to have him decorated, and then I'm going to train him to bite womankind on the ass. That's going to be his work," Logan said grimly, "going around the world and biting women on the ass to give them a disease."

Sally began to laugh. "You're crazy, Jack." She patted the top of his head. His hair was definitely thinning, not like Hamilton's. Peter had a crop of hair as thick as a mattress. "Jack, Jack," she said, "forget all this. We'll be friends. I'll take your part. I'll even confirm your lies—about taxes, contracts, anything you want . . ."

He looked at her, astounded. "What the hell do you mean lies? Sally, I never lie about taxes and contracts. . . ."

She ignored that, continuing, "I've always liked you, otherwise I'd never have . . . Never mind. I didn't give you anything precious, did I, like a cherry, so we're even. I'll work for you and I'll stroke your ego. But nothing else."

Logan's square face was still hopeful. "Just now and then?"

"Now and then, what?"

"I can . . . look at you? You're my girl, right, Sally?"

"Sure," she said indifferently, "I'm your girl—your Girl Friday, Jack."

But it wasn't enough for him. He had worked himself close to her, and now he flung his face at her chest, his stubby nose nudging her breast. "Sally, tell me what you want," he cried out. "Let me wallow. I'll do it!"

"Jack, stop it!"

The determination in her voice was enough to make him pull away and collapse on his haunches. He looked at her lengthily, his eyes gone small and glittery. "You never even let me eat your little pussy!"

"No." Sally felt she might easily begin to scream. "That's for Mona."

"It's not the same. That's too old. It's like Grand Central Station."

Sally grunted with distaste. Clinically, she said, "Jack, I'm not trying to insult you, but I think you're a little perverted."

"No, no! That's just it. I'm not. What I like is youth, Sally. I adore youth. There's nothing unhealthy about that."

"Maybe you're into your male menopause," she suggested.

"No!" Logan scrambled to his feet, looking around, as though there might be somebody present who'd overheard. "I don't want to talk about it anymore, Sally. What you've said is quite enough," he said, stretching the words. "I quit!"

"Good."

The crisis seemed past. Logan smiled slyly. "Remember, I'm still your father and I'm not going to let you get in trouble with that bastard Hamilton."

"Okay," she said, standing up.

"I could just fire your ass," he said, repeating his threat.

"Well, then, do it. Just because you gave me a job doesn't give you the right to come over here and feel me up all the time."

"You bitch," he muttered, sneering. "Are you a virgin? I'd just like to know—you fight like one."

Sally felt her cheeks flush. "Well, I'm not, Jack. When I was in college, I screwed the entire senior class at West Point."

"What! Two thousand guys? Sally, goddamn it," Logan howled, "you're just like your mother. God, you've got a mouth on you."

"So you're going to get even with her by using me," she taunted him.

Logan's right eye began to twitch. "That's enough," he said. "That's it. I'm going now. Who needs you?"

"Right. Cherish Mona Prissian."

He looked disgusted. "Cherish *her*?"

"Sure. She's not a bad woman, and she likes you, doesn't she?"

"Not very much," he said. "She's using me."

"And you're using her. So why don't the two of you use each other and live happily ever after?"

He snorted. "You do have a beautiful way of putting things, Sally." He pulled himself up and walked in the direction of the front door. He turned and said, "Just remember, you're on sufferance now. One false move and out you go."

Her face was stiff. "All right, fine."

Logan straightened his body, got through the door with some dignity, and slammed it behind him. He hadn't even said good-bye.

Sally let loose a sigh of relief. Hell, the things that happened to people. Would anybody believe it? It didn't matter whether they did or not. She was happy she'd finally turned off the tap, closed the book, cut the motor. It hadn't ever been a comforting relationship. She would start paying her own way now.

Sally crossed to the door, shot the dead-bolt, and hung the safety chain. She picked up the ashtray containing Logan's dead cigar—like a dog turd, she thought—and carried it into the kitchen alcove. She watched it grind into the waste-disposal hole. Jesus, sheer relief.

Sally stripped off her jeans and then the shirt, feeling soiled. Next on the agenda was a shower. And tonight? A tuna sandwich and some beer, television . . . sleep, dreams.

First, she went to the telephone and dialed Hamilton's home number.

"Hello . . ."

"It's me," she said. "You got home all right, I see—One-Hung-Low."

Hamilton's laugh was quick. "One-Hung-Low?"

The sound of his voice made her tingle. But his laugh made her laugh too.

"Chinese," she said.

"I see," Hamilton said thoughtfully. "Well . . . that was a good lunch. I enjoyed it."

"So did I." Holding the phone in her left hand, she put her right hand to her breasts and felt the nipples. They had tensed. "I . . ."

"What?"

For want of anything else to say, Sally told him, "I'm starting Chinese language lessons."

"Whatever for?" Hamilton demanded, as if he didn't know.

What could she say? Christ, *what* could she say? That she wanted him here . . . now?

"Whatever for?" She repeated what he'd said. "*You* don't speak any Chinese, do you?"

She was aware of his puzzlement, then his caution. She could almost see him staring at his hands.

"No, I don't speak Chinese," he said slowly. "What's that got to do with the price of bagels?"

"Well," Sally said daringly, "I thought since the Chinese are our friends now, somebody . . . might . . . someday . . . need a translator."

"Somebody?"

"Yes, you know—somebody," she murmured. "Peter, tell me something—what are you doing for dinner?"

Guardedly, he replied, "I thought I might have something to eat."

"What?"

"Hell, I don't know, Sally." He paused again. "Maybe a hamburger."

"Where?"

"Christ, I don't know, kiddo."

"Hamburger Hamlet—the one where Sunset turns?"

"That's . . . a possibility, I suppose."

Before he had a chance to say anything else, she cried, "I'll meet you there at seven-thirty, One-Hung . . ."

Six

It was Nathan Sinclair's eighty-eighth birthday, and he and the boys were going to celebrate in style. A big chocolate cake with a white icing inscription reading "11 × 8 = 88," like a mystical Druid formula for longevity, was centered on the circular mahogany table next to his recliner chair.

The berobed lad named Paul sat stiffly next to the locked door, his hands braced against each other in spiritual fashion. Now and then, while Nathan talked into the intercom, Paul lifted a hand to scratch his shaved hand, or dropped the other to have a fling at his balls under the yellow robe.

Wade French was in the anteroom, on the other side of the door, listening to Nathan and then respectfully answering Nathan's questions or acceding to his commands. Wade French had not seen Nathan Sinclair in five years or more, and there was no way he was going to see Nathan now, even on the eighty-eighth anniversary of the old man's birth, not that French could be aware of the importance of the day. This day Nathan would spend, as he did all others, with Paul and Paul's brothers, Simon, Shuster, and Babylon, the latter called Baby for short. The four young men would each have a piece of the chocolate cake, and Nathan would have two, despite anything doctors might have to say about liver, spleen, kidneys, bladder, heart, lungs, or asshole.

Then, later, there would be a surprise.

Nathan realized his voice was hollow and echoing. He was rather deaf now and he talked too loudly in compensation, for he did love to hear his own voice.

And whether he shouted or whispered, they all had to listen.

He was in the process of lowering the boom on Wade French. If there was one thing Nathan Sinclair could still enjoy, it was lowering the boom.

"French, French! Listen to me! I've had the book read to me. It is dirty and rotten! *Powerhouse* is the House of Sinclair. It's about *me*."

Wade French's voice trickled out of the box, so quietly that Nathan could not make out what he said. Nathan bellowed at French to speak louder.

"Mr. Sinclair, it's very difficult. . . . The disclaimers are there."

"French, I do not give a *fuck* about disclaimers. The book is about *me*. That vermin, that traitor, that scumbag, that miserable son of a bitch Felix James has libeled *me*, slandered *me*. That son of a bitch is the only man alive who knows all those stories about *me*."

"And Virginia," French interjected, "Virginia Preston."

Nathan's voice jumped an octave higher in rage. "Virginia Preston is a *cunt*. That part on *Moisturizer II* is made up. She's got the boat perfect in every detail but, I tell you, French, Virginia Preston did not—ever—give me a blow job. Never! Would I allow such a *cunt* to touch my private parts? Would I, French, *would* I?"

"No, sir." French's voice was as quick as the brown fox.

"French," Nathan said, trying to keep calm, "there is no court of law, no judge, who wouldn't agree with me. That Benedict Arnold, Judas Iscariot, Quisling son of a bitch—after all I did for him. *French*. Are you listening?"

"Yes, sir."

"Then listen *good*. I put that scumbag through

school, French. Me, I supported that bastard. I did! *Me*. And now . . ."

And now, what? What Nathan Sinclair knew was that he wanted to spread devastation across the land.

"French, I'll tell you something that nobody knows. I want you to send Felix James a message. Tell him that I, Nathan Sinclair, *me*, fucked his wife, yes, Evelyn James, once . . . no, three times . . . no, more than that! A thousand times! Yes, on his desk in the executive wing of Sinclair Towers. I did that, yes, *me*, I did it every time he was out of the city." He laughed delightedly, vengefully. "They didn't know that to put in their goddamn book, did they? Did they, *French*?"

French did not seem very excited by the revelation. There was a long pause before his voice returned over the squawk box. "Mr. Sinclair . . ."

"What?"

"Mr. Sinclair, that's unbelievable."

"What!" he screamed. "I tell you it happened, French, and I want you to pass that message to General Benedict Arnold Felix James. I want it to *hurt* him. *Do you understand*?"

French's voice was more of a groan than an obedient, "Yes, sir."

"And, French, I want them *fixed*. I don't care how. Sue, French! Sue those motherfuckers. Sue them and their goddamn publisher for ten million, fifty million, a *billion*. Get an injunction on that book, French. *Do you hear*?"

"Yes, sir."

"Force them to take that book off the shelves of every goddamn bookstore in the country, out of every supermarket and drugstore, and out of every airplane terminal."

Nathan stopped for air. Paul looked concerned, but Nathan waved frailly at him. He was not to be deterred.

"French, I want them *destroyed*. I want them ruined."

"It'll take time, sir."

"Time? All I've got is time. *Do it*. Hurt those cocksuckers!"

Paul was watching him, devouring his words as if they fell from heaven. His eyes flickered angrily, for a wounded and defiled Nathan Sinclair was a wounded and defiled Paul . . . and Simon, Shuster, and Baby. Paul listened carefully as Nathan Sinclair lowered the boom.

"And let me know when you've done all that, French. Let me know *when . . . where . . . how*."

"Yes, sir."

Nathan lashed out at the intercom, striking the "Off" button so viciously that he splintered the long fingernail on his right forefinger. Another nail, goddamn it, he muttered to himself. How dare this keep happening? He glanced down at his feet. The toenails were too long. It was painful to have them trimmed. The merest pressure of any sort sent shooting pains up his legs. But the pain never reached his head or heart. He would get better and soon. Sons of bitches, there was no reason he couldn't live forever.

What he had told French was true. He had fornicated with Evelyn James, among others. Nathan laughed to himself. As a younger man he had always told himself that when the day came, like this, he would be able to comfort himself with the memory of all the women he had fornicated. And it was so . . . Of course, the memories were often incomplete and often unsatisfactory, for it had all happened so long ago. Twenty years? Yes—or longer. Evelyn would remember if he asked her. He had always liked Evelyn; she had always enjoyed him. She was an angel compared to that slut Virginia Preston and a virginal Mary in person when stacked up against that other cunt, Perfidia, who had been his so-called wife until that night off Capri when she'd met the Frenchified German Nazi faggot Thurnsteil.

But they would *all* get theirs. Except Evelyn. If he did ever happen to die, he was going to leave Evelyn money and, someday, yes, he was going to have the boys call Evelyn and get her up here to see him.

Thurnsteil had died and in his dreams Nathan commended the nasty Nazi son of a bitch to the devil. And so was Perfidia's daughter Naomi dead, that little tramp who'd had the gall to ask him for money—she had something to *tell*. What had she had to tell? There was nothing! Decadent, all of them were equally decadent. But slowly they were being picked off by a friendly Lord. Nathan would outlive them all.

He barked at Paul. "You heard all that? Those bastards! I want them hurt, fixed. Punished. Ruined. If I owned a prison, I'd send them all up for life or to the electric chair. I'd hang them on piano wire. Paul, I want their balls scorched, I want their cunts fried in thirty million-dollars worth of oil."

Paul's head jerked, and his eyes blazed like beacons.

"Coke!"

Paul stood up and went into the kitchen next to the large bedroom, Nathan's command post on Park Avenue. The drapes were drawn, but Nathan knew it was mid-morning. He had seen the "Today" show, and it would be about eleven by now. In the afternoon, before the party, he was going to see a cowboy movie.

Paul brought him a glass of brown liquid. His drinks had to be lukewarm because Nathan could not bear coldness against his gums. Paul aimed the bent straw at his mouth, and Nathan sucked. Then, almost at once, he felt drowsy.

The first reminder that he had fallen asleep came with a sensation of wetness at his crotch. He had spilled the drink.

"Wet!" he roared irritably.

Paul was at his side instantly. "Wet," Paul yelled in his ear.

"Yes. Dry! Dry! Bedpan!"

At six P.M., more or less, Paul and his brothers assembled in the dark room that was Nathan Sinclair's nerve center. From here, he still took an active interest in the day-to-day business of his empire, adding shingles to the House of Sinclair and now and then clearing the cellar of rats like Felix James.

In his sleep during the afternoon, Nathan had dreamed fitfully of Felix, the man he had loved more than any of his wives. Felix, smooth, white-bodied youth, so young, wholesome, handsome, a waif when Nathan had first invited him into the House of Sinclair. Nathan had sent Felix to Yale and then watched him go off to war . . . and return, a captain, beautiful, still youthful. Felix had become Nathan's personal assistant, later vice-president for corporate public relations and heir-apparent to the Throne of Sinclair.

Then Felix had left him. First, by marrying Evelyn, and finally over such a personal matter that even now Nathan could not think about it. It was not, as everyone believed, because Felix had let Perfidia slip through his fingers that night in Capri. It was something else, and it had been Nathan's mistake. In his dream, Nathan had wept, but only in his dream, for he had no real tears left to weep when he was awake. At least, they—rather, Felix—had not put *that* in the book.

Felix, beloved, traitor. No love was more hateful in the end than the misunderstood variety. . . .

Paul and his brothers carried white plates and silver forks into the room. Wielding a long butcher knife, Baby began to cut the cake. He placed one slice on each of four plates and two slices on the fifth. The last he handed to Nathan.

Paul and his brothers surrounded him. They might have been his sons. They *were* his sons. They sang to him.

Happy Birthday to you, Happy Birthday to you . . .
Happy Birthday, dear Nathan Sinclair, Happy Birth-
day to you, oh beloved one . . .

They sang beautifully. They were his own House of Sinclair choir. Acid burned in Nathan's tear ducts. In some confusion, he plunged his fork into the cake and tried to shovel a huge piece of it into his mouth. Some of it arrived there neatly, but more of the gooey sweet fell on his soiled pajama top, and there was stickiness on his hairless chest.

"Clean."

Paul mopped him with a tissue and took the fork from Nathan's trembling hand to feed him the rest of his cake. The other boys watched, beaming joyously. They were happy for him and to be with him on his birthday. In unison, they cried out.

"Surprise . . . Surprise."

Simon darted to the door and flung it wide. Outside, in the hallway, Nathan saw a long, wheeled table and upon it a big, round object trimmed on the top with tall candles. Simon pushed the table into the room.

Surprise. Surprise. Happy Birthday to you . . .
Happy Birthday to you.

At the high note of the second "Happy Birthday," the top of the big fake cake flipped open, and a naked girl jumped to the floor. She waved her arms and yelled excitedly. She was black-haired, Nathan noted appreciatively, and she had enormous jugs, the kind he liked best. They drooped to her bellybutton.

"Happy Birthday, Nathan," she screeched.

Was this, he wondered, the same girl they'd had last year? *Had* was the word, since they'd each had her here in the big room while the others watched. It was all right, Nathan had decided a few years ago, because it only happened once every twelve months. It was a sort of ceremony to celebrate spring.

She did not look familiar, but the act was the same. She lifted her hands above her head and danced around his chair in her bare feet, bumping her belly at him and shaking her ass. Nathan felt a flush of warmth rise from beneath him, a stirring of life in his crotch.

The black-haired girl bounded toward him, her hands holding her jugs aloft and shaking them in his face, touching his cheeks with nipples, which were the size of powder puffs. Now Nathan could see her face. She was pimpled around the mouth, and acne glistened on her forehead. He was tempted to cry, *"Unclean!"* but resisted because the boys would have been disappointed. They were most careful about choosing the right girl—it would not do to hire one who'd shout from the rooftops afterward that the great Nathan Sinclair was really nothing but a dirty old man.

The girl's eyes were glazed, devoid of understanding. She obviously had no idea where she was and, if he hadn't known his boys better, he'd have sworn she'd been drugged to the asshole.

"Nathan, Nathan," she babbled, "what do you want most for your birthday?"

Nathan shook his head from side to side. He didn't know. Yes, he did know, but he was not going to tell her so soon.

"Nathan, Nathan," she screamed in a singsong voice, too close to his ear. "Nathan, Nathan, I've been thinking. . . . Far beyond the northern seas . . ."

He hated that. It sounded so faraway and final. And he could wait no longer.

"Suck," he roared, his voice quaking, *"Suck. . ."*

"Yummy," she cried, almost hysterically.

Paul pulled the blue light wool blanket off Nathan's hips. The girl seemed to jerk backward. But no, that could not be. Not from the sight of Nathan Sinclair. His was a presence to be worshipped. The boys worshipped him, and so must she.

She picked up the shaft of light in two fingers and massaged it for a second with her thumb.

"But, it won't . . ." she began to say.

What! What was this! Never. Paul tapped her on the shoulder and put his finger to his lips. She nodded uncertainly, not seeming to understand.

"Suck," Nathan bellowed.

He saw Baby's hand on the girl's head, and the head descended.

The boys began to sing again.

Happy Birthday to you . . . Happy Birthday to you . . . Happy Birthday beloved Nathan . . . Happy Birthday to you.

Nathan closed his eyes, soothed at last by the laving sensation. His mind drifted away toward an awareness, finally, that some rusty mechanism or other had been triggered. Later, he told himself, he would watch the gang bang. Nathan basked in restful, heavenly sun, a warmth that in his imagination bathed all the House of Sinclair products, so clean and bright in their blue and white packaging.

In the dark, some time afterward, Nathan was not sure when, he awoke. He swore angrily. He had missed the gang bang. From somewhere in the outer rooms, a thin scream lilted toward him. Somewhere, people were having fun. Paul and his brothers opened the door, then closed it again. They came and went, through the bedroom and into the kitchen . . . and back. The tables had been removed, and the remains of the cake. He watched them, shadowy figures in their robes, rustling.

The girl, he remembered the girl. A slut, naturally, a wanton and ruined creature, not worthy of consideration, or life. Seeing and ministering to Nathan Sinclair had been her moment of glory. Such a girl was chosen each year for the ceremony of the renewal, to wit his birthday. Tomorrow, like the day after Christmas, Boxing Day in England, they would have the feast. The feast of the sacrificial lamb, the boys called it.

Nathan was too tired now to think about it.

Seven

"Are we over Ohio?" Virginia asked. "Tell me when we're over Ohio, and I'll order a big drink."

"At eleven A.M., Virginia?" Felix asked grumpily.

"Doesn't matter. Whenever I fly over Ohio, I have a drink to my first husband . . . dear Orville."

"Orville Jones." Naturally, Felix knew the name, although he had never met the man. After her move to New York, Virginia had dropped the "Jones" and reassumed her maiden name. "Do you ever hear from him?"

"No." Virginia shook her head pensively. "Thank God, no. Sally does. But I don't. I let him carry on as though I never happened. He's been married again for over twenty years. I think she was an airline hostess."

"Interesting," Felix said, adding ironically, "very interesting. You told me once Orville is an accountant."

"Yes." She was not going to discuss it. She hailed a flight attendant. "Bring us a couple of bloody marys, please."

"Virginia, I don't want a drink."

"Come on, Felix, be a sport. Think of it this way—it's a new departure for you. You've never been on your *own* book tour before."

Felix nodded but said nothing. Think of it this way indeed. He frowned to himself. Evelyn had laid the ultimatum on him: if he went on a tour with Virginia, it was a matter of conjecture whether he'd have a happy home to which to return. Evelyn had gone back to Maine, and she was emphatically *not* joining them in California. Marvelous, he told himself, just bloody marvelous. Felix had called her from Washington, and she had talked to him distantly—distant in more than miles—from her stone house on the rocky coast. The book tour had been arranged weeks in advance, he'd tried to explain, and it was not something he could duck out of now, as much as he wanted to be with her and as much as he deplored being thrust into such a high-profile situation. After all, a really successful P.R. man was one who stood forever in the shadow and manipulated. Felix James was a star-maker, not a star. But Evelyn would not listen. She was adamant and finally just plain nasty. Before blistering him with a frosty good night, Evelyn had informed him that Wade French was "getting together the necessary papers" and that she hoped he, Felix, would accept the inevitable with good grace. The question had occurred to him then: was Evelyn taking advantage of this circumstance to do something she'd always wanted to do, or at least had wanted to do for some time now? Wade French? That dark suspicion came to him at the same time—Wade had been divorced from the lovely, if brittle, Irene not more than a year before.

Just marvelous, bloody marvelous, he repeated to himself. So they had written *Powerhouse*, and Nathan Sinclair was furious. It was altogether possible, he realized helplessly, that he would be facing two lawsuits, one for divorce and the other for *Powerhouse*. Felix downed half his bloody mary.

"Felix! I thought you didn't want it. Take it easy." Virginia pressed his hand. "I have a question for you, darling," she said, as if reading his mind, "did you put anything of Evelyn in the book?"

"Certainly not."

But this was not precisely true. As a mark of affection, teasingly, he had inserted one tiny private thing. Evelyn, at the most intimate spot on the inside of her thigh, was marked by a small brown mole. The latter had been implanted for posterity on the lush body of one of Marcel Power's girlfriends. Evelyn, naturally, had spotted the mole in the book, and she appeared to resent this one, harmless disclosure more than she did anything else, even the fact he had written, or collaborated on, what she termed "smut." Did he, Evelyn had demanded harshly, intend to infer that she'd had something, anything, to do with the old tycoon? Of course not, Felix had said sharply. But the denial was not good enough.

Virginia pulled him back to the American Airlines flight, to his bloody mary and the fact he was sitting with her in a comfortable first-class seat, an author about to be celebrated.

She laughed huskily. "I've got them all in—Orville, Jack Logan, a cast of hundreds."

"Virginia!" His nerves whipped him. "I don't think you should ever, ever say so. I'm beginning to regret we wrote the blasted book."

Virginia shrugged and laughed lightly. "Botheration, Felix. No regrets now. Never explain, never complain."

He should not be surprised at her, not ever. He knew about Virginia, and he hadn't any illusions about her or her lifestyle. Virginia was not a bad woman just because she was . . . well . . . promiscuous. Fortunately, she'd always been discreet. The wonder of it was that he always enjoyed so much being with her. And they had been together much over the years.

"Buck up, Felix," she said.

Felix chuckled and picked up her hand, bringing it to his lips. "Virginia, I should spank you. You are too much!"

"Felix, would you like to spank me? Oh, my! I've heard of men like you. Felix!" She laughed. "You're turning red. You see, it *is* a brand-new departure. . . . Evelyn is very angry, isn't she?"

"More than that."

73

Virginia pursed her lips. "Well, I think that's just plain silly, if not stupid. Felix, damn it, she knows we've never fooled around." She ignored his wince of pain. "And why she'd be angry about the book is beyond me. Felix, all it is, really, is a lark. Nobody is going to take *Powerhouse* seriously. They shouldn't. It's only what the reviewers call a *romp*. They're fools if they do take it seriously."

"Well . . ." He hesitated, for what he was about to say was probably not true. "She'll get over it. I know she will. Evelyn is just too . . ."

"Goddamn serious," Virginia said crisply. She held up her glass. "Felix, darling, here's to us. You know how much I love you—in a comradely fashion. Is that the way to describe us? Comrades? Whatever, here's to us." She touched her glass to his. "Let's have another. Then I've got to get to work. I've got to write a column."

Felix was impressed, as always. That was another thing about Virginia. Whatever else she might be, she was a damned hard and dedicated worker, and her syndicate should be very proud of her. He himself could no more have considered bending mind to work right now than he could have jumping out of the plane.

He picked up the morning paper as Virginia ordered their second drink. They'd had coverage in Atlanta— one of the social columns. Cozily, Virginia put her head against his shoulder and read along with him. She kissed him on the earlobe.

"Felix," she said mischievously, "I know we'll get a rave review in Los Angeles."

"Virginia!" he said with exaggerated dismay. "Lenny Thoreau? Descendant of the solitary philosopher?"

"Is he? Well, he's a nice man, I know that. We'll see him again in California."

"I wouldn't be at all surprised," Felix murmured.

She laughed again, warmly. "Life is brief, Felix. *Vita*

74

brevis and long in the ass, you've heard? Now, tell me, is it kosher for me to write about a party given for us? I should mention Earl. He's such a friend."

"Earl is one of the nicest men in New York City."

"He didn't charge us a nickel—did he?"

"No." Felix shook his head. "Only for the caviar."

"God," Virginia mused, "he is such a nice man."

Virginia took a long legal pad from her attaché case and with a gold Tiffany pen began the doodles preliminary to serious composition.

"I'm drawing an airplane," she said.

Felix glanced down. "Virginia, really! I *should* spank you. Phallic symbols . . ."

She gasped and turned a face of innocence to him, then thrust the tip of her pink tongue out in mock defiance. God, she was such a devil. Felix shivered. How could this be when she looked so wholesome? Her skin was spotlessly smooth, her light blue eyes as clear as crystal, her blonde hair lustrous and impeccably brushed. Virginia gently put her fingers on his wrist and, mesmerized, Felix stared at the back of her hand. It was small-boned, hardly bigger around than his thumb. The fingers . . . they were much longer proportionally than one might have guessed from her body.

"Felix," she said, taunting him a little, "I'm beginning to think you *have* made the departure. Did you ever hear of a thing called the Mile-High Club?"

"No." But he thought he knew what she'd say it was.

The transparent eyes twinkled. "Supposedly, you get some kind of a silver pin if you can honestly say you've made love in an airplane. . . ."

"Not on the ground, though."

"No, upstairs, at least five thousand, two hundred and eighty feet. It'd have to be on a night flight, I suppose, unless you wanted to be really daring." Felix did not look at her. "We're going to be doing an awful lot

75

of flying in the next couple of weeks, Felix," she warned him teasingly.

Felix grunted, "I'm already a member, Virginia."

She stared back at him, her eyes wide. "What! I don't believe you."

He nodded. "During the war. I've never told anybody. There was a WAC . . ."

"Felix," Virginia almost screeched, "I cannot believe it!"

"It's a fact," he said evenly, "but, Virginia, that was a long time ago, you know."

"Jesus Christ," she said, annoyed, "don't apologize. I think that's wonderful. Felix, it changes my whole view of you. Why didn't you ever tell me that before?"

He shrugged. "There was never an occasion. Besides," he said glumly, "I'm too old now to try for a cluster on my silver pin."

"No way! Felix, I've always thought the one thing you've been lacking is a little spice in your life. You've never had a mistress, have you? You're so faithful, it's tiresome. Always old Evelyn." This time, her mention of Evelyn's name was not so tolerant, but more cutting and cruel.

"Yes, that's right," he said, "always old Evelyn."

Virginia realized instantly that she had wounded him. "I'm sorry, Felix."

"It's not like you to talk like that, Virginia. I'm older than you are, you know. I *am* stodgy. I am a bore, Virginia."

"You're *not* that much older than me, and you're the funniest, nicest man I know."

"Virginia," he said stubbornly, "I know what I am." And he didn't feel bad about it. There was nothing much one could do about the way one was. "I've never felt the need to play around. I don't know—maybe my sex drive is too weak."

Virginia shook her head disbelievingly. "Don't be

76

naive. There's no such thing as a low sex drive. It's all in your mind and has to do with proper stimulation." Her expression became more analytical. "Felix, I can't think why we've never . . . I mean, heavens, we've been alone enough, traveling around, even back on Sinclair's boat. In fact, it's a little insulting, when you come to think about it, that people have never jumped to the conclusion . . ."

He interrupted. "I think Evelyn has jumped to that conclusion, if it's any comfort to you. But, yes, it is amazing no one else has." He frowned. "Probably because they think I'm such a stick-in-the-mud."

"You're not insulted, though?"

"No," he smiled, "that doesn't insult me."

"Even after twenty years? Haven't you ever wondered how I look without my clothes on? Tell the truth."

Felix shifted uneasily in his seat and started the second bloody mary. "The truth is," he said, "that I have seen you without clothes. I've seen you skinny-dipping over the side of *Moisturizer II*."

Playfully, Virginia snapped her fingers. "Of course. Off Capri. Now *that* was a trip. *Quelle voyage!* Remember the night when you all went ashore without me? When Perfidia first met Putzi von Thurnsteil?"

Felix nodded. Yes, that had been a night of nights. Virginia, with a tummy ache, had stayed aboard with Nathan, who'd been a fairly ancient number even then. And thus, it had fallen on Felix to escort Perfidia and Evelyn for a drink and some dancing at the Miramare Hotel. Somehow, like two meteors colliding, it had happened. The two strangers, Putzi and his friend Lutzi Dopplesegel, had boldly joined them, and Putzi made no bones about his instant fascination with the dark, gypsy looks of Perfidia Sinclair. Perfidia, for her part, had fallen into a near faint at the sight of the tall, platinum-blond German whose eyes were as cold as snow and as blue as the sky. Putzi had been a member of the old Bavarian nobility, and he behaved as though it were, indeed, his seigniorial right, even duty, to sweep Perfidia off her feet. Of course, it had to be said that he made a striking opposite to old Nathan. The two had danced to the point where Felix became worried not only about the time, but the future. Whatever happened on such outings as these, he was responsible. Before he had managed to get Perfidia and Evelyn out of the Miramare and back to the *Moisturizer II,* however, the deed had been all but done. The dashing twosome rendezvoused the next afternoon, and by five P.M. Perfidia was pregnant, although that fact didn't become known until they had all been back in New York for a couple of months. It turned then into a messy and nasty affair, but Perfidia came away from her five years with Nathan in sweet financial shape. It had been enough for her to pursue and capture Putzi von Thurnsteil, to get rid of Lutzi Dopplesegel, and then to keep Putzi captive in his Capri villa for the rest of his days.

Sadly, Felix said, "They say Perfidia's daughter is a raving beauty."

"Yes," Virginia said. "I visited them a few years ago, you know. The daughter's name is Marina. She'd be about sixteen now. She looks like Naomi, you remember?"

"I hope," Felix said devoutly, "that she doesn't behave like Naomi."

"No, she seemed like a very well-behaved little child. But Felix," she said, "don't make moral judgments. You can't have any way of knowing what happened between Peter and Naomi."

"Except that she deserted him," Felix said primly, "and that, briefly, Peter was even suspected of killing her."

78

"Well, that was silly. Peter Hamilton could never be a murderer. He's too intelligent . . . and too lovable."

"Oh, yes?" Felix glanced at her. Her judgments were so simplistic. "Lovable? That's got nothing to do with it, Virginia. Men do kill."

"No, not Peter. I'm looking forward to seeing him again. Aren't you? Our old gang has really broken up, hasn't it?"

"That old gang of mine, yes." And a little more breakage was in the offing, he thought.

"Haaah," Virginia sighed, "you'll have to admit it was great fun being mixed up in one of the great love affairs, that of Baron Putzi and the third Mrs. Sinclair."

"Our heroine," he murmured, beginning to worry again. "The wonder is that she got the double-gaited nobleman away from that other guy."

Virginia laughed. "Perfidia put him in thrall. He never had a chance." Thoughtfully, she went on, "Doesn't she make one hell of a heroine, though? Too bad Grace Kelly isn't available. She could have played her to a T."

God, he thought, all the memories and how many of them he and Virginia had used to their own purposes in *Powerhouse*. All told, it had been quite a night that night off the coast of Capri. Not long afterward, in the shambles of the aftershock, Felix had left the House of Sinclair.

Again, Virginia yanked him back to the present. "Felix, speaking of being undressed, I've never seen you without your clothes. But naturally—you're not the type to go skinny-dipping off *Moisturizer II*. What an archiac expression, by the way."

"Virginia," he replied laconically, "tell me, why is it we're having a discussion like this after twenty-odd years?"

She chuckled intimately. "Maybe because it's odd

that after twenty years, we don't know more about each other. Maybe the book *has* untied a knot of some kind."

"The departure you mentioned—I'm kind of old to be departing."

"Felix, for God's sake," Virginia exclaimed, "you're not even fifty yet. Stop talking like an old man. Someday, I'm going to spank *you.*"

For some reason, the jocular threat unnerved him. Of course, now and then he had taken a carnal peek at Virginia. It would have been unnatural if he hadn't. But, as the saying went, deed had never overpowered thought. And now? His life was changing, no doubt of that, so much that it was frightening to think about it. If what he had begun to suspect was confirmed, that Wade French was having his way with Evelyn, and with Evelyn's wholehearted concurrence, then what was there to bind Felix to his vows?

But an affair with Virginia? The idea seemed so outlandish that he was embarrassed even to fantasize it. Virginia had never so much as hinted that she might find him a desirable bed companion, and it had always seemed to him that they could have shared a bed without anything of a sexual nature transpiring. No, their partnership would continue to be just that—a social and financial contract.

All the same, he couldn't stop himself contemplating when, or how, an alteration of state might occur. When—at what point—might he start lusting for her? For Felix knew he was capable of lust.

As if to bring the hypothetical moment within range of reality, Virginia casually put her hand on his knee. Felix was aware of a jolt of recognition. Now? So soon? But even his precipitous surge of nerves was spoiled by the knowledge of all the men Virginia had made love to. The lurid fantasy developed rapidly, numbed the nerves, and made his stomach toss. With jealousy? Reproach?

He pushed it all aside. He was old enough to know better. Virginia was fine, marvelous, enchanting as a traveling companion and working partner. If he asked, or became suddenly hungry for more, he would be asking for trouble.

Eight

"May I speak to Miss Prissian, please?" Hamilton said into the telephone.

"You *are* speaking to Mona Prissian," the female voice said briskly. There was a suggestion of the London West End stage in the voice but also an overlay of California: MGM, Paramount, and Universal Studios.

"Ah, Miss Prissian, my name is Hamilton. I'm calling at Jack Logan's suggestion. His ex-wife Virginia Preston has just written a book, a novel . . ."

The Prissian voice snapped like a guardsman's leather. "I'm aware of it. I'm to have the lead in the film version."

"Yes, so Jack said. I'm . . . that is, *we're* inviting a few people to a party at my house for Virginia and her co-author Felix James, and we'd like very, very much for you to come."

"Yes . . ." She paused. "Yes, but I haven't read their book yet. How can I get a copy?"

"Surely, the studio . . ."

"Them? They refuse to let me see anything until the script is ready. They don't trust me. They're afraid if I read the book, I might not like the script."

"Well . . ." Hamilton chuckled. "I could lend you my copy—if you don't tell Jack."

She laughed heartily, with full throat, pleased, it seemed, to be able to pull a fast one on Logan. "How very kind. When could I get it?"

"Well . . ." Again he hesitated. "I could get it to you this afternoon, I suppose. I have to be in Beverly Hills."

"Oh, could you? How kind."

Why? he asked himself. He had better things to do than play delivery boy to Jack Logan's mistress. But they did want her at the party. And he was curious. He had always been curious about Logan's women, and that was a fact. He was also fascinated by the juicy, no, ripe voice.

"Do you know where I live?" Mona Prissian asked.

He did not, and she described the route. First, he must turn off Sunset Boulevard into Benedict Canyon. . . .

Mona Prissian had always been famous for her knockers, if not especially renowned for her acting ability. Hamilton had seen pictures of the upper-story but had never faced the structure in person. It had often been said that Mona Prissian looked the part of a well-scrubbed and straight-laced English schoolmarm. True, she hailed from Devon, which also produced heavy cream. But she had spent almost the whole of her career in California, having been stolen away from the Rank Organization by the first Hollywood mogul who'd met those knockers head on.

Mona had medium-long russet hair, a gigantic and healthy pile of it. Her complexion was milky white, despite California. She was dressed carelessly in a royal blue bikini and not too well covered by a blue terry robe, the initials *M.P.* embroidered over one outstanding breast. Her mouth was large, and a fresh coat of lipstick had been hastily, therefore sloppily, applied before she opened the door.

Advertising himself, Hamilton held his copy of the book in front of him.

"*Mr.* Peter Hamilton," she exclaimed, the sound apparently rising from dead center of the remarkable bosom. "Mr. Peter Hamilton, and *such* a kind man to bring me the book. Do come in for a moment! I'm sitting out by the pool."

She led him by the hand through the house and, with a flurry of patting and stroking, placed him in a chair. Mona Prissian obviously believed in touch. She arranged herself under a big blue poolside umbrella, explaining that she had to be extremely careful to avoid the full rays of the sun. The doctors, you see, and so many of her friends said one could, if one were not cautious, be withered brown as a mummy and just as cracked.

"That's right," Hamilton said. He pointed flippantly at her robe. "I know that means Mona Prissian—the initials. Are you also a Member of Parliament?"

"Ha, ha," she laughed with precision, staring him in the eye curiously. "If I am, then they'd have to say those were pretty important members, wouldn't they?"

"Well . . . very impressive anyway," Hamilton said daringly.

"A drink?" Mona asked.

"If you're having something . . . I wouldn't mind a beer."

He had to admit that he was more curious now than before. If Mona did, in fact, play the third Mrs. Sinclair, Jack Logan's job of casting would be on the nose. Mona, in an unmistakable way, did look like the bitch goddess Perfidia of sixteen or so years ago. The hair would have to be changed, and that was about all. Perhaps dark contact lenses for the eyes.

Mona picked up a crystal bell from a glass-topped table at her side and jingled it. The sound summoned an abbreviated Oriental man from the house. He was dressed in baggy black pants and a white buttoned top. "Wang," she said, slowly and distinctly, "please bring a glass of beer for Mr. Hamilton and a glass of Perrier for me." Next she hefted the book in her hand. "It *is* a big one, isn't it? I must get right to it. My friends who've read it say it's very . . . what do you say? Explicit, *n'est-ce pas?*"

Her use of the most obvious French phrase dropped like a clanger between them. "A trifle, yes," Hamilton said.

"All the better. I do like explicit books. I'm a fan of what are called Gothic romances—not the genteel ones, but rather those that take one beyond heavy sighs and ripped bodices."

Mona, Hamilton thought, was a real one, real Hollywood, despite her effort to hang on to the English tartness of voice. He accepted the beer from the little man called Wang, recalling what else he knew of Mona Prissian. She had never shown much except silhouette and cleavage in any of her films—now and then, in the earlier, striving days, perhaps a flash of tit and nipple. Lately, she had been quoted as deploring full-frontal nudity on the screen and as quite despising simulation of the sex act. If that hadn't been necessary in *Mrs. Miniver,* then why now?

"I must fall into the water," she announced. "Suddenly, it's unbearably hot . . . just walking to the door."

Hamilton sipped his beer and watched as Mona stood up and dramatically flung aside her robe. She turned to give him the full treatment. For thirty-five or whatever she was, it had to be said Mona was in good shape. Her legs were smooth and unmarked. The bottom of her bikini stretched snugly but not too tautly across restrained hips. He did note little puffs of excess flesh around the navel, but when she raised her arms, as she did now, stretching her body toward the sky, these disappeared. The vaunted superstructure hung neatly and naturally inside her bikini top.

Mona hurled him a dazzling smile, which reflected, with appreciation, his own obvious admiration, and then threw herself into the blue-green water. Hamilton congratulated himself. He was happy he'd come to see her. Whatever her relationship with Jack Logan, it clearly had not immunized her against other men. What a bastard he was, Hamilton told himself smugly. Not Jack Logan; he, Peter Hamilton.

From the far side of the pool, her voice rippled toward him. "I'm not clear on your position with Jack Logan. Do you work with him at Logan Productions?"

Notice, he told himself, she did not say "work for," rather "work with." She wasn't ready to assume he was a lower man on Logan's particular totem pole.

"No, we're just friends—from the old days in New York."

"But you *are* involved in the film business?" She seemed anxious for him to say this was so.

"I make documentaries."

"Oh? Is there still a market for documentaries?" He was not surprised she sounded disappointed. He was disappointed too, for he was astute enough to know that while Mona Prissian might, as Sally Jones gossiped, have humped every producer in town, she was not going to hump him. This, for the simple reason that Mona was unlikely ever to star in a documentary about pigmies—or Chinese panda bears. One of those knockers was as big as a whole pigmy. "What sort of documentaries?" she asked.

"Cousteau-type things. The Congo, the Amazon."

"Like the *National Geographic* magazine," she said. "Bare-breasted tribal women standing under trees in the rain forest. I'm fascinated by that kind of thing."

Mona was in mid-pool, floating on her back—not a difficult feat, he told himself, supported as she was by those Mae West things. She tilted her head over her shoulder. "In that case, I'll tell you something about Wang. Wang is *unique*—in that, he's a *eunuch*." Mona laughed, almost deliriously. Obviously, this was one of her standing jokes. "I bought him in Singapore."

87

"Bought him?"

"Yes, it can be done, Peter. I *will* call you Peter. I was over there making a pirate movie. He was happy enough to leave the place, I can tell you. He adores me."

"How did he become a eunuch?"

"I haven't the faintest. Maybe he was born that way."

She reached his side of the pool, stared up at him, and smiled. Although Mona was possibly lacking a few mental buttons, Hamilton thought, she might be a more genuine person than he had thought.

"Do you think there are any more like him in Singapore?"

"No." She laughed throatily, showing big white teeth, English teeth, good for gnawing on bones. "I got the last one. He's darling, Wang. He understands what I say, and he never talks back."

"Never?"

"I have never heard him talk. I think he's mute."

"God," Hamilton mused, "a mute eunuch. It could only happen in Hollywood."

Mona placed her chin on folded hands on the edge of the pool. "Tell me about Felix James," she urged. "I know about Virginia Preston already. I've always read her columns, and Jack has told me a little."

How much? he wondered. "Felix," he said, "is one of New York's biggest flacks. No, I shouldn't call him a flack. Actually, Felix is a very classy P.R. man, and he handles only the best clients."

"Personal or corporate?" She knew the difference.

"Both. He's been at it for years. He's very trusted. He'll launch a debutante if he likes her. On the other hand, he's capable of defusing the most delicate corporate flap. When I was a reporter, I could always trust Felix. He never dumped on me. If Felix said it was so, then it was so."

"He sounds like the most *precious* kind of man," Mona exclaimed. "I definitely cannot wait to meet him." Rolling her tongue inside her generous mouth, she continued. "Now, Peter, tell me about *Powerhouse*. I'm told the female lead is a woman who . . ."

"Yes," he drawled, "very much a woman *who*." He tried not to sound too hateful. "I think you resemble her very much. Physically, that is—except for the hair."

Mona understood. "But she is *not* nice. Good. I don't like to play *nice* women. This woman, though, is she a real-life or made-up character?"

How much should he tell her? It was not going to be any great revelation that Pauline Power, in the book, was the spitting image of Perfidia Sinclair. *Spitting* was the word.

"In real life, she's a woman named Perfidia Sinclair," he said. "We won't mention *that* name again. She's Pauline Power in the book."

"Perfidia," Mona repeated, "what a marvelous name. Do I look like Pauline Power?"

"Yes, but she's dark-haired. Her hair is jet black."

Mona tossed her head. "That's only an incidental thing." She held out her hand. "Peter, please pass me my Perrier—and a cigarette. Light it for me, please."

Hamilton pulled a Pall Mall out of an open pack on the table. How long since he'd seen a woman smoke a Pall Mall? He tapped it on his thumbnail and lit it carefully. He did not want to get hooked again by lighting other peoples' cigarettes. He slid forward on his knees to hand it to her. She seized his fingers, then impulsively kissed his knuckles, wetly, leaving a red lipstick mark.

"Thank you, *Peter*," she said huskily. "You know, Jack never talks much about Virginia."

He remained on his knees, looking down at her. He could see straight through the notch in her bikini, down to where the bottom started and where a knot of dark hair was sticking out of the top of it. About Virginia . . .

"It might not be the kind of thing Jack likes to talk about very much."

"A stormy marriage?"

He could not resist saying, "The *Titanic* would have sunk twice sailing through it."

"Virginia's daughter works for Jack. He adores her." He nodded. Adored? That much? "Sometimes," Mona said, "I'm jealous. But I don't think it's anything of a . . . you know . . . sexual thing."

"I'd be very surprised if it was," Hamilton said reassuringly. And hurt and insulted too if Logan proved to be such a pig after cautioning him to stay away.

Absently, Mona put the Perrier to her lips, swallowed and took a deep drag off the Pall Mall. "I'll tell you about Jack, although you probably know him better than I do." Her eyelids batted. Christ, he hoped she was not going to play ingenue for him. "Jack does not love me very much, *Peter*. We do sleep together now and then, but I fear he doesn't really love me. He wants to use me, you see. He wants me for his films. I've always resisted taking parts in his horror films— with the murders and blood and sharks and maniacs because I know all he wants is my bosom. Peter, do you think it's *right* that a serious actress should be exploited because of her *breasts*?"

"No," he said.

"But this—*Powerhouse*," Mona argued. "This is something I can do. It's a dramatic role, and people will see my *face*." She laughed ruefully. "You know, Peter, if it weren't for my *bosom*, I think Jack would just walk out without saying 'Boo!' "

"No, do you really think so?"

She noticed that he was doubtful and coldly demanded, "I see you think I'm too tough a woman to be victimized." He denied that, even as he was wondering who was humping whom and to what end. "I'll tell you," Mona said sharply, "sometimes I do become vastly annoyed. Sometimes, I feel like pulling up stakes and going back to New Mexico. I have a horse ranch down there. I feel like telling Mr. Jack Logan where he can put his part."

Hamilton smiled mildly. He was not impressed—Mona was merely exercising her temperamental license. Nonetheless, he felt it was time to detour. "Do you raise Arabian horses?" he asked. He remembered what Logan had promised—that he was going to have racing colors tattooed on his hairless Chinese dog.

"No, I raise *hell*," she said hotly. "Just ring that bell on the table, and I'll show you what I'm going to do to Mr. Jack Logan before we're finished."

Hamilton lifted the bell. Crystal chimes pealed, Wang's very own signal. The small man hurried from the house.

"Wang," Mona commanded, "I want you to do your trick. Your *trick*, please, Wang—for Mr. Hamilton."

Wang hissed and bowed. He whirled back into the kitchen—Hamilton assumed he had been in the kitchen—then reappeared carrying a long two-by-four. He put the piece of wood over the mouth of a barbecue fireplace near the pool house, nonchalantly stepped back, and then attacked.

Loosing a wild shriek, Wang jumped forward and swung the heel of his hand in an arc. When hand met wood, the latter splintered, the two ends flying up in the air.

"Whew!" Hamilton said, "some *trick*. But I don't think it's unique."

"Wang," Mona said, clucking delightedly, "that was marvelous. Thank you ever so much. You see?" she asked Hamilton.

"I thought he didn't speak."

"He doesn't. He only screams when he breaks some-thing—not dishes. Never dishes, he's very careful. He can do bricks too." Wang was gathering up his ends of wood. "It's karate training, of course," Mona summed up. "You can see why I'm never worried about being alone."

"But, seriously," he said, "you'd never use that weapon on Jack Logan—would you?"

"I might. Peter, come in the pool."

He shook his head. "I should hit the road, Mona."

"*Peter*, come on in. You've got nothing to do. You look all hot and bothered." She winked at him. "It's me, I know. I give off a sexual discharge." Her nose twitched. "Electrical, I mean."

He could not disagree. Mona, possibly excited by Wang's show of force, had become a sexual being, a nimbus prepared to swallow the whole world of men. Her eyes glittered greedily at him.

"Mona . . ." He didn't know what he should do.

"Like you said—it could only happen in Holly-wood," she mocked. "Come on. I'd like to feel a little flesh. I'm sick and tired of being Jack Logan's play-thing."

She was direct, that's for sure. Playing with Mona, however, had not been on his list of musts for the af-ternoon. But once more, he was drawn by simple curi-osity.

"I suppose you want a game of water polo," he said.

Mona dropped her mouth, then spurted a stream of water toward him. "Peter, strictly in fun. There's noth-ing I can do for you and there's nothing you can do for me—in a professional way, I mean."

"Mona . . ." He placed his right hand over his heart. "Mona, you are tempting me severely. What about Jack?"

She considered that for a second, and winked again. "Bugger Jack. Not literally, of course. There are suits in the pool house, duckie." She pointed at the low-ceilinged pavilion next to the rambling wood and stucco house.

He debated the odds. "Okay. I suppose if I don't, you'll get Wang to break my arm."

"Precisely," Mona chuckled.

He found a suit that was too big for him and slipped out of his clothes. Emerging from the pool house, he stood watching her, finishing his beer. He realized that Mona was now undoing her bikini top. When it was free of her shoulders, she threw it up on the tiles, then braced her feet on the side of the pool and pushed herself forcefully backward. There was no good reason he shouldn't look at her; indeed, he knew, he was supposed to look at her. So he did. The famous Prissian knockers glimmered in the water, twin porpoises, red nipples like porpoise noses flashing in the wavelets.

He had been wrong about Mona. She didn't give a damn whether he had a job for her or not. He hoped she didn't intend to hump him there in the pool, however. He had tried that once, and it was very strenuous, although thrilling.

"Come on, Peter," she called. "Don't be a sissy. And don't worry about Wang. Wang hears no evil, Wang speaks no evil, and for goddamn sure Wang sees no evil—not in anything I do."

"All right then."

He dove in, nearly losing the suit over his knees. He pulled it up and kicked toward her, underwater. The long Prissian legs waggled, and she laughed when he surfaced beside her. She placed her hands on his shoulders and moved close. The twin Mount Prissians flattened on his chest, nipples hard. "You're in good shape," she flattered him. "You've got an Eastern body, flat and bony and nervous. Jack is already a California *pudge*, like a Fijian chieftain on a diet."

"I do play tennis most days," he said.

"Will that do it?"

"They say it helps."

"Jack does what he calls *work out*," Mona sniffed. "Which means he puts on his jogging suit and has a bloody mary for breakfast."

"That is very funny," he said.

"Is it?" She smiled quickly and then clamped her mouth voraciously on his lips, thrust her tongue between his teeth, and grunted happily. Hamilton felt himself borne away. There was not much a man could do to resist such an onslaught, even if he had a mind to. He allowed himself to sink toward the bottom of the pool, taking her with him, and had the singular pleasure of pushing his face into the Prissian cleavage. Her body shook, and she wrapped her legs around him. When they came up for air, she said shakily, "Here, Peter, or in the house?"

"Mona, I've got a lot of party invitations to deliver."

She groaned, "Peter, I love you. You're a funny man. Could we become thick?"

"As thieves? I don't know."

Her eyes were close to his. "If you're thinking about Jack again, forget it. He's got nothing to do with this. I need somebody for the fun of it. To touch. No ties. Just touches. You're not married, are you?"

She did not know about Naomi. But, he thought, realistically, not everybody in the world had to know about Naomi. Mona probably never read a newspaper, and in any case, her attention span was no doubt measured in seconds.

"No, I'm not married."

Beneath the water, he could feel the intense warmth of her belly and aggressive crotch. There was about Mona a raucous, distinctly animalistic quality that was, at the very least, stimulating and a relief from the usual

94

nasal-toned patter in this part of the world. She seemed to grow, before his eyes, into a sort of voluminous sex organ. In her way, larger than life, Mona resembled Virginia much more than she did Perfidia Sinclair. Thank God for that. Her eyes heaved passionately, and she pressed against him. He held onto the side of the pool for dear life.

"I feel a certain reciprocation," Mona muttered, and laughed again, from deep inside. "I've always thought it should be very good in the water, in suspended animation. As in a spacecraft, out of touch with gravity."

"We should know soon, now that they're taking lady astronauts."

"A stroke for woman's liberation, whatever that is," Mona agreed, flashing white teeth. "In space like that, nobody could complain they were always on the bottom. You know—don't breathe a word of this—Jack likes to be on the bottom. I find it off-putting but, of course, it doesn't muss my hair."

What was he supposed to say to that?

"I'm sorry you don't seem to think very well of Jack."

She shrugged, closed her eyes, and energetically bumped against him. In the next few minutes of erratic conversation, their bodies plastered together in the lukewarm water, he discovered that Mona's life had not always been smooth. She'd had a demanding and not ragingly successful career and had been married twice, the last time to the Russian-English composer Uri Norris.

"And believe it or not," she said urgently, her mouth fastened to his neck and her thick hair trailing in the water, "I was very faithful. It was Uri who fell in love with the first violinist." Too bad, Hamilton commiserated. "Yes," she went on, "especially since the first violinist was a man with a mustache. I had no idea he was gay. I guess that's when I realized that the best revenge, like it's said, *Peter*, is to live well. You could help."

He did want to help, God knows he did want to help in any way he could. "Mona, it's not often a man gets the chance to make love to a famous movie star person with such lovely knockers."

"Knockers?"

"A great American expression, dating back to the Civil War. There was a Union general named Knocker. During the Battle of Gettysburg, he was heard to yell, 'I like girls with big tits,' and from then on his men always called tits 'knockers' in honor of the general."

Mona pinched his thigh and grabbed his sword in her right hand. "You are incorrigible, Peter. . . . It's not a derogatory term then?"

"Not where I come from." He had decided his best strategy was to be a bit flippant. He could not take this seriously. He had, since Naomi, never taken it seriously, this stage business between man and woman. This was the reason Sally Jones troubled him just a little. She was pressing him too hard. . . . He was not totally convinced he should make love to Mona, just for the reason of his emotional integrity. He didn't really want to cuckold the pudge again, although it gave him a minor kick to know that he could. "That's what I like about old Hollywood," he said. "Guy comes to deliver a book, and he winds up taking a swim."

"And that's not the half of it. *Peter*, take my breasts—my knockers—in your hands. *Please*."

He moved his right hand from poolside and put it on her left breast.

"So light," he said, "like a soufflé."

"Like a little duckie," Mona said breathlessly, "like a little duckie with a red nose." Hamilton laughed and nodded. "Insured by Lloyd's of London," Mona added seriously.

"I can believe that. How much is the premium?"

"Peter, it runs to the thousands every year."

"But God," he said, "it's worth it. I wonder if the Lloyd's bell will ring if I pull you underwater?"

Mona giggled when he grabbed her around the waist, again planting his nose, eyes, and chin in her endowment. They drifted slowly toward bottom, then he let her go and, dodging her seeking legs, kicked toward the other side of the pool.

"Whew!"

"Shit!" she exclaimed, for she had noticed Wang's reappearance. This time, the eunuch karate champ was carrying a plug-in telephone. He used an outlet by the table and brought the instrument to Mona. Hamilton realized he had been saved, for the moment, by the Bell system—either saved or denied a romp, whichever way you looked at it.

Mona climbed the steps and sat down. Sitting barebreasted, she braced one forearm on her knee and laid the knockers across it, nipples aimed like ship guns at his head. She picked up the phone, assuming a very annoyed expression. "*This* is Mona Prissian." She frowned more fiercely and raised her eyebrows at Hamilton. "Oh, hello, Jack. Yes, Jack, all right, Jack . . ." Pause. "Yes, we'll be waiting. . . . Yes, we." She opened her mouth, eyes sparkling. "Yes, Mr. Peter Hamilton is just delivering a very personal invitation to his party. . . . Yes, *we'll* be here, Jack." She put the phone back together. "Your friend Logan approaches. He was phoning from his car."

"Like LBJ. Did you ever hear the car joke about LBJ?"

"I don't wish to," Mona said icily. "Car jokes make me carsick." She tumbled back into the pool and

97

breast-stroked toward him. Again she placed her hands on his shoulders. Looking him in the eye, she said, "I could tell from the tone of his voice that your good friend Jack Logan thinks that you've just porked me."

"Porked you?" He hacked a laugh.

"An old English expression," she said, face straight. "It dates back to the Henry VIII. One night whilst at dinner, he looked up at his princes and said, 'You know, chaps, I like eating pork better than fucking.' From then on, as a matter of respect, when his court said the word *porking*, they meant fucking."

"But it's not derogatory?"

"Not where I come from." She put her lips to his and nibbled. "But as for you, we're going to have to delay what Jack suspects we're already done. Shucks, as they say in the movies."

"Mona . . ."

"You're going to be embarrassed when they get here?"

"They?"

"Sally Jones is with him and, even now, they are near. Jack called from Sunset, just as they passed the Beverly Hills Hotel."

"Holy Christ—I better get dressed."

"Peter," she protested, "you are pusillanimous? A *cringe*?"

"No, not a cringe. But I think it would be smart if you put your top back on."

"I will not," she said determinedly. "Mona Prissian always swims *sans* top and often *sans* bottom as well."

Hamilton was palming her breasts in the water. Like little duckies, yes. But she was not good for her threat. In a second, affixing to his face a last toothy kiss, she walked to the shallow end of the pool and picked up the bikini top. The knockers remained in peaky stance. He supposed that at some point she'd had them underpinned with silicone. He had to wonder if Jack Logan was telling the truth about Mona having her superheated beaver run tightened for a closer fit. It didn't matter much now, either way.

He heard the car pull up outside and then the heavy tones of Logan's voice.

"Duke! Come on, boy. . . ." Christ, he was bringing the hairless wonderdog with him. "Duke! Come on, you dumb son of a bitch, *heel*, you bastard. March. Follow me. Sally . . . goddamn it, kick him, will you?"

Hamilton was rehooking the metal tabs on the back of Mona's bikini top when Jack Logan and Sally Jones came out on the terrace. Behind them was the strangest dog Hamilton had ever seen. Duke was quite bald all over, white-skinned and totally hairless. The dog's eyes were pink, watery, and depressed. Duke did not walk like a dog. He slouched sideways. His knee joints were knobby, and he was big-assed and small-chested, like some women. Duke's tail was like a piece of string, and he slobbered.

Mona exclaimed, "Jack, you've brought the monster! My God! Peter, this dog is positively prehistoric. It used to be a fish."

"Goddamn it," Logan growled, his eyes switching from Mona to Hamilton, "this dog is a pure-bred Chinese temple son of a bitch." His voice became sarcastic. "Well, this is a cozy little scene."

"Hi, Sally," Hamilton said. Her eyes were flat and deadly, like a snake's. She didn't answer.

"Jack, *dearest*," Mona squealed. She was back to playing little tootsie, Hamilton realized. She sprang toward Logan and planted a lippy kiss on his tanned cheek. "How was your day? And Sally, dear, hello . . ."

"A shitty day, as usual," Logan spouted. Still staring at Hamilton, he sat down at the glass-topped table. "Don't you have a pool of your own, buddy?"

"Sure I do," Hamilton said, smiling. "Mona invited me for a swim. She said I looked hot."

"Hot! I'll bet," Logan growled.

"We were talking," Mona said brightly, "about you."

"About me? What?" Logan demanded.

"Only good things, duckie." Mona's eyes were mischievous. "Sally, how *are* you?"

"Just fine, duckie," Sally said blackly.

Hamilton decided it was high time for another diversionary maneuver. "Is this animal really your attack dog, Jack? I have to tell you, he looks very meek."

"Yeah? Show him a rat and watch him go," Logan grunted. "Show him an intruder on my *turf* and watch him turn into a killer."

Duke shambled away from them, picking a spot on the other side of the pool under a bush, where he could see but not be noticed.

"He don't like the sun," Logan explained. "He gets sunburned, like Mona here. He's got very sensitive skin."

"Then how in the hell are you going to get him tattooed?"

"For some reason, this kind of a dog doesn't mind that. The Chinks have been doing it for years. In fact, these hairless types *like* it. It makes them fiercer."

"You sure he's not just some kind of an albino?"

"Pete, he's no fucking albino," Logan said impatiently, "and stop making fun of him. Otherwise, you're liable to lose your leg."

Hamilton kept it up. "Does he bark?"

Sally stared at him angrily. "If you don't stop talking about this goddamn moron dog, I'm going to start barking." Still glaring at him, she said sternly, "Get dressed."

100

"What?"

"Get dressed. You're going to take me home."

"I am?"

"Yes, you are. Get dressed, you horse's ass."

Nine

Sally didn't say anything until he asked her where it was in Westwood that she lived. Her fingers knotted rigidly in her lap, she sat staring straight ahead at the street.

"This is what you drive? A goddamn Pinto?"

"Sure," Hamilton said easily. He couldn't figure out why she was so angry. "It's got four wheels and a motor. What the hell more do you need?"

"You son of a bitch," she muttered, by way of reply.

"I'm a son of a bitch because I drive a small car? You sound like Jack Logan."

"You miserable son of a bitch," she said again. "What the hell was going on there? I'll get even with you. Fuck you, Peter Hamilton."

Enough, he thought. He pulled the car over to the curb and stopped. Grimly, he said, "What the hell are you talking about, Sally Jones? What do you suppose was going on—not that it's any of your business either way."

Her eyes were wet with fury. "I think you screwed that big cow, that's what! How *dare* you?"

Hamilton drew a long, calming breath. "Just tell me where you live. I'm taking you home and dumping you. What a bad-tempered little bitch you are!"

"I suppose it's those gigantic tits that grab you," she said sarcastically.

"Yes," he grunted angrily, "as it happens, I am nuts for big tits."

"You would be! You're nothing but an adolescent. Kids like big tits, not grown men."

He was annoyed, very annoyed, but at the same time, for some infuriating reason, he felt like laughing. Things like this—a man could not take them seriously. "You're so right, Sally Jones. I'm an adolescent, and that's why I don't dig you—you've got little tiny ones."

Not quite so tiny, he judged, but even so . . . He was not prepared for the slap. Her right hand flashed across and landed with a *splat* on his cheek. "Son of a bitch!" she cried.

Hamilton grabbed the hand before she could recock her arm, then whapped her lightly across the face with his left palm. "You insane little . . ."

Sally struggled, her muscles tight, but he managed to hold her. She began to weep in frustration, and then he did start to laugh. She pulled furiously, trying to get away. "I'm going to kick you right in the balls."

"No, you're not, the car's too small for that."

She butted at him with her head, and he threw her a shoulder. She went after his neck with her teeth and, before he realized what had happened, her face was against his, her mouth was open, and she was crying. She kissed him.

"Goddamn it," he exclaimed, "stop that!"

Sally bit his lip, not hard enough to draw blood, but hard enough to hurt.

She drew back, smiling tremulously. "Peter Hamilton, you belong to me!"

He dropped her hands and turned his head away. "Now I've heard it all. What the *hell* are you talking about?"

"Just that. You belong to me, hot stuff."

Steadily, he looked at her. Yes, it was as he had feared. "You're too young to own property," he muttered, "and I still don't know what you mean. I don't remember signing anything." Christ, he thought, what was this? She was crazy. She was beyond Virginia. And he was not going to stand still for such a silly thing.

"You bastard," she said softly, "I've dumped my chum . . ."

"So?"

"Because of you."

"So?" he repeated, more irritated.

"Goddamn it, Peter Hamilton, don't you understand? I'm in love with you!"

"You're not."

"I am."

"Impossible," he snarled. "I won't accept it. I won't take the responsibility. I don't even like you very much. Keep out of my hair, Sally Jones!"

She merely smiled, rattling him more. Women were such goddamned idiots! They could never accept anything so beautifully simple as *No, no, a thousand times no. I'd rather die, sweetheart, than say yes.*

"You've got it all ass-backwards," she said, total conviction in her voice.

"No, I don't," he said, feeling desperation piling upon him like a swelling tidal wave. "You're young and you're stupid, mostly young . . ."

"Sticks and stones," she interrupted blithely. "I know what's going on. You're scared." She was watching his face, that tolerant look pursing her lips, that look no man could ever hope to match. "You're scared . . . and you're ashamed because you slept with my mother."

He turned, hot, embarrassed. "Sally, you're full of . . ."

"Shit?" she inquired pleasantly.

"And you have a filthy mouth," he said, endeavoring to look sickened. "You should write the Webster's dictionary of filth and obscenity."

"Maybe I will," she murmured, "but in the meantime, take me home."

"I will, gladly, if you'll *please*, finally, tell me where in the *fuck* you live."

"Ugh," she said, "you talk awful, Peter Hamilton. No, you still don't understand. I want you to take me to your home."

Had he known that was coming? "I won't. I refuse."

"Then I'm just going to camp in this tacky Pinto. Because I'm not telling you where I live."

"Jesus," Hamilton groaned, as hopelessly as he could, "Sally, please, cut it out. You can't do this to me."

"Yes, I can," she said stubbornly. "I'm absolutely serious."

"Sally, I have no wish to be arrested for statutory rape."

"Asshole," she exclaimed tenderly. "I am twenty-three."

"Maybe by the calendar—no other way."

She folded her arms. "I'll just sit here all night."

"I'm getting a phone call from New York," he lied.

"Well—then drive home, for heaven's sake, Peter."

He sighed. "Good God . . ."

"He won't help you," Sally said quietly, "because He believes in love. Drive home. I won't molest you. . . . I just want to see where you live."

"That's all? You promise that's all?"

"Yes, duckie," she said sarcastically. "Big bad girl is not going to do anything to you."

Cursing to himself, Hamilton started the car. He was nervous. He didn't say anything until he'd negotiated the streets behind the Beverly Hills Hotel and found Beverly Drive, which led him into Coldwater Canyon. His house was up in the crest of the hills.

Finally, he said, "Sally, you're a little pain in the ass."

"Is that the best you can do?"

"I'll think about it." He did but could only come up with a question. "Sally, why are you doing this?"

She looked at him as if he were some kind of moron.

"Jesus, because I love you. Haven't you heard about love, Peter Hamilton?"

She could have put it better. "Yes, I have," he said haltingly, "and that's part of the trouble. But forget that," he went on strongly as she tried to backtrack. "I remember you were in love with this other guy and, boy, did you dump him fast."

"No," Sally said thoughtfully, "I wasn't in love with him, and anyway we agreed, in a very mature fashion, to dump each other. He saw reason," she continued, talking fast. "He was married, and he wasn't going to marry me. Besides, he had his kids and . . . and his wife was pregnant. Actually, Peter, wasn't I good . . . and kind?"

He nodded. "Yeah, kind of kind. A funny kind." She *was* insane, popped out of her shoes.

"And," Sally went on, her mouth going sixty miles an hour. "Besides, I want my own children—with you. Little ones with curly hair and cute buns and all."

Hamilton was ready to park the car again. "Sally . . . Sally, I'm going to have an accident if you don't shut up!"

"Well, you don't have any," she accused him.

"So? Is that a crime? I hate children. I *don't* want any."

She laughed, the sound splattering him. "You do!"

"I don't, goddamn it, not necessarily, not at all. My God, my God," he groaned, "what is this? Sally . . . I thought your generation decided the world was too terrible a place to drag another kid into."

"Balls," she drawled. "See—you agree."

"I don't agree to anything," he exclaimed. "You're some lousy example of the liberated woman."

"Balls," she repeated. "Being liberated, as you know, dear man, doesn't mean you don't have kids. If I didn't have one with you, I'd do it with somebody else. I think it's about time for me, don't you? You

107

don't want to be *too* old." She put her hand on his arm and stroked. "All being liberated means is that you have kids but you don't get married."

"Married?" Was that a horrified shriek he had produced? Hamilton knew about this, he knew all about it, and now he also knew that he was lost. Somehow, sneakily, she had introduced him into the Sahara of her emotions and already he was a lost one-man patrol. There was no good trying to establish the generation gap; for one thing, he admitted, there was not quite a generation between them. But she was so young. She didn't fit into his plans. All he wanted was to play tennis and travel. But there was nothing he could say to her that she would condescend to hear. Or? He assembled himself for strategic retreat. "Good that marriage isn't important to you," he murmured. "Because I don't intend to marry you." He paused. "What am I saying? I don't intend to do *anything* with you."

"So, who asked *you*?"

Hamilton's house was teased, like a fan dancer, by two tall eucalyptus trees with wispy, droopy branches. It sat unobstrusively on a curl of the hilly road, nondescript in front, with white-painted clapboard sides and shuttered windows.

"Press that button there," he told her wearily. "Remarkably, it will open the garage door."

She did so, and he drove inside and stopped. A door led from the garage into a small kitchen, bricked and chromed, and then into a big living-dining area. A set of brick steps dropped from the living room to a wide terrace.

"I thought you said you had a pool," Sally said.

"A Jacuzzi," he muttered. "That's a pool, isn't it? Not everybody has an Olympic pool, you know. Will that make you change your mind about me?"

"What a phony," she said. She looked around. "I

don't see how fifty people are going to fit in this dump."

"Dump? Of all the . . . They'll fit if we use a shoe-horn. I open the doors and they overflow outside."

Sally stood critically, her fists on her swivel hips, her shoulders tense. "Well . . . they're going to fall over the edge."

"So? Small loss," he sneered. "I do hope the humble dump meets with your approval." Virginia was like Sally: forward, aggressive, too frank. He caught himself. Virginia resembled Sally? Before, he'd thought Sally resembled Virginia.

"How long have you lived here?" she asked.

"About a year."

"Since . . ."

"Yes."

"Well," she repeated, doubtfully, "it *seems* comfortable enough. I'll make a few changes."

"Change what? You're not going to change anything."

"I didn't say I didn't like it," Sally cried. "Don't be so sensitive. What's upstairs?"

"Two bedrooms," he said, not looking at her.

"Ah . . ."

She was trying to be cute, but he didn't bite. He opened the terrace door and stepped outside. There were more trees, and beyond the end of the terrace, a tangle of underbrush lay beneath what was reckoned a fair view of one sector of the Los Angeles skyline. Some people said it had a *great* view, and Hamilton supposed it did, if one liked to look at street lights leading to infinity and then only on clear nights.

"Where's *your* manservant?" Sally demanded sarcastically. "Don't you have a Wang? I know you have a wang—but do you have a Wang?"

He didn't trip over that. "I don't have a manservant.

I have a cleaning woman who comes in three times a week."

"No cook?"

"No, no cook either." He stared implacably down the hillside. "How does the view suit you?" Sally was standing beside him. She was almost as tall as he was. Her father, he thought acidly, must have been a normal-sized man, not a midget like Virginia. "I suppose you're going to say the view is tacky too."

"Did I say anything?" she laughed. "You *are* sensitive. I was going to say it looks the typical bachelor pad—messy and slightly crummy."

"Oh, thanks. I'm not sensitive. It's just that you . . ."

"What?" She slipped her hand in the crook of his arm. "Peter Hamilton, if you're going to say I'm a ball buster, I'll get mad."

"Did I say that?" He stared at her large, liquid, startling blue eyes. "But now that you mention it . . ."

"You rat!" she cried. "I'm not. I am not a ball buster. I'm a fun-loving girl. You're thinking of my mother."

"I am not thinking about your mother," he said stoutly. "I don't believe Virginia is a ball buster. . . . *And* I wish you'd stop assuming there was something between us."

"I've read the book. I told you I'd be looking out for you."

"Well, I'm not in it, am I? I told you I wasn't and I'm not."

She nodded. "That's true. I couldn't find you." Her eyes fell away from his gaze. "I don't know why you don't like me."

"Sally, I never said I didn't like you. When did I say I didn't like you?"

"In the car," she said plaintively. "You said I was a pain in the ass."

Patiently, comfortingly, he said, "You got me mad. I

110

didn't mean it. I just find you . . . I don't know . . . astounding."

"And I frighten you."

"Yes." Well, not exactly, he admitted to himself. But she was not a tranquilizer either.

"Why?" Sally asked anxiously. "I want to know. That's something I need to know. I don't want to run around scaring people."

"Sally," he said, feigning deep thought, "I just don't know. Maybe it's the sharpness of your intellect."

"What?" Her face broke. "You prick. You're kidding around with me."

"It's true," he maintained. "You do have a sharp intellect. You also run at me, head on. I can't dodge. I mean . . . ordering me to get dressed like that at Mona's."

"Well?" She frowned. "Don't you like to know where you're at?"

"Yes."

"Then you should like me for my frankness," she said, relieved, "even if you don't like me for anything else."

Hamilton nodded. He thought that just maybe, for a moment, he had the upper hand. "I admire you for *everything*, Sally. You're terrific. You're beautiful. You've got the body of a ballet dancer and the mind of an Einstein. You're honest and unassuming—and you swear like a truck driver. What else is there to say about you?"

"That you love me."

"Well, I'm not going to say that."

"Not at all? Ever?" she wailed. She shifted to face him, placing her long body two inches from his chest. "That can't be true, Peter Hamilton." She glared at him insistently. "I know that you love me a little bit. I do know that. I can feel it. You love me marginally, yes, that's it. You'd like to be able to love me, but you

111

are timid. I can understand that. You don't want to commit yourself . . . again. I appreciate that. I'm *very* reasonable."

"Oh, my God."

"Are you going to faint?" she asked innocently. "Come inside and I'll make you a drink. Pull yourself together, old cock."

"All . . . right. Yes, make me a drink. I think I might faint."

"That's what I said," she chuckled. She took his arm, helped him across the terrace and up the steps, then pushed him down on the long couch facing the open door. "Now," she said, "What is it you'd like?"

"Get the Russian vodka out of the freezer," he murmured. "Get a glass and fill it up, on ice. A slice of lemon."

"Yes, sir."

"Sally," he said weakly, laying it on, "I don't have any dope in the house."

"That's okay," she said brightly, playing along, "I'll have a vodka too."

Hamilton did, as a matter of fact, feel a little paralyzed, as if, perhaps, he'd fallen and bumped his head or been KO'd by Muhammad Ali sometime last week and was still recovering. His arms and legs were draggy, and his brain shot through with holes. He sat, his hands on his knees like an invalid, listening as Sally clattered around *his* kitchen, banging closet doors and muttering to herself. It didn't take her very long to find her way around. In a moment, she was at his side with a glass—vodka, clear, steaming cold from the freezer. She gave him the glass—rather, inserted it in his fingers.

She sat down carefully beside him. "Cheers," she said brightly. "Here's mud in your eye and grease on your axle."

He turned blankly, blindly. Was she real? Hamilton

112

had always figured there must, somewhere, be a person like Sally, but he had given up expecting to meet her. "You know," he said, "you really are . . . unbelievable."

"But nice," she said cheerfully. More softly, she added, "I'm better than you think I am, Peter Hamilton."

He nodded and that seemed to make her happy. He sipped some vodka and turned his eyes back outside. "That helps."

Sally held her glass in her hands between her jean-clad legs. In a small voice, she said, "I guess you know by now that I want everybody to love me. The shrink said I'm kind of self-defeating in that department."

"You've been to a shrink?" For some reason, he had always found the idea of psychiatric help somehow repulsive. He had never been able to believe in his heart that people shouldn't be able to heal themselves. Logically, he knew he was wrong.

"I went for a couple of months after I got out of college," Sally said. "I had an identity crisis. I thought I should be my mother."

"But now you *do* know who you are," he said. "I can see you do know that."

"Yes." She was solemn. "Of course, he told me I had to get over coming on like a stormtrooper. Nobody loves stormtroopers."

"I see." What did he see? "Look at it this way—it might be a little exaggeration for you to go on about . . . loving me. What you really want, maybe, is for me to love you."

Sally lifted her glass and held its cold lip against her front teeth. "I guess that could be partly true."

"Therefore," he said persuasively, "you don't really . . . love me, right?"

"Yes, maybe that's it," she said doubtfully.

"Oh, I see. God, Sally, you do jump around."

113

"There!" she cried, abruptly turning. "You do want me to love you. And I do. I think I do, anyway, and isn't that half the battle?"

"Battle? Stormtroopers? Hell, Sally, I knew love was emotional warfare. But Sally, I'm not ready for Vietnam again."

"You were in Vietnam?"

"A few months, that's all."

"You're scarred."

"No, I'm not scarred. Christ, all I did was a TV thing, got drunk a few times and then out."

"But you are scarred," she insisted. "From your marriage."

Reluctantly, he said, "I suppose so. There's no point in denying it. I felt as if I'd been knifed too, so I must have a scar somewhere."

Sally turned her legs toward him. She put her lips on his cheek but did not kiss. Hamilton felt the warmth of her breathing and the whisper of her eyelashes. God, he thought, she was clever. In a word, a woman. She wasn't wearing perfume, but there was a fresh scent on her, possibly a little sweaty. She didn't move, and a deep silence descended, except for her breathing. Now, if he hadn't known before, he realized what was happening and where it was going to end. He had to shake himself out of the past and into the present.

He moved first—he put his right arm around her shoulder, and she edged closer. Her mouth was at his ear now; a flutter of her tongue made him gasp, and she giggled. He turned his head and their lips met. They kissed. Her lips were soft and quick. A small essence of vodka joined them, and then she drew a deep and trembling breath. She closed her eyes, for once speechless. They stayed like that another long moment, until she opened her eyes.

"Now *I'm* afraid," she whispered.

"Of what? All I did was kiss you."

She shook her head deliberately. "I don't want to do anything you don't want to do."

"Nothing's going to happen," Hamilton said, although he knew it was not true. "We'll drink up and then I'll drive you home. By the way, where the hell is your car?"

"I left it at Twentieth," she said. "But look, I'm not saying I want to leave. I can't go back there. He . . ."

"He, what?"

Worriedly, she asked, "What if he's, you know, lurking around? He said he probably couldn't let me go."

"Oh, for Christ's sake," Hamilton sighed, feeling his desire recede. "I'll check the place out. Then you can lock your door. Don't let him in."

"What if he breaks down the door?"

"Don't you have a gun?" he demanded irritably. "Better buy a big cannon. . . . Call the cops!"

"Oh, Peter." Sally shifted ground rapidly. She lifted her face. "Kiss me again, Peter, just once more."

Naturally, he thought cynically. "Sally, stop kidding around. Now's the time for you to make your retreat, gracefully." Blackly, he threatened, "This is your last chance. No more teasing."

Her voice was miserable. "I'm afraid you may not like me," she murmured shyly. "I don't have big ones like Mona Prissian."

"I'll be the judge of that," he said. "So far, they seem okay to me." It was the first forward remark he'd made, but he was not about to be finessed by her quivering lips. Now was the moment: put up or shut up. Either way, he'd know.

"I hope you think so," she sighed.

"Sally, I'm not a man of steel."

She kissed him again, her eyes pressed tightly shut. Out of nowhere, like a hummingbird, the tip of her tongue darted daringly. Scarcely moving her lips, she whispered, "Am I going to seduce you, or not?"

"I thought I was seducing you," he said. "Jesus!"

"Peter," she said, "there's no seduction involved, not if both parties are game. Remember, a kiss is the first bounce in the basketball game of ecstasy."

"What's that?"

"An aphorism. I just made it up."

"Holy Christ," he muttered, "people get killed for saying things like that, Sally."

"I apologize," she said, smiling. "Want to hear another?"

"No." He shoved her away. "I've got to have another vodka. You make me very nervous."

She handed him her glass. "Me too. I'll have a little bit more."

"You're nervous too, aren't you?"

"Sure I am," she said. She grinned up at him, then lifted her arms over her head. "Oooh," she cried, "I'm in heaven." She fell over on her side on the couch, wriggling.

Hamilton went into the kitchen and got the icy Stolichnaya out of the freezer. It poured like syrup, gleaming, into their glasses. Well, it was done, he supposed, all but the plucking. He glanced toward the garage door and thought of Virginia, just for a second. It wouldn't have surprised him at all if she'd burst in. But then immediately the presence, if it had been that, was gone. Virginia was gone.

But was she? When he carried the glasses back into the living room, Sally was staring toward the edge of the terrace.

"What is it?" he asked.

"I'm trying to figure out why I should fall in love with you. Or why I should think I'm falling in love with you. What's so special about you, Peter Hamilton?"

"Not a thing." He sat down on the edge of the

116

couch and took her hand. It was slim and warm. "And what's so special about Sally Jones?"

"Plenty."

"That's right," he said quietly, "you are very special."

She snuggled her body against his knee. "Do you mean that, or are you just saying it for effect?"

"No, I mean it," he said.

He laid his hand on her back, palm against her spine, with the fingers spread. Slowly, he caressed her. She shivered and he felt her muscles loosen. She smiled gratefully. "That's very nice."

"You are tense."

"Wouldn't you be? I'm not experienced like you."

"I'm not *that* experienced."

"I don't . . . Let me ask: do you really want me? I don't want to disappoint you, you know."

"Sally, it's not as if we're going on a suicide mission. Relax. Or maybe you don't really want to."

Christ, he could not get over the worry that he was somehow taking advantage of her.

Huffily, she said, "I'm not some kind of a groupie, you know. I told you I loved you."

"You said you *thought* you loved me."

"I just said that—for no reason. Now you're going to find out I'm not a virgin, and you'll probably be hurt."

Hamilton looked at her, nonplused. "Sally, if I thought you were a virgin, I'd be out in the street screaming for help."

"How the hell do you know I'm not?" she demanded.

"I don't. You're the one who's been making so much noise about being shacked up with a guy. I just figure you were doing more than playing Monopoly."

Impatiently, she said, "But it's possible, isn't it, that's all we did do?"

117

"Yes, that's possible," he admitted.

"But not probable, right? The next thing you're going to want to know is all about my other love affairs—you think I'm like Virginia."

"Sally," he said, "I'm tired. Listen . . ."

She lifted her hand and laid a finger across his lips. "No more . . ."

"In the nick of time, Sally."

She moved her hand to the back of his head and drew him down. Self-consciously, she kissed him again. Hamilton caressed the soft lips with his own, slowly, and her breathing became measured, more focused. She shifted her legs, straining. Once again, the big blue eyes popped open. "The kiss," she murmured. "The kiss . . ."

"Don't say it, not another one of those things."

"I won't."

Her head fell back. She was smiling, her tongue caught in her teeth. Waiting.

"Now," Hamilton said, "I'm going to open your shirt, little miss, and remember, you asked for it."

"Do it then," she urged.

He did so, opening the flannel shirt to bare skin. The right breast was immaculate, rose-tipped. He brushed it with his mouth.

"Oh . . . oh, I never thought you would. Yes."

Ten

The *Chicago Tribune*'s review of *Powerhouse* was what Virginia called a stinker, and she said so on the Prentice Baumgarden show. Virginia, Felix learned again, was never at her most tolerant at seven A.M.

"What a marvelous welcome to the Windy City," she said grumpily as soon as Baumgarden was through with his initial words of welcome and explanation of who they were and what they were doing on his "Bright Eyes—Bushy Tail" wake-up hour.

"And we take a burst of forty-five caliber poison," Virginia went on. "But never mind. What can you expect in the Windy City except wind?" Baumgarden chuckled and lifted his plastic coffee cup to her in mock toast. His voice was the opposite of his face, the latter long and gastric, the former deep and mellifluous.

"Of course, mommies and daddies," he said sweetly, "everyone should understand that Virginia Preston is really Eve. And Eve writes a syndicated column from New York City called *Bites from the Big Apple.*"

"Right on," Virginia sniped. "And so much for the *Chicago Trib . . .*"

However, it still had to be said, and Virginia did, that reviews did not bother them, not in the least. The main thing, she told Baumgarden and his millions, was that the book was being talked about. Trashy? So what? Had Mr. Baumgarden taken a close look at the bookstores lately?

"Felix and I are not worried. The last review is the one that counts: are they buying your book or not?"

Baumgarden pointed out that the word was that *Powerhouse* was going to be a big movie deal.

"Exactly," Virginia said. "Felix and I are looking forward to working with Jack Logan on that. Jack is a dear friend—and before you ask, I'd better say that he's also my ex-husband."

"Really?" Baumgarden sounded astonished. But he should have known that from the biographical data he'd had in his hands for at least a week. For sure, he hadn't read the book, but he might have taken the trouble to read the background. "And what about the paperback sale, Virginia and Felix?"

"It'll be six figures," Virginia predicted.

Neither of them knew this to be true, but it didn't matter.

"Really?" he cried again. "Congratulations, Virginia and Felix! Now," he went on insinuatingly, "word of mouth is that *Powerhouse* cuts pretty close to the bone. Tell us now, you bright and obviously prosperous people, is the truth stranger than fiction?"

Virginia looked confused, so Felix fielded the loaded question. "Sometimes, Prentice," he said casually, "but not in this case. *Powerhouse* is fiction and a lot stranger than the truth—in fact, far removed from the truth. It's *fiction*, and it's catalogued in the Library of Congress as fiction. There's no resemblance in this book to actual people, whether living or dead."

"And," Virginia interjected sharply, "if they're living, that's especially true."

Whatever the tone of the reviews—and, by and large, the critics found *Powerhouse* to be a "page turner"—Virginia and Felix triumphed wherever they went. Naturally, they had built-in clout. They were well-known personalities in their own right, book or no book. Virginia's columns appeared in one or another of the daily papers in the larger cities and, over the years,

Felix had become acquainted with the affluently social or socially affluent, the low-keyed underground that really ran the country.

On each of the two days they spent in Chicago, there was a cocktail party in the evening, followed by a formal dinner. Many of the honorable matrons had made a point of buying *Powerhouse* and reading or skimming it before bringing it along for an autograph. No one seemed particularly put out, or even interested, that the book was richly laden with scandal and sex. Of course, there were *some* intriguing comments.

One of Felix's oldest friends and one of Chicago's foremost names was Adele Fleishpacker. During dinner at the Matrixes, Adele was his table partner. Over a spicy wurst salad, Adele whispered conspiratorially, "Felix, I am quite astounded. Quite. I had no idea!" Felix shrugged ever so slightly and grinned shyly. But then Adele did something that was very un-Adele-like. Chuckling in a peculiar manner, she slipped her hand under the tablecloth and found Felix's penis beneath his napkin. She squeezed it, quite roughly. Felix was so startled, he almost passed out. As it was, he dribbled gravy on his tie. He summoned a chuckle, but even as he lifted his napkin to dab at the spot on his tie, Adele did not let go. Despite the circumstances, Felix was perplexed by a mild tumescence.

He leaned forward, putting his elbows impolitely on the edge of the table. "My dear," he mumbled, "I don't think you should take the book seriously. It's what we—Virginia and I—call a romp."

"Some romp, old friend," Adele said flatly. Anyone watching them would have concluded that she was issuing a severe reprimand. Her face was that stony. "You are a sly one, Felix. You quiet ones do run deep." Her next outrageous aggression was to invite herself to the hotel for breakfast the next morning. "There's something I want to ask you about, Felix," she muttered, a fevered smile toying with her cheeks. "I think perhaps you can be of help to Horace and me."

Felix told Virginia about the incident later. He tried to be cheerful about it but, actually, he was mired in a dark and fatalistic mood. For, before leaving for the Matrixes, he'd already had the phone call from Wade French—the separation papers had been drawn and they'd be served on Felix in California. Would Felix mind telling Wade where he'd be available? Yes, he would mind, very much. There was also, French continued brutally, the matter of Nathan Sinclair. Altogether, French concluded, it was not going to be duck soup for Felix James and Virginia Preston. Felix sensed there was something more French wanted to tell him, or ask. But he hung up before French could elucidate.

"So," Virginia crowed with delight, "you invited Adele here, you rascal?"

"Virginia—Adele invited herself."

She laughed brittlely. "I'm surprised and I'm not sure I approve. Don't worry. I'll chaperon."

"That won't be necessary, Virginia. I can take care of myself."

"I'll bet I know what's made her curious," Virginia said.

"Tell me, then."

"The cunnilingus bits. It's got to be that, Felix. Cunnilingus is something they've never heard about in Chicago. The question, however, dear boy, is do you know how to perform it?" Virginia peered at him distrustfully. "I'll bet you never learned it from Evelyn. Maybe on that B-29 during the war."

"So?" She could be insufferable. He felt an unaccustomed hostility rise within him.

His tone of voice confused her, for once. She did not know what to make of him now. She stood up, placing her empty glass on the table.

"Well," Virginia said, "good night, coauthor." But she didn't leave. She stood there, clicking the catch on her pocketbook open and shut. "Good luck in the morning," she muttered, striding into her side of the suite. She didn't shut her door all the way, but Felix did not take the bait. He sat for a moment, then went into his bedroom, had a bath, and slept.

Virginia was still asleep when Felix let Adele in at eight-thirty. She didn't waste any time. "I've already had my breakfast, Felix. Horace and I always eat breakfast at seven A.M. before he leaves for the plant." She smiled bravely and braced her shoulders. "I've brought the book. Now, here, I've got it marked. On page thirty-eight, you say . . ."

Virginia had been right about Adele, in every respect.

When it turned Sunday, they were in Dallas, with the day off until a six P.M. cocktail party at Magda Henderson's. Magda was another of Felix's old friends. It was Felix who'd introduced Magda's daughter, Cynthia, to New York society some ten years before. Since then, of course, Cynthia had been married and divorced twice. Now she was living with a baseball player in Houston. No, one could not say that Cynthia had turned out supremely well, but Magda couldn't hold Felix accountable for that. Putting things together had nothing to do with their falling asunder.

A full morning of rest was welcome, Felix told himself, and Virginia certainly agreed. She was stretched out on the couch, still clad in her plaid robe and furry mules. They'd finished a light breakfast and the Sunday morning papers. There had been generous mentions: a book review that found *Powerhouse* to be "fascinating froth" and paragraphs in the social columns. No big deal, the latter, Virginia dismissed them, when one considered she was always extra kind in New York to visiting society columnists.

Even in the morning, Virginia looked stunning. And that despite the fact that the evening before had been long and tedious—at least that part of it they'd spent together at the Philpotts. Virginia glanced over her shoulder toward him. The famous skin bloomed, and her eyes were fresh and bright. Felix didn't think it was necessary, or wise, to ask where she'd gone after the strawberries and cream and demitasse at the Philpotts', and then until closing time at the hotel bar—and, evidently, until much later than that. He'd waited in the bar, ogled a couple of party girls, then wearily come up to bed. He was still a little hung over.

Whatever she'd been up to, he knew, it had evidently been in the company of the young oil heir, Vince Murgby. Well . . .

Felix lifted his cup and finished what was left of his coffee. Quietly, he returned cup to saucer and pretended to busy himself with another look at their long itinerary. "We'll arrive in Los Angeles a week from today," he mentioned.

"Don't tell me your troubles," Virginia quipped sharply. He looked up. "You're wondering, Felix?"

"About what, Virginia?"

"What I was doing last night."

"No, no, not at all, Virginia. As to Los Angeles, I can bear it, if you can. I know you've always said you hate the place."

"I almost wish we were going straight to Honolulu," Virginia said moodily.

"But we'll be with friends. Your daughter . . ." Virginia frowned. "Peter. Even Jack."

"Felix, I don't know that I want to see Jack after all. Maybe we could skip Los Angeles altogether and spend the whole time in San Francisco."

Felix looked at her quizzically. "And there's Lenny

Thoreau. Mustn't forget about Lenny Thoreau, Virginia."

"Yes, Felix," she said irritably, "and don't forget about last night, either."

"What about it? I came back here, had a couple of drinks, and went straight to bed."

"That's all?" For some reason, she was miffed. "I thought you might have gone off with that little barracuda you were sitting next to."

He laughed. "Miss Bronski? Hardly."

"Well, Felix," Virginia stated carefully, "you did seem much taken by her cleavage. I was watching you."

"Were you now?"

"Yes, I was," she said sharply. "Felix, I'm beginning to think this whole thing is too much for you. I hope you're not going to begin playing literary lion." She nodded for emphasis, and then informed him, "Believe it or not, *I* went to look at a ranch. That young Murgby man drove me out to look at his little spread—his *town* ranch, a mere one thousand acres. The big one is in east Texas."

"Very impressive, I'm sure."

"Felix," she snapped, "are you trying to make me angry?"

"Certainly not, Virginia. Would you like me to order some more coffee?"

She stared at him, perplexed. "Yes," she said, "and some ice cream. I want some walnut ice cream."

Felix took his time dialing room service, humming and studying the menu. He watched Virginia out of the corner of his eye. Preoccupied, she had turned to stare out the window at the wilderness of downtown Dallas. The skirt of her robe fell away from her knee, revealing a piece of well-rounded thigh. But she did not notice.

He replaced the phone and stood up to cross the

room and take her empty coffee cup. As he bent down, he could see the beginning curve of her breast at the top of her robe.

"Oh, thanks," she said. She motioned toward the end of the couch. "Sit down, Felix. I've got to talk to you." When he had put himself next to her feet, she said soberly, "Felix, I hope you're not going haywire."

"Well, no," he said mildly, "I don't think so."

"These women—they're throwing themselves at you."

He smiled thinly. "Not so I've noticed. The men, far more at you."

"Felix." She shook a finger at him. "Now, I don't want you to be jealous."

"Jealous?" He rounded his voice, as if to say this was far from his mind. "Why should I be jealous?"

"That's just it. You shouldn't. I've always thought of you as a man of the greatest generosity of spirit."

"And so I am."

"But," she said perplexedly, "then why are you making so much over the women?"

"Well, I'm not, Virginia." He laughed self-effacingly.

"*Well*, I think you are, and the reason is that you're jealous. Otherwise, you wouldn't do it."

Impatiently, he demanded, "Virginia, tell me which way you want me to be. I try my best not to react at all. But since you want to know, I'll tell you frankly, Virginia, it's not pleasant for me to see you squander yourself on every Tom, Dick, and . . ."

"And Vince?" Now she was behaving as though he had insulted her, rather than responded to incitement. "On every little piece of tail that comes down the pike, eh, Felix?" she jeered.

"Virginia!" His face flushed and he rapped her on the knee with the palm of his hand. Her body jerked at the gesture, and her robe moved to expose the plump little paw of her femaleness. Felix could not help himself. He stared.

She hooted mockingly, "If crotches could talk, eh, Felix, what stories they could tell."

He was terribly embarrassed. "I was not thinking that, Virginia! I wish you'd not talk like that."

"Felix, it's not a serious subject," she said calmly. "It's like our book, a romp. You know, it *is* true that we're not going to live forever."

Sarcastically, he said, "Gather ye rosebuds while ye may . . ."

"Yes." Virginia's eyes, surprisingly, filled with tears. "Poor Felix, I'm sorry. I am cruel to you."

She held out her arms, and he was drawn forward. She kissed his lips softly and closed her eyes in apology. He was fascinated, for never before had he seen her surrender. She pulled away for an instant, as if undecided about something, then, apparently having made up her mind, returned to the kiss. Her mouth opened slightly, and her hands tightened on his shoulders. Thickly, she said, "Felix, I think it's about time you took off your ridiculous clothes."

"Virginia . . ."

"No arguments, Felix. After all these years, the time has come."

He nodded against her face. "I guess you're right."

"Don't guess. *Know.* The time has come."

He stood up and untied his dressing gown. Virginia rose and took his hand. She led him into her bedroom. The sheets were in disarray, but the smell of her sleep was still on them. She slid onto the bed and beckoned to him. Carefully, he stretched out beside her. He kissed her this time, and she caressed him. He ran his face from her lips to her throat, then her breasts, perfect rounds of velvet. The nipples were small, patrician; they puckered when he touched them with his tongue.

127

Virginia sighed and shuddered when he reached her navel.

"Ah, Felix," Virginia said luxuriously, "isn't this perfect for a Sunday morning? Much better than the funny papers."

As he had known all along, Virginia was perfectly formed. It was trite to think of her this way, but she was like a little doll. All her components had been joined with precision. Felix slid his hand to her crotch, its well-groomed pubic hair, and private paraphernalia. The clitoris was right there, to hand, located exactly, prominently, as in the medical books. When he touched it, her entire body focused on it. "No, Felix," she breathed, "please not with the finger."

Felix ducked his head obediently into the musky smell. There it glistened at his nose. He nudged it with the tip of his tongue.

"Yes, Felix, there is a Virginia," she moaned, "and she's right there."

Virginia was exciting, as exciting as he'd always known she would be. Her body was mysterious, complex, and replete with hidden riches; it was more than a naked body. She touched him, making approving noises, and he trembled before her lips. God, yes, she was exciting in arousal. She was a perfect lady about it too. She left him no doubt that he was satisfying her greatly and this was a stimulation in itself. Very soon, she was ready for him. Her eyes, he saw, were shining in anticipation, and she kissed him again, fervently. "Felix, dear Felix . . ."

She pulled him over her and between her legs, spreading them wide and gathering him into her snug, again so orderly, interior. Hands spread on his buttocks, she expertly manipulated his body, pulling him forward. Virginia made love neatly with no wasted motions, like a marvelous piece of machinery. Her every movement counted for something, each signaling the

128

forward march of passion. Normally restrained, and never one to express himself violently during the act of love, Felix heard himself panting.

Even Virginia's climax was orchestrated. She loosed herself the first time with one short exclamation, the tip of her tongue in her teeth. Felix continued, bearing down with the greatest force he could muster, and she opened her mouth, panting, and put it to his, gushing sweet, warm breath, while jiggling herself to another small pitch of fulfillment that paralleled his own spending. Felix cried out hoarsely with the wild discharge, like flame in his loins. Virginia's face became wreathed in a childlike smile, and she pulled him into the depths, hinging her pelvis under him in one, two, three final drawing movements. Then, slowly, naturally, as if slipping gears back to neutral, she subsided and was finally quiet under him. "Felix, that was lovely."

But he was out of his mind. He kissed her. "It was . . . catastrophic, Virginia."

The man from room service arrived at their suite at about the same time as the phone call from Orville Jones, of Toledo, Ohio.

Felix, dizzy and disturbed, slipped back into his paisley robe and went to the door. The white-jacketed waiter put the fresh coffee and Virginia's ice cream on the table by the window. Felix tipped him a dollar-and-a half.

Virginia's voice emerged stunningly from the bedroom. "Orville. After all these years!"

Felix left her in privacy. He sat down and poured himself coffee. He could not help listening. He crossed his legs and flexed his muscles. He didn't know whether he felt glorious or terrible.

"Orville . . ." Virginia was evidently trying to get a word in edgewise. "Orville, the book is not scurrilous, and it's got nothing whatever to do with you. Orville, do you realize you're talking about a period of time that's more than twenty years ago?"

Oh, Christ, Felix thought, double-damn. Was this even more trouble? First Evelyn's mole and now Orville's . . . what?

"Orville," Virginia cried, "it's not going to make a laughingstock of you. Nobody even knows you were married to me. Of course we were on TV in Chicago, and so what?"

She was listening again, and Felix heard her gasp anxiously. "Yes," she muttered angrily, "yes, I know Sally is in California. Yes, we *are* going to be in Los Angeles too. Orville, goddamn it, no!"

Felix fancied he could hear the babble of words spewing out of Ohio.

"You're behaving like a child, Orville. You know, I can hardly remember your face, let alone your scrawny body. And I don't *care*. You're not silly enough to think you're the first farm boy who screwed a girl in a haystack in a barn. And your pants were just as hot as mine—so there!"

And that was that. Felix heard the phone being slammed down. Virginia shot into the living room of the suite, her face red and angry. Felix grinned at her.

"What the hell are you laughing at, Felix? That was Orville Jones."

"So I gather."

"He hung up on me!"

"I don't wonder," Felix said calmly.

"He thinks he's in the book, the goddamn fool!"

"Well, he is, isn't he?"

Virginia paused in mid-fury, then nodded. She chuckled. "Where's my ice cream, Felix?"

All Felix could think of was that Virginia looked as elegant standing up as she did lying down. She whipped the cover off the serving of ice cream and spooned into it. "Funny," she murmured, "ironic. I think I was eating ice cream at a church social the first time I ever laid eyes on Orville."

"That is ironic," Felix agreed.

"God," she mused, "just imagine. Twenty years and he still pisses me off." She shook her bare shoulders and ate voraciously. "Best thing after sex is ice cream," she said.

"Aha! That's why you ordered it? You knew we were going to bed?"

Virginia nodded cleverly. "I had an idea we might. Just think, Felix—about the only 'victim' we haven't heard from yet is Perfidia Sinclair."

"God," he groaned, "not the hellion of Capri. Perfidia would never sue, would she?"

"She better not," Virginia said stridently, "and she'd be ungrateful if she did. She comes out of the book smelling like a rose. Nathan is the one who gets all the heat. Besides which," she added spitefully, "Perfidia so much as opens her peeper, and she'll never again be mentioned in Eve's column."

Felix nodded appreciatively. "Perfidia should particularly like the part about the affair with a sitting president."

"You said it!" Virginia finished the ice cream and put the dish on the table. She smiled eagerly at him, eyes glowing. "Felix, you were the master stroke." She slid up next to him on her bare feet, pressing her hip against his cheek. Felix wrapped his arm around her, turning her slightly so he could kiss her belly. "Felix, let's go back to bed."

"Yes," he said. He gazed up at her face. Her lips were parted, expectant. "You know, Virginia," he said emotionally, "everything is changed now. You've got to promise me, Virginia."

"Promise you what?"

"About *us*. This doesn't change anything between us. Whatever else happens. Even if . . ."

"If what?" she asked. "You mean even if we never go to bed again?"

"Something like that," he said haltingly. "What I really want is that, whatever happens, we're always going to be the best of friends."

"Well, naturally," she cried. "And I hope I'll be able to keep you from shooting off like an errant rocket."

"I wouldn't do that in any case," Felix said.

"Oh no?" She glanced at him, amused. "What I didn't tell you—speaking of errant rockets—Orville says he's coming to California."

Eleven

Had Virginia been in New York, there was no doubt she would have had the "scoop" on the arrival in the Big City of Perfidia Sinclair von Thurnsteil and her nymphet daughter, Baroness Marina von Thurnsteil, heiress to the declining estate called Thurnsteil bei Isar, near Munich, Germany.

It was left to Suzy and Liz Smith to record the fact that the former reigning beauty, Perfidia, former wife of "ailing" cosmetics king Nathan Sinclair, was paying her first visit to New York in more than fifteen years. Everyone would recall, said the columnists, that Perfidia had been a principal in a devastating divorce action and then gone into voluntary exile on the fabled Isle of Capri to live out one of the love affairs of the century with the man who had been called the handsomest in Europe, namely, Baron Putzi. Putzi, all his dear friends in New York and Palm Beach regretted to hear, had died "suddenly" in the late autumn of the previous year.

Wade French made a habit of scanning the gossip columns because many of the people mentioned there were friends of his, and even strangers sometimes turned up in the legal frays of the future.

Thus, French was not surprised to hear again from Perfidia. She was staying, Perfidia said, at the Plaza Hotel, and she would love to see him. There was so much to talk about. "Not least, *caro*," she murmured, amused, "this book that dear Virginia and dear Felix have written about me."

133

Oh, oh, French thought. "Fido . . ." he began to say.

"*Caro*, we no longer refer to the Baroness von Thurnsteil as Fido." She paused haughtily. "Please come at five," she said, taking it for granted that her wish was his command, "and we'll have tea. It has been a long time, Woof-Woof."

French grinned to himself, remembering many things. He chuckled. "Baroness, we no longer refer to Wade French, attorney at arms, as Woof-Woof."

Perfidia's voice cracked in a nasal cackle. Her laugh was among her least attractive attributes.

After they'd said good-bye, French recalled, for he couldn't put memories aside any more than anyone else could, how their nicknames had evolved. During the Sinclair divorce proceedings, Perfidia had tried her best to win him to her side. She had *done* her best too. God, he thought, it would be terrible even now if Nathan Sinclair were to learn about it. For French, judiciously, wisely, carefully, had manipulated the settlement very much to her advantage. It had been either that, or revelation and ruin. Perfidia, he reminisced with a certain satisfaction, *was* that bad, and *he* had been weak and stupid. He had committed the unpardonable. She had shot his ethical parachute full of holes. Even after all these years he shuddered. And now he shivered with mortification when he reminded himself of what Nathan Sinclair had told him about taking advantage of poor Evelyn whenever Felix had been out of town.

None of them who'd had any contact with Nathan Sinclair had come out of it in good moral health or with peace of mind.

French, sitting at his imported teak desk with its brass fittings, inhaling the leather scent of ancient and modern law books, was half in love with Evelyn. Strange, he mused, her very coldness was like an

134

aphrodisiac. She was bitter and brittle, terrifying. She detested men, it seemed; therein lay the challenge, her unique fascination. Evelyn had informed him, perhaps as a necessary bit of information in the initiation of the separation proceedings, that Felix had never, never satisfied her in a physical sense at any time during the long marriage. Not that it mattered, Evelyn said distantly. Naturally, the bald statement was enough to incite almost any man to try to do better.

French slowly buttoned his vest, tightened the knot in his Princeton school tie, and shrugged himself into his snug suit jacket. He needed another crack at the old diet.

French cabbed to the Plaza, planning his arrival as close as he could manage to the dot of five. He would not be early; he would not be late.

Perfidia, ah Perfidia! She was sitting by herself at a table in the Palm Court. He stopped outside to look at her. She had not changed an iota since he'd last seen her, fleetingly, in Rome, five years before. They had taken tea at the Villa Borghese, and there had been no question then of reliving the past, for Putzi was still alive and Perfidia, madly enough, was totally devoted to the rarified German baron. Many people suspected that Putzi was a raging fag, but if Perfidia knew this, it did not seem to bother her in the least. She had been able to talk of nothing but Putzi and her darling daughter, Marina. Both had stayed behind in Capri while Perfidia attended to business in the capital. Fido and Woof-Woof had not surfaced again.

Perfidia was dressed in black, in what French thought looked like a modernized Fortuny dress, pleated and body-hugging. He was familiar with *La Mode* since one of his hobbies, not one he talked about much, was his collection of period ball gowns. Perfidia's costume, while the ultimate of chic modesty, nonetheless outlined the breasts and emphasized the line of her waist. Perfidia looked . . . what? Firm, yes, that was the word and, as always, extremely well tended. What set her off from the biddies having their tea in this palm-shrouded oasis was the hat—it was a black, soft felt slouch hat that framed her face in mystery. Under it, her face was implacable, the eyes turned in, arrogant. Perfidia was not interested in anybody else. She would not be watching for him; it was up to French to find her.

Her hair was waved in a short European, or maybe peculiarly prewar Italian style, and French noticed instantly the teardrop emeralds she was wearing at her ears. Perfidia lifted a cigarette in an ivory holder and put it coolly to her lips. Almost imperceptibly, she glanced at her watch. She would have seen it was five P.M. She frowned. The rings glistened on her fingers.

French entered the Palm Court, and she saw him. He strode to the table.

"Fido," he said. He couldn't resist.

"Woof-Woof." Perfidia smiled her slightly lopsided smile, at once sardonic and amused. Her eyes, smoldering and black, fastened upon him.

French sat down next to her and leaned to kiss her cheek. He smelled her perfume, the same, as if it had been used and recycled.

"It's wonderful to see you again, charming Baroness."

"And you, Mr. French."

"Well," he said, summing up the five years, "you look marvelous."

"I never change," Perfidia said, smiling aloofly. "Now I'm a simple widow in my widow's weeds." She looked at him. "You've gotten a little beefier, Wade."

He huffed a chuckle. "Time thickens all men. But not women—at least not you, Perfidia. You look better than ever."

"Possibly," she drawled, "mourning becomes Perfidia? And you, Woof-Woof, you're divorced, I heard—or read. Somebody else? Were you carrying on?" she asked lightly.

He felt he should nod self-confidently. "Yes, Irene was tired of me. I took up with a little . . ."

"Showgirl?"

"Well, yes." Of course, it wasn't true. Actually, it had been a legal secretary, and Irene had discovered their love nest by pure accident.

Perfidia chuckled fondly. "Woof-Woof, you are a sly old dog."

"You're not so bad yourself, Fido."

She stared at him for a moment, then teasingly asked, "I suppose you've completely forgotten by now how we got our little names?"

French colored to a proper shade of red. "Not for a second." The derivation of Fido and Woof-Woof would not be considered very polite in the circles to which French had become accustomed.

"I'm surprised," Perfidia said thoughtfully, "that Virginia didn't know about that, too. She seems to have everything else in that book. The sex is just overpowering."

"But how could she know that?" he demanded gallantly.

"You might have told her," she said. "I know how Virginia twists men around her little finger. And she *did* put in everything else, down to the last grunt and groan. How did she find out?"

He shrugged. "I don't know. Maybe intuition, reading between the lines. Is it actually so very close?"

Carefully, ominously, Perfidia said, "It is goddamned close, Wade."

"That's what Nathan says too."

Irritably, Perfidia said, "It's blatant. She's got me doing everything with that old man." Words came to

137

her lips sweetly. "She has made a big thing of the fellatio, very important to Nathan, of course." She ignored his squirming. "It is surprising, therefore, that she didn't, somehow, discover about you and me and doggie-style."

"Jesus, Perfidia, don't say it out loud."

"Well?" she demanded, then relented. "I'm just happy Putzi isn't alive to read the book."

"There's never been a murmur about us, not a murmur."

She frowned, her dark eyes malevolent. "It's comforting to know some things are sacrosanct."

French nodded and cleared his throat. "If it's all right with you, I'm going to have a Scotch instead of tea." He lifted his hand for a waitress and ordered a Black Label on ice, no water.

"Remembrance of things past upsets you, Woof-Woof?" she asked, smiling bitingly.

"No, no, I've always thought of that . . . interlude . . . with the greatest pleasure. There's never been an adventure like it, Fido, before or since."

She nodded reluctantly, not willing to admit there had ever been a "tops." She bent forward so that the brim of her hat bridged their faces. "It was the circumstances that made it exciting, Wade. The danger. You defending the old man and me on the other side of the fence."

"But didn't I come through for you?" he asked smugly.

"Yes, I give you credit for that, Wade. You did me well—in *all* respects."

Perfidia poured more tea, and they were quiet while the waitress placed his drink before him.

"We made a good pair, didn't we?" he asked.

"Rascals, both."

"No, not rascals—friends, helping each other."

"You would think of it that way, wouldn't you?"

Perfidia put her tongue on her lips, testing the lipstick, and her left hand to the side of her face. Again, the rings registered in his mind. "How is the old fool? I presume you're still serving him legally."

"Nobody sees very much of him anymore."

"You do."

"Now and then," he lied. It wouldn't mean anything if he told her he hadn't seen Nathan personally since he'd last seen Perfidia in Rome.

"Good," she said, suddenly vibrant, "because I have a very important project for Nathan to become involved in."

French's laugh was brief and astonished. "I think . . . you must be joking, Perfidia. The old man flies into an apoplectic rage whenever he hears your name."

She placed a long fingernail on her nose, dead center. "Tut-tut, don't say that, Woof-Woof. How could that be, after all these years? Dear, there must be forgiveness, finally. He'll die soon, won't he?"

French shook his head. "I doubt it."

"But I *know* he's eighty-eight years old now. He must have just had a birthday. He can't last much longer."

Her voice was a little ghoulish, and French was dead set against getting her hopes up. Besides, Perfidia had already had all she would get of the Sinclair fortune. "Some people never die," he said, smiling. "What is the project, exactly?"

"Of course! Save Capri!"

"Oh? I didn't know Capri needed saving, Perfidia."

"Wade," she replied briskly, "the island is sinking, and my beloved home is sinking with it."

"I haven't read anything about this, darling."

"Nonetheless, it's true, Woof-Woof." Her eyes burned with meaning. "I happen to know Capri is sinking."

"But, Perfidia," he protested. "I've been there. The

island is made of solid rock. How can the goddamn thing sink?"

Patiently, she told him, "Rock rots. Do you realize Capri sank one centimeter into the Mediterranean just last year alone?"

He shook his head. He could not believe this. Then, on the other hand, he realized he did not have to believe it, not for Perfidia's purposes. "I know you're not serious, Perfidia."

But she insisted, "I am serious and my project is serious too. I want one million dollars from Nathan Sinclair, and I won't take no for an answer."

Perfidia induced perspiration, and French felt it now, breaking out on his forehead. "Perfidia," he said, "it's Venice that's sinking, not Capri. This is a game. Nobody is going to fall for it."

"It is no game," she said fiercely. "If Venice is sinking, so can Capri. Nathan always loved Capri. He loved to park *Moisturizer II* off the coast. Don't you remember?"

"I remember all too well," French said sullenly. "But I'll remind you I wasn't there the last time he anchored off Capri."

That was when it had all happened. The reminder didn't put her off. She pressed five scarlet fingernails into the back of his hand, like talons. "You mean when I *disgraced* myself?" she cried softly. "No, you weren't there. But everybody else was. By the way, how are they all? Is Virginia still laying every man she can get her hands on?"

"I gather so," he said, happy to get away from the subject of a dissolving Capri. "Virginia doesn't change. Felix is the same, except that Evelyn is divorcing him. She's angry about the book."

"Evelyn? Why should Evelyn be angry? She's not even in the book, Woof-Woof."

"Yes," he said uneasily, "but she thinks she is, and

140

that's what counts. The person who's really angry is Nathan. He wants to sue them for millions and get an injunction on distribution. Jesus!" he cried. "I can't do— that. There is still a First Amendment. If I start a libel action, that just calls attention to the goddamn thing. Perfidia . . ." He was broadsided by a horrible suspicion. "Perfidia, you're not going to sue, are you?"

She laughed outrageously, tossing her head. Even in the chaos of his thoughts, he noticed how smooth her neck was. Could it have aged so kindly? But there were few lines on her face, merely fine crisscrossing creases at the corners of her eyes.

"Sue?" she cried. "No, I'm going to say that everything in the book is true!"

Now French began to see what she was getting at. It was simple: one million dollars. God, he told himself sardonically, it was such a relief to discover that Perfidia had not changed at all. The shock was that he, Wade French, was hereby appointed to get the one million dollars out of Nathan Sinclair.

"Where's your daughter?" he asked dully, trying to avoid the moment of truth.

"Upstairs, resting. She still hasn't gotten over her father's death. She loved him very dearly."

"Well," he said curtly, "she would, wouldn't she? He *was* her father."

"Yes," she said, looking wan. "But Marina loved him a little bit more than that."

French leaned back and handled his glass. What on earth did she mean?

Somewhat bitterly, Perfidia went on, "Marina has, or had, what one might describe as a very strong father fixation."

"I don't see anything so unusual about that."

Perfidia glared at him. "Don't you see what I'm trying to say?"

"No," he said uncomfortably.

"I mean to say the relationship was incestuous. Yes! That's what I mean. So," she said angrily, "I've lost both my daughters. First, Naomi to that man Hamilton and then to a murderer—probably Hamilton, if the truth be known. And now, Marina."

French shook his head wearily. "That's not so pleasant, is it? Why couldn't you—"

"What the hell could I do?" she exclaimed. "Maybe it's partly payment for my own deeds. But whatever, that's the way it is. I pretended it wasn't there. I turned my head, gave parties, gadded about. But it went on. You see," she said dismally, "when Putzi died, it was very sudden, a heart attack. We were in bed—Marina was in bed with us."

"At her age?" French felt his eyes widen.

"Yes." Traces of tears showed at the rims of her black eyes. She gripped his hand.

"She's only a child," French muttered.

"Seventeen now," Perfidia said. "Beautiful. And ruined. She's tried to ruin me too. She *has* ruined me. I love her too much. I can't do anything. I am powerless."

"Jesus Christ," French whispered. "That's depressing."

"Yes, isn't it?" Her smile was frightful. But then she snapped her fingers impatiently. "You're the only person who knows this. I thought you'd understand. After all, you're a lawyer, and surely lawyers hear such things all the time."

French placed his hand over hers on his arm. He patted. "I'm sorry," he said soothingly. "Is there anything I can do?" He felt it was polite—and politic—to make the offer.

Perfidia pulled her hand away. "No. Now Putzi is dead, I hope it'll go away. She'll snap out of it, I know she will."

"Yes, of course. She's only a kid, Fido," he said

142

comfortingly. "She'll go away to college soon, won't she?"

"In Rome, yes."

French chuckled. "She'll meet some handsome Italian stud."

Perfidia drew in a sharp breath. "She's met plenty of Italian studs already. She tries them out. Nothing has come up to Putzi, ever."

Slowly, French asked, "What was so special about Putzi?"

"Well . . ." Perfidia hesitated, smiling inwardly again. "Don't be shocked. Putzi was insatiably lustful. We . . . uh . . . spent whole weeks in bed, the three of us. It was . . ." French cupped his chin in one hand, fascinated. "Delightful," Perfidia admitted scornfully. "Yes. Heavenly. I have to say it was."

French slowly began withdrawing his sympathy. This sort of thing, he knew, was sickness. Yes, and he *was* familiar with the phenomenon within the courts of the law. "Where are you going from New York?" he asked evasively. "Back to Italy?"

"No, we're going to California. Marina has never been there, and I haven't been in Los Angeles since I can't remember when. I believe Virginia and Felix are headed there too. And I do want to see Peter Hamilton," she said. "I want to look him in the eye and ask him if he killed Naomi."

French shook his head. "I happen to know that Peter was completely cleared of any suspicion of murder."

"*Caro*," Perfidia murmured, herself again, "don't say things like that. I have to know. Besides, I want him to meet Marina."

"Fido, Fido," French said painfully, "are you purposely torturing yourself?"

"Perhaps."

Perfidia passed her tongue gently across her lower

143

lip, showing the tips of teeth that were distractingly yellow. She hugged her forearms under her bosom. Her dark eyes were wounded. But then she revived her haunting smile. French was conscious of a familiar tug of desire in the pit of his stomach.

"Woof-Woof," she pleaded, "you will get Nathan to help save Capri, won't you?"

Slowly, French nodded. "Yes, of course, Fido. I'll try, although I don't know how I'll approach it. If it doesn't work out, you will understand, won't you? It could be very ticklish. He . . . his men watch his finances very carefully."

"Darling, Woof-Woof, all I ask is that you do your best. You *could* explain to him how I feel about the book, how *much* I enjoyed the story of our love affair. Woof-Woof, tell him how much I love him still, despite everything, despite his cruelty to me. Tell him that at last perfidious Perfidia has a *cause* and that he can make one last, grand philanthropic gesture."

French held up his hand. "Cut it out, Perfidia, there's nothing I can tell the old bastard that's going to make him feel good about it. Admit it! You're not finished with him yet. That's what it amounts to, isn't it?"

Her eyes glittered with sincerity. "No, Woof-Woof, I'm giving Nathan an opportunity to do good and to feel good about it."

"Come on, Fido, you're talking to Woof-Woof," French said emphatically, leaning back and hooking his thumbs in his vest. "It's the last hit, that's what it is. It'd kill him if he had to do it."

Perfidia's mouth lurched to the side in her least attractive expression. "Good. If kindness kills, then he'll go happily. Woof-Woof, don't misunderstand me. I *am* determined to have Nathan contribute. After all, Capri doesn't sink every day."

He smiled pleasantly. How he admired her nastiness.

144

In this way, she was very like Evelyn. He liked nasty women.

"You're marvelous, Fido," he congratulated her. "I can't get over it. I guess I've always loved you."

He got no relief from her eyes. "No, Woof-Woof, you're a lover of realism because you're an attorney."

"You would have made a great attorney," he said.

"Yes," she agreed devilishly, "I would have made a great crooked attorney. Not upright and honest like you, Woof-Woof."

Perfidia put her left hand on his shoulder, gently pressing, then ran her long fingernail along the line of his chin. French trembled at her touch.

"When you've finished your drink," she said, "I want you to come upstairs and meet Marina. You'll find her precious."

He knew he was at a precarious turning point. It was clear that Perfidia again was bent on making him her accomplice.

"Well," he said, realizing he had no time to maneuver, "I'd like to meet her. If she's your daughter, she must be a fascinating little creature."

"Of course she's my daughter," Perfidia laughed. "And she's not so little either. She's as tall as I am."

"And you're no shorty," French said quickly. "I have to make one phone call."

"You can do that upstairs."

"No, it's a business thing. I'll do it out in the lobby."

What he had to do was tell Evelyn that he was tied up, taking a deposition, and wouldn't be clear until close to midnight.

Twelve

Orville Jones was tall and, as Virginia had reminded him on the telephone, his body was scrawny, even at the age of fifty-five. Most men put on weight, at least a paunch, when they passed forty. But not Orville. He ate like a horse. He was known in his household as the "garbage can" because he put away leftovers as fast as any disposal unit. He had not gained an ounce of weight since his army days.

Which returned him to the point he would make with Emily before he left for the office. An old army buddy was having a reunion of sorts in Los Angeles this coming week, and Orville planned to attend. Yes, and for once, he was going to tell her, he was going by himself. He had reached the breaking point and damned if he was going to rot in Ohio.

Orville stared at himself in the mirror. His eyes were more owlish these days, and his cheeks were gaunt. Emily said often enough that he looked like a scarecrow, and so did his kids, Bertie and Betsie. But they were away at the state college, and they didn't bother him anymore, except when they needed money.

At least he would smell good. He picked up a bottle of Pierre Cardin after-shave and splashed it liberally on his face. Now was the moment. In his bathrobe, Orville marched into the kitchen and picked up the coffee Emily had poured for him. She was standing in front of the window, her gut propped on the sink. She was watching something outside in the yard.

"Morning," Orville said.

"Hi."

He drank some coffee. "What's going on?" he asked.

"Nothing," she said, not turning. "Over next door. A couple of dogs are screwing."

"How nice. Well, it's spring." He stared at her bulky behind. He might have added that if this was so, then it was the only screwing happening anywhere in the neighborhood.

"Where's the eggs?" he asked.

"Coming up."

Emily trundled around. A fine transformation, Orville thought. Is this what happened to airline stewardesses when they put their feet permanently on the ground? The doctor had told her that she was bordering on hypoglycemia or some such mysterious sickness. But Emily did not give a damn. Whereas Orville ate and ate, he didn't have much yearning for sweets. Emily gobbled cookies and candy all day long. Even now, a gooey Mars bar dangled from her fingers.

"Jesus," Orville said, "you eat candy for breakfast too?"

"Why not?" she demanded. "If it suits you, try it on."

"What the goddamn hell is that supposed to mean?"

"Every cat to its own kaboodle."

"I see," he nodded, "that explains everything."

She glanced at him and slammed the frying pan down on the stove. Her eyes were like little diamonds in the folds of her cheeks. "The doctor says I'm compensating for something," she muttered. "Probably for you."

"Right." He leaned back in the kitchen chair and watched as she cracked two eggs into the pan. "Well, Emily, you can compensate for something else next week."

"How's that?" she asked indifferently.

"I'm taking a week off, and I'm going to Los Angeles to see an old army buddy of mine. I heard from

148

him yesterday. We—some of the boys—are having a reunion."

"Los Angeles," Emily repeated thoughtfully. "I've never been there, not even when I was flying. Do I get to go?"

"No. This is a stag party."

"You guys have plenty of stag parties right here," she pointed out, reasonably.

"This is different. We were all in the Big Red One."

He'd explained to her so many times that the Big Red One had been his army division in Europe. But she never remembered—either that, or she preferred to play forever dumb.

"And what're you going to do out there?"

Orville shrugged. "Drink beer. Go to porno movies. Probably get laid fourteen or fifteen times."

"Boy!" Disgustedly, she shoved two pieces of bread into the toaster. "If it's getting laid you want, that can happen on the home front too, you know."

"Can—but don't."

"Oh yeah, who says?" Emily demanded belligerently.

"Says me."

"Oh yeah?"

Emily turned away from the stove and with one hand flicked Orville across the cheek, not roughly, but not playfully either. Jesus, he thought, was she going to pop him? She'd done it before, and not rarely. There *was* such a thing in the world as husband-beating. Not many people talked openly about it, but it did happen. Emily had popped him more than once.

"Just sit still, Mr. Smart Ass," she ordered.

She turned off the gas and then turned on him. Emily reached under his bathrobe and grabbed him by the pecker. She yanked on it a couple of times, and Orville was irritated to feel himself going stiff. Despite his emaciation, he never had any trouble that way, and during the few times they had reached the point of mutual irritation that enabled them to get excited, he had enjoyed these early morning bangs in the kitchen.

She hiked up her extra-large morning gown and straddled Orville's knees. She weighed a ton. Emily pushed her big bosom in his face, holding him by the shoulders.

"Just suck on those for a minute, mister," Emily grunted, "and we'll see what's what around here."

Orville put his hands on either side of her breasts and pressed them around his face. He made the wheezing, snorting sounds she liked, holding the distended nipples up and out of the way of her belly button. Emily groaned hoarsely and heisted her hips further up on him. She grappled for him and succeeded in forcing his pecker into her. She huffed elaborately, and Orville extended himself as best he could around the meaty arc of her gut. She bounced up and down and, he realized, began flaunting the insidious smell of sex rampant.

"We'll see about getting laid, mister!"

Emily was practically pushing him through the seat of the chair, lifting and falling, loosing her entire weight upon him. Then, goddamn it, if it didn't happen. There was a splintering sound as the hind legs of the chair gave way. And then they were on the floor. Orville's pecker felt as though it had been wrenched out of its socket. Emily let out a sharp cry of pain. Slowly, he untangled himself. But Emily just sat there, bare-assed on the linoleum. She held her ankle and began to weep with rage.

"Son of a bitch," she howled, "look what you've gone and done with your getting laid. My ankle is broken."

"Probably sprained," Orville said miserably. "I told you you got to lose weight. Look at that goddamn chair."

"All you care about, the goddamn chair," she hollered. "Look at my ankle."

Orville looked. Her thick ankle was swelling up.

"Shit," he said disgustedly, "now I've got to get you to the doctor. How in the hell am I going to get you dressed? And to the car? Jesus, I can't carry you. Remember how I carried you over the threshold when we were first married? You must have weighed ninety-eight then. Now you weigh a hundred and ninety-eight. You're as big as the whole fucking house, Emily."

Emily commenced to moan. "You don't love me anymore," she wailed.

But Orville was past control. Now was his moment. "If I loved fat ladies," he said cruelly, "I'd go to the circus." She could not touch him now.

"Oh, you son of a bitch," she sputtered, "and you're going out West and leaving me like this."

"Yes, with a big cast on your foot. I hope they don't have to amputate."

He began to laugh wildly. It was true—*now* indeed was his moment, his time to flee. Emily could not catch him now and pop him. He would hide her crutch or take the spokes out of her wheelchair, whichever they gave her, and he would be gone. The moment of freedom. He stopped laughing and looked down at her.

"What I better do," he said thoughtfully, "is call for an ambulance and some strong men. There's no way I can get you to the car."

"Are you going to the doctor with me?" she cried.

"I gotta go to work, Emily."

"Goddamn it," she shouted, "if I could get up, I'd pop you!"

He shrugged and went into the living room, where they kept the phone. He sat down calmly, listening to her infuriated sobbing. He fingered his pecker. It ached a little, but it would be in good shape for Hollywood, that he promised himself. He thought of Virginia.

Little had he known when it happened, how much he was losing when Virginia waltzed out. For the millionth time, he wondered why she'd left. They had been in love, or at least he thought they had. And the hours in the sack had never again been so good.

But, facing it, he knew that Virginia had wanted the world, not Toledo, Ohio. And now she had it.

But it was also Orville's moment. He would make a point of seeing Virginia in California. That's why he was going.

Thirteen

Hamilton woke up and looked at his watch. It was eight A.M. He rolled over. She was gone. But her jeans were still hanging over the back of the bedside chair.

He got groggily to his feet and looked out the window to check the day. A heavy haze hung in the valley between his house and the city. Then he saw her. Sally was standing on the terrace, like an apparition in the dull light. She was naked, her back to him, and he saw that she was cradling a mug of coffee in her hands. Steam rose around her face. Sally was quite still, gazing into the nothingness, her head erect, back straight. The slim roundness of her buttocks seemed to quiver in the morning chill.

She was beautiful like that. And yes, he *was* in love with her. He hadn't really told her so yet.

Sally had mounted her campaign, invaded his territory in a series of lightning forays that he could not have countered, even if he'd known how. Her car was parked outside and she had moved in her armory of jeans. Jeans, she had said, are the basics of the wardrobe of love. Move the jeans in, and it's serious.

Sally stepped closer to the edge of the terrace, and he wanted to shout for her to be careful. But she was nimble. And she was unconscious of the world. But in this weather, there was no way anyone could see her. Only the birds. They were squawking in the trees, clearing smog from their pipes. Sally wouldn't have cared if the world *was* watching. She was unaffected about her body, about everything. Virginia, in her more sophisticated way, was not much different. But Virginia was in the past.

Sally stooped to pick up something, a leaf, and he saw the soft roll of her left breast.

Not looking up, she said, "I know you're watching me, Hamilton."

"I'm watching you, Jones," he said through the open window. "I didn't hear you get up."

"You were sleeping like a log," she said, "as well you might, after the workout I gave you. Better than tennis, old cock."

"More fun," he agreed. "You made coffee?"

"Yes, do you want some?" She turned to look at him, her oval face serious. "I'll bring you some. The way to a man's heart is through his percolator. But you've got to buy a coffee grinder."

"Oh, yeah? I'm coming down."

"I want to buy a dog too," Sally announced, before he could move.

"What? Not a monster like Logan's, I hope."

"No, a puppy."

"Yeah, a puppy, but what's it going to be when it grows up?"

"A Labrador, a pure black Labrador."

"And who is going to take care of it, may I ask?"

"Me."

"And what about when *you're* at work?"

She grinned up at him. "I'm not going to be at work. I'm going to quit Jack and work for you. You work at home, so I'll always be here."

"Sally—goddamn it, I haven't even offered you a job."

"Don't be churlish, One-Hung. Why do you think I'm learning Chinese? And I can type. I'll be your girl Friday."

"I thought liberated broads didn't like being girl Fridays."

154

Sally laughed merrily. Her voice was like a bell in the mist. "I'll be for Monday, Tuesday, Wednesday, Thursday too."

"And what about the weekend?" He was drawn along by her happiness, forgetting his reservations.

"On weekends," she exclaimed, "I'll do double duty, overtime. I'm going to turn on the Jacuzzi—is that all right, sir?"

"But of course," Hamilton said, "my Jacuzzi is your Jacuzzi."

Sally strolled to the other side of the terrace and briskly pushed and pulled the controls that turned on heat and soothing waves in the little pool. Heavy steam hit the cool air, and the froth of surface action began. She thrust a toe in the water. "It'll be ready in a minute. Coming down?"

"Yes, Jones," he said, "I'm coming down." Hamilton took a couple of towels from the closet at the head of the stairs and paced slowly down the steps. She was in the kitchen by the coffee maker.

"Hamilton, you're naked as a jaybird," Sally yelped.

"So are you, in case you didn't notice."

"See," she said, "with a grinder, we'll get a better class of coffee." She shrugged at his disinterest and poured coffee into a mug. "Come on."

"You give good coffee," he commented, tasting it.

"Yes, coffee is the aroma of post-coitus," she murmured.

"Come again?"

She didn't answer but merely smiled in that knowing way. She was feeling very secure now, Hamilton thought, knowing that she had him.

They climbed into the Jacuzzi, and Sally slid toward him on the seating step. The smoothness of her body was linked to his with the liquid massaging of the jets. She held her coffee high, in her right hand, and slipped

155

the left along his leg to his thigh, then to the pit of his stomach.

"I can't get over that thing," she muttered. "It's getting hard again."

"Sally, I'm beginning to think you need a seventeen-year-old kid. I'm an older fellow, you know."

"Not so I'd notice," she said. She kissed him quickly. "I suppose the same thing would happen, with any woman doing that."

"Probably," he agreed.

She rammed her tongue in his ear. "Hamilton, you rat! Remember one thing—you're mine now."

Hamilton set down his coffee mug. He placed his hands on her waist, just below the gentle beginning swell of her breasts. "Sally, you've been here—how long, now?"

"Since Monday night, not very long."

"Yesterday, you called in sick," he reminded her. "Today is Wednesday. What are you going to do today?"

Calmly, she said, "Today, I'm calling in to quit."

"Listen," he said, "is that smart? I mean . . ."

She poked him in the stomach. "What? You don't want me around? You think it might not work out and then I'd be out of a job too? Hamilton, I'm reckless. I'll take a chance if you will." Her face changed, smile surrendering to concern. "Seriously, just once—do you want me here? If you say you don't, I'll go. I'm not kidding."

Hamilton moved his hands across her perky breasts and put them around her throat. "You beast. What are you doing to me?"

"Nothing. Nothing at all. I'm giving you my semi-virginity. Or is it neo-virginity?"

"You could drive me crazy," he warned. "I wouldn't want to go crazy. Think of it the other way around.

Suppose you jump up and leave *me*? What would I do then?"

Solemnly, Sally said, "I'll not leave you. I promise. I want to go to China."

"Yeah," he said sarcastically, "that's what you see in me. A ticket to the mysterious Orient."

"Slow boat to China," Sally murmured.

Hamilton nodded. "So you've taken possession of me. But I notice you haven't moved your shoes and boots in yet. I won't be sure until the boots are here."

"That's tomorrow," Sally said. She winked. "And I've got some kitchen stuff too. Dishes—a few, you know, a pot and a pan."

"Stale bread and curled-up bacon. Yes, I know. I saw it in the refrigerator. And a half-bottle of wine that's turned to vinegar."

He had driven her over to her apartment the afternoon before to pick up the jeans and shirts, a skirt or two, an umbrella, and a basket of unwashed panties. Sally didn't own any bras.

"I'm going to give up the apartment," she said earnestly. She put a hand on each of his cheeks. "There's something I have to tell you. I want to be very honest with you."

He drew back. He had a feeling he did not want to hear this. "About the guy . . ."

"Yes," Sally said. "When I make the call to quit, that'll automatically cancel the apartment."

Of course. It was obvious, wasn't it? "Jack?" His stomach turned. "Jesus Christ, Sally!"

"It was a friendly arrangement," she said slowly. "Old times' sake and all."

"The guy was *Jack*?" he exclaimed disgustedly. "Sally, if I'd known that . . ."

"So what, Peter? Does it matter? Listen, nothing happened. I mean *nothing*."

"Nothing? But you led me on, Sally," he protested.

"Sure. I had to. I wanted to get you interested." She kissed his mouth, drawing out the evil. "Jack had ideas, ambitions, but nothing happened, I swear. All he ever really wanted was a little feel."

"And you let him? That's revolting. That bastard!"

"Once or twice," she admitted, making a face. "It was hard to keep him off, and it didn't really seem to make much difference. He *is* a lonely guy—Prissian leads him a hell of a chase. So what if I let him feel my tits a couple of times? That's not the end of the world."

"*Whoo*!" Hamilton exhaled air. "Just like that. You're pretty cool, aren't you?"

"Got to be," Sally said knowingly. "Tough world out there. He never got to the bare skin."

"Yeah, shit! That makes a lot of difference, doesn't it? Look, hot stuff, I'm going to have to think about this."

"Goddamn it, Hamilton, I didn't even know you then. And you didn't know me. I'll bet you've done some pretty shady stuff that you wouldn't even tell *me* about."

She had him. He didn't dare answer. He remembered how recently he'd fondled the bare duckies on Mona Prissian's broad chest. Truth was, he didn't have much cause for complaint. But he was not about to admit it. He scowled. "How do I know I can trust you now?"

"And how do *I* know I can trust you?"

They stared at each other. He studied her eyes, the short, straight nose, the mouth, its rosy red lips. The chin was just slightly prominent at the bottom of the face. That stood for stubbornness. As far as he was concerned, she was beautiful. Other people might think the face—and its structure—was too strong. Maybe, but it was not ordinary.

After a second or two of intent observation, Sally's

lips quivered. She smiled and winked. "Okay then, old cock?"

"Jesus," Hamilton sighed. "I love you, Sally. I don't know why. I think basically you *are* a pain in the ass."

"Maybe—but I'll keep you on your toes. Remember, a pain in the ass is the first twinge of . . ."

"Stop!"

"Do I get my dog if I agree to become your mistress?"

"Yes."

"You promise? I don't want jewelry, you know, like most other mistresses. I want a dog . . . and a coffee grinder."

"Yes, Sally," he murmured. "I promise."

"Then I love you too."

He lowered his head, laughing, and allowed the Jacuzzi jets to beat him around the forehead. He needed that. "You come cheap."

"I'm a real tart, Hamilton." She laughed gleefully. "Come on, let's go upstairs. I want to lick you all over."

Sally called her office at ten A.M. and did what she'd said she would do. She quit. There was a great deal of sputtering at the other end of the line but on Sally's end only finality.

Logan called back ten minutes later and demanded to speak to Hamilton. "You son of a bitch," he snarled, "I'm not letting you use my tennis court anymore."

"Shove your tennis court, Jack," Hamilton said. "Does that mean you won't be coming to the party?"

"What!" Hamilton could see Logan's dark face twisting with disgust, but still cunning. "Why won't I? Just because that little asshole quits me to go to work for you? Just because you've stolen my most valuable assistant? The fuck I won't be at the party! Jesus Christ, Pete, I'm paying for it, ain't I?"

The call from New York was the next item on the morning agenda. It interrupted them in bed.

"Peter . . ."

Did he recognize the voice? There was the familiar harsh and not very musical ring to it. It was the voice of the witch of Capri.

"Perfidia."

"None other, dear boy," Perfidia said emphatically. "I'm in New York City, and I thought I'd advise you I'll be in California Sunday. Be a dear and reserve a suite at the Beverly Hills Hotel for me and Marina."

"Perfidia," Hamilton said slowly. "It's been a long time. We haven't talked since . . ."

"Yes," she took him up swiftly, "not since . . . last year."

Perfidia had not come over for the funeral. She had remained in Capri, there to receive the slashed corpse of her oldest child, the misguided and tragic Naomi.

"It's my first visit to California in many years," Perfidia said coldly. "I hope it hasn't changed too much."

"Hardly," Hamilton said dryly. "You know what they say. Beneath the phony tinsel of Tinsel Town lies the real tinsel."

"Clever. Yes, you were always a clever boy, Peter. That's why Naomi loved you so."

"Yes, possibly."

"You knew Putzi died," she stated.

"I wrote you a note, Perfidia," he reminded her.

"Yes, you did. Thank you. I appreciated that." But she had never said a word to him about Naomi. Not a word. All the instructions had come from Baron Putzi, then only a few months away from death himself. Putzi had not been a bad guy. The one trip to Capri that he and Naomi had made had not been a barrel of laughs

160

or reeking of familial affection. But he had carried it off as best he could, in the presence of those three somewhat gruesome Meissenlike figurines. "I'm looking forward to seeing you, Peter," Perfidia said, high drama in her voice. "I *must* talk to you."

"And you will," he said quietly. "I'll reserve a suite. Where are you now, Perfidia?"

"Why, I'm at the Plaza. Didn't I say? I've been having tea with Wade French. You remember him."

Hamilton had met French some years before through Virginia and Felix, most likely during the time he'd first come to know Naomi. Naomi: the craziest blonde God had ever created, and the most passionate. Thinking of her made Hamilton turn and wink at Sally. How did they compare? Did they compare at all? Naomi, spread on a bed, was a shaking, quaking sex machine. She would have been crazy with impatience at this interruption. Sally lay quietly, her hands folded under her head, staring placidly at the ceiling and listening. Sally was a bit wild, but she was not wanton, he judged. He believed her—she would not leave him high and dry, as Naomi had. No, the two were not the same. Sally was a human being.

The next voice he heard thumped into the receiver. "Hello, there, Peter."

"Wade, nice to hear your voice again," he responded automatically.

"I'll most likely be coming out to California at the same time as Perfidia," French said heartily. "I've got to see Felix when he gets there. Say, sport, any chance you can get me a room at the Beverly Hills too?"

"I'll take care of it."

"Sorry to put you out."

"Old friends," Hamilton said. "No problem."

"We'll get to the hotel on our own. Don't worry about a car or anything."

"Okay, fine."

"I'll see you, sport," French boomed.

Hamilton put down the phone and returned to kneel on the bed beside Sally.

"That was Perfidia Sinclair von Thurnsteil, the black queen of Capri. She's coming to Los Angeles," he said.

"Gawd," Sally grumped, "what a collection we're going to have here. Virginia, Felix . . . them."

"And Wade French. You haven't heard of him most likely. He's a lawyer. Something of a son of a bitch himself, I'm led to believe."

Sally made a rude sound with her lips. "Fuck 'em all. Let's get back to our anatomy lesson."

Hamilton lay down beside her, his head cocked up on his hand. He bent to kiss the buds of her breasts, and quickly she moved to place him within her snug smoothness. She rocked carefully beneath him, breathing steady satisfaction in his ear. She arched, her belly tightening, pulled in and thrust her chubby mound at him, reaching and seeking.

Fourteen

Wade French had once bought himself the services of two whores in Paris, France, but they had been nothing compared to Perfidia and her daughter. He understood now how Baron Putzi von Thurnsteil had died. As it was, after another whiskey downstairs and a brief rest, French was still worried about the pounding of his heart. He was, he thought fearfully, damned close to fibrillations. He paced his exertion carefully—out of the elevator and down the hall to Evelyn's pied-à-terre.

"Wade," she remarked, as she opened the door. "Come in. Dear, you look tired. Was it a very boring deposition?"

"No, no." He shook his heavy head. "Interesting. It just took such a long time."

"Shall I make you a little snack?"

"No, no, Evelyn. Might I just have a wee Scotch?"

No, he thought, as he watched her bustling around the living room, it had not been boring. It had been thrilling—and shocking. Evelyn rearranged a stack of magazines, turned on some music, then finally clunked ice in a glass and poured in a hefty Scotch. Christ, he thought, she was so fussy, she'd have washed the drapes if he hadn't stopped her.

"Why don't you sit down, Evelyn," he suggested. "Don't worry about me."

"Oh, yes," she said. She sat herself in a chair opposite and clasped her hands on her knees. She stared at him expectantly.

"Well, Evelyn," French said carefully, "it looks like

I'll have to be going to California myself to deliver those papers to Felix. He's being . . . uncooperative."

"Wade, I thought they had process servers in every city."

"Yes, they do," he nodded, "but he won't tell me where he'll be."

"Check the hotels," she said petulantly.

"Evelyn." He scratched his chin. His beard was prickly; he hadn't had time to shave again. "I'd feel better about it my way. Besides, I'm hopeful for a reconciliation, you see. Two old friends, both of you. I'd hate to see . . ."

"Wade, it's over between Felix and me," she said irritably. "There's not going to be any reconciliation."

Her face was long. Her plucked eyebrows lifted with emphasis, and her thin lips tightened. Evelyn was a handsome woman, he told himself, but she could be repellent too in middle age, even to her perfume, which added an acrid bite to the air in the apartment. French shifted in his chair. He had to tell her about Perfidia, and now was as good a time as any. "Did you know Perfidia Sinclair has arrived in town?"

"No!" Evelyn did not bother with anything so frivolous as gossip columns.

"Yes. She called this afternoon. We talked a little while on the phone." There. That was enough.

Evelyn's face brightened with malice. "Is her daughter with her?"

"Marina von Thurnsteil. Yes, I believe so."

Oh, yes, indeed, Marina was in town all right. And then some. French was embarrassed to remember their matinée. At first, it had been somewhat off-putting to be blown by Marina while her mother watched, now and then extending a hand to squeeze his balls, all the while smiling gratefully, as if French had been helping the child with her arithmetic. But quickly he had realized that what was happening was nothing out of the

164

ordinary for them. Later, in the bedroom, he had done his best to make love to Perfidia, recalling with some delight the days of Fido and Woof-Woof, but Marina would not stand for it. She wanted everything for herself, and she seemed to enjoy making her mother suffer.

Evelyn made a gesture of speculation by putting her finger between her lips and caressing her front teeth. "you know," she said, "it's funny, but I've always half suspected that Marina isn't Putzi's daughter at all."

This was idle speculation, as far as he was concerned. "Whose then?"

"Sinclair's."

He shook his head. "If so, then why all the scandal? If she'd been Sinclair's, then the old man wouldn't have made all that noise."

Evelyn shrugged. "Maybe Perfidia wanted him to think it was Putzi's. Maybe she just wanted her freedom. It was a perfect excuse, and there was never a blood test, was there?"

"I suggested it," French recalled, "but Nathan wouldn't have it. Nothing was to defile his body, and it seemed enough for him that Perfidia announced it to the world—the *whole* world, remember—that Marina was the result of her torrid afternoon with Putzi von Thurnsteil."

"On the magical isle of Capri," Evelyn hissed. "Nathan was very hurt. He was very, very insulted and wounded. I remember . . ."

Did she, French asked himself. Yes, according to Nathan, she would have remembered.

"Nathan," French said, fondness buttered on his voice. "Even then he was over seventy years old. Everybody assumed that he was past fathering a child."

Evelyn shook her head. "Plenty of seventy-year-old men become fathers. I am *sure* he had it in him."

"Sure?" he asked archly. "How can you be sure?"

"Oh, yes," Evelyn said, smiling secretively, "I'm sure."

What was she going to tell him? He watched her warily. Evelyn thought of him as such a correct and proper man of the legal cloth. "What makes you so absolutely sure?"

Evelyn laughed curtly. "I had an affair with Nathan, that's how I can be sure, and it went on until he was at least seventy-five. I suppose you wouldn't know that, would you? I can tell you, now that you're *my* lawyer."

Lamely, French asked, "How would I know a thing like that?"

Evelyn laughed again, this time gaily. "It was more a matter of corporate concupiscence than anything like love, Wade. I suppose you are very shocked?"

"Evelyn," French said, shaking his head, "I'm not shocked at anything anymore. Do you mean you thought you'd help Felix get ahead by . . . giving yourself to Nathan Sinclair?"

"I suppose that's it," she agreed. "I used to visit Nathan at the corporate offices. Nothing," she recalled acidly, "seemed to delight Nathan more than making love on a conference table. But that's a long time ago now, Wade, and Felix never knew how much I helped his business career. He's always accused me of *never* helping him. But God, Wade, if he knew how many of his accounts I've wined and dined and bedded over the years, he'd have to give me his whole company in our settlement."

Despite his effort to remain cool, French snapped, "Why, Evelyn, I couldn't bring that up! *How* many, Evelyn?"

"Countless," she said flatly. She reached for his glass. "Let me freshen your drink."

God! He had known she was cold and calculating. But she was so bloodness too and unemotional. French groaned—it seemed to be his day for hearing confessions. First, Perfidia and now Evelyn. "Father" French was in session.

She handed him his glass. "I knew you'd be surprised to hear this, Wade, but it's as well that you know it now. You've always thought of me as some sort of distant planet, cold and frozen in outer space. *My* outer space: Maine."

"I am astonished," he admitted softly. French recrossed his legs, feeling the sharp crease in his trousers. "But I never thought of you as cold—or frozen. Inaccessible, I guess."

"Yes. Inaccessible. By definition, cold."

"No," he disagreed, "not cold. Removed from ordinary life—the way ordinary life is lived. You've got an ethereal quality about you."

"Ethereal?" she repeated, not much happier with that designation. "A creature of whimsy? I'm not a creature of whimsy, Wade."

"Ethereal doesn't mean whimsical," he corrected her stiffly. "Ethereal to me implies an indefinable spiritual quality. That's you."

"Spiritual?"

"Yes, I think so. You have a distinctly spiritual quality, yes, I'm sure."

Evelyn chuckled tersely. "Wade, I'm afraid I'm not very spiritual. More the other way around, if anything."

"Not hellish!" he laughed.

"No?" He didn't understand what she had on her mind, but she made herself a little bit clearer by kneeling before him and staring fixedly into his eyes. "Wade, how is it that *you've* never asked me to go to bed with you?" French was speechless. His mouth hung open. "Wade, answer the goddamn question," Evelyn commanded. She sounded like that man from the D.A.'s office.

167

"Evelyn, it . . . I . . . it never occurred to me to ask."

"Ask!"

"Evelyn, please," he murmured, "I've got to collect my wits." The bother was that he knew there was no possibility he could be of service to anyone more that night. It would take him at least a week to recover from Perfidia and Marina. "Evelyn, Felix is a good friend—an old friend, I mean."

"Shut up," Evelyn said forcefully. "Isn't it noble about Felix being a good friend, though? I *told* you it's all over between us. I am unbound. I've always been unbound and especially now when I think about him sleeping with Virginia Preston."

"We don't know that he is."

She bleated disbelief. "Stop it, Wade. Don't be naive. We can take it for granted that he is. Do you think for a minute that Virginia Preston would let that little fish escape the net that's caught every shark in the ocean?"

Sorrowfully, putting her off, he mumbled, "I suppose you're right but . . ."

"Jesus, Wade," Evelyn sneered, "you're such an honorable man, aren't you?"

She was not paying him a compliment, not in that tone of voice. She was indicting him for being a sap. "I try to be," he said, too piously.

"I see," she said, climbing to her feet. "The fact is that you are not going to ask me to go to bed."

"Evelyn, just now I couldn't. I wouldn't feel right about it."

She smiled caustically. "It's not every day that I'm rebuffed, my dear man."

French understood that now was the time for him to go. He silently placed his glass on the table by his chair and stood up. "I'm very sorry, Evelyn, but I do have a certain code."

168

"Ethics? Don't make me laugh."

"Yes, a code of ethics," he proclaimed. "You may not appreciate this, but, ethically, since I'm serving as your attorney and am therefore legally involved with the defendant, it would be most improper . . ."

"What?" she demanded. "Don't give me that party of the first part and the party of the second part crap, Wade." She put her knuckles under her chin. "The fact of the matter is that you don't find me attractive—or appealing."

"Evelyn," he said sternly, "that is not true. But you must understand, there's a time for everything, and this is not the time. Later, after all this is settled, then, well, nothing would give me more pleasure, or do me more honor, than to ask you for your love. *Later*, if you find you love me a little, we might . . ."

"Ahem, ahem," Evelyn mocked him. "You're talking about marriage, possibly?" She stepped back. "That is not important to me. What's important is sex, plain *sex*. I don't think I ever want to marry again. I don't want to be saddled with a man on a day-to-day basis. It's not necessary anyway, is it?" Her eyes were digging, probing. "I'll explain what I mean. I like my sex two or three times a week. Raw. Unrefined. No touching words of 'I love you' and all that malarkey. Just pure *sex*."

"Evelyn," French whispered, "Evelyn, you dismay me." He matched her withdrawal with a retreat of his own. "Evelyn, you *stun* me."

"Stun you?" she hooted. "I'll stun you, Wade."

With that, Evelyn hiked up her matronly skirt and confronted French with bareness. She was wearing nothing underneath. He would never have suspected that Evelyn's crotch was so heavily furred with dense brown hair. It crinkled and curled and swept up her belly and down her thighs. Her eyes blazed at him, and

169

the crotch seemed to snap, as if somewhere in there a set of teeth was set chattering.

"Evelyn," he cried, reeling back, "please . . ."

For the second time that night, there was no escape for Wade French. Evelyn's eyes held him. He could not get past her to the door, and he knew that if he tried, she would lift a hand and turn him to stone.

Then she did lift her hand. She thrust out her hand and curled the index finger in a come-hither crook. She walked toward the bedroom and turned, pulling him forward with her imperial finger. French almost stumbled as he followed. Without a word or further command, Evelyn lay down on the edge of the bed and spread her legs. God, he moaned to himself, it was plain enough what she wanted. "Evelyn, I see that you are quite beside yourself."

What was it with these women? First he had heard Perfidia's dread confession and now he knew Evelyn's deadly secrets. Well, he supposed someone had to be the good Samaritan. Resigned to this, he took off his blue pin-striped jacket and vest, then removed his Princeton tie.

"Evelyn . . ." Wasn't she going to say anything?

"Shut up!"

Without further ado, "Father" French took communion.

Fifteen

It was Paul, faithful Paul, who stayed abreast of the media as it concerned the affairs of Nathan Sinclair, and so Paul was aware of the arrival in New York of Perfidia and her daughter just as soon as Wade French was.

He decided, without discussing it with Boss Man, to send Shuster and Babylon to the Plaza Hotel on an exploratory mission. They would establish the lay of the land on Fifty-Ninth Street, and then headquarters would be in a position to make further plans. Paul understood how Boss Man's mind worked. When he discovered what Paul already knew, that Perfidia and Marina von Thurnsteil were here in the same city as he was, he would go berserk. Mere geographic proximity to the hated baroness would be enough to send Boss Man around the bend.

Paul issued his orders. This was to be strictly a look-see, he warned the two boys, nothing more than that. Find out which room Perfidia occupied and then observe comings and goings. They might have to lurk around the hotel for hours on end, but if that's what it took, okay. Get a shoeshine, buy a paper, anything, but be careful. There was to be no trouble with the police outside or the house dicks inside the Plaza.

They were to go incognito. Naturally, the boys didn't wear their robes when they went out among the masses. They were very, very low-profile. Babylon was assigned a curly blond wig, which made him look a little like the late Harpo Marx, and Shuster wore a slick brown hairpiece. What with his three-piece

Brooks Brothers suit, Shuster resembled nothing so much as an ambitious Young Republican, or perhaps overfed Wade French's younger brother. Babylon, well, he was cute in his fright wig, all dimples and bright-as-a-button blue eyes.

"Carry on!" Paul muttered.

The two boys walked from Park Avenue and arrived at the hotel just in time to observe Target One—Perfidia—hustle down the steps and into a cab. They recognized her instantly from the updated mug shots Paul had shown them. Perfidia's face was grim as death and brooding, like a storm coming in from the sea, Babylon told himself. It was easy to see why Boss Man disliked her so much.

After she'd gone, they strolled nonchalantly into the lobby, circled the Palm Court, studied menus and, one at a time, went downstairs to have a leak in the men's room next to Trader Vic's.

They had been on station little more than an hour when Shuster nudged Babylon in the ribs and danced his eyes in the direction of the elevators.

Baby was stopped cold. Baroness Marina von Thurnsteil was a vision, an angel incarnate, whose sleek black hair shone like metal under the lobby lights. It was cut short and close to her head. Baby had never seen anything so beautiful. Her cheeks were bright, and her eyes darted with excitement. She looked around—for her mother? To make sure her mother wasn't there? She wet her lips, bright red, Cupid shaped. Dynamite, Baby thought. He could not move. He stared. Marina did not notice them—why should she? As she turned and swept toward the entrance, Shuster hit him in the ribs with his elbow.

"Wake up."

"Pretty," Baby said.

They followed her outside. Marina turned left under

172

the canopy and walked toward Central Park. Careless of the heavy traffic, she ran across the street toward the carriages lined up waiting for fares. Gaining the other curb, she turned and lifted her arm. Baby thought for a second she was waving at him. Seeing only her, he stepped forward.

It was then that a taxicab ran over the toes of his left foot.

"Oooowwh!" Baby howled.

The cab driver slowed for just a second. "Whyancha get outa da way, you fuckin' asshole!"

Never mind. Marina whirled at the sound of his voice and really saw him for the first time. A startled smile flicked across her angelic face. She laughed, showing small white teeth. Baby forgot the hurt. He was stunned. She lifted her arm and did wave at him then, *at him*.

"Shit," Shuster snarled. "You've broken our cover, stupid asshole."

"Don't call me names," Baby said. "He . . . ran over foot."

"Shut up, creep," Shuster told him. "I hope he broke every bone in your little tootsies."

"It's bad to say that. Buy me a hamburger."

"Jesus," Shuster muttered. "Fucking moron."

Already the girl was gone. Her hired carriage moved smartly away under the power of a beautiful white horse. Gone. Baby felt tears in his eyes.

"Come on," Shuster said roughly, "I'll buy you a hamburger, you stupid idiot."

But it was not that Babylon was stupid. It was just that he had gotten out of the habit of speaking very well. They didn't talk in the presence of Boss Man, and in three or four years—whatever it was—what chance did he have to practice his vocabulary?

Babylon came from Scarsdale, New York, the broker belt. He had been educated well enough in grade

173

school. Then he had run away from home. He'd come under the influence of Paul, Shuster, and Simon sometime around then. They'd found him in a gutter in SoHo, where he'd been working as a porno model, sniffing glue and other things, whatever was offered. By now, Babylon's brain was slightly uncoordinated. But his real name was not Babylon. It was George. That he remembered.

For a second, Baby considered running after the carriage, but Shuster grabbed his arm and yanked him away from the busy corner. Shuster walked him to Fifty-Seventh Street and into a delicatessen. They stood on line and ordered two hamburgers and Cokes. When they were sitting alone at a little table, Shuster said, "Why'd you have to yell like that, stupid?"

"Not stupid. The man ran over my foot. She is very pretty, the girl." Baby stopped seeing Shuster as he nibbled at the hamburger. Instead, he was seeing beautiful things—clouds drifting through a blue sky, the brightness of the girl's eyes. Baby saw forests and murmuring brooks, waves beating on a seashore and golden sand. About his body, too, he imagined long fingers and tasted red lips, redder than anything.

"Baby," Shuster said, more calmly, "you're dribbling catsup on your tie."

Tie? Oh, yes, he was wearing a tie. She was so different, the beautiful girl, from his friends. Friends? He didn't need friends if he had golden sand and blue sea and red lips and soft body, beautiful things to see.

"Pay attention, I said," Shuster hissed. "Wake up, for Christ's sake, stupid!"

"Not stupid," Baby said irritably, not wanting to be bothered. He put down his hamburger and stared at Shuster. "Bad!"

Shuster reached across the table. Baby felt his grip. Shuster was bruising his skin; he'd done that before, too often. Very carefully, Baby put his right hand over

Shuster's. He squeezed Shuster's knuckles, gently at first as a warning for Shuster to stop. Then, as Shuster pinched him harder, Baby ground Shuster's knuckles. Shuster gasped with pain, and Baby smiled.

"Stop it, idiot! Stop *it*!"

Baby let him go, and Shuster yanked his hand back to his side of the table. There was sweat on his forehead. He held his fist with his left hand.

"Fucking idiot, what're you doing?"

"Bad!" Baby repeated. "You are bad men!"

Shuster's face turned even whiter. "What do you mean?"

"Very bad what you do," Baby said complacently.

"What *we* do?"

"You hurt the girl."

"What girl?" Shuster's eyes were anxious.

Baby smiled at him. "Birthday girl."

Shuster tried to sneer at him. "What birthday girl?"

Baby hit himself on the chest. "I know," he said slyly. He didn't want the hamburger now. He stood up. "Good-bye," he said.

Shuster leaped to his feet. "What you mean, good-bye?"

Baby didn't answer. He turned and went toward the door. Outside, in the clear air, he hurried along the street, back toward the hotel. Behind him, he could hear Shuster panting.

"Where're you going?" Shuster exclaimed. "Baby, come on, don't be that way. We were just playing."

Baby turned and glowered. He held his fist under Shuster's nose. "Go away! Go away, bad man."

"Are you crazy? Where in hell are you going?" Shuster yelled.

"Going to get the girl," Baby replied reasonably. That was what he wanted to do. He was going to get the dark-haired angel. He loved that girl.

Shuster tried to pull him around, but Baby wrenched

175

his arm loose. "Go away!" He was of a single mind. He passed the Plaza and crossed the street into the park. He pulled off the jacket of his suit and slung it over his arm. He began trotting. He *would* catch the white horse. He was determined to do that. After he'd run a hundred yards, he stopped and looked back. Shuster was standing by the carriages, his arms stiff at his sides and an expression of fury and incomprehension on his face.

Shuster knew he had blown it. He didn't know what he was going to say to Paul, and he considered taking off himself. It was that serious a thing—to lose control. Instead, getting his story together, he walked back to Park Avenue. The simple explanation was the best— Baby had run away. One minute he had been there and the next minute he had disappeared. Shuster was certainly not going to tell Paul that the idiot had taken off after the girl, daughter of Number One, the slut.

When he came worriedly off the elevator, he saw that Paul was busy. Wade French, the pompous and self-important attorney, was sitting in the anteroom, waiting for the intercom to come to life. French looked worried too.

Paul resumed what he had been saying. "I told you, Mr. French, that Mr. Sinclair is having his nap."

"Then, wake him up, for Christ's sake," French exclaimed angrily. "It's an urgent matter."

Paul considered this carefully, only then noticing that Shuster was alone. A look of concern crossed his bland face and, holding his robes around his chubby body, he came around the desk.

"Where's . . ."

Shuster whispered, "The little prick ran away."

Paul's eyebrows tightened. "Gone?" he exclaimed loudly, forgetting French.

Shuster nodded.

Paul said, "We'll talk about *that* later." Scornfully, he turned back to French. "Sit there. I'll see if he'll confer."

Shuster lowered himself into an easy chair on the other side of the room. For all French knew, Shuster might have been another client. He must have looked nervous enough. French folded his hands on his knee and stared at Shuster with open contempt. Then he looked at the bare walls. They didn't keep any of those phony art reproductions in this office. This place was strictly business.

After what seemed a long time, Paul came back. He glanced lethally at Shuster, then coldly at French. "Pick up the phone. He'll talk. But make it quick."

French cast another baleful look at Shuster. "What about him?"

"It's all right," Paul said. Or was it? The look in Paul's eye said that it was not impossible that Shuster would be cast into the cold. Shuster began to perspire into the armpits of his Brooks Brothers suit. He knew what they'd say. Baby would have to be found and put away, one way or another. The best thing would be if they could get the moron committed to a state booby hatch, where no one would pay any attention to anything he said.

The Boss Man's voice boomed into the room. "Yes, yes, French."

French, of course, hadn't said anything yet. "Good afternoon, Mr. Sinclair."

"Good afternoon, my ass, French!"

A great beginning, Shuster thought. "Mr. Sinclair, we have a problem," French said.

"A problem! So what else is new, French?"

French passed his hand across his forehead. "I have to report . . ."

"Speak up, for Christ's sake!"

177

French plunged ahead. "The Baroness von Thurnsteil is in New York."

"*Whattt!*" The Boss Man's voice was a screech. It rattled the room. "What did you say?"

"Perfidia Sinclair is in New York, sir."

Shuster saw Paul cross his arms. That meant he had not told Boss Man yet.

"Jesus H. Christ! Why wasn't I told this?"

"I don't know," French said maliciously, smiling at Paul. "I'm telling you now."

The next was a moment of dread silence. Boss Man's voice dropped to a wheezing whine of rage. Even Shuster, much occupied with his own misery, felt stimulated by Nathan's anger. The bitch! How dare she come to New York? She must know they all hated her. Wasn't she aware that revenge was their profession, their line of work? Shuster's intestines curled like an enormously long snake.

"Well! Speak up, French! Why is that cunt in New York? Why?"

Slowly, French got to the point of the visit. "Mr. Sinclair, she wants money."

Again, frenzy swept into the anteroom. "*Whaaat?*"

"Yes," French said slowly, as if enjoying the moment. "Money."

Boss Man had no trouble hearing now. "How? Why? I'll be goddamned!"

"Mr. Sinclair," French continued, "she wants a million dollars."

Boss Man strung together a volley of epithets, panting. "I'll see her dead first!"

Paul looked at Shuster, and Shuster felt the snake of his intestines spit venom. Boss Man put things in their proper perspective.

French muttered, "It's the book, sir."

"The what? Speak up, goddamn it!"

"The book, sir," French exclaimed. "*Powerhouse*. She sees herself in it."

Boss Man's voice turned to a cackle. "Well, she ought to," he bawled. "She *is* in it. And what's she going to do about it?"

"Sir," French said loudly, "sir—she says she's going to swear it's all true. She's going to say there's more. She's talking about writing the rest of it herself."

Boss Man screamed, then abruptly stopped. The next sound was a whimper. "Oh, the miserable lowdown cunt! French, French, are you there?"

"Yes, sir."

"Goddamn it, French, that's blackmail, nothing short of blackmail!"

"Yes, sir," French agreed. "It is. It's blackmail."

"French! French! What are you going to do about it? Tell me what you're going to do!"

French shrugged his pinstriped shoulders. He glanced at Shuster, then Paul. "There's not much I can do about it, sir. She has her position. She wants the money—for her charity."

"Her *whaaat*?" Boss Man was amazed.

"Her charity. A cause," French shouted. "To save Capri."

"Save Capri? Are you insane, French? Why should she save Capri?"

"It's her home, Mr. Sinclair," French said.

Boss Man roared, "Her fucking home can fucking sink into the fucking ocean for all I fucking care!"

French nodded patiently. "That's what I told her, sir. But she insists—either . . . er . . ."

Boss Man loosed a long drawn groan of frustration. It sounded as though he might be crying. No, the following noise was a bellow.

"Why doesn't she just die . . . die . . . die?"

Paul winked at Shuster. Then he frowned. He remembered that Baby was missing in action.

179

"She seems to be in very good health, Mr. Sinclair."

"Yes, yes! I'm sure she is. It's unfair! I want her destroyed, French. If she opens her mouth, sue. I'll take every nickel she stole from me. Do you understand?"

"Yes, sir," French said. There was a bemused smile on his face now, as if he had passed the frontier into the Second Terrestrial. "Sir, she's also threatened to reopen the divorce settlement." Again, there was that heart-rending whimper of hurt from the other room. "She says she can prove the child is yours, that Marina von Thurnsteil is really Marina Sinclair, that you impregnated her before she ever met Baron Putzi. . . ."

"Oh, *oh*, oh, *oh*," Boss Man sputtered. "No, please, French! Why are you torturing me?" His voice faded, then came back. "Impossible, French. I never touched her on that cruise. She wouldn't let me in her cabin. French, a witness! There must be a witness that she fucked Putzi Thurnsteil."

"There is one witness."

"Who, who, *who*?" Boss Man yelped.

"Evelyn James, sir."

"Evelyn? Yes. Yes, Evelyn," Boss Man mumbled hopefully. "She was there, French."

French nodded somberly to himself before he answered. "Yes, she was there, sir."

"Can she swear to it, French? Was she in the room? Was she? Can she swear to that, French. Can she?"

"Yes, sir," French said tiredly, "she can swear to it, sir. She was in bed with them."

Shuster gasped so loudly that French turned his head. Was there no end to the evilness of these people?

"Oh, oh, oh!" Sinclair was breathing hard. "This is a disgusting thing you're telling me, French!"

"Life," French said philosophically, "is often disgusting, sir."

180

"French, don't talk shit to me! Would Evelyn so testify?"

"I'm sure."

Boss Man absorbed the message, then ranted, "And how much would *she* charge, French?"

"Evelyn is your friend, sir," French said with dignity.

Boss Man began to weep loudly. "Thanks be to God I have one friend left in the world."

Only one? Shuster wondered about that. Surely, they were all Boss Man's friends except, now, for Babylon, who had deserted the flock. But Shuster's faith was intact. Babylon would return. Babylon would die without them.

"French," Boss Man said in an awed voice, "it is awful for me to accept that Evelyn James would go to bed with two such whores."

French said quietly, "Evelyn is an adventurous woman, sir. But give me your orders, sir—what shall I do about Perfidia?"

There was a long pause as Boss Man sorted out his thoughts. Finally, he muttered, "Pay, French. But not now. Put the money in escrow. She's to get the money when she leaves the country—if she lives that long."

French frowned. He didn't quite understand what Sinclair was saying. The words, however, were the signal for another swift exchange of dark looks between Paul and Shuster.

"Jesus . . . Jesus . . . Jesus," Boss Man panted, and then the intercom went dead.

French stood up, scowling. "You heard," he said. "He authorized me to put one million dollars in escrow for Perfidia Sinclair von Thurnsteil. Are we agreed on that?" Paul nodded jerkily, an unpleasant—frightening—look on his face, if French interpreted it correctly.

"Very well," French said, "I'll take care of it. I'll be

sending the paper over for him to sign." He motioned toward the closed door.

Baby ran up and down Central Park, holding his jacket in one arm and his blond wig in place on his head with his free hand. He ran and ran. He must have covered five miles in twenty minutes. He overtook one carriage and looked inside, then another. Finally, after an hour of breathless exertion, Baby was ready to give up. He was sopping with sweat, and his lungs smarted.

Then, suddenly, he saw her. He spotted her gleaming black hair and burst forward with one last effort. He raced up to her carriage. She looked out and smiled, then stuck out her tongue at him. Baby jumped up and into the carriage. The driver, feeling the weight, turned with a curse and lifted his whip.

"No!" she cried, "don't strike!"

Baby threw himself back on the cushion beside her. He was breathing so hard, he could not speak. It didn't matter. Marina stared at him mutely. Astonishment and pleasure made her eyes alive.

"What is your name?" she finally asked, slowly.

"George," Baby said. "I . . . love . . . you."

Marina's eyes blinked. "You love me? Why?"

"You . . . are . . . beautiful."

"Yes," she said. She seized his hands and pressed them to her breasts. He could feel the soft outlines under his fingers. These were . . . tits. George knew the word. "You are beautiful too," she said. *"Junger Mann, du bist wunderbar."*

"I love you," he repeated, finding his mouth again.

"Ja?" She laughed. "Will you come with me?"

"Yes," George exclaimed, "yes!" He would never leave her now.

Her eyes danced with fire, and she planted her lips on his cheek, then his mouth. Her lipstick was like glue.

"My *mutti* will so like you," she cried. "You will come with us to California, yes?"

Wade French knew that in a few more years Evelyn would have passed the point of iron-gray hair and reached her blue period. Was that what he wanted? A middle-aged woman with blued hair, when available to him were two black-haired devils, one not quite as young as the other?

For a moment, as he strode back down Park Avenue, French remembered the diamonds on Perfidia's fingers and the emeralds at her ears. And then he thought of the villa in Capri, the olive groves, a symbol of good Italian living, even church of a Sunday at the local parish, St. Boffo's of the Upstanding Mammaries. Yes, that was the very place for "Father" French. Did a New York pied-à-terre and cold house in Maine measure up to any of that?

There were a couple of things he had to do. When he reached the Plaza, he called Evelyn and told her Nathan Sinclair might very well need her at some time in the future to testify to the fact that Perfidia Sinclair had, indeed, engaged in intercourse on that faraway day in Capri with the Baron Putzi von Thurnsteil and that, like a handmaiden of old, she had witnessed the coupling.

"That I did, Wade," Evelyn said waspishly. "I practically put it in for him. And I knew that he seeded her."

Despite himself, his better judgment, French was embarrassed. "Evelyn, you don't know how painful this is for me."

"Distasteful, is it, Wade?" she demanded scornfully. "But these are the sorts of things an attorney has to deal with. And if I do testify?"

"You will not go unrewarded," he said uncomfortably.

"Good. No *p* without a *q*, you know."

183

"Yes."

"What time are you coming over, Wade?" she demanded. "I'm dying to see you. It's been a couple of days now, hasn't it?"

"Yes, Evelyn. Well, I've got a little more business to attend to. I'll be at your place about seven. Dinner?"

"I'd love it, Wade." She was chuckling.

"See you later then, darling."

He stepped out of the phone booth, smiling at his cleverness. As always, he was playing both ends against the middle. He rang Perfidia's suite. She answered the phone snappishly.

"Hello," he said, "I'm downstairs. I have some things to tell you. May I come up?"

"Might as well," Perfidia said. "Everybody else is here."

Thus did Wade French first meet George. When he walked into the suite, Perfidia was a study in suppressed violence. Her face was angry and her lips as tight and red as a knife wound. She did not say a word. She took his arm and pulled him across the room, flung open the bedroom door, and pointed. *"Regardez!"*

He did not recoil, as she might have expected him to do. He was not surprised anymore. Entwined in the bed were two figures, one Marina. The other was a bald-headed youth with wild blue eyes. Plainly, they were copulating.

"Grüss Gott," Marina called out cheerily. "Here is George, my friend."

French looked at Perfidia. She scowled nervously and slammed the door.

"For God's sake," she barked, "let's have a drink. I come back here and what do I find? She's picked up this little bastard in Central Park. What the hell am I going to do about that, Wade? Suppose he's diseased?"

He shrugged. What else could he do? And what did

184

he care, if the truth be known. "I'll pour a Scotch," he said.

Perfidia flopped down on the couch. "Make mine a double on the rocks. Jesus Christ!"

As he made the drinks, French said mildly, "You wanted her to get connected. Good-bye, father fixation."

Perfidia only glared, then reluctantly nodded. "Do you think so? If *I* really thought so, I wouldn't mind so much. It might give me a little relief."

He understood what she meant. "Play it by ear," he said nonchalantly.

French handed her the Scotch and sat down beside her. He touched his glass to hers, then tried to put his lips to her cheek. Perfidia pulled away.

"Cut it out," she growled. "Do you know this little bastard is coming to California with us?"

"Really? Who says?"

"*She* says." Perfidia thumbed at the bedroom. "I don't have any control over her at all. As you see, she drags any old trash off the street. And now . . . that. And *he's* coming to California."

"So?" French demanded irately. "Maybe he's Prince Charming in disguise. Don't you want the child to be happy?"

"*Caro,*" Perfidia said irritably, "do cut it out, will you?"

"All right. Do you want to hear my report from the front or don't you?"

"Yes. Let's hear it. Go on."

"Well . . ." French smiled triumphantly. "It's done—almost. He's going to put a million in escrow—for when you leave the country."

Her surly face cracked into a wicked smile. "So! He was scared!"

"You scared him. I passed along the message."

"Good!" Perfidia crowed. "Let's up it to two million."

"Darling," he said quickly, "don't be greedy. Nathan will fight like a tiger if you push him too far. He'll do it for one million just to keep you out of his hair."

"No," she said decisively. "He's scared. If he'll buy one, he'll buy two."

French drank some Scotch. "No," he said stubbornly, "I'm telling you, Perfidia, he won't. He wasn't happy about it at all. Besides, he's recruiting Evelyn."

"What the hell for?" Darkness swept across her beautiful, smooth face again.

"Evelyn will testify that you really did go to bed with Putzi that afternoon in Capri."

She didn't get it. "Well, of course I did. He doesn't need her to swear to it."

French explained, "You see, part of the ammunition was that I told him you might reopen the divorce settlement. You *might* say the child—little Marina in there—is really his."

Perfidia's eyes closed down to slits. "You said *that?* Clever you! For all I know, she is his."

"I thought it was clever," French said, patting himself on the back. "The only thing is, Evelyn would tilt the case. She'd say she was practically in the room when Marina was conceived."

"As she was," Perfidia said, smiling.

"Perfidia . . ." He made a *tut*ing sound. "How . . ."

She laughed raucously. "We were quite a little group, weren't we, Wade? Nothing like now, so deadly dull and moral."

"Yes, so moral," he said.

"Oh," she exclaimed, "you mean those two in there? Wade, they're only innocent babes. They don't even know what they're doing. Let them go!" She laughed breathlessly, throwing her hands in the air and spilling Scotch on him.

186

French leaned toward her. "Stay together, Perfidia," he warned solemnly. "This is a very crucial time, no time for any slips. I'm going to draw the papers tomorrow. He'll sign by the time we leave for California."

"Tomorrow! Tomorrow is another day, Wade, darling bundle of a man! You've done so well, as always. Come to me, dear pear-shaped man. Let me kiss you."

Perfidia applied herself to his dry lips, her bejewelled fingers on his face. The tonnage of the single diamond-edged ruby on the middle finger of her right hand jolted his eye. He assumed it was not, could not be, paste. Perfidia was not a woman to wear a fake stone.

"Perfidia . . . Fido," he murmured, "you know I'd do anything for you."

"Yes, Woof-Woof, I know."

"Oh, Fido, Fido," French whispered, his voice trembling with emotion, "when you're gone . . ."

"Woof-Woof," Perfidia cried, "you'll come and stay with me in Capri, for as long as you like. Will you make love to me freely and as a friend?"

"Incessantly," French pledged. "But do you think Marina . . ."

Perfidia didn't let him finish his thought. "No, no," she said emphatically, "she'll be cured by then. Maybe this young man, whoever he is, will make her forget Putzi." She considered the prospect, the hope, calculatingly. "If so, then it's worth the freight to take the bald-headed little shit to California."

"Yes, well worth it." He was telling himself that it would certainly not do to have Marina clawing at his ass in jealousy every time he tried to mount Perfidia.

"Ah . . ." Perfidia sighed wearily, leaning back on the couch. "Ah, darling Woof-Woof. Woof-Woof always takes care of his old friend Fido, doesn't he?"

"Woof-Woof," French cunningly grunted.

Sixteen

"The entrance fee to happiness," Sally declared nervously, "is a hearty chuckle."

Hamilton felt in his pocket for cigarettes, then remembered he'd given it up. "Sally, please," he said. "Your insouciance is deadly before lunch."

Sally pretended it was he who was on edge. She slid closer to him in the back seat of the limousine to peck him on the cheek. "Come on, Hamilton, it's not the end of the world."

"No," he said gloomily, "the end of the world is around the next corner."

Ahead, along Century Boulevard, he could see that stupid flying saucer of a restaurant shackled to the parking lot, signifying Los Angeles International Airport. Already the tempo of the traffic was a crawl.

"Don't be bashful," Sally said. "After all, you and Virginia *are* good friends. She smiled significantly. "I think you are all aquiver at the prospect of seeing your future mother-in-law again."

"Wait a minute. Future mother-in-law? I thought we agreed marriage was for the faint-hearted."

She laughed, mocking him. "Just a *finger* of speech."

Hamilton shook his head and closed his eyes. He was thinking how idiotic it was of them to venture into the crowded airport when Virginia and Felix could just as well have come into town in a cab. But she was right about Virginia: what *was* she going to say? He knew Virginia well enough to know that her reaction to the fact that her daughter was shacking up with Peter Hamilton could be extreme and embarrassing.

189

Sally was off. "It doesn't matter to me one spit," she said, then snapped her fingers, "whether or not you were one of Virginia's lovers."

Hamilton eyed the little bar that faced him in the back seat of the car. Perhaps it was time for a hit. Champagne was cooling in a built-in ice bucket, waiting to be cracked.

"Goddamn it, Sally . . ."

She stared insistently. "Do me the honor of owning up. Were you, or weren't you?"

"No, were *not*."

He was never going to admit it to her. He had learned that one never confessed. As much as she might think she wanted to know, she did not really want to know.

"All right," she said slowly, "so we could have invited them to stay with us."

"No! There's not enough room in the house. They're going to have interviews and drinks with people and all that. They're better off at the Beverly Wilshire Hotel."

"Excuses," she said. Her voice was getting more jittery, the closer they got to the arrival gate. He understood why she was tense. Sally's friendship with her mother had always been a tentative one, a matter of truce. They were close enough, but they were also so much alike that they recognized each other coming and going. Sally too was more than a little concerned about how Virginia would respond when she discovered, as discover she must, that they were living together. By now, Sally had moved everything out of the apartment that Jack had paid for. They had even looked at dogs. "Don't worry, kiddo," he said, "it'll be okay."

"So who's worried?" she demanded. "Why should I worry? Do I look like the type that worries a lot? Worry is the first signal of breakdown."

"Oh, shit," he said. "I don't know what type you look. You're dressed like a clown."

That meant, per usual, in her faded jeans, checked shirt and, for this auspicious occasion, a startling, shiny orange chino jacket over the lot of it. Sally had washed her hair just before leaving the house, and wet curls clung to her neck.

"Like a clown?" she repeated, wide-eyed. "Now you're trying to give me an inferiority complex."

"Impossible," he grunted.

The criticism didn't slow her down in the least. She popped another salient thought. "Why didn't you put Virginia and Felix at the Beverly Hills Hotel with Perfidia and her entourage? I am disappointed there isn't such a thing as a Marquis de Sade suite anywhere."

"Good thinking," Hamilton said, happy enough to change the subject. "What I figure was that they might not like to be so close to each other. After all, sweet buns, Perfidia *is* the main character in the book. It's just possible she's mad as hell."

"So brilliant." She smiled scintillatingly. "You're so brilliant. You should be an ambassador."

"Sure. You'd have to stop wearing those jeans."

"With all the little junior ambassadors running around the embassy," Sally exclaimed mockingly. "How exciting."

"Yes, very."

She put her mouth to his ear and whispered, "I'm serious. I'm pregnant."

"Impossible," he said again. "Look, Sally, the driver keeps staring at us in the mirror. He thinks we're nuts."

"Never mind, old cock," she said blithely, "let him think what he wants. He ain't seen nothin' yet. But you're going to find out. I stopped taking the pill."

"Damn it, Sally, you'd just better jump right back on the Pill. I don't have the money to support you *and* fourteen kids."

191

She pulled away and pouted. "Who said anything about fourteen? All I want is one at a time."

"Just remember one thing," he said sharply. "We're not having a kid unless I vote yes too. Right now, I'm more interested in life*style* than bringing new life to the planet." He paused, then delivered the knock-out blow. "And remember one thing—if you get pregnant, you are *not* going to China. Presuming we go to China."

Softly, Sally said, "You're a prick, Hamilton." Then she brightened. "So I do get to go to China?"

She had him again, he thought, right by the balls. He was proud of her. She was too clever. "Yes," he sighed.

The driver was confused. He was trying to ease into the curb behind a Holiday Inn airport shuttle and to keep an eye and ear on them at the same time. Hamilton grinned and shrugged at the rearview mirror. He was trying to say he was not responsible for this crazy woman.

"Uumm," the driver said. "I can't park here for long—unless you see them."

Hamilton scanned the sidewalk outside the PSA terminal. "I don't see them."

"I'm not surprised," Sally muttered. "You're very shortsighted."

"No, as a matter of fact I'm farsighted. I see far into the future."

"Your eyes, Hamilton, are in your . . ."

"Sally, stop it! That's enough. You're shocking this man."

She smiled arrogantly and leaned forward, demanding, "Am I?"

"Uh huh," the driver said. He pulled his chauffeur's cap down on his forehead.

"See, Sally, he doesn't know what to say to you."

"Bullshit!" She opened her door and jumped out of the car.

"I'll circle," the driver said.

Hamilton followed Sally into the baggage claim area. Sally had already found them. She had both arms around Virginia.

"Sally," Virginia was saying, "how marvelous to see you." She gently pushed Sally away. Virginia, it struck Hamilton, was definitely not Earth Mother.

Felix looked tired, but his eyes lit up warmly when he saw Hamilton. He also looked relieved. "Peter."

"Hello, Felix, how are you?"

They shook hands, and Felix did something then that was very unlike the old Felix. He put his arm around Hamilton's shoulders and hugged him gently. For a second, he thought Felix was going to kiss him.

"And Peter!" Virginia cried, shaking Sally's arm away.

Virginia put her hands to his waist and shoved against him, pressing. She lifted her face, lips poised for his kiss. Hamilton saw that Sally was watching alertly, but there was nothing he could do about it. He lowered his head, intending to kiss Virginia on the cheek, but she was not having that. She sought his lips. *How could he forget?* That's what she was signaling. A shiver flashed down his back and into his thighs. She reminded him then of her other trick. No one could know, but as she kissed him, he felt the urgent little push of her cushy mound against his leg.

"Hi, Virginia," he said. "You look wonderful. All this travel seems to agree with you."

"No," she disagreed, still peeking up at him privately, "what agrees with me is seeing you again. It's been so long."

A miserable look crossed Sally's face, then a frown. He was going to answer for this. Hamilton backed away from Virginia as quickly as he could. Almost, but

193

not quite as suspiciously as Sally, Felix also witnessed the embrace.

"Bags down yet?" Hamilton asked, flustered.

"All but one," Felix said.

"Get a porter," Sally snapped.

"Yes," Hamilton said.

When they were in the car, Virginia started the conversation by saying, "I hate this goddamn city."

Hamilton chuckled. "The Big Orange? How can you say that?" Virginia had not changed. How long had it been? She looked exactly the same—just like Sally. Where, in which part of the face, did the difference in age make itself evident? Feature by feature, they were almost identical: the same nose, eyebrows darker than the blondeness of their hair, the same light blue eyes. Even the same facial structure, oval and rounded to a strong, neat chin, and the throat. So where was that generational definition? It was not possible to say. It had to do, Hamilton decided, with the skin and the manner in which it hung on the bones.

"Goddamn," he declared boisterously, still trying to establish for Sally his own identity, "I don't think I've ever seen you together. But don't they look like sisters, Felix?"

"I'm taller," Sally said distantly.

"Yes, you are, honey," Virginia agreed, not a seam in her voice. "Maybe a little, just a little, too tall."

"I *know* I'm too tall."

"They do look like sisters," Felix said, as if he were passing judgment on a portrait.

Virginia turned to look at him indulgently. "Do you think so, Felix?" she drawled, smiling. "Felix has become an absolute expert on women, you see," she commented. "You wouldn't believe the transformation in this man in two short weeks."

194

"Now, Virginia, don't exaggerate, please," Felix said softly.

Hamilton realized Virginia's guns were turned on Felix. He wondered what had happened in San Francisco. Or Texas. Chicago?

Smoothly, Virginia continued, "Felix met the most charming woman in San Francisco. Her name was Veronica, wasn't it, Felix?"

"Veronica Stickel," Felix murmured uncomfortably.

"A toothsome product of all the fog and rain. Built like—what is it they say, Felix?"

Felix was irritated. Abruptly, he replied, "Like a brick shithouse, Virginia."

"Ah!" she gasped. "You see," she told Hamilton, ignoring Sally, "Felix and Veronica had lunch yesterday. Felix has become very interested in modern art."

"Really?" Sally butted in. "That's nice."

"Yes." Virginia turned steady eyes on Sally. "Nice, too, that you've come out here to pick us up, you two busy people."

Virginia clearly was very annoyed with Felix. Icy silence descended in the back of the limousine. Hamilton had to intervene. "Hey! Champagne, courtesy of the house. Felix?"

"Yes, please," Felix said.

"Virginia?"

"Of course, Peter dear."

Growling, Sally said, "And for me too, Mr. Hamilton."

Virginia's eyebrows wagged.

Hamilton opened the champagne. "Sally, hold the glasses while I pour, please."

"Yes, hot buns," she said, "it'll be a pleasure."

Virginia's eyes swiveled between them. Only Felix seemed numb to this bit of electricity. He sat looking out the car window as southwest Los Angeles whizzed past.

"Felix," Hamilton asked politely, "how's Evelyn?"

Felix's eyes jumped back into the car. "Evelyn? Oh . . ." He laughed briefly. "I *think* she's fine. We're getting divorced. I guess you wouldn't have known."

Hamilton's mind made the agile leap: divorce— ergo, lawyers. "Wade French is coming into town with Perfidia Sinclair. You knew?"

Virginia shook her head. "I heard she was in New York. I didn't know she was coming to California. Why?"

Hamilton shook his head. "She said she hasn't been out here in a long time. She's anxious to see you."

"Son of a bitch!" Felix swore, again uncharacteristically. "More trouble. French will be delivering me the legal stuff, I suppose," he said gloomily. "Nasty. Does he know where we're staying?"

"No, but I guess it'll be easy enough to find out."

"Felix is absolutely paranoid about Wade French," Virginia said spitefully. "Felix, don't be stupid. One would think you're not a man of the world. Evelyn probably found out about Veronica Stickel."

Sullenly, Felix said, "Virginia, please don't be silly." He groaned, then forced a smile. "Well, as we've learned to say, damn the torpedoes and full speed ahead." He lifted his champagne glass, offering a mock toast to Virginia.

She smiled acidly. "You see, children," she said, "it all happened when Veronica Stickel accused Felix of not knowing anything about the female orgasm."

"Virginia . . ." Felix seemed to pale.

Sally giggled. "The female orgasm," she said gleefully, "is the first shot in the sexual revolution."

"Sally!"

Sally clinked her glass against Virginia's. "Here's to orgasm," she said. "But listen, Felix, if you wanted to hide out from Wade French, you two should have stayed with us."

The mere word, *us*, dropped like a bomb in the back of the car. Sally threw it out so innocently, seemingly unpremeditated. He might have known better. She had been rehearsing the detonation since morning.

Smiling brightly, Virginia lifted champagne to her lips. Carefully, she sipped, then lowered the glass.

"*Us?*" she asked.

Sally nodded vigorously. "Peter and I are living in a delightful little house in the hills. It should belong to the Seven Dwarfs. It has a Jacuzzi and a big deck and a kitchen and living room. . . ." She rattled ahead, even to the number of rooms and closets and what he kept in the bar. Hamilton sat there, nodding and smiling like a zombie.

"I see," Virginia said slowly. "You two are living together in a cute little house in the hills. Well . . ." She ran her tongue over her teeth, as if sharpening them, but then with deceptive meekness, she said, "Well, that does come as something of a surprise. But . . ." She lifted her glass again. "What is it they say, Felix, man of the world? *C'est la vie*, or something?"

"Yes, Virginia," Felix said, "that's what they say."

Virginia tried to look amused. "Well, Peter . . ."

She didn't have to finish the thought. Everything was implicit in the tone of her voice.

"Strangest thing," he murmured. "We got together to talk about your party. We had lunch."

"And one thing led to another," Virginia concluded. She should know how one thing led to another. She was an expert in adding one thing to another.

"Isn't that something?" Hamilton demanded.

"That," Virginia said, "is *really* something. I'm . . . well, astonished, I guess. I *guess* that's the word."

Felix spoke up. "That's the word all right, Virginia," he said ironically.

"What the hell is so astonishing about it?" Sally demanded. "It's the same old story. Man and woman."

"Woman?" Virginia echoed her, sardonically.

"Yes, woman," Sally said stoutly. "In the full bloom of sexual and physical maturity at twenty-three years of age."

"Twenty-three?" Virginia exclaimed. "Surely not! Dear girl, you can't be more than sixteen. Why, if you were twenty-three, that would make me, my God, at least forty-one years old."

"Forty-one is not so old," Felix said.

Virginia cut him cold. "How old is Veronica, Felix?"

"Thirty."

"You see," Virginia said coldly. "A forty-one-year-old can't hope to compete with a thirty-year-old."

"Balderdash," Felix muttered.

"Felix," Virginia said, "I don't think you should drink any more tap water in out-of-the-way cities."

Felix laughed heartily and slapped his leg. "You see, Sally, your mother has lost none of her joie de vivre!"

Christ, Hamilton thought, he had never seen Felix like this. Solemn Felix had come uncorked. He remembered his discussion with Jack Logan.

"Felix," Virginia said bitingly, "has turned into a satyr. I don't understand him anymore, not at all." Recklessly, she plunged ahead, as if determined to wound somebody. "He's the classical enigma—the black cat in a dark room chasing . . . pussy!"

"Virginia!" Felix yelped. She had hit home.

"Don't worry about Sally," Virginia said. "I'm sure she knows all the words. If she doesn't, Peter will teach them to her."

"Now, Virginia," Hamilton said, "that's not fair. I'm guarding Sally like a precious piece of porcelain." He smiled in what he hoped was infuriating fashion.

"Bullshit," Sally said.

"Sally," Virginia said severely, "you must not use such awful words." Gently, she slapped Sally on the knee. "I suppose you learned that from this lout."

"Lout?" Hamilton cried, as if outraged. In truth, he was not planning to take any of it seriously. "Sally picked me up, you know. I thought from the beginning that she was too young for me."

"As she is," Virginia sniped. "And when are you going to stop wearing those jeans, Sally? And that awful jacket?"

"After I'm married."

"You'll never get a man dressed like that," Virginia said.

Hamilton smiled as he watched the two of them. Virginia wouldn't be caught dead in jeans. It had always been dresses for her, with hems that hit kneecap. Virginia made the best use of her legs. They were like forceps for snaring the most agile of specimens. Smooth and subtly rounded calves, the perfect little ankles and tiny feet. Did he remember? Could he forget?

"Don't worry about me," Sally said grimly.

"But I do, sweetie," Virginia said, glancing at Hamilton. "I do worry about you. Peter," she said, "you are a big, bad man, taking advantage of my daughter like this."

"Like hell," Sally interrupted furiously. "I took advantage of him, *sweetie*. I *seduced* the poor bugger!"

It might have turned stormy. All it would have needed in the way of revelation was for Virginia to announce to them publicly that she had beaten Sally to the punch. Hamilton knew that Virginia was debating whether to let them have it with both barrels. He looked at his watch. Christ, it was taking forever to get back to town. And he didn't know that they'd make it without a huge blow-up.

Felix saved it for a moment. "I wonder," he mused, "why Perfidia has really come over from Italy."

Virginia allowed herself to be diverted. The subject of Perfidia was endlessly fascinating to her. "For sure not to sue us," she snapped. "Is that horrible daughter of hers with her? I understand she's one jump ahead of the funny farm, that ex-sister-in-law of yours," she said to Hamilton.

"I don't know anything about her," he said awkwardly. "But I think she is with Perfidia."

"Well," Virginia said mercilessly, "Naomi *was* bonkers, wasn't she? Wasn't she a nymphomaniac, Peter?"

Felix shook his head reprovingly. "Virginia, that's not a nice thing to say."

"Well, I don't feel very nice," Virginia said doggedly. "Not that Perfidia's all there, either. I'm sorry, Peter. I shouldn't bring it up."

"Forget it. I'm not making any excuses for her, or anything else."

"Goddamn right," Sally added emphatically.

Felix again stepped in diplomatically. "It's past, all of it," he said. "We deal with the present. What's for tonight?"

They spent the rest of the time in the limousine discussing Virginia and Felix's Los Angeles schedule. There was to be a dinner that night at the home of the Burton Mildbitterses, one of those old Los Angeles families, patrons of the arts and protectors of social purity, then the next night at the home of Felix's old friends, the Sacks, Herbert and Nora. The Sacks had known Felix since their days in Washington, when Herbert had been an under-secretary of something or other. Nora had been cultivating Virginia from time immemorial.

"Do you know them?" Virginia asked Sally.

"How should I? *Why* should I?"

"Darling," Virginia said, gently prodding, "you must begin meeting more people." Sally shook her head indifferently. "Now, tonight, darling," Virginia continued, "you absolutely cannot wear jeans. Do you own a long dress?"

"Why should I?"

"Well, you must have one for tonight," Virginia said determinedly. "If you don't have one, go out and buy one."

"He'll have to buy it for me," Sally said, grinning at Hamilton maliciously. "An earned dress is an increment on the sliding scale of emotional investment."

"I beg your pardon?" Hamilton pondered what she'd said. "I see it as a belly-flopper on the slippery slope toward bankruptcy."

Virginia clucked impatiently. "What in the world are you two idiots talking about? Now, tonight—I'm told the radio man, Morris Scarlatti, has been invited."

"He's not coming tonight," Sally said. "He's coming to *our* party."

"And also Jack Logan," Virginia went on, undeterred.

"My former boss," Sally said.

"Former? What do you mean? I thought you were doing so well."

"I quit," Sally said. "I'm working for Hamilton now, this guy here. We're going to China."

"*If* you show more respect," Hamilton said.

"Blah!" She stuck her tongue out at him.

Virginia decided to ignore them. She was in the midst of the party list. "Rita Mildbitters said she was inviting a solid social mix—Hollywood, a few of the leading lights, the social set from . . ." She reeled off the names of choice bits of Los Angeles and Beverly Hills real estate. "Jack is supposed to bring that actress who will play Perfidia in our book."

"Mona Prissian." Hamilton supplied the name.

"What's she like?" Virginia asked.

"A bombshell."

"A cow," Sally said nastily, "a cow with big tits."

"Sally!" Virginia reprimanded her absently. She

clicked her thumbnail against her teeth. "Do you suppose Rita has invited Perfidia? And Wade?"

"Murder!" Felix exclaimed.

"We know Rita is the first person Perfidia would call in Los Angeles," Virginia pointed out. "My, my, that'll be fascinating."

The trip from the airport ended at the Beverly Wilshire Hotel. With relief, they all climbed out of the stuffy limo. Felix saw to the baggage while Hamilton paid off the driver. Sally and Felix sauntered into the lobby and, deliberately, he knew, Virginia lagged behind.

When the others were out of earshot, she looked at him engagingly. "Well, Peter, I had looked forward to seeing you again. I didn't expect *this*, not in my wildest imagination."

Hamilton shrugged. "Virginia, what can I tell you? She's so much like you. I fell like a ton of bricks."

Virginia's eyes widened sorrowfully. "You're in love with my daughter?"

"That's about it. What can I say?"

"Peter," she said slowly, sadly, "you are a *very* son of a bitch. Heavens, what can I say? Maybe . . . I suppose you were getting too old for me anyway. You know I like them young and quick."

"Yes, Virginia."

"Yes . . ." She eyed him shrewdly. "So I lose a daughter and gain a son. Incestuous little son of a bitch that you are. I hate it."

He knew it hurt her enormously. It reminded her of years, age. He tried to smooth it over, but his words did not come out very well. "Virginia, you were always . . ."

"Always what?" Her eyes were vulnerable, then defiant. "The best lay of the latter days of the century? I

202

still am, Peter, and I'll stay that way for the *rest* of the century!"

"Not only that, Virginia. More than that."

"Darling," she asked surely, "what else is there but that?"

Seventeen

Virginia was alone. Sally and Peter had gone dashing up Rodeo Drive to buy a dress—Christ, like two children. And Felix was having a nap in the next room.

She was tired too, as tired as Felix, from the parties and nonstop interviews. The latter had begun to run together. Washington, Atlanta, Dallas, Houston, Chicago . . . where else? San Francisco. Yes, San Francisco. Felix and that goddamn woman. Virginia knew he had slept with her; he didn't need to say so. But it was silly and unproductive to brood.

She crossed the room and opened Felix's door. He was asleep, his face placid, his mouth lapsed slightly open. His black hair was surprisingly unruffled. He was sleeping like a dead man.

Virginia slipped up to the side of the bed and stared down at him. She sat down and carefully extended herself beside him on the bed, on top of the covers. She could feel his warmth, but she did not disturb him. She lay there like that for a half-hour.

Suddenly, he was awake, and then startled when he realized she was stretched out beside him.

"Virginia," he said.

"Don't move. Don't touch me."

He did not understand. She just wanted to be there. His eyes were dark and liquid from his sleep, and he studied her face perplexedly. All she needed was a little reassurance. Virginia folded her hands on her stomach.

"Virginia," he said softly, "I know you've been upset with me."

"No, no." She shook her head. Felix was a tender man, she gave him that. She thought how easy it would be to settle for Felix. Settle? A form of surrender, giving up. Felix lay motionless. Was he waiting for her to make a move? She would not. He was troubled and confused enough already without her demanding more of him.

The trouble with these California parties was that the cocktail hour went on far too long, and that was what had happened at the Parkmans' in San Francisco. By the time they'd sat down to dinner, most of the guests were pickled, including the woman, Veronica Stickel, whom Virginia had been baiting him about in the car.

"Felix," Virginia murmured now, "you know I don't blame you. She practically threw herself at your feet."

"We were only talking about art," he muttered.

"You'd buy California school?" She looked at him mockingly. "I think you bought something else along with it, Felix."

"She led me on, Virginia," he confessed. "She challenged me almost."

"One should experience everything, Felix," she said, feeling numb. Why? "I mean, I don't blame you, Felix. Really." Virginia turned her head to look soberly at him. But she did blame him. She did mind, she admitted to herself.

Felix moved his arm, as if to embrace her. "Virginia . . ."

"Don't touch me, Felix."

"You *are* angry with me."

"I am not! I'm not standing in your way, Mr. Wandering Minstrel." She put her feet down on the floor. "I'm going to have a bath."

"Virginia," he said in a low voice, "we don't have to get dressed for a couple of hours. Stay here," he cajoled.

"No."

Without looking at him again, she went back to her side of the suite, ran her bath, and undressed. Comforted at last, she was reclining in the tub when she heard the phone ring, then, faintly, Felix's voice.

Next, there was a knock at the bathroom door.

"Yes, come in."

Felix stuck his head in the crack of the door. She was spread before him covered in bubbles. She smiled distantly. "Yes?"

Was he going to step inside? No. His face lengthened. "That was Peter. They're going to pick us up at seven-thirty." He stared at her. She glanced down. One of her nipples had pricked a bubble.

"All right, Felix," she said. "I'll be ready."

In the car, driving back to the house of the Seven Dwarfs, Sally had sat beside Hamilton silently, hugging the long Giorgio's box. And when he turned into the last canyon, Sally had suddenly burst into tears. "Hamilton, no man ever gave me anything like this before. I suppose this means I'm ruined, I'm a kept woman!"

"Sally, where in the hell do you get these ideas?"

"I made you miserable and you thought you had to buy me off."

"Goddamn it, I bought you the dress because I wanted to."

She was still muttering and moaning when they got into the house. "Hamilton! You're too good to me. I don't deserve it."

"Yeah, you do." He remembered what Virginia had said. "You do because you're a good lay."

"Oh, you rat!"

Nonchalantly, for he was feeling good, he said, "I wonder where the seven dwarves have got to."

"They're probably in the back room screwing," Sally said.

She put the box down on the living room couch and turned. Hesitantly, she asked, "How do you think it feels being insulted by your very own mother? That's what she did, you know. She insulted me."

"No, she didn't. She was surprised. You hit her with it like throwing a mackerel in her face."

Sally nodded and looked pleased. "Yes, good. And I don't care now that you slept with her. And that's as plain as the chubby little nose on your face."

"Wrong again!"

"I don't care, old cock," she said softly. She surrounded him. "I love you and I'm going to give you beautiful babies."

"Oh, my God! Sally, didn't I warn you?"

She stamped her foot furiously, nearly getting his shoe. "Christ, I don't know what's wrong with you, Hamilton. You don't understand anything. Why do I know this when I'm so young and you're as old as the fucking hills?"

"What is it I don't understand, sweetie?"

"Idiot," she said, "don't you know that when you're so in love with somebody that you can hardly talk, all you want is to reproduce them? To try and try? Can't you get that through your thick skull? I want more you's."

He grinned at her. "One's not enough? I thought one of a kind would be sufficient."

"Blast you, Hamilton, you make me so mad I could pee! You are impossible," she yelled.

"I'm not. I am very possible."

She vented a long groan of despair, then began to laugh. "You do love me, Hamilton, old cock. Don't say you don't!"

"I cannot lie, Sally," he said. "I love you, Silly—I mean Sally."

Eighteen

"What is this shit," Jack Logan demanded, "about Virginia and Felix getting sued?"

Hamilton shrugged. "Seems old Sinclair has got his nose all out of joint over the book."

"Christ!" Logan's shoulders shook. "After all the money I've sunk into it already? And what about her?" He pointed his nose at Mona Prissian. "If we have to call it off now, she'll go apeshit."

"Well . . ." Mona was standing by the bar in the Mildbitterses' atrium rumpus room, talking to Felix and Virginia. They were undoubtedly discussing the book. Mona was wearing a very tight-fitting red satin dress, which trailed to her heels but whose bodice spread like a tide from the nether-swell of her breasts. She was exhibiting her talent fully. Jack followed Hamilton's eyes. "Pete, you got to admit she's got a great set of tits."

"Outstanding," Hamilton agreed.

"Yeah," Logan said proudly. "Big, the way I like 'em. On grown women, that is. On little girls, they got to be small, of course. Like Sally," he said nastily.

Hamilton nodded easily. Logan could say whatever he wanted. It wouldn't bother him, not this night. Logan was a schmuck anyway, he told himself. But at least he'd had the brains to change from safari dress into a dark blue suit, this coordinated not exactly in the most understated way with a red shirt and bright blue silk tie. Logan still looked very California. "Virginia looks terrific, doesn't she?" Logan said admiringly. "She kissed me on the lips."

"That's because she likes you, Jack."

"Yeah, I suppose so," Logan admitted blandly. "I think she always did like me, even when we were splitting. I've even wondered about us getting back together. That'd be rich, wouldn't it, Pete?"

"Jack, you wouldn't dump Mona!"

"Ha! Wouldn't I?" Logan laughed scornfully. "You bet your ass I would. She doesn't amount to much, Pete." He stopped gazing at Virginia long enough to glance skeptically at Hamilton. "What you see is what you get—a big pair of tits and that's about it. But you? I can see you've fallen ass over teakettle for Sally." There was an element of wonder in his judgment. "Jesus, robbing the cradle."

"So," Hamilton said coolly, "I've heard stories about you robbing a few cradles yourself, Jack."

"Bullshit," Logan disputed. "Not on your life. I'm too smart for that. Anyway, I'd never marry another bimbo unless she had a ton of money. I'm after the mega-bucks now, Pete. I admit it!"

"Sally told me you were paying for her apartment," Hamilton said casually, thinking that would take some of the wind out of Logan's sails. "She told me how generous you've been to her."

The remark didn't faze Logan in the least. "What the hell," he said expansively. "I figured, why not? I've got it." He switched his attention to Sally, who was standing near the door of the atrium, talking to Burton Mildbitters, a frail old man leaning on a cane. Sally was paying close attention to Burton, and he seemed to be enjoying it. "Look at her," Logan said. "She looks wonderful in that dress. I don't think I've ever seen her in a dress."

What Sally had chosen for his first big investment in her was a much-ruffled Zandra Rhodes, a flowing experiment in the use of transparent materials. She had even treated her mouth to a generous slash of lipstick.

210

It didn't surprise Hamilton to see her entirely at ease and poised. There was nothing timid about Sally.

Hamilton murmured, "She's a knock-out all right, Jack."

And she was! So far, she'd won every round.

People were still arriving for before-dinner cocktails. The Mildbitterses could always rely on the sparkling attendance of the rich and famous, for before his retirement, Burton Mildbitters and the movie business had been in lifelong alliance.

Rita Mildbitters was holding forth to a small group on the other end of the bar. In her hand she gripped a large glass, which sloshed Scotch as she spoke. She was a white-haired lady, slightly stooped, wtih chubby cheeks and very mischievous eyes. Hamilton thought to himself that, in her younger days, Rita Mildbitters must have been a very remarkable woman. She still was.

They were to eat at eight-thirty, at least according to the wording of the invitation. It was already a quarter to nine.

Hamilton returned to the matter of the book. "Jack, you wouldn't dump *Powerhouse* just because of the rumor of lawsuit, would you?"

"Christ," Logan sighed, as if much put upon, "I couldn't handle any more problems now, Pete. What if Sinclair did manage to get an injunction on the goddamn thing? I wonder what the legal position would be then?"

"What do your lawyers say?"

"Shit, *they* don't know. What they say is, sit tight." His eyes hardened. "Say, Mona has fastened right onto Felix. I wonder if he'd like to keep her? If I could hook him onto Mona tonight, it might give me a chance to make out with Virginia."

"Gosh, Jack, you're just an old romantic, aren't you?"

211

"Yeah, I am. I could say I needed to talk a little business with Virginia."

"She won't talk business with you," Hamilton pointed out. "They've got an agent in New York."

"I know," Logan sighed. "But I mean past business, not about the book."

Hamilton nodded. Why not? "Try Felix out," he suggested. "You heard he's getting divorced from Evelyn, didn't you?"

"All the better. He *is* getting rid of the old bag then. We were wrong about him, Pete, dead wrong."

What might have been *the* entrance of the evening now took place. Perfidia Sinclair von Thurnsteil swept into the atrium like a large blackbird. She was covered in a flowing black chiffon dress, self-caped in the back with scalloped wings. Behind her, in attendance, marched stolid Wade French. Although the party was not supposed to be formal, he was wearing a tuxedo and black tie.

Perfidia rushed across the room to Rita Mildbitters and bent to kiss the hostess lovingly on both cheeks. "My dear . . . my darling," Perfidia sang.

Hamilton did not move. He was, as always, mesmerized by the sight of Perfidia. It was as if time had, as they said, stood still. Had *any* of them really changed? It did not seem so. Grief had laid only a caress on Perfidia's smooth face and her jet-black hair was shaped to her head as perfectly, hair for hair, as a blackbird's feathers. She talked animatedly to Rita Mildbitters, while her eyes charted the room. She took note of all, impressed by no one. Finally, she saw Hamilton and smirked.

Wade French shook hands perfunctorily with Burton Mildbitters and went straight to Felix. They nodded and touched fingertips. Then French's hand flicked to an inside pocket, and he drew out an envelope. He handed it to Felix. Felix James's face hardened. He

212

barely looked at it: he folded it once and shoved it into his suit pocket. There, it had been done, Hamilton realized. French had served him the papers. Didn't he need some sort of signature? Hamilton saw Felix's lips form an exclamation. He gasped. Felix had obviously told French to go fuck himself, for French's face turned red and he wheeled away. He came face to face with Hamilton. "Hello, Peter," he said tensely, still embarrassed. "Long time, no see, sport."

"Wade," Hamilton said, "you know Jack."

"Jack Logan, of course. How are you, Jack?"

"Just merely wonderful," Logan said. "And how's our legal eagle? Just a polite question, Wade; don't start the clock."

French frowned. He was too ponderous to go for that old joke. Hamilton had never liked French very much and, having seen him use such an inauspicious moment to deliver Felix trouble, Hamilton liked him less than before.

"You came out here with Perfidia, Wade?" he asked curiously.

"Of course," French said swiftly. "You know, we were never personal enemies, even though I had to defend Nathan in that case."

"No raised eyebrows, Wade?" Logan asked.

"Why should there be?" French replied curtly. "I'm talking to you, aren't I?"

"Sure, but you were on my side then," Logan said chirpily, then shut his mouth.

Hamilton put the needle in. "What was that about? I didn't know you guys ever had legal business."

"Nothing significant," French said carelessly. "This is quite a grouping of people here."

Logan had gone completely silent. Hamilton asked, "Where's Perfidia's daughter?"

"At the hotel, Peter. She wasn't invited. She'll enjoy

213

American TV more than a party anyway." He smiled too fondly. "She's with her . . . brother."

"I didn't know Perfidia had had another kid!"

"No, no, this is a boy she's adopting," French explained. "He's the son of an Italian nobleman. A great friend of Perfidia's. The mother and father died in a tragic plane crash. Maybe you read about it."

Logan shook his head. "Plane crash every day these days," he muttered.

"His name is George Minelli," French informed them. "He's a beautiful little blond-haired kid."

"Perfidia has become quite the do-gooder, hasn't she?" Hamilton asked.

"Yes, she certainly has," French said enthusiastically. "One reason she's come here is to try to raise money for her dearest charity."

"No fooling," Logan said.

"Yes. It's called 'Save Capri,' " French said devotedly.

Logan's was an obvious reaction. "Capri needs saving? From what? Tourists?"

"No, no, the island is sinking, like Venice."

"Well," Logan laughed, "if it's sinking, how can they save it?" He snickered. "Why don't they cut it loose and tow it to Long Beach? They could park it next to the *Queen Mary*."

"Jack, this is serious," French said. "Don't let Perfidia hear you talking like that."

Hamilton had had enough. "Excuse me," he said. "I'd better say hello to Perfidia." It had to happen sooner or later.

He edged toward Perfidia and Mrs. Mildbitters. She saw him out of the corner of her eye, turned, and presented him a cold cheek, which he kissed reservedly. "Hello, Perfidia. It's good to see you again."

She smiled, not believing it. "Rita, please excuse us. I must talk to Peter, my former son-in-law."

As they walked away, Perfidia got straight to the point. "I can't tell you how much I miss Naomi."

"So do I."

"Do you? Do you, Peter?" She froze his blood with her intense stare. "Did they ever find out who did it?"

He shook his head. "Not a clue. There were oodles of fingerprints. But they didn't match up to anything."

"Peter . . ." Perfidia gazed into his eyes, "I *have* to know. Did you kill Naomi?"

Clearly, Perfidia had been unable to accept the fact that Naomi had been murdered senselessly, for no reason. He stared back at her, just as darkly, trying to penetrate her opaque eyes. "No, Perfidia, I did not. You know very well I did not."

"But, *caro*," she whispered, "it had to be a crime of passion."

"Why? Would that make you feel better?"

Perfidia nodded. "Yes. Unless it *is* a *crime passionel*, it seems to me that being murdered is just pointless."

"I see," he said stiffly. "You would think that, wouldn't you? Well, Christ knows, I had motive enough. She ran away, you remember," he said brutally. "She was shacked up at the beach with that bastard Scanlon. *They*, whoever they were, caught Naomi and Scanlon at a very awkward moment. While they were . . ." He stopped.

Perfidia closed her eyes. The lids were soft, dusky hued. "No more. I know what you're saying."

"Well . . . there you are. That's the way it was."

She nodded. The eyes opened a crack. "I never really believed you did it."

"But I could have."

"But you *didn't*."

"No, I didn't." He couldn't decide whether she was satisfied now, or more frustrated. She took a cigarette out of a smooth leather evening bag. "Perfidia, let's

215

forget it. We're still around. . . . How's your daughter?"

"Marina?" Her eyes glowed. "Perfectly splendid."

"Wade said you're adopting a boy. Congratulations."

She chuckled, dismissing it. "It's not as if I'm giving birth, Peter. What about you, Peter? You haven't remarried, have you?"

"Uh uh." He was not going to tell her anything. Let her find out for herself.

"Nothing on the horizon, either? Maybe you should meet Marina."

Hamilton smiled self-effacingly. "I'd like to meet her. I'm sure she's a beautiful girl."

"Ravishing," Perfidia hissed. "More beautiful even than . . ."

"Naomi? Then she must be an absolute marvel. Maybe I'll ask her out for a date."

"Oh no, she's much too young for you. And active." Perfidia nodded. "She's a goer and a doer, Peter."

"So am I," he said. "I'll bet she's a passionate number too," he went on softly, for her ears only. There wasn't any good reason he should treat Perfidia with great care. She had never been nice to him. "That's the one thing I remember about Naomi. God," he said soulfully, "was she ever passionate. Her whole life was passion."

Perfidia's face was like a thundercloud. "I have no wish to hear this."

"Perfidia," Hamilton pressed, "she took after you, that's what I'm saying. I *know* that you're a very passionate creature."

She nodded unwillingly, looking for sarcasm, but his face was set sincerely. "I am. What do you mean, though? I hope you're not making a pass at your ex-mother-in-law, Peter."

"No, stating a fact, that's all. Besides, I see you're with Wade French." He raised his eyebrows.

Perfidia smiled impishly. "A convenience, dear Peter."

He laughed. "Perfidia, you're a triumph of the species."

"My, my," she murmured. She was affixing her cigarette to a long holder. "How fervently you flatter me."

"As I should. You're in a class by yourself," Hamilton said, and he was not being facetious. "I watched when you made your entrance. It was fabulous. You knocked them dead."

She nodded, smiling with pride. "Yes, you're right, Peter. I *am* in a class by myself. That's why it's so hard for me to replace Putzi. He and I were in the same class."

Her attention was caught by the sudden flurry of party activity. "I see Virginia is here, and Felix, my old friends. I suppose Virginia is afraid to approach me—that's why she's hanging back. I'm not angry about the book, not at all. I love it! Virginia and Felix have captured us to a T, Nathan and myself." She grimaced. "That's probably where you got the idea I'm so passionate. Still, it's not so bad to have that sort of reputation, is it—especially as one gets on."

Hamilton flattered her again. "I'm sure Virginia wasn't stretching the truth."

Perfidia flicked ash off her cigarette. "She certainly didn't leave anything to the imagination, did she? Everybody knows exactly how I look stripped naked."

"Yes, I think I do anyway," he smiled.

"Uuum." Perfidia stared at the mirror behind the bar. "The perfect courtesan. Black hair, undyed but *never* uncoiffed, even in dishabille, the eyes fevered with desire. Yes, that's me. Magnificent breasts, rounded tummy, long and sinuous legs, and all that . . ." She breathed somewhat strenuously, glancing at him in the mirror, beside her. "All that geared for love, as they said. Remember that Marlene Dietrich song in

217

The Blue Angel? From head to foot, I'm geared for love."

He was much taken by this narcissistic self-examination. "You really are like that, aren't you? Just like Naomi."

"I'm afraid so, Peter," she said. "Beware! Don't play with me. I might call your bluff."

"Me? Shucks, Perfidia, I'd be scared to death."

Fortunately, Sally appeared at his elbow. "Hi there. What are you two up to?"

"Perfidia," Hamilton said, "Meet Sally. Virginia's daughter."

Perfidia smiled with the tolerance an older woman tries her best to muster for vibrant youth. "I remember you when you were the tiniest tot, darling." She inspected Sally, doing everything but lifting her to check her weight. "Beautiful. You look just like your mother."

Unsmiling, Sally said, "So I've been told. Here she comes now."

"Perfidia," Virginia began, rather timidly for her, "you look utterly ravishing."

"Just like Pauline Power, you naughty thing! Virginia . . ." Perfidia shook a long fingernail at Virginia's face. "You *captured* me, Virginia."

Virginia blushed. "No, no, Perfidia, it's not you."

"And Nathan is not Marcel Power either? Bosh, Virginia, you can admit it to me. I don't care. I *relish* it. *I'm* not going to sue you. Nathan is such a nasty old reprobate, I should have thought he would be terribly flattered. After all, you made him out to be a . . ." She glanced at Hamilton. "Such a passionate fellow, which he was *not*. In fact, nasty as he is in the book, I'd say you made him better than he really is. . . ."

Virginia feigned concern. "Oh, dear, everybody seems to think it's you two. But that's not what Felix and I had in mind. Oh, certainly not. The Powers are strictly fictional."

"So you say, darling," Perfidia exclaimed loudly, her voice hoarse. "Well, darling, all right, suit yourself. I found Pauline Power to be fascinating, although it seemed all she did was . . . well, you know."

Sally spoke up strongly. "I agree. I thought she was a great character."

"Yes, dear," Perfidia said. "But she'd have to be, wouldn't she?"

"Anyway, Perfidia, darling," Virginia said sweetly, "Felix has to take credit for all the sex scenes in the book. Heavens, I wouldn't have known how to write those."

"Of course, dear," Perfidia said.

"There's Felix now," Virginia said. She had been watching him the whole time. He was still deep in conversation with Mona Prissian. His shiny hair looked as unreal under the bright overhead lights as a toupee. His face bristled with intelligence, and Mona listened raptly, her mouth slightly open. Plainly, Felix was charming the daylights out of her, or the pants off her, Hamilton noted. Virginia frowned fleetingly. "I think it's time, Peter, we broke that up."

"Poor Felix," Perfidia said. "Wade was bringing him some legal papers tonight."

"He brought them," Hamilton said.

"Good," Virginia snapped. "At least, we'll have that behind us." Then, with a sly look at Peter and Sally, she asked Perfidia, "Have these two proudly announced to you that they're living together?"

"Indeed?" Perfidia looked at him with pain in her eyes. "Why didn't you tell me that, Peter? I'm almost your mother, you know. Not in age, of course."

"Virginia, I have not been bragging about it, if that's what you mean," he said.

"Darling," Perfidia said to Sally, "be careful. Peter has a vile temper."

"I know. He's a beast."

219

Falsely, Perfidia charged, "He used to beat my daughter up, and that's why she ran away from him."

"I know," Sally said flatly, "he gave me a black eye yesterday."

"Sally! That's not true," Virginia said.

Hamilton placed himself in jeopardy. "Actually, Perfidia, she ran away because she had raging hotpants for that no-good son of a bitch Scanlon."

Virginia groaned. "You two are terrible! Peter, that is an awful thing to say about somebody who's come . . . to a dreadful . . . You should apologize."

Hamilton bowed to Perfidia. "I'm sorry. I apologize, Perfidia. But the history books are going to say, nonetheless, that Naomi was very passionate and she would have made love to a doorknob if all else failed."

Oh, shit, he asked himself, why had he said it? It was a terrible thing to say. But she had lied. She *was* a bitch and she had it coming. Besides, whatever Naomi had been had been because of inheritance and Perfidia's schooling.

"Peter!" Perfidia's aplomb failed her. "How could you? Good God!" Her voice lifted, raspingly, and a number of heads turned. Perfidia put her hand to her face, as if she might faint. Then she whispered, "You are a *shit*. I always knew it."

Jack Logan broke up the confrontation. He eased up and put his arm around Virginia's waist. She was still glaring angrily at Hamilton.

"Children, children, what's going on?"

"I was just telling Mr. Hamilton that he's an absolute rotter," Perfidia said coolly, "and I mean it."

"Well," Logan said, "I've always known that. So what else is new?"

"Soothing, soothing, Jack," Virginia said, smirking. "I'm *happy* to see you, Jack."

"Virginia," Logan oozed, "I'd like to talk to you privately while you're here. Could we get together?"

"Well, of course."

"Can I take you to lunch tomorrow?"

She studied him judiciously. "Just me, all by my little self?"

"Yes, just you and all by your little self."

"Jack," she said eagerly, "can I come to the studio? I'd so like to have lunch at the Twentieth Century-Fox commissary."

"Beautiful," Logan said.

"And I won't bring Felix, will I?" Once more, Virginia looked over her shoulder at Felix and Mona Prissian.

"No, for God's sake, don't bring Felix."

"My," Perfidia said, "now that's a treat. Would you invite me too? Could I bring Marina and my son?"

"Sure," Logan said, "what about the day *after* tomorrow?" Perfidia thought that would be okay. "I'll send a car for you," Logan promised. "You're at the Beverly Hills Hotel?"

"Don't send a car for *me*," Virginia said. "I'll cab. I'll be there about eleven, Jack, tomorrow."

Sally said, "You'll love it, Mommy dearest." She coughed and stuck a knuckle to her nose. "Oh, I think I'm catching a cold," she announced. "Do we have to stay for dinner?"

Hamilton, still ashamed at his outburst, said, "Are you ill, my dear? You sneezed."

"Internally," Sally said. "I didn't want to interrupt the conversation."

"I guess I should get you out of here if you don't feel well," he said quickly, seizing the opportunity. "We wouldn't want to spread germs among the mighty."

"Sally!" Virginia said angrily. "There's nothing wrong with you!"

"I don't feel well, Mother," Sally whined. "I feel a little nauseous."

"Sally, you stop that—at once!"

Sally pouted. "I can't help it if I don't feel good. I think I'm getting the curse." She cut a quick smile at Hamilton.

"Sally, goddamn it! Do you have to do this to me? Rita Mildbitters asked you especially because of me." Virginia glared at Hamilton. "You two—honestly! A pair of children!"

Perfidia interrupted. "Let her go. Good God, you can't argue with them, darling. Sally is probably bored out of her wits listening to us. As for him . . ." She did not look at Hamilton. "I wish he *would* leave."

"Done," Hamilton said, lowering his shoulders. "I'm slithering away. Watch me slither."

"Snake," Perfidia growled, her final word.

Nineteen

Orville Jones had made his move. After stashing her crutches in the garage, he packed his bag and, leaving Emily bawling on the sagging living room couch, her foot in a heavy cast, Orville had said so long, two-ton. He stood in the doorway to absorb her blood-curdling threats for a moment, registering them in his head so he would always know why he'd left. Then little Orville was off to see the world.

Now, he was in Hollywood, California. He'd caught the airport bus into town and found himself a cheerful little motel on Sunset Boulevard. It appropriately enough, was called the Sunny Nook Motel, for it lay in the heart of nooky-land. Who hadn't heard that Hollywood was paved with gorgeous girls yearning to give it away?

But a night later, Orville still hadn't found one of them. He *had* discovered the corner of Hollywood and Vine, the place most people called the center of the world of entertainment. Orville had himself some chicken at the Colonel's and then decided to stroll down the boulevard. He stopped first to inspect the hand prints outside the Chinese Theatre. This was a sight to see, a national monument on the scale of the Washington Memorial. Orville had never been a movie nut; that had been more in Emily's line until the time came when her ass was too big to fit into a seat in the movie theatre. Now she was dependent on TV, a far cheaper form of entertainment if one took into account the cost of candy, popcorn, and Dr. Peppers, in addition to the price of a ticket.

However, Orville had always respected the entertainment business for the brilliance of its financing. He might, he acknowledged, be a dope in many ways, but he did understand figures and accounting machines.

To his chagrin, he had begun to think that Hollywood Boulevard, despite the hype, was a street of freaks and crazy people. There must, he thought, be a place in Los Angeles that was not as alien to him as this. And then he realized that if there was anything to Hollywood at all, it was the Hollywood of the past. Therefore, as he walked along, Orville concentrated on the golden stars planted in the sidewalk, each bearing the name of a Hollywood great, most of whom were dead but a few who were living as well.

The stars he most wanted to see were those belonging to the memory of Clark Gable and John Wayne, two of Orville's all-time heroes. And Marilyn Monroe, yes, of course. Jesus, did he ever remember her! Emily had looked faintly like Marilyn when they were first married, before she began her career in gluttony.

But that was past tense, he told himself. Orville put his hands in his pants pockets and felt his bank roll, then his pecker. He would try to keep both intact. He imagined, with horror, going for one of those loud and flamboyant hookers he'd spotted working the boulevard, losing his money and picking up a case of clap, or worse. Christ, he thought, risking that would be equivalent to sticking your pecker in a red-hot furnace. Orville decided, sadly, to stroll down to Sunset and head back to the Sunny Nook. He turned at Vine Street and headed south.

It happened to him in a quiet place just after he passed the theater called the Huntington Hartford. He was pushed from behind by what felt like an army of barbarians. Something soft hit him at the base of the skull, and the next thing he knew, he was on the sidewalk, blood gushing from his nose. Somebody was going through his clothes with a thousand hands—and into his trouser pockets. Orville was so stunned, he could not move.

Strangers muttered over his body. "Fuckin' turkey . . ."

They had the money. He tried to turn over, but somebody kicked him, and things turned black. Son of a bitch, he told himself as his head began to clear, he had been mugged good and proper. He struggled to sit up.

A police car stopped at the curb in front of him, and an officer spoke to him from the window, without even opening the door to get out. "Trouble, pal?"

"Some sons of bitches knocked me down."

"Drunk, huh?"

Orville shook his head groggily, trying to sound reasonable. "No, I'm not drunk. I'm a visitor from Ohio, and somebody just mugged me and took all my money."

"What'd they look like?" the officer asked, with a bit more interest.

"I couldn't see them. I was on the sidewalk. They got me from behind, the dirty rats."

"It only happens about two hundred times a night around here," the officer said sympathetically. "Didn't anybody tell you this is a jungle? It's not safe to walk around alone."

"*Now* you tell me."

"Where are you staying?"

"Down on Sunset Boulevard at a motel," Orville said.

"Get in the car," said the officer. "We'll drive you back. You don't look too good."

Orville managed to get to his feet. He opened the back door of the police car and got in.

"You smell of booze," the officer said.

"I had a beer at dinnertime."

225

"Are you sure you're not drunk?" The officer glanced at his partner, who was driving the car. "Maybe we ought to run this guy in. You got any money?" he asked Orville.

"I told you—they took my money." Orville pulled a handkerchief out of his back pocket and put it to his nose. Blood. But it had stopped bleeding.

"Vagrant," said the officer who was driving the car. "Fuck 'em, let's run him in. Half drunk, public nuisance, no money, vagrant."

"I'm not a vagrant," Orville exclaimed. "My name is Orville Jones."

"Identification?"

"They took my wallet, for Christ's sake. Look, let me the hell out of the car. I'll walk back to the motel. Listen, I was in the Big Red One during the war. I'm out here to see a buddy."

"Your buddy can bail you out," said the officer sitting up front in the passenger seat.

Orville was shocked. He had never been arrested before. And now, not only had he been mugged in this sewer of a city, but they were about to arrest him for it.

"You got any witnesses as to your misadventure?" the officer-driver asked scornfully.

"No," Orville said. "In this asshole place a dozen people would walk by and not stop. Come on, let me out."

The car stopped at a light. Orville searched for a door handle. Of course, there weren't any.

"Shit," the driver said, "he's trying to escape. Shoot him, why doncha?"

"Nah," said his partner, "I might hurt him."

"Shoot him in the head, and we'll say he was resisting arrest."

Orville knew they were baiting him. "You guys are pretty funny," he muttered.

The driver made a *tsk-tsk* sound. "What'd he say? Is he insulting law officers, this man who says he's . . ."

"Orville Jones, from Toledo, Ohio," Orville yelled.

"He insulted us," the driver said. "He called us funny, and not only that—he insulted our fair city. Wait till the mayor hears about this."

His partner tittered. "Yeah, what a nerve. I suppose I should've put the cuffs on him. Can you imagine? Resisting arrest, insulting law officers, threatening the mayor, defaming the city, drunk and disorderly, loitering and vagrancy."

Orville could not believe his ears. "Hey, what the hell are you talking about? I didn't do any of that. Listen, back home I'm an accountant, and I'm pretty well respected around the city."

"So what?" the driver snarled. "Respected in Ohio and then you come to our state, our beautiful city, to raise hell—piss in our alleys, get drunk, screw our hookers—and then insult the police and city officials. You married back there?"

Orville didn't answer at once. Should he own up to Emily?

"Don't be evasive," the driver's partner said.

"No."

"No next of kin and no visible means of support," the driver commented. "Mister, you are some kind of sad sack."

Orville at last had a sensible thought. "I've got a daughter here in Los Angeles."

"Oh, yeah? Who?"

"Her name is Sally Jones."

"Haw, haw! A likely story. Who ever heard of a broad named Sally Jones? You got her phone number there, Orville?"

"She is *not* a broad," Orville said angrily. "And I don't have her home phone number, but I know how to get in touch with her in the morning."

"Well, man, that does it," the driver said. "You'll just have to spend the night in the cooler then. In the morning, you can call her, and she can bail you out."

Orville's voice was so low, it hardly carried. "I'd be ashamed to ask her. I haven't done anything—except get mugged."

"Then what's to be ashamed?"

Wearily, hopelessly, Orville murmured, "Did you guys ever hear of Franz Kafka?"

The officer in the passenger seat turned around to smile curiously. "What division does he work in?"

Twenty

Virginia was feeling terrible the next morning, even worse than she had the afternoon before. It now seemed definite that the whole world had passed her by, leaving her sitting in the dust. Seeing Hamilton again had, at first, sharpened her perception of past merging with present. But then to find out he was living with her own daughter? Was this fair of God?

Then Jack. Even Jack caused her to feel uncomfortable, and he was older than she was, just a year. But he looked, in his California rebirth, like a youth, and *he* made Virginia feel decrepit. Why had she accepted his luncheon invitation?

And Felix. Felix had flown out of her orbit. Felix, her only secure bridge from past to present.

Virginia was in her bathroom, on *her* side of the suite, preparing herself for the outing at Twentieth Century. She was doing her face with special care this morning. She was a little tired, but the face was the same, the body was the same. She was Virginia Preston, the one and only Eve. She *had* to pull herself together.

Was it the men? Hamilton had somehow deserted her. She *knew* Felix had deserted her. Jack? He was still, at least partly, in love with her. But so what? She couldn't go back, not with Jack anyway, although in Hamilton's case she would have made an exception. Anyway, the thing with Hamilton had never been in the category of heavy affair; it was more a series of chance encounters, easy, not demanding in an emo-

229

tional way. And then, of course, he had met Naomi, and that had been the end of that.

Naomi was Perfidia's work. Virginia paused, her lipstick in midair. Of course, that was it. Perfidia's influence, her presence, whether actual or extrasensory, ran like a spider's silken thread through their lives. The night before, she had become uneasy again as she was reminded of Perfidia's power, the power of her mind, her intuition, her hatefulness. Virginia had always wondered if, by some genetic accident, Perfidia's brain had been vented into an intelligence not normally available to a human being. And if not intelligence, then some more acute understanding of people and how they behaved and how they could be manipulated—or abused.

Virginia wished Perfidia would go away. Yes, it was in the limousine, when the announcement had been made that Perfidia was in town, that things had begun to go sour.

Perfidia had been the star of the Mildbitterses' party, not she and Felix. Toward the end of dinner, after only a few perfunctory words about *Powerhouse* and Felix and Virginia, Rita Mildbitters had gotten into what, for her, had suddenly become the real focus of the evening—Perfidia. Sweet, beautiful Perfidia, welcome back to our golden shores! Poor Perfidia, a thunderation of sorrow over Perfidia's bereavement. And finally, Rita had rambled into what became almost a funeral oration over the spirit of Putzi von Thurnsteil, that dear, witty, charming German playboy, now planted, Virginia had no doubt, on the side of a hill in Capri, where he would eternally have a beautiful view of the azure Mediterranean.

And then, for God's sake, Perfidia had had the nerve to make her pitch: Save Capri. No one in the room believed it was anything but an outlandish idea. Yet, with a smile of dedication warping her lips, Perfidia had convinced them that Capri was sinking—and sliding toward Arab North Africa. Even Felix, normally so cynical about such things, had gone for it. But then, he had been only half listening; the other half of him was in a swoon. He was sinking, too, into Mona Prissian's cleavage.

Rita Mildbitters was setting up a committee. Yes, wouldn't she though. Save Capri. The California ladies loved to set up committees. Mention any good works, a cause, and a committee materialized overnight. Certainly, naturally, there would be a Save Capri Ball by the end of the year, with proceeds going to another committee, which would be established in Capri itself to fund a scientific study of the geological underpinnings of the island. Virginia knew Perfidia well enough to know that a good chunk of the money would end up in another benefit: Support Perfidia!

Shit! Disgusted, Virginia finished with the lipstick. To hell with all of them. She looked perfecto! And, having arranged everything in her mind, she felt better.

Then the phone had to ring. "Mother," Sally said, without prelude, "I have some news for you."

"Something good, I pray," Virginia said. "Are you feeling all right today, Sally? You little phony. Still, I have to say you didn't miss anything. I wish I'd left too," she added venomously.

"I feel great," Sally said. "The news—you better sit down."

"I'm sitting in my boudoir," Virginia said impatiently. "What is it?"

"Your . . . my . . . Mr. Orville Jones is in Los Angeles."

Virginia screamed lightly. Was it never to end? Was *all* the garbage of the past landing on her head? "Oh, my God," she cried. "That is the last straw! The very last straw. I'm going to kill myself."

"No, no, Mother." Sally began to laugh. "He's here

231

with Peter and me. He's outside sitting on the terrace having coffee. He's in a kind of shock. We just got back from the police station. He got arrested last night."

"Oh, Jesus, oh, Christ," Virginia whispered in anguish, "another ghost. I can't handle any more ghosts, Sally. Why are you telling me this? He's not *my* father, Sally. I don't have any responsibility to Orville Jones. What did the stupid bastard do to get himself arrested?"

"Nothing," Sally said, "nothing at all. In fact, it was the reverse. He got mugged on Vine Street, and the goddamn cops picked him up for vagrancy and threw him in the slammer."

Virginia sighed. "How very splendid. That'll make a nice item for the papers."

"Shit, Mother," Sally said, "who's going to put an item in the paper that a guy named Orville Jones from Toledo, Ohio, got mugged?"

"You never know what the papers will do," Virginia said, again feeling very weary. "They find out I was married to him and it'll be in the papers."

"Well, too bad," Sally said stiffly. "The question is what the hell are we going to do about him?"

"I'll tell you exactly what to do. Take him out to the airport and stick him on a plane back to Ohio."

"No," Sally said slowly, "he says he's never going back to Ohio. Mother, he wants to see you."

"No!" Virginia shrieked. "Never! I'm not seeing him!"

"That's what I thought," Sally said calmly. "But, we've . . . I've got to do *something*. He lost all his money, identification, everything." Then with determination in her voice, Sally continued, "He has got to get a job. You know, whether you like him or not, he's a very good accountant. What I was thinking—Jack should hire him. From what I know about Jack's business, he could always use a good accountant, the more creative, the better."

"What the hell do you mean?" Virginia demanded coldly. "Is there something fishy about Jack's business?" She was thinking about the book. Was Jack setting them up?

"No, nothing fishy," Sally soothed her, "but artful accounting is always useful in the movie business. Haven't you read about all that in the newspapers?"

"Sally," Virginia said, groping for sanity, "Jack is not going to hire my first husband to work for him."

"Mother!" Sally was emphatic now. "Will you ask him? I know you're going over there today."

"No," Virginia cried. "Never. I won't! Why should I? I have no right to ask Jack for something like that."

Sally did not respond immediately. Virginia knew she was thinking fast. Sure enough, along she came with another zinger. "Jack will do it for you. And if you don't ask him, Orville will be over to see you and Felix to get some ideas about his future—without Emily."

"Emily?" Virginia echoed her. "Oh, yes, Emily, his wife."

Sally's laughter tinkled. It would have been so pretty if it had come in another guise. "You know what my dad said just now? Well, you know, he was in a very bad state of mind after a night in the drunk tank. Anyway, he was crying a little, and when he saw me he said I remind him so much of you. He's *never* stopped loving you, Mother."

Virginia nearly dropped the telephone. Tears of rage and frustration were running through her light mascara. Her stomach churned. She thought she'd be sick. "Sally, that is revolting! Why are you doing this to me?"

Sally sighed. "I suppose there isn't any chance of you two getting back together," she murmured.

"Sally! Be realistic." She knew that her daughter, her own daughter, was deliberately torturing her.

"Mother, the little baby always likes to see her mummie and daddy together, you know."

Virginia managed to say, weakly, "Sally, you are disgusting. God, are you insane?"

"He's my father, Mother."

"I know that, damn it. I wish I could say you'd come of an illicit union with a polar bear or a mongoose—anything but Orville Jones." Virginia saw Orville's face: his gaunt clumsiness, an undernourished bag of skin and bones.

"That's not a very nice thing to say to me, Mother."

"I'm sorry," Virginia stammered. "I don't mean it that way. I'm not saying you're a mongoose or anything. A goose maybe . . ." She laughed erratically. "Look, all right, you've got me. I'll do it. I'll mention it to Jack. I don't like doing it but I will. God knows, I don't want him hanging on *my* neck—or on yours." She considered the situation. It really wasn't such an onerous thing to ask of Jack. And the answer would be easy: either yes or no. "He hates his wife, you say?"

"I didn't say," Sally replied. "But, yes, he does."

Small wonder, Virginia told herself. Orville Jones was not likely to find *anybody* to measure up to Virginia's specifications. "Sally," Virginia asked curiously, "did you ever meet her?"

"I went there once. They had two fucking awful kids. I never went back. I saw him in Chicago on my way out here. Mother, he's not a bad old coot, you know."

"Old?" Virginia snapped. "Why should he be old? Is everybody over the age of thirty old?"

"Not Hamilton," Sally said coolly.

Ah, Virginia shivered, she was rubbing it in again. "I'll say one thing for Orville Jones," she sneered. "He's a goddamn farmer and a bore."

"No, no, Mother," Sally protested. "He's an accountant, and a good one. Remember that for Jack. He worked for Price, Waterhouse once."

"Yes, dear," Virginia said slowly. "All right, all right! I'll ask. I've got to get dressed now. Sally, *don't* give him my best regards. All right?"

God, Virginia thought to herself while she was putting on her clothes, double-damn. It was worse than before. Hamilton . . . Logan . . . Orville Jones . . . Felix? Yes, Felix, and where in the hell had he gotten to? She had realized while on the telephone with Sally that Felix had already left, and without saying good-bye. He didn't want to tell her where he was going. Felix had mentioned at the shank end of the evening that the delightful Mona Prissian was deeply concerned about the dimensions of the character known as Pauline Power. It was not impossible, Virginia thought sourly, that Felix had gone off to give Mona a bit of coaching when, Christ, all he had to do was tell her to observe Perfidia Sinclair.

Well, so be it, Virginia thought angrily. Everything was out of her hands now, and she didn't care anymore. She was sick and tired of them all, just plain fed up. For all she cared, they could all sink, like Capri, drown in the memory of long ago. God, Virginia yearned to get back to New York, back to her column, where she had everything under control.

She remembered she had to call Lenny Thoreau, the critic she'd made love to those eons ago high above the East River. Yes, yes, perhaps Lenny Thoreau was the answer to her douleurs. She found him in her address book and dialed eagerly. Thanks be, he was at home. He answered promptly, and the first thing he asked was when he was going to see her. Yes, Lenny would help release her from her misery. Virginia said there was nothing she'd like better than to come to Venice,

California. She hoped *this* Venice was not sinking, she chirped playfully. No chance, Lenny giggled, at least not until the earthquake. Virginia thought she could make it by three-thirty.

Again, her view of the world took a turn for the better. Virginia even whistled a little as she finished dressing. She put on a blue-figured silk dress that was cinched with a narrow black belt at the waist, slipped into black patent leather shoes and, carrying a light blue wool blazer, opened the door of the suite and stepped into the present.

The cab drove her to Twentieth Century on Pico Boulevard and, after being cleared through the gate, straight to the door of Logan's bungalow. Outside, a sign read: JACK LOGAN PRODUCTIONS.

His secretary escorted Virginia directly into Logan's office. He was sitting with his feet up on his desk, scanning the *Hollywood Reporter*, the show biz publication. Logan heaved his feet down and himself up in a single eager motion.

"Virginia! On the nose!" He turned to his secretary. "Close the door, will you, Beverly—and take Duke with you. My dog," he told Virginia proudly.

"Come, Duke," Beverly said. But Virginia didn't see any dog.

"Duke," Logan grumbled, "go on, you son of a bitch!"

Obediently, a long white-skinned dog emerged from beneath Logan's desk. Casting a wounded look at Logan, he meandered toward Beverly. She nudged him with her foot and closed the door.

"That dog," Virginia murmured. "He lurches."

"Maybe," Logan said, "but he worships me—and he's the only human being that does."

"Jack, a dog is not a human being."

"Oh, no?" he cried. "Haven't you ever heard about dogs with a human soul? They're very big in China."

"Okay, Jack," Virginia said patiently, "if that's what grabs you."

Logan beamed. "Virginia, you look magnificent. Please sit down."

Mildly, Virginia said, "You're looking pretty good yourself, Jack."

He was dressed in a red cotton sport shirt and white slacks, his tan dipping off his face and into the open neck of the shirt. Virginia assumed Jack was tanned all over. He had never been one for half measures.

"A sight for sore eyes, eh?" he demanded boastfully.

"You mean you're a sight for sore eyes?"

"Well, *you* are, doll."

"Jack, it's nice to see you again. I don't know whether you're exactly a sight for sore eyes, though."

"Whatever grabs you, doll," he exclaimed jovially. He helped her into a leather chair and returned to his mammoth executive throne. "Virginia . . . Virginia . . ." He gazed at her benevolently, and she felt small. Then she realized his chair was hiked up higher than the one in the front of the desk. "What I thought we'd do, Virginia, is walk over to the set—they're working on interiors for my latest picture. It's called *Blood in the Surf*. We just finished *Roller Derby Capades*."

"Jack," Virginia said, "you've done so well."

"Yeah, I agree. Of course, I'm not saying these flicks are great art or anything like that."

"I have to confess I've never seen any of them."

"No." He paused and looked at her. Jack had never been able to tell when she was making fun of him. "Well, they do what they're supposed to do. Kids see 'em in the drive-ins and get it off a little. There's enough sex, you see, as much as we can tuck in around the story." Easily, he warmed to his expostulation, staring up at the ceiling, his tanned hands cathedraled

237

under his chin. "*Roller Derby Capades* is a good example. What you do is get a lot of girls with big tits—they bounce like hell when they're skating—and of course they have fights and all, rip off their jerseys. It lets you see a lot of skin."

"Is that where Mona Prissian fits in?" Virginia asked.

Laboriously, Logan laughed. "Mona? Not likely. She'd never play in anything like that. She's an *artiste*," he said sarcastically. "Mona's for *Powerhouse*—if we make it."

"You're afraid of Sinclair."

"Goddamn right I am. You can't fight that kind of money. But, what the hell, Virginia, it'll turn out all right, I promise you."

"I hope so," she said.

"Me, too." His face darkened. "Ten thousand a year is a lot of money—when you think that you probably make more than I do, even in your bad years."

"Yes, yes, Jack, but remember," she reminded him quietly, "we did agree. Most of your friends you know because of me. Your success out here is my success too. It's my introductions that help you get production money. Am I right or wrong?"

"You're right, Virginia," he said.

"And," she said pointedly, "we never talk about the past." His eyes grew anxious as Virginia applied the final persuasion. "Nothing . . . no more trouble out here, I hope."

"Virginia, please," Logan said imploringly, "don't even hint at it."

"I don't," she said smiling winningly. "I really do talk you up, Jack. How many people have said, 'Virginia sent me'? Lots, don't forget."

"How could I forget?" He tried to smile boyishly, but the allusion to his "slip" had knocked a hole in his ego. He tried to cover up by saying, "I've always been

238

in love with you, Virginia. You know that. You were always good to me and good *for* me."

"Yes," she said. "I've never had any hard feelings, either."

"Hard? Jesus, I still get hard feelings whenever I think of you." He laughed boisterously. "I'm getting hard feelings right now, just looking at you."

"You haven't changed at all, have you, Jack?"

"And why should I? And disappoint all my fans?" He looked at her sadly. "I suppose there's no going back, is there, Virginia?"

"Where to? I wouldn't want that."

The problem, however, was to lead him *forward* so she could broach the subject of a job for Orville Jones.

Logan nodded sorrowfully, then asked, "Did Felix make a connection with Mona Prissian?"

"What connection?"

"Felix was much taken with Mona," Logan said slyly, "and she with him. Don't think that *I* give a damn."

"Nor I," Virginia said evenly. "But isn't she your girlfriend?"

"Yes and no." He smiled. "On and off. Now and then. Here and there. Once in a while."

Irritation reentered Virginia's air space. Felix! The bastard! So that was where he'd gone. It made her sick to think of it, but she didn't allow herself to reveal any concern to Logan.

"Felix mentioned that Mona was . . . puzzled by Pauline Power."

"Yeah, puzzled, all right," Logan chattered. "I can't figure Felix out. He was always such a deadbeat, and now he's swept Mona off her feet. Maybe it's all got to do with divorcing that battle-axe. I'll betcha anything he's out there right now, advising Mona on how to make it big in society. By the way, she fell hook, line, and sinker for that Save Capri bullshit. Did you see how she was kissing old Rita's ass last night? Mona sees her chance. She's going to get into L.A. society. Christ, *what* L.A. society?"

"And *you* don't care."

"Not if she stays out of *my* hair and as long as she doesn't come to me looking for a Save Capri donation. I hope Felix gives her everything she wants—whatever it may be. And," he cried, "speaking of our friends, boy, do I have a bone to pick with that guy Hamilton. You know, he stole Sally out of here. He never asked my permission, either. And I always considered I was her guardian. That's what you wanted—for me to keep an eye on her."

"Did I say that? I'm not so sure, Jack," she said sharply. "You're not exactly the type of man to keep an *eye* on young girls."

Logan's face fell. "Virginia, goddamn it—one mistake! You know I was framed. That kid's mother . . ."

Virginia held up her hand. "No, no more, Jack. I don't want to go over it again. It's past. We agreed."

Logan stood up and came around his desk. He surprised her vastly by falling on his knees next to her chair.

"Jack!"

He commanded tears to come to his eyes. "Virginia, I've always worshipped you."

"Stop it, Jack."

But he wouldn't. He began to sob wildly and thrust his face into her lap. She couldn't push him back. "Virginia," he cried, his voice muffled, "I can smell it. It smells just the same."

Virginia started to laugh. "How does it smell, Jack?" She *had* been married to the man once.

"Heavenly," he bawled into her thighs. "Virginia, please, can I, just one more time?"

"What do you want?"

"I want to worship—at your shrine. I want to drink of the holy fount."

"Jack, that's horrible." It was also one of his oldest lines.

"Come on, Virginia, let's sit on the couch. *Pul-ease.*"

"Why should I?"

"Because you've always been a kind woman."

He had a sort of answer for everything, but should she allow herself to weaken? After all, what difference would it make if she did weaken? She thought of Felix, of Mona Prissian. "Jack," she muttered, "I didn't mean for this to happen. I shouldn't have come here. I made a hell of a mistake."

"No, no, the only mistake you made was kicking me out."

She shook her head, although he couldn't see her do it. "No, I didn't kick you out. We separated. I thought that was the nicest thing I could do for you, under the circumstances. You know very well, Jack, that I wasn't behaving myself either."

"I wouldn't have cared, Virginia," he lowed, "as long as you stuck by me."

"The past, Jack, is past."

He took his left hand from where it had been anchored on the chair and jammed it under her dress. She felt his knuckles and thumb on her nexus. God, she told herself, this too? Was there no escape? Thinking, *knowing* it was the wrong thing to do, she let her hand drift to his belt. His body buckled forward. She felt for his thing, hidden in his pants. It was hard but no bigger than before. Once, Jack had talked of having a transplant, an extension put on, but he hadn't. And that was the thing about Jack. He was stubby and therein lay his frustration and anger and insolence. His underendowment had diverted his sexuality. Virginia worked the zipper down and put her hand inside. He was hard, like a little red radish, she thought. Jack

241

must have been standing behind the door when these things were handed out. Moreover, he had never been convinced that it was not so much a matter of how much you had, but how you used it. She smiled, thinking of Hamilton. He was hung like King Kong, compared to Jack Logan. Sally, the little bitch, now that belonged to her.

Virginia toyed with him until he began to weep, as he tried to get his head under her skirt. As philosophical as she was about it, she realized her panties were getting damp. The moment had come.

"Jack, will you do something for me?" she asked, as if nonplused by rapture.

"Anything!"

"Will you hire Orville Jones to work for you as an accountant? He's very good at it."

"Oh, Jesus!" His head bobbed up. "Orville Jones? Isn't that . . ."

"Yes. It is. He's just come in from Ohio. He got mugged last night."

"No more than the asshole deserves," Logan said cruelly. "What do I need with him?"

"He needs a job," Virginia said tearfully. "I'm thinking of Sally. Sally shouldn't be saddled with him."

"Serve her right," he said grimly, "and Hamilton too."

Virginia ever so carefully caught the knob of his little thing between her thumb and forefinger. "You won't believe this, Jack," she murmured, looking him in the eye, "but I believe in being kind to my former husbands. Haven't I been kind to you? Aren't I . . . now?"

Logan's eyes made as if to roll up in his head. "Yes," he gasped. "You say . . . he's . . . a good accountant?"

"The best. Inventive, I'm told. He used to work for Price, Waterhouse."

Logan's eyes sagged and his breathing faltered.

"Come," Virginia suggested soothingly, determined to get it over with, "let's sit over on the couch."

Logan nodded, speechless, and helped her to her feet. The couch, long and leather, like the chair, occupied almost a whole wall beneath dozens of publicity pictures. Virginia sat down, sliding her silk back on the leather. Logan knelt before her again and put his hands on her knees, nudging them apart.

"No, no, Jack." Virginia patted the leather. "Sit up here, by me." She parted his jockey shorts and hauled out his thing. It was blustery and red, thick but abbreviated. "Jack, it's cute," she said.

Harshly, Logan said, "It's not the cock for a man like me."

"It's fine, Jack. Didn't I always say so? How come it's not tanned like the rest of you?"

"It doesn't tan," he said, "no matter how long I stay out in the sun. I dunno—that's just the way it is, I guess."

His face was alive with anticipation. He was not quite sure what she was going to do. What Virginia emphatically didn't want to do was to get her dress soiled. It was going to be a long day—she had another stop to make, in Venice. Tentatively, Virginia leaned down and put her tongue on the blunt end of his thing.

"Ooooh!"

"Like that?" She looked up and smiled at him maddeningly. "What was it we were talking about?"

"I dunno," he lied. "I can't remember."

"I know," she said. "We were talking about Orville."

Logan's head drooped back on the leather. He groaned. "Tell him to get his ass over here tomorrow morning, Virginia. I'll hire the son of a bitch, but only as a favor to you. Remember that. Just like Sally. If he fucks up, he's out on his ass."

243

"Of course," she said smoothly. "Now, you won't forget you promised?"

"No, no." He lifted her head and put his thick lips to her mouth. He thrust his tongue forward, and Virginia bit it teasingly. "Virginia, please let me . . ."

"No, Jack, *my* way."

He tasted vaguely of talcum powder, and she had no doubt that every morning before leaving for the office he dunked his stuff in a can of it, just in case. She applied her lips to it again, chewing thoughtfully, making his body buck. If Sally knew what she was doing for Orville Jones . . .

Then, naturally, it all had to go wrong again. The office door bounced open behind Virginia, and she heard a gasp.

Logan bellowed, "Beverly, cantcha knock, for Christ's sake?"

"Sorry, *Mr.* Logan."

Jesus, Virginia thought instantly, a witness! But what the hell did she care? It was a witness against him too.

He puffed outrage at the intrusion, and Virginia withdrew her mouth for a moment. "Forget it, Jack. What does it matter?"

She continued. Beverly had probably performed on the couch too but, all too obviously, she had not expected the famous Virginia Preston to be caught in such a predicament. Virginia had to finish with him quickly and get herself to Venice. To hell with lunch. She'd be early at Lenny's.

Seconds later, Logan yelped and came in her mouth, not very massively, she calculated. He sighed again in expiration. "Where's your executive bathroom?" Virginia asked.

He pointed languidly. "In there."

Virginia crossed the room. His private bathroom was wood-paneled and several rude pictures hung above the sink. Virginia carefully redid her makeup and grinned at herself in the mirror. She was not past it—the old power was still there, undiminished.

Logan was on his feet, standing at the window, staring out at the bustling studio street. He turned and grinned sheepishly. "You still didn't let me do what *I* wanted to do."

"Another time, Jack," she said casually. She declined his offer to sit down again.

"When's next time, then, Virginia?"

"Next time, that's all. Who knows where or when?"

"Christ, Virginia," he beamed, "you sure haven't lost any of your old pizzazz, I'll say that for you."

"As good as Beverly?"

He looked blank. "Oh, Beverly."

"Jack, now you haven't forgotten what you agreed?"

Reminded of it, he scowled. "Virginia, is that the only reason you blew me?"

Virginia grimaced. "Jack, what a distasteful way of putting it."

He chuckled, falling right back into Logan character. "Didn't taste good, doll?"

She ignored it. "You are *not* going to forget?"

"No, no. Tell the dimshit to get over here tomorrow morning."

"You'd better not forget, Jack," she warned, "or all hell will come down on your head."

"That's it—head," he exclaimed, full of himself now, "that's the word."

But Virginia was tired of the word game. "Just remember, I haven't forgotten about your little . . ."

Horror raced across his face. "I won't forget, Virginia. Jesus! Let me off the hook, will you? All I'm saying is, he doesn't deliver the goods and out he goes."

"Fair enough, Jack." She went to the door. "I'm seeing you at Peter's party, right?"

"Yeah. Christ, Virginia, do you have to rush away? I wanted you to see the set."

"Another time," she said again, smiling slyly. "Now, Jack, keep exercising it and it'll grow, just like any other muscle."

He grinned foolishly. "What a bitch you are, Virginia."

Beverly was sitting at her desk outside, glaring blackly at her typewriter.

"So long, Beverly," Virginia said.

"Did you think so?" Beverly demanded haughtily. "I never did."

Virginia had no recollection of how long it took to reach the place called Venice. Then the driver announced that they were there. Evidently, at some point in time, a madman had thought to recreate old Venice along the Pacific coastline. The ruins of canals were still to be seen and, in some, trickles of rank water along with rusty tin cans, old tires, and rotting cardboard. Lenny lived on a street that Virginia supposed resembled beach neighborhoods the world over. It was lined with old clapboard shacks, new condominium buildings, and masses of cars with no visible place to park. Lenny's building was a rococoed and musty-looking stone house on a corner.

Not feeling very safe, Virginia paid off the cab driver and, gripping her pocketbook fiercely, crossed the sidewalk to the entrance. She found the name Thoreau and pressed the bell. Almost instantly, a buzzing sound popped open the heavy front door. She pushed her way into a grimy hallway.

From above, vacantly giggling, his high-pitched voice reached her. "Virginia? Virginia, it's Lenny. Come up two floors."

Ah, Virginia thought, smiling, the voice of friendship, a port in the storm. Lenny was the present, at last, and he was not of the past. She climbed the steps energetically, even then feeling erotic pressure between her legs. Yes, dear God, she wanted love in an uncomplicated manner.

Thoreau, bearded, his tongue laving his lower lip, was waiting for her at the door. "Virginia," he cried.

"Oh, Lenny!" Nearly in tears, she flung herself at him, feeling the youthful muscles in his shoulders and legs. She pressed against him and kissed his hairy mouth.

"Come on in, Virginia. Come on in."

She followed him into a short entry, which led straight into a kitchen chaotic with pots, pans, wire bags of fruit and vegetables, and what seemed like a thousand small cans of seasoning scattered over counters and chairs. In one corner, an ancient refrigerator shuddered as it turned on. The stove was filthy, stained red around the burners by boiled-over spaghetti dinners of the past.

"Looks like you had a feast," she smiled.

The place was very bohemian, but then that's what she expected of Lenny. Lenny was for real. Through an archway, she saw a living room that was, perhaps, twice as big as the kitchen and just as messy. Books were piled everywhere, and magazines were heaped against the walls. The ashtrays were full, every one of them, with pipe cleanings.

Timidly, Virginia advanced. To her left was a broader archway, and this led to the bedroom, almost completely filled up by a large headboard and a mattress on a frame.

Upon the bed lay a chubby girl with frizzy hair and horn-rimmed glasses. She was wearing a pair of black panties and a black brassiere that did its best to contain a burst of boobs. The girl looked up from the book she was reading. Virginia, heart quaking, saw it was one of Erica Jong's. Virginia was frozen to the floor.

"Hey!" Lenny cried out happily, "Virginia, this is Studs. Studs, this is Virginia."

"Hi, Virginia," the girl said. "Actually my name is Betty."

Coldly, Virginia asked, "Shall I call you Studs or Betty?"

Thoreau laughed shrilly. "Call her Studs," he advised. "She wouldn't recognize Betty."

"Yes," said the frizzy brunette, "do please call me Studs."

"Well, all right, Studs."

"Hey!" Lenny said. "Here. Take off your jacket and sit down."

"Thank you," Virginia said. God, she was so depressed now, she could have screamed. She sat down in a straight-backed chair, between two tall piles of books.

"Hey!" Lenny shouted again. He bent and kissed her again, fully on the mouth. She moved her lips against his, never mind about Studs, who could not have been less concerned anyway. Perhaps she would be leaving soon. "Welcome to my pad," Lenny said. "How about some wine, Virginia? I've got a pretty good bottle of California stuff in the icebox."

"That'd be nice," Virginia said.

While Lenny was in the kitchen, Virginia looked at Studs and Studs stared at Virginia, her eyes wary. She was not so unconcerned after all. Feeling ashamed, Virginia supposed he had told Studs about this little old lady he'd laid in New York. Yes, that was about right. Studs seemed to be measuring Virginia with her eyes, as if for a coffin.

"Lenny told me you're one of the most fascinating women he's ever met, Mrs. . . . . "

"No, call me Virginia. That's *my* name."

248

"He told me you were beautiful and you *are*."

"Am I? I think he was exaggerating."

Studs shook her head. "Made me jealous."

"Hey!" Lenny called from the kitchen. "Come on—you're *both* top hole."

Quite a way to put it, Virginia told herself dryly. But again, for the umpteenth time that day, she asked herself, what the hell? At least she was not among enemies, as far as she knew. But it was a bother that she'd expected he'd be alone.

Thoreau carried three wine glasses and a bottle into the living room. "You staying there, Studs?"

"There's no place for everybody to sit," she said. "It's comfy here. You could all sit on the bed if you want."

Thoreau looked at Virginia—daringly? No, not quite.

"Suits me," she said. What the hell.

"Okay, everybody in the sack," Lenny cried.

Studs fluffed up the pillows and moved to one side. Lenny put the glasses and bottle on the top of a packing case that served as his nighttable and jumped into the middle of the bed. He held out his hand for Virginia. She kicked off her shoes and crawled up beside him.

"Now," he said merrily, "shall we have a joint?"

He acted, Virginia told herself critically, as if he'd been smoking pot all day. "A little wine first," she said hopefully.

"Right-o," Studs said. She passed a glass of wine across Lenny to Virginia. A second glass went into Lenny's hand, and Studs lifted the third.

"Hey, cheers," Lenny said. "I love it!"

"Music," Studs said. She reached behind the packing case and found a radio. Slow music filled the room.

Virginia closed her eyes for a second, trying to establish in her mind where she was and what she was

249

doing here. It was not exactly the most sophisticated way to spend an afternoon. She tasted the wine. "Good," she said, "relaxing."

"Chardonnay," Lenny said. "Good, good. Relax, Virginia. You look a little tired. Wow! Look at me, parked in bed with two luscious women."

"Lucky you," Studs said. So saying, she pushed herself down lower on her pillow. Her breasts humped up, and Lenny moved his hand and pinched Studs's nipple. Now what was happening?

"Virginia," Lenny said daringly, "what do *you* say we get Studs to take off her brassiere?"

"Would she?" Virginia asked quietly.

"Well, why not? Go on, Studs, you'll be more comfortable. You don't like to wear clothes anyway."

"So true," Studs said. "Here. Unhook me." She rolled over.

Virginia held Lenny's glass while he undid the back of Studs's bra. A welt from the elastic rose on her back. When she turned again, the breasts, no surprise there, were heavy and slightly veined around big brown nipples. Lenny chortled.

"Looka-that, Virginia! Aren't they great?" He sounded like a little boy. "You know, I love it! I love women's breasts in free fall, swinging around, like Studs's."

"Silly bastard," Studs said. "I'd like to see yours," she told Virginia.

"But why?" Virginia asked.

"Why indeed?" Lenny exclaimed. "Go on, Virginia, why don't you get out of that dress anyway. It's going to get all wrinkled."

What the hell! "All right," Virginia said placidly. "I don't mind if you don't. I'm not as impressive a sight, though."

"Listen," Studs said complacently. "It takes all kinds."

Virginia got up and, as they watched her, she removed her belt, then undid the buttons of the dress and stepped out of it. In the archway, telling herself she had to be crazy, she unsnapped her own modest bra and pulled it off, leaving herself, like Studs, dressed in bikini panties.

"Well, there," she said.

"Hey! Great! I love it!"

Lenny jumped off the bed. "I'm taking off my pants," he announced.

Oh, my God, Virginia quailed. But she needn't have worried, for, unlike that night in New York, today he was wearing zebra-striped bikini shorts under his corduroys.

Back on the bed, the three of them lay side by side, like a line of stiffs.

"Now," Lenny said, "how's that? Better?"

"Much," Studs decided. She licked the rim of her glass. "What's that sticking up there?"

Virginia had already noticed it, the jutting thing straining his shorts. This was it, she told herself, and what had she gotten herself into? A threesome, something she'd never experienced before. And in Venice, California.

"Well, what did you expect?" Lenny demanded excitedly.

Studs winked at Virginia. "Since we've all seen it before, you might as well take it out."

Lenny squirmed and his thing poked up through the opening in the shorts. *"Voilà!"*

Virginia almost cried out. The thing was engorged and trickling eagerness.

Idiotically, he asked, "Well, how's it going in California, Virginia?"

"It's fine. We've talked to a lot of people," she said.

"Well, that's how it is," he said thoughtfully. "Studs,

251

you know, Virginia has got so much sex in that book of hers, you wouldn't believe it. All combinations . . ."

"I should read it," Studs said.

Virginia had to put them straight. "There's nothing in *Powerhouse* like this."

Lenny guffawed. "You left that out, didn't you, you little rascal, Virginia."

Virginia laughed. "Maybe this'll be in the next book."

She could not take her eyes off him. His thing stood there without visible means of support, aimed at the ceiling.

"How's the party scene here?" Thoreau asked, as if he were trying to ignore it. "Lots of parties for the book?"

"You're invited to one tomorrow night at Peter Hamilton's," Virginia said.

"Oh, yes, tomorrow night. We'll be there, won't we, Studs?"

"Am I invited?"

"Of course you are, Studs," Virginia said.

"Then I'll be there. You can count on me."

"Good." Virginia didn't know what else to say. "I like your apartment, Lenny, so nice and close to the ocean." She could hold off, if they could.

"The sea air is very good for you," Lenny said earnestly. "I try to get out there every morning before I start working. I do most of my work here. I seldom have to go to the office."

"That's handy," Virginia said. "I always like to work at home too, when I can."

Surreptitiously, she was comparing the size of their breasts. Studs's were wild and undisciplined. Lenny was right—they would swing and flop. Her own were neat, Virginia always thought, a good handful but muscled and firm. She would not have traded. As if he'd read her thoughts, Lenny dropped his head her

252

way and put his bearded face to her left nipple. It hardened and he touched it with his lips.

"I love it!"

Virginia could hardly contain herself, Studs or no Studs, she wanted desperately to grab his thing, and she didn't give a damn. Why should *she* be a lady?

Lenny pulled back and smiled at her. "Virginia is one hell of a writer," he murmured.

Studs's eyes popped myopically behind her glasses. "You're not by any chance bisexual, are you?" she asked Virginia.

"Not that I know about," Virginia replied coolly. "What about you?"

"I don't know. I've often wondered."

"Well, I don't know," Virginia mused thoughtfully. "I've never had occasion . . ."

"To try?" Lenny whinnied. "Now's the time to find out, girls." He drained his wine and exuberantly tossed his glass into the other room. It bounced off the dirty carpet. Teasingly, he contorted himself to put one hand on Studs's right breast and the other on Virginia's left. "Nothing like this in the book," he said.

"No," Virginia said. Slowly but surely, she was losing patience.

"How did you dream it all up?" Studs asked.

"Purely imagination."

"Ah!" Lenny exulted. "The imagination! Nothing like it. That's what separates us from the apes."

"Are you so sure?" Studs demanded. She looked at Lenny, then at Virginia. Virginia knew what she was saying, but it went clear over Lenny's head.

"I wouldn't say we're that far away from the apes," Virginia said, agreeing with Studs.

"Oh, come on!" Lenny protested.

Virginia realized then that the two younger people were as hesitant about this as she was, maybe even more so, although they had obviously discussed beforehand how they were going to make her live up to the book. Virginia's only point of reference was to think of Perfidia. How would magical Perfidia have dealt with this situation? Without blinking an eye, that's how. But Perfidia was crashingly evil and she, Virginia, was not.

Nevertheless, she thought, she would tempt them. Very deliberately, Virginia put out her hand and wrapped it around Lenny's thing. His eyes bugged. Then, calmly, Virginia dropped her wine glass on the floor and, with one eye on Studs, changed the position of her body so that she could reach his thing with her mouth. But she didn't touch it with her mouth. She breathed on it, as one might have done to a pair of glasses, Studs's glasses, before cleaning them.

Studs emitted a gasp when Virginia dropped Lenny's thing and moved the hand to her breast, covering the nipple and jogging it. Studs immediately closed her eyes. Virginia was astounded at herself, but what the hell? This was amusing, merely an experiment that she knew now was going to lead to nothing. She felt Studs's hand groping for her. Never had female hand touched Virginia there, except perhaps in grade school.

Lenny dissolved in confusion. "Hey! I love it!" he neighed.

Virginia slid her hand to Studs's belly and into the top of her panties. Studs gurgled with fright, and her muscles tensed. "Hey!" she cried.

Laughing, Virginia withdrew her hand and clasped it in her other over her chest. It was skin, she thought, yards of skin stretched across a bed in Venice, California. Merely skin and so what? She was more depressed than ever because she knew she was not interested. She was nothing but a piece of skin herself, like the hide of an endangered species.

She glanced at Lenny. He was staring at her, not understanding anything she might be thinking. Studs lay

254

supine, looking a little sullen. "Whew!" she breathed, her chubby cheeks puffed out.

"Say," Lenny asked uncomfortably, "I was wondering, Virginia. Do you keep writing your column when you're away from home, like this?"

"Why?" she demanded. "Do you want a mention? Well, folks," she continued mockingly, as if reading from a column, "guess what Eve did in California? *Can't,* can you? Well, Eve took a little trip down to Venice, California, to have a little afternoon threesome at the bohemian digs of Lenny Thoreau, boy book critic. The other party was a little girl called Studs. . . ."

Lenny was wounded. "Well, what do *you* want to do?"

"That, dear boy, is up to you."

"Well . . . shit . . . I don't know," he cried petulantly. He was not so cool now. "I don't know where to start."

"Be logical," Virginia said impatiently. "You're going to have to screw one or the other of us first."

"Let's vote," Studs muttered. "I vote for you, Virginia."

"And *I* vote for me," Virginia said harshly. "Because I don't think I'd like seconds. Lenny, who do you vote for?"

Cautiously, for he didn't want to insult either of them, he said, "You voted for *you.* I love it! But I don't know if I can with the other watching."

"I'll close my eyes," Studs offered.

"But you'll hear," he cried. "I make a lot of noise."

Virginia sat up. "This is silly," she said. "I'm going. This ain't for us, as any fool can plainly see. Look at you." She pointed at Lenny's thing. "You've lost your stand."

"Well, Christ, what did you expect? I'm not a piece

of lard." But he laughed uproariously, out of habit. "I love it!"

"Are you disappointed?" Virginia asked.

"Yes!" Lenny shouted.

"No," Studs said.

Virginia put her feet on the floor. "Can I catch a cab downstairs?"

"Plenty down at the corner," Studs said, relieved.

Virginia dressed rapidly and slipped her shoes on. Was she desolate? No, strangely not at all. Perhaps because she knew she'd have felt far worse if she'd gone through with it. She'd never have forgiven herself that and, as it was, she had enough things already to live down. Doing a threesome would have meant far too much exposure of her private self.

When she was ready to go, Virginia came back into the bedroom. She put her hand out to Studs. "So long," she said. "It was nice meeting you. He's right," she said, motioning at Lenny, "you do have good boobs."

Studs shook her head. "No, yours are much more aristocratic."

"True," Virginia agreed. At least she could take that with her.

Lenny came with her to the door. When she had gotten to the bottom of the stairs, he called after her, "Virginia, I love the book. I love it! Virginia, I love you too."

Bullshit, Virginia thought. A sort of calm came down. To hell with it, she told herself.

Twenty-One

Felix found Mona Prissian to be absolutely overwhelming, both physically and in the hyperactivity of her mind. The latter was a clutter of beliefs, misconceptions and bigotry, a chaos of memory and half-learned truths. Her understanding of the world was almost infantile. Somehow, she had decided that, having conquered show business, she would now become a mover of society. She did sense one thing—she was never going to make it with Jack Logan as her guide and mentor. But did she realize, he asked himself drolly, that he, Felix James, did not undertake to make a woman a social star because he admired her breasts? He did it for money.

They had had a light lunch prepared by her manservant, something concocted out of tuna fish, lettuce, and tomatoes, and seasoned with a bit of spice—precisely what, Felix did not know, except that it was hot. Now they were sitting in what Mona referred to as the "study," a small room next to her boudoir. It was a study, he supposed, by virtue of long shelves of collected works by such people as Dickens, Dumas, and the like. If any of the books had ever been opened, Felix would have been surprised to hear it. Books like this, he thought churlishly, one bought by the yard when furnishing a house.

Mona was not a well-read person, but cultivation dripped from her lips. They had been talking about *Powerhouse*.

"I could tell from the book," Mona said, "that you're a person of immense refinement."

"Not really," Felix said breezily. "I've just been around a long time. I buy good clothes, I wear them well, and I have a good barber."

Mona nodded, her eyes flattering him. "You are couth, most couth," she said, "as opposed to uncouth, don't you see?" She tittered nervously, and he wished she would stop trying to impress him. He was impressed already. "I love your shirt and tie."

"Nothing special," Felix said. "Merely my uniform. A wool blazer suit, button-down shirt, and club tie."

"But the yachting patch on the pocket and your gray flannels, pressed to razor sharpness? No, you look very elegant, Felix, very, very elegant."

Felix chuckled modestly. "I don't belong to a yachting club. If I'm asked, I say it's the West Egg Croquet Club."

Mona let out a laugh that was nothing short of hearty. "You're a devil. So clever." She leaned back in her chintz-covered armchair—Grand Rapids maple, it looked to be—her coffee cup cradled in her large hands. She tossed her head, sending her titian-shaded hair into a raucous tumble. And she smiled. *Did* she smile! Her white teeth were set wide as a trap. It was then, perhaps, that Felix understood he did not have the upper hand. He could assure himself smugly that *nobody* got free advice from Felix James, but he knew suddenly that Mona was not going to pay him anything, except maybe in kind. He became even more convinced of this when she leaned forward. Her breasts bulged against the front of her red-zippered terrycloth sheath, a pool dress that left her long arms free to the shoulders and displayed her throat, the swell of bosom, and then her very long legs. Despite her fulsome figure, Felix noted, her ankles were small, a sure sign of classic beauty no matter what existed further north.

"Felix," she asked earnestly, "what would you advise? I mean, where should I start?"

Felix sipped coffee, then set cup and saucer down on the beveled-glass table. "Well, for starters," he said, folding his hands in his lap, "if I were you, I'd join a few of the very select Los Angeles women's groups. The best, of course, is the Blue Ribbon, those women who work for the Music Center. Yes, become active there, Mona."

"Work permitting," she said.

"Naturally. But you see, as much as you can do, what with your busy schedule, the more they'll appreciate you. From there all else will flow. They'll begin thinking of you not as merely an actress—I mean, that's how *they* think," he said, laughing self-effacingly. "They'll start thinking of you as a *woman,* a woman committed to social causes."

"Yes," she said, her eyes bright. "I see. Now, what about that charity from last night? To Save Capri?"

Felix smiled distantly. "I'd go for the Blue Ribbon, if I were you. I have a feeling Capri will take care of itself."

She took the point. "Baroness Perfidia—she's Pauline Power in the book, according to Peter Hamilton. Was she, is she, really such a woman as you describe?"

Felix smiled carefully. "There might be certain similarities."

"Jack said that part is *me.* Is that supposed to mean I'm so similar to Perfidia—Pauline?"

"No, no," Felix said hastily, "I shouldn't think so. I think he was talking about physical type, a big girl. But whatever, actresses are not supposed to be carbon copies of the wantons, or whoever they're playing. Are they?"

"Oh, no, by no means. But I wonder what's in Jack's mind."

"I'm sure Jack sees you as a marvelous actress who could play any part," Felix complimented her.

"Yes." She thought about it. "That's true. I *can* play any part. Do you think I could play such an evil woman as that, though, Felix?"

"Of course. You're perfect for the part." Oh, blast, he told himself, he had not said it right. "I mean, you could throw yourself into the part, with perfection."

A smile crinkled her full lips and zigzagged across her teeth. "You *are* refined," she exclaimed softly. Mona crossed her legs, and the red sheath pulled away from the white underside of her thigh. Solid flesh, he could see, not puffy or spotty with cellulite bumps. She leaned forward, placing her forearms on her knees. "And now, tell me. After I slay Los Angeles society, what do I do next?"

"Ah," he said, for now she was edging back toward the money part of it, if money *was* going to play a role. He knew the process by heart. "The next step is New York. Usually the most convenient route from California is via Palm Springs and Palm Beach. There are certain parties in the two 'Palms' that are a must. And then New York. But Mona, now you're running into high finance."

"Money?" she said. "What's money!"

"You can get away with it here for a lot less," Felix said. "In New York, you start pitching against the heavy hitters. Eventually, the campaign you're talking about demands a really big income to keep it going. And, my dear, you *are* still a busy woman professionally. Don't forget that."

Mona blushed. "I love it the way you say 'my dear.' So refined."

She confused him, gushing like that. "It's just a figure of speech. Everybody says it."

"Not like you do," she murmured. She leaned so far downward that she might have fallen on the table. "Give me your hand, Felix, your right hand."

He did as she bid. She ran her right index finger

over the lines in his palm. "Umm," she mumbled, "my word, Felix, you *are* a man of accomplishment. *And,*" she cried, "the best is yet to come." She closed his hand tightly, making it into a fist, then pried it open for closer inspection. "Yes, yes. Money, power, and influence, you'll have it all. Felix, what sign are you?"

"Gemini," he said. Secretly, he hated this kind of thing.

"Like me!" She bent and put a wet kiss next to his thumb, then ran her tongue along his life line. Felix jumped. Mona looked at him calculatingly. "Gemini. The twins. Dual personalities, creatures of mood and impulse. Lovable but sometimes cruel. Am I right, Felix?"

"I've never believed in it, Mona."

"Ah, but you should. Don't be a *skept*. Why shouldn't we believe it? Is there anything better to believe?"

"Science," Felix said.

"Science? I don't understand science. I can't even add—although I *can* count." He didn't see what the difference was. It must be a reference to money and the making of it. "Felix," she went on warmly, "tell me, do you think I could look the part of a person in society? You know, many people say actresses look so cheap and flashy. I don't look like that, do I?"

"Not at all and that's the truth. I've noticed you don't wear much makeup."

"That's so," she said with satisfaction. "I hate makeup, and it's very bad for the skin. I have to wear so much of it when I'm working. At home, nothing at all. In fact, you know," she said confidentially, "when I'm home alone, I don't even wear clothes most of the time. Unless . . ." She laughed shyly. "Unless I have a guest as refined as you are."

Oh, Felix thought, the invitation to the waltz. But

what about her servant, this little man called Wang, who looked like an agent of the Koumintang?

Mona didn't give him a chance for indecent speculation. "Felix, tell me, what would you write for me? What adventure?"

Felix laughed. "Ah, *that* would be telling."

"Tell me, Felix," she pleaded. She touched his knee.

Felix closed his eyes and was silent. Then he said, "Somehow, I see you aboard a fast sloop, off the coast of Rhode Island. The weather is foul and the wind is in your hair. . . ." Her eyes were intent. She nodded. "I don't know if you're alone. No, I see a man, the captain. Mona, the captain calls, 'Come below, *me hearty*.'"

She chuckled lithesomely. "And who's sailing the boat if I go below?"

"Maybe the first mate," Felix suggested, smiling. "Anyway, there you are, down below. God, what do I see!"

"Tell me, Felix!"

"This captain is a mountain of a man; his name is Dean. I suppose you're wearing a . . . uh, tight sweater."

"Well, of course," Mona chuckled.

"All right—you asked for it, *me hearty*," Felix said grinning. "He meets you at the bottom of the ladder, or companionway, and he grabs you in his arms. He probably kisses your neck."

"Just as I like it," she agreed. She licked her lips. "Then what, Felix?"

"Oh," he said evasively, "I couldn't go into all that, Mona."

"Felix, I'm hanging on tenterhooks."

"All right," he continued, short of breath. "What he does, he slips his hands under your sweater. Well, Mona, that *is* what happens in situations like that." She nodded, her eyes warm. "Okay," Felix warned, "I'm

262

going on, even if you're shocked. Well, naturally, you come close to fainting. Dean, this mountain of a man, places you reverently on a bunk. . . ."

"Yes," Mona said softly, "your imagination is visual. You should write for the movies, Felix. Then what? Tell me instantly."

"So you're on the bunk, right?" he asked. "You are quivering with delight. Naturally, with a man like this. His eyes, God, they're dark pits of passion. He says, 'Gel, if you're wearing a bodice, I'll rip it straight off you.' "

"But," Mona objected, "I am *not* wearing a bodice. This is not a Gothic. I don't have anything on under the sweater."

"Of course not," Felix said impatiently, "I'm getting to that. Dean removes your sweater, and under it you are wearing nothing because you like the feel of virgin wool against your virginal booz-ooms."

Mona hooted. "Virginal booz-ooms—that's a good one!"

"I see you are also wearing loose corduroys, fly fronted, men's style. Dean, all the while staring into your limpid eyes, puts his mouth to . . . uh, your sweet booz-ooms. Naturally, this brings you to raging desire."

"You bet your sweet bippy," Mona exclaimed. "If anything does it, that's it, when the mouth hits the booz-ooms. Felix, masterful! Continue, pray!"

"Well." Felix rubbed his forehead. "Mona, heavens, I don't want to exaggerate—if you insist." He could see that she did insist. She leaned back in her armchair and crossed her arms over her sweet booz-ooms, all the while staring fixedly at him. "Slowly, Dean puts his hand to your . . . He lowers his hand and toys with the zipper of the trousers. By now, of course, being a woman, you are bucking with passion, like an untamed mare. . . ."

Mona tittered and crouched forward again, absorbing the recitation.

"Dean pulls the zipper. Underneath, you are wearing nothing." Felix smiled cleverly. "Nothing. For you like the feel of rough corduroy against your—on your thighs."

"Yes, that is quite so," Mona murmured. She inhaled sharply.

"Suddenly, his face is at your—suddenly, he lowers his face, and you feel his heavy beard on your . . . You feel his beard. You feel his rough lips. You groan."

"I'll say." Mona groaned.

"The groan blots out even the sound of the heavy sea. You feel his lips, his, yes, tongue. . . ."

"Yes," Mona sighed, closing her eyes, "on my candy box."

"Well, yes," Felix said hesitantly. "The while, of course, you are aware of his . . ."

"His sword." Mona supplied the word.

"Yes, apparatus, if you will."

"Uh huh," Mona cried, "and what I want is to put it in my mouth!"

"You do?"

"Of course I do, Felix," Mona said scornfully, "what the hell kind of woman do you think I am? Is *he* going to have all the fun?"

"You're getting ahead of me," Felix said primly.

"I know what happens, Felix. How does it end? I suppose the goddamn boat sinks under us."

"That would be a tragic ending," he said.

"So? I'm meant to have a tragic ending," Mona exclaimed. "It says so in my horoscope." She jumped up. "Felix, you kept talking about this man Dèan. The man I see in that story is *you*."

"Me?"

"Yes." Mona stood beside him, terrycloth rubbing

the side of his face. "You want to, don't you?" He didn't say yea or nay, but she knew it was a yea. "Come with me, Felix. This will probably get me banned from the Blue Book, but I'm determined to make love to you."

Bashfully, Felix stood up. "Mona . . ."

"Just follow me, Felix."

Her boudoir was done up in soft shades of rose and peach and apricot. The bed was large, as it would be to accommodate her commodious body. Mona slammed the door and unzipped her sheath. It fell to the floor at her feet. Underneath she was naked.

Mona chuckled. "Nothing underneath, Felix, because I love the feel of virgin terrycloth against my virginal body."

"My word!"

"So refined," Mona murmured. She stepped up to him. "Take my breasts in your hands, Felix, and squeeze them, gently."

Respectfully, he did so and she breathed shallowly. Politely, he passed his thumbs over the puckered nipples, leaving prints behind, he thought wildly, for posterity. He began his circumnavigation of her body, tracing a route down her ribcage to her slim behind, across her hips to her belly, so lush. Mona moaned and produced low-keyed panting.

"My refined man," she said, "I've been fantasizing about you since last night."

She pulled off his tie and unbuttoned his shirt, and as he shrugged out of his blazer, she was already loosening his trousers and then telling him to lift first one foot, then the other. In a trice, they were in bed between pink-colored sheets.

"As I suspected," she said fiercely, "a perfect little body, and much refined. Your waist can't be any bigger around than mine. Ummm, your skin is clear and smooth."

Mona mouthed his neck, his chest, and his stomach, leaped to his legs and chewed at his kneecap, grunting and growling the while, and panting as she changed the venue of her white teeth. Intermittently, she slammed her chest down on his face and banged her breasts against his nose. She seized his balls in her strong fingers and kneaded them demandingly. She took no notice of anything Felix did in recompense. She could not possibly be transported to a higher state of pure lust. Then, finally, ravenously, she put her mouth to his penis and gulped, sucking and slurping noisily. Mona was an animal, Felix told himself desperately. But that was all right. It was all right! For he had never met an animal before.

"Frrh, grrh, uuum, aarh."

He was soon wet with sweat, and when he managed to get his hand between her legs, he discovered that she was producing scads of oily, sticky sexual fluid. A heavy, almost smoky odor of sex began to saturate the room.

"Grrrh, haaah, uuumh, aarh."

Mona slid on her breasts up and down his body, as if she were surfing, halting to grab his penis between the booz-ooms. Then she gulped him again, while shoving her wet vulva in his face. Timidly, he put his tongue to it. That was the least he could do.

"Oowweh!" Mona screeched at the top of her voice.

That did it. He expected Wang to rush in waving a meat cleaver.

"Oowweh!"

First she was on all fours above him then, in a flash, on her back. She grabbed him and pulled him between her legs, then locked him to her with her ankles. Under his chest, her breasts rolled. Felix felt infinitesimal inside this raging, labyrinthine wind tunnel. She needed something larger than he had to offer, he told himself.

But she did not mind. She pulled in, tightening, and screamed. "Oowweh!"

Felix became part of her flesh. What was happening was astonishing because he was not any smaller than she was. He was just as tall and must have weighed more or less the same. But, for some reason, she *was* bigger, she was *gigantic*. Perhaps, he thought wildly, it was because there was so much of her on the surface: the breasts, for one thing, suctioning him to her. Each time they met, there was the impact of *thwack,* or *thump.* And underneath, she was like a stampede of a hundred horses.

Making sense for a second, she muttered angrily, "Actresses are hot, Felix, hot, hot, hot. They need it for their art, art, art. Bear down, Felix, bear down. Oowweh!"

He dug his fingers into her buttocks, holding on for dear life, trying mightily to manage those untamed loins until, understanding that he was not to be bested, she subsided a little. Biting on one of her nipples, he dug his toes into the mattress and paced her. Her belly caved and inflated, and finally she commenced the slow, labored, demanding but defeated panting that signified she was approaching a climax. When it came, with a terrible scream, he thought Wang would now certainly rush into the room.

Finally, her lust receded. "Felix," Mona groaned. "Did you come?"

Yes, he had, he knew, but he was not sure when it had happened.

"Woooh!" she exhaled happily.

Felix flopped over. He was exhausted, make no mistake about that. His legs ached, and his shoulders were stiff.

"Can I ask you a question?"

"Of course, sweet one."

"Are you always so passionate?"

Mona turned her head toward him and smiled moistly. "No, not always. Only when I *want* so desperately."

"I hope I didn't hurt you," he murmured. He moved his head to the Prissian breasts and, chuckling to himself, remembered the joke about the mouse screwing the elephant. How could he have hurt *her*?

"Yes, you hurt me, Felix, you hurt me most delightfully." She stroked his back and, giggling, reached for his balls. She held them in the palm of her hand. "You are worth your weight in gold, Felix. But tell me, now that you know about me, do you think I'll be able to make it in polite society?"

He propped his head on the luxurious breasts and put his mouth to a silken nipple. What was that about a fee? Mona gave off the scent of after-sex, of release, like a sky swept clear of rain. This was woman, vulnerable and loving. Passionate. Sweet, mad, lustful. The pure sweaty smell of her was like a restorative. He could almost feel his hair growing. Good God, Felix thought, had he finally found *her*?

Twenty-Two

Sally looked him in the eye. "Do you like my old man? You don't have to, you know."

"I like him all right," Hamilton said. "He seems like a nice guy. I'm just finding it a little hard making any connection between him and you."

"You think I'm not like him?"

"There's very little resemblance," he said.

Sally couldn't see much either. Glumly, she sat down on the edge of the bed and put her chin on her hand. "Hell, I'm probably not even his kid."

"Why do you say that, Sally?" he demanded. "Of course you're his kid."

He was not in the best of moods, she thought. Naturally enough. Visiting the Hollywood Division police station was not everybody's cup of tea, and since Orville was a complete stranger, it had been a bit above and beyond his call of duty to Sally.

"Why do I say it?" she repeated. "Easy. Because it's just as likely Virginia was screwing around in Ohio. She did enough in New York—you ought to know."

He walked to the window and looked outside. "I'm not dignifying that crap anymore," he said.

"Well, don't," she said. "I don't care. Christ, the whole world is unhinged."

"Sure," he grunted. "Maybe your old man is actually the Great Caruso or somebody like that. What the hell difference does it make anyway? As far as I know you're Sally Jones. You'd still be Sally Jones even if you were really Sally Schlumbagel, heir to the Schlumbagel bagel millions."

"Goddamn you."

"Don't goddamn me. I didn't get drunk and wind up in the can," Hamilton chuckled.

"You never take me seriously," Sally charged. "You treat me like a child."

"You are a child."

"You think I'm nothing but a nut out of the Tower of Babel . . ."

"That's Bedlam," he said. "The Tower of Babel signifies decadence."

"So now I'm decadent."

"Yes, you really are decadent, Sally," he said sarcastically. "Your riotous life has been one of hedonist diversion beyond my ken."

Sally did not know why she felt so tired and frustrated. The only reason could be the sudden appearance of Orville Jones. "You drive me crazy, Hamilton," she said softly, tears filling her eyes. "You're so blasted intellectual. You know just everything, don't you?"

"More than you do, that's for sure."

"Bullshit! I'm just as smart as you are," she cried. "I don't really need to work for you. I may not even go to China."

"Yeah?" He turned and looked at her. "What the hell are you crying about, Sally?"

"Nothing. I'm just mad."

"At what? What did I do?"

"Nothing. I don't know why I'm crying. I'm mad at the world."

"The world?" He began to laugh. He hugged his chest and laughed at her, making her feel more furious than before. "What has the world done to you?"

She shook her head. She didn't know. She couldn't explain it. She stood up and went to stand beside him, arms hanging forlornly. "He's sitting on the terrace."

"He says he wants to drink beer all afternoon. Let

him. Sally, I don't think you should have told him you're my keeper."

She smiled at him. "Why not? How else am I going to explain my presence in this household?"

"Just plain secretary would have been good enough."

When Orville had pulled only slightly out of his funk, he had become intensely curious about their arrangement. What exactly, he asked Sally, did she do for Peter Hamilton Enterprises? Sort of girl Friday, she had explained innocently. But more than that, she'd been hired to keep an eye on him. He was prone to depression and now and then was seized by epileptic-like fits. The doctors insisted somebody always be nearby. Orville had cast an anxious eye at Hamilton, a little worried that Sally was so close to a madman of sorts. But he had been nicely impressed by the house. They had installed him in the small downstairs study, over his protests. Orville had insisted to Sally that he could wire for money. He could take care of himself.

"Well," she said, "he won't be here long. Virginia'll get him that job with Jack."

"Working for Jack Logan?" Hamilton said. "I don't know."

"Jack pays," Sally said, "so what's the diff?"

"I don't know," he said. "It might be all very well working for Logan on the non-money side, but I wouldn't want to see your old man get caught holding the bag. I have the distinct feeling Logan's financial structure is built on sand."

"No, no," she said. "Orville's too smart to get caught like that. He's so honest, he'd probably turn Jack in."

Hamilton laughed again and tucked his arm around her waist. He kissed her on the forehead. "See," he said, "you *are* just like him—honest, frank, and straightforward."

271

"Yes, that's so." She rubbed her body against him. "Anyway, thanks for being so nice . . . and understanding."

"I wouldn't do it for anybody else."

"Listen," she said, "enough chitchat. Do you love me, like you said, or are you just pulling my leg?"

"What time is it?"

"About four-thirty."

"We've got a couple of hours."

"So?"

"Tonight we're supposed to go over to those friends of Felix's for dinner—the Sackses."

"I don't want to."

"Why? Don't you want to see your mother again? She *is* your mother, even if you're not sure of your father."

"Jesus," Sally sighed, "you're really after me."

"Yes, I am."

"What about him?"

"He's happy enough, isn't he? You can tell Orville I had one of my seizures. Which is true. A sudden seizure of lust."

Sally smiled from far away. She knew it was lust, but what else was it? He had this very, very bad habit of being flippant with her. She still didn't quite know where she was with Hamilton, despite all the words and the playing.

From down below, there was a rumble of song. "Roll me over . . . in the clover . . ." Orville's voice was hoarse, just a little raucous. "Roll me over . . . lay me down . . . and do it again . . ."

Hamilton chuckled but Sally said, mildly panicked, "He knows what you're doing."

Hamilton murmured something inconsequential, pawing her around the bed, like a butcher handling a piece of meat. And what could she do? Nothing. She was a sex object. But she wanted *him,* and that was the difference. He was not rough, she admitted. He caressed her breasts in that gentle and amazed way he had, exploring, kissing, and tasting. She felt him against her leg, and then his hand spread over her crotch like a fig leaf. He was warm.

Again, the tones of Orville's song drifted upward. Sally smiled into Hamilton's shoulder. Orville. She had never known him. But he was not a bad man, and Sally knew there was more beneath the surface than met the eye.

She put her arms around Hamilton and rocked him on her body. He was so warm and full of life. She closed her eyes, thinking only of his body against hers. His lips. She was ready.

"Hamilton, honey, come in from the cold."

"Sally, can't you wait until I've finished with the preliminaries?"

"You have finished. I'm ready. Now."

He positioned himself above her as if he were preparing a push-up, then slowly came down. She reached for his entry, bit by bit, until he was fully linked within her to her . . . what? Heart? Soul? Tears came to her eyes again, a different flavor of tears. "Hamilton, very easily. Very tenderly . . ." She stroked his back. There were yards of him.

It was so marvelous, Sally mused, and God must be good to have come up with this brilliant arrangement of things. Just as easily, during that seven days of hyperactivity known as the Creation, God could have made them all hermaphrodites, if procreation was the sole purpose of all the fooling around. But no, God, very, very wisely, she thought, had chosen to make it beautiful and fulfilling. Hamilton was right. What reason did she have to be mad at the world?

Despite what he might think or however she had tried to lead him on, Sally was not widely experienced.

She'd had her flings and a couple of brief love affairs. But nothing had ever been serious or long-lasting, and the sexual encounters had been merely silly. She sighed and let herself whisper, "Hamilton, we're so lucky. Aren't we?"

He looked into her eyes. His were studious, very green so close up, with minuscule flecks of yellow, like butterfly wings, deep inside. Emotion, yearning, gushed into her throat and she lifted herself, tightening around him. At once she felt a gathering of nerve ends, like a bouquet, and a spinning sensation from her lips downward, spiraling dizziness. Deeper, deeper, he pushed. And then it happened, the rushing of energy toward her center and waves of release, as if she were being thrown into the air by a dozen strong men. He finished before she reached the peak, and then, as his muscles began to relax, he was kissing her with a kind of desperation, still spending the last, when she finally burst. She heard herself gasping, then squealed.

She could not speak right away and didn't want to. That had been the best. The very best and it would get better.

Hamilton rolled over on his side, but she could still feel the beating of his heart along his arm. "I've had it," he sighed.

"I know," Sally said softly, "you've just unloaded a bunch of vital fluids, and your body resents it."

"No," he said, "the body doesn't resent it. The body is very pleased."

"Well," she said, "well . . ." She put her fingers on his face, running them under his eyes, down his nose, across his lips, along his chin. "That's the one that did it."

"Sally." He chuckled very softly. "Enough with getting knocked up."

Chill spread across her sweaty body. "I know I am."

"I hope you're right," he muttered, his hand over his

eyes, far away. "Then at least we could stop talking about it so much. You've got some kind of a fixation. Do you want to be or not? I can't figure out what you want."

"Yes, I do, honestly," she murmured. "Are you listening to me, Hamilton? And I *don't*—blast you, Hamilton, what is it *you* want?"

"All I know is I want to go to China," he mumbled.

Sally turned to face him, her head next to his on the pillow. "Tell me about it."

"If it turns out right, we'll go in the early fall, when it's not so hot. We go with cameras and crew up the Yangtse River toward the headwaters. Nobody's been up there in years."

"Looking for those cute panda bears."

"Yes, cute! That's where they come from. Sally, it'll be a hell of a project. Just great!"

"I'm coming."

"Yes, you are," he said solemnly. "Your name is on the list in Washington for visas."

"You didn't tell me!"

"I'm telling you now."

"Oh, Peter!" She kissed him violently. "I'll do anything. I can cut film, you know. I can write."

He laughed in her ear. "You're going to be a grip."

"What? Carry the gear?"

"And tote that bale too. You better get back on the pill," he said.

"I hate the goddamn pill. It's unnatural."

"Then you better get in touch with the Pope. He's got a birth-control method that's foolproof. It's called abstinence."

Sally said happily, "I've heard of that."

"Well, I'm telling you—seriously now," he said. "This is going to be a very strenuous trip."

"I'll do whatever you want—as long as we're together, Hamilton. I just want to be *with* you," she insisted.

"Will you follow my orders?" he demanded sternly. "I demand complete obedience—especially from my grips."

"I'll grip you anytime you say," she promised. "A grip, they say, is God's prelude to the grapple and then the saddle."

"Ah, Sally, Sally, what am I going to do with you? Those nights in camp will be long and tedious."

She grinned. "Don't worry. I'll just shoot off a few aphorisms once in a while to keep everybody on their toes."

"Yes, that's what I'm afraid of. Confucius will probably cartwheel in his grave."

She yelled happily as she jumped off the bed and went into the bathroom, slamming the door. Sally sat down and listened to her jolly tinkle, as they called it in polite circles. She washed and threw some of his after-shave lotion on her body, rosy and flushed with having loved him. She came out and leaped back on the bed, crouching on her knees beside him. His dick was shriveled and lifeless, asleep on his thigh like a lazy watchdog. "Look at that thing," she said. "Surfeited."

"You expect it maybe to sing and dance for you?" he said, yawning.

"I expect more respect." She snapped her finger at it. "Punk!" She took the end of it in her teeth. It tasted a little bitter but began to perk up with the attention. Such a marvelous thing, she thought, ever flexible and adaptable. Everything women had was inside them, except their boobs and, according to the sociologists, that was merely an accident, another trick of clever God's to get men's eyes off women's asses and around to the front where they belonged. Women didn't even come as men did, and why was that? Simple, my dear Hamilton, because women had to take the sperm within themselves to hide it along with their big, true emotions. Men, yes, were all on the surface.

He grew inside her mouth, the flaccid going hard. Sally climbed on top of him and guided it inside her again. Hamilton's eyes were blank, and he stared stupidly at her, a tiny smile on his lips. Bastard—he was so proud of himself.

"I love it," she sighed, closing her eyes.

"Well, it's just something you can't resist, I guess."

"Don't be so conceited," she muttered, her teeth clenched.

God, she was so close to the threshold, just thinking about him, that she came again almost immediately, whimpering and then falling forward so he could put his arms comfortingly around her. Sally began to cry shamelessly. Her tears ran down, wetting his chest. It was ridiculous. Why was she crying? He didn't say anything. He just petted her and smoothed her hair.

"Goddamn it, Hamilton, why are you so secretive? Why won't you say it?"

"I did say it. You're coming to China."

"No!" she wailed. "Say you love me. I don't want to screw around with somebody who doesn't love me. It's a waste."

"I said you're coming to China—would I take you to China if I didn't love you?"

"Say it!"

"I love you, Sally," he said seriously.

"I don't believe you!" Why?

"Oh, shit," Hamilton said. "Just a minute." He groped for a notepad and a pencil on the nighttable by the telephone. He leaned on his elbow and scribbled, then handed her the piece of paper. "There!"

"Sally Jones: I love you. Sincerely yours, Peter Hamilton."

"Ha!" she cried. "It looks good in writing. Gimme the pencil."

Underneath his scrawl, she wrote, "Peter Hamilton: I love you too. I love you to distraction and you drive me crazy. Sincerely yours, Sally Jones."

He read it. "All right, I'm going to frame this and put it over the bed. Then, whenever you have any doubts, you can just look up at it."

Sally nodded. "All right, that's a good idea. But you better put it on the ceiling because I expect to be spending most of my time on my back."

"Sally," Hamilton exclaimed, laughing. He grabbed her again. "One thing—don't change, *ever*."

Twenty-Three

Wade French talked briefly to Evelyn James in New York during the afternoon. Yes, he had handed the papers to Felix.

"And what did he say?"

"He was very annoyed," French said. "Evelyn, I miss you ever so much, dear."

"And I miss you, Wade," she said. "I'm . . . I can't help remembering that night, those few nights of ours. It was heavenly, Wade."

"Stellar," he agreed soberly, even though he was not all that happy remembering it. French was a straight-ahead sort of man when it came to the emotions, and he preferred a classical straight-ahead sort of screw.

"What you did to me . . ." Evelyn's words reached across the continent, coming out at the California end in a moan. He hoped she did not elaborate; phone calls *were* sometimes monitored. "Wade, when are you coming back?"

He wondered what the hell was ailing her. She'd told him she liked her men twice a week, about as often as the hairdresser. But, impatient as he was, he could not afford to brush her aside. Not yet, anyway. "Darling . . . I should be back in a few more days. Now that I'm here, there are a few more odds and ends of business to attend to."

More *odds* than ends, he told himself, if one was thinking of Marina and bald-headed George.

"Darling," Evelyn said, "I'll be waiting. Kiss-kiss."

French made a face to himself. "Yes, kiss-kiss."

But, well, so what? He was smiling deeply within

himself, satisfied with his juggler's expertise, as he strolled down the hall. He knocked on the door of Perfidia's suite.

"Wade," she greeted him profusely, "come in. We're *all* here."

She indicated George and Marina with a movement of her arm. It swung loosely within a voluminous and silky Japanese kimono. She was holding a glass of champagne in her hand.

French glanced at the two kids. Dressed in identical T-shirts and jeans, they were seated next to each other on the couch, facing the TV set, which rattled and honked with the electronic exertion of one of those game shows.

"Jesus, Perfidia, don't these two do anything but watch TV? Why don't they go downstairs and go swimming or something? The hotel is famous for its pool."

She shrugged indifferently. "Has there been any communication from New York, Wade?"

"No," he said, shaking his head heavily. "But have no fear, the contribution—that's all been taken care of."

"*Dear* man," Perfidia said. She moved, gently swaying, he realized, away from the door, taking his hand.

As they passed in front of the TV set, George impatiently waved his hand, signaling them to get out of the way.

Perfidia trilled a nauseous laugh. "Rude, isn't he, the little bugger. But so dear!" She belched lightly, behind her champagne glass. "Well, Wade, we'll just leave the children here and go into the other room, where we can talk."

Perfidia closed the bedroom door behind them and placed French in one of the two armchairs by the window. She arched her black eyebrows toward the champagne bottle, nestled in an ice bucket on a long bureau facing the bed. French got up and found a clean glass. He poured himself champagne and sat down again. Perfidia lowered herself to the edge of the bed and crossed her legs. The kimono fell away, as she meant it to, revealing for him the smooth calf and introductory inch or two of thigh. Perfidia's skin was so smooth and unblemished, he told himself, as perfect as if it had been meticulously sandpapered.

"Wade," she asked slowly, wetting her lips with more champagne, "what should I do about Peter Hamilton?"

He didn't know what she meant. Why would she want to do anything about Peter Hamilton? He muttered that there was nothing that occurred to him to do with, or to, Peter Hamilton.

"He was rude and piggish to me last night," Perfidia said. "He was insulting. You know," she continued broodingly, "I'm still not convinced he didn't have something to do with Naomi's death. It's possible, isn't it, that he paid somebody to kill her?"

Reluctantly, he agreed it was possible. "But, Perfidia, I don't think there's anything in it for you. The police investigated thoroughly."

"Still . . ." She smiled. "I could hire a detective, couldn't I?"

"Of course, you *could,* Perfidia. But I don't think anything would come of it. And I'd hate to see you waste your time and energy—and money."

She smiled again deeply. "Money is very precious to you, isn't it, Wade?" She seemed to be stripping his soul with those eyes.

"Well, yes," he admitted, lowering his head to stare at his hands. "Isn't it to you?"

"Primarily, yes, basically and primarily. But it would give me a great deal of pleasure to unmask Peter Hamilton, if there is anything there to unmask. He tried to make a fool of me, you see."

"Well, I wish you wouldn't . . . I . . ." He stopped and looked at her. Would she be receptive now to what might be a very forward suggestion? "I visualize things in quite another manner."

"Indeed?" The plucked eyebrows rose. She emptied her champagne glass and held it out to be refilled. The kimono slipped away from her bosom, and French was treated to a sight of the famous Perfidia Sinclair breasts, firm, large, and strong with nipples so red, they were almost black like her hair. Perfidia was aware of his eyes; she smiled savagely. While he shakily refilled her glass, she put one hand on the right breast, absently touching the nipple. "Wade, don't spill. Tell me what you visualize."

"Well, if you'll . . . permit me to say so. God, Perfidia, that is so beautiful."

"Yes, isn't it?" Her smile verged on a leer. "You mean the champagne?" Christ, yes, didn't he know that she was evil? She'd used this body on him before, and he'd willingly been victimized. He could not resist. Perfidia was half mad, somehow unbalanced. Why was he about to ask her for an alliance, a permanent one? Naturally, it would mean ruin.

"Perfidia," he said humbly, "what I see is your enjoying your stay in this country! What's past is past, isn't it? Then you'll go back to Italy—at which time the Sinclair contribution to Save Capri . . ."

She interrupted him with a mocking chuckle. He realized she was more than a little drunk. "Aha! My vision is of *you* as the man who came to dinner at the Villa Putzi and never left!"

French returned the champagne bottle to its bucket. Next to it was a bowl of strawberries. He helped himself to one, nervously stalling, and licked his fingers. "That had occurred to me, too. You'll need someone to manage the money now, darling, since Putzi isn't there to do it."

Haughtily, Perfidia said, "*I* always managed the money. Putzi was so stupid, he couldn't even count." She laughed shrilly. "You're wondering about me and Putzi? Yes, it's true—Putzi was very stupid. His blood-line was run down, Wade, like an old clock. Look at Marina, for God's sake. She's practically a moron."

"Perfidia! How can you?"

"Goddamn it, it's true, Wade. You ask why? Why did I do it? I'll tell you. I was fascinated by his platinum hair, and he was a fag. I *wanted* a fag. But I turned him, Wade. It's rarely done, but I did it. It was a matter of challenge, of honor, if you like. I twisted him around, like mastering a tornado. And I did it, too, to spite Nathan Sinclair. But Wade!" She gulped air. "I love Capri. I've never loved anything, or anyone, else."

"Perfidia," he stuttered, "I know. I understand. I've always figured . . ."

"That you would join me in Capri?" She laughed, the sound like a peacock's scream. "Why not? Why not, indeed? But do you love me, Wade?" she demanded coldly.

"Yes, I do," he said, his words rushing, "I always have."

"You're fascinated, I know," she said wickedly, "but that's different from love. Putzi loved me. No, he *adored* me."

"I worship you!"

"Do you?" she mocked. "How could you prove it, Wade?"

"In any way you like, Perfidia. I think I've proven it already. Look how much I risked for you . . . before. And now, I'm proving it again. One million dollars is nothing to sneeze at, Perfidia, and I managed it. Signed, sealed, and delivered—after you go back to Capri."

Her smile was like a cut in a steel plate. "My, they're *all* so anxious to get me out of the country.

Wade, you don't know me very well. I'm not an easy woman. I have *very* unusual tastes and demands."

"Perfidia . . ."

"I'm not talking about whips and such, Wade!"

"Whips?" He faltered. "You're joking."

She was toying with him, laughing at him. She was *so* amused. "Wade, darling, come over here," she said. Obediently, his knees trembling, he went to her. Perfidia ran one hand down the back of his leg. "Kiss me, Wade." He bent and kissed her lips. The taste was acrid from the champagne, like iron filings. Perfidia sighed, her eyes far away. "Capri," she said softly. "There is an ancient custom, a betrothal ceremony of sorts. I learned about it from Putzi."

French nodded, his lips dry. She was trying to frighten him, perhaps scare him off, but he remembered the jewelry, the villa, the Sinclair millions, the last million and the millions she'd had earlier. His will strengthened.

Perfidia pressed his leg and smiled. "Wade, I've ordered up those strawberries and cream for a very particular purpose. On Capri, we always eat strawberries and cream in the spring."

French smiled understandingly. "Everybody likes strawberries and cream, Perfidia."

"Yes, they do, don't they?" She pointed at the bowl. "Bring them here, Wade." He brought them to her. Perfidia lifted the spoon at the side of the bowl and dug in. "Very good," she said, her mouth full. "You'll like them, Wade. Sweet."

"Yes, I already had one. They're very sweet." He turned to his chair.

"Just a minute," she said. Eyes glittering, she drank some more champagne and then, holding the bowl in one hand, she lowered herself from the bed to the floor. She stretched out and pulled the kimono away from her body. The body gleamed, dusky skinned, in

284

the afternoon sun that slanted through the blinds. French began to shake. She was built like a goddess; she was worthy of Zeus himself. Perfidia lay placidly, grinning up at him fiendishly. Then, to his unutterable amazement, she selected a strawberry from the bowl and tucked it into her vagina . . . and another . . . and another. Then she smeared whipped cream on her thighs. "Enjoy, Wade," she said, "enjoy . . ."

"Perfidia . . ." He was perspiring.

Gently, she said, "The spring rite on Capri, Wade."

Christ, he felt his heart murmur. What was she asking? Why was it these women wanted his face and nothing else? What was it about his face, red as a Beefeater's, blunt-nosed and thick-lipped? The lips?

"Wade," Perfidia said gently, "if one wants to live on Capri, one must indulge in the native customs."

"Yes, Perfidia," French grunted. "Tradition is precious."

He removed his suit coat and loosened his vest. Not chary of paying obeisance to tradition, he knelt at her parted legs. Her look was expectant and demanding too. Yes, he would have to do it. He ducked his head. It was not exactly the same as ducking for apples in a barrel, but he owned that there was a similarity. He found the first of the strawberries with his tongue and sucked it free. Perfidia gasped loudly. "Good, Wade?"

"Delicious strawberries," he muttered.

"If it's too . . . traditional for you, just say so."

"No, no, not at all," he murmured, licking cream and chewing quietly. He was afforded, in the interim, a close look at her apparatus. It was impressive, no doubt about it, and French could see why Perfidia had made it as a top model all those years before. He became engrossed in the . . . tradition. Actually, it was not unenjoyable, and he began to concentrate so single-mindedly on what he was doing, he realized just a moment later, that he failed to hear the bedroom door open. His first inkling of another presence in the room came when hands reached around him to unbuckle his belt and then, roughly, pull his trousers and boxer shorts off his hips. Cool hands grabbed his testicles and squeezed. French grunted with surprise. Perfidia opened her eyes and gazed along her body into his eyes.

"It's only Marina," Perfidia sighed.

"Oh." Crouched on his knees, elbows on the floor, he continued ducking for the strawberries. Perfidia arched her hips a bit so he would have easier access. French was careless of the giggles behind him until he remembered George. That reminder came along with a stab of pain. Good Christ, no! French's body jerked, but he could not get away. Marina had her arm under him, gripping his nuts and holding him in place. He felt another heavy thrust into him. French choked and cried out. When he looked up at Perfidia, in anguish and pleading, she smiled crookedly and patted his head. Christ almighty, he was being raped, by the three of them. Yes, raped! French groaned and gasped, and he began to cry. Then roughly George wrenched away from him. French fell on his side, but even then Marina did not let go. She was giggling idiotically. French bellowed and tried to get her hand away from him.

"George! George!" Marina yelped, her crazy face gaping, *"Wunderbar."*

George stood above them, smiling. "Yeah, Marina, honey." He stared at French patronizingly. *"She* wanted me to," he said simply.

French groaned. "You dirty little cocksucker. You've ruined me."

George frowned. "Not a cocksucker."

"Well, whatever you are, you little son of a bitch."

"Don't be silly, Wade," Perfidia eventually drawled. "Ruined? How could you be ruined? This sort of thing has been going on for centuries."

286

"Yes," Marina said angrily. "Silly man." As if to emphasize the point, Marina dropped her head and bit him sharply on the cock.

French howled. "Jesus! Perfidia!"

"Marina! Stop that!"

French staggered to his feet, pulling up his shorts and trousers. "Perfidia, was this necessary? Did you have to do this to me?" he cried. Tears were still pouring down his cheeks.

Perfidia laughed. "Still want to be the man who came to dinner, Wade?"

"Perfidia, Perfidia," he said brokenly, "you . . . lovely! But him?" He pointed at George. "Why?"

George smiled. "Because it was there, Mr. French."

"*Mutti* . . ."

"Marina, just stop it. Stop babbling!"

French lowered himself gingerly in the chair and put his head between his hands. It was surely the end of him now.

"Wade," Perfidia cautioned him, "it's not Doomsday, after all."

"For me it is," he mumbled. He was ashamed, so very ashamed. "Why did you let them? I'm humiliated, defiled. It ruins a man, for Christ's sake, Perfidia!" he exclaimed.

Her eyes were furious. "Oh, bother, Wade! Admit it! You liked it. You were surprised but you liked it. Next time, you'll like it even more."

"What? What do you mean, next time?"

"Oh, you're just like Putzi, *au fond.*"

"I am not a pervert!" French howled. Guiltily, he looked at bald-headed George.

"*Mutti* . . ." Marina crawled toward her mother and crept into her arms. She began suckling Perfidia's breasts. Perfidia's eyelids sagged.

"*Marin-chen,*" she whispered, "my little girl." Perfidia was not embarrassed. She stroked the girl's hair, as French watched blindly. "Woof-Woof," Perfidia murmured, "oh, Woof-Woof, what am I to do?"

"Fido?" he said meaninglessly.

Perfidia's expression was tragic. "You see now, Woof-Woof?"

"I don't know," he muttered. "I don't know what I see. What am I supposed to see?"

"How it is with us on Capri."

This was the way it was on Capri? French's mind was aflame. He did not understand anything, except what had happened to him. Slowly, French felt anger growing within himself. Harshly, he said, "I don't understand any of this, Perfidia. Does this all satisfy you?"

Thoughtfully, her hand in Marina's black hair, Perfidia said, "No. I guess the man who wrote Oedipus never thought of all this, Wade."

French was exhausted, wounded, but he would never admit that he was bowed. Sickness swept up from his stomach, and he tasted vileness, not strawberries and cream, in his throat and mouth. Holding his hand over his mouth, he rushed into the bathroom, closed the door, and threw up. He gagged and cursed, cursed and gagged, and finally spewed it all out.

The three of them were watching when he emerged.

Perfidia by now was lying in the bed. Marina sat beside her, holding her hand, and George stood at Marina's side, the three of them a living tableau of decadence.

"Well, Woof-Woof?"

Levelly, French said, his voice hoarse from his vomiting, "You want to know if I can bear it? Is that it? I can, yes. I can bear anything."

Once again, in his mind's eye, he saw the diamonds and the rubies covering Perfidia's fair body, the villa in Capri surrounded by citrus and olive trees. Next time, he thought, he would make her wear her precious

288

stones while they were in vile embrace. He saw her, a single strand of silky pearls at her neck, a ruby in her navel, and diamonds stuck in her snatch. He would withdraw them, one by one, with his lips and tongue. Yes, that would be more pleasurable even than traditional strawberries.

French circled to the side of the bed. He put the back of his hand against Perfidia's cheek, roughly shoving George out of the way.

"*Mutti . . .*"

Perfidia's face lengthened solemnly. "Yes, darling, perhaps this is your new father." Perfidia's bare shoulders shook, and her rounded breasts quivered. Was she laughing or crying? She was laughing.

"What about *him?*" French demanded.

"My new son?" Perfidia asked. "The dear boy? He'll be with us too, Woof-Woof, never fear."

Marina blinked happily. "Woof-Woof," she chortled.

George dropped suddenly to his hands and knees in front of the bed. He lifted his bald head and howled, "Woof-Woof! Woof-Woof!"

Perfidia screamed with laughter. "Oh, yes, dear!" she gasped.

French felt his face burning. But he smiled. Just as evil as they were, he was. "Very amusing little son of a bitch, isn't he?"

Twenty-Four

When they arrived at the Beverly Wilshire to pick up Virginia and Felix, they discovered there had been a change of plan. Perfidia had called a few minutes before and asked them to come for drinks before they went on to the Sackses'.

"Must we?" Hamilton groaned.

"Poor Peter," Virginia said. "I know . . ." She pressed his arm. "Did she give you a *very* bad time last night?"

He repeated what he'd told Sally. Perfidia still believed he had bumped off that crazy kid of hers.

Felix shrugged impatiently. "She's a very disturbed woman, dear boy. Forget it."

Virginia's laugh was spiteful. "Do you think we got her right in the book, Felix, *dear?*"

"Not half right enough," Felix said. "We erred on the side of kindness."

"Well," Hamilton said, "screw her anyway."

"I wouldn't if I were you," Virginia said coolly. "It might be an experience you'd live to regret."

Sally turned on them abruptly. "God, please stop talking like that! It makes me sick!"

Virginia was taken aback. "Does it offend your tender sensibilities, little dear?"

"Yes!"

"Virginia," Felix said softly, "I think Sally's right. You shouldn't . . ."

Virginia turned on him furiously. "You! You're a fine one to talk, Mr. Felix James."

Hamilton was embarrassed for Felix. Maybe Felix

understood why she was angry, but Hamilton certainly didn't. "Let's get in the car," he said.

"No," Virginia said irritably. "I'm not going in that crummy Pinto, Peter. Let's take a cab."

Sally snapped, "Why don't we just call the whole thing off?"

"Shut up, Sally," Virginia said. "Listen, I don't want to see Perfidia any more than the rest of you. We're only going because . . ."

"Because why?" Felix demanded.

For a second, Virginia was perplexed. Then she snarled, "Because I want to find out what she's up to with Wade French. And so do you."

Perfidia had reserved a large banquette in the corner of the Polo Lounge and, much to his chagrin, Hamilton found he was being placed to the right of Marina von Thurnsteil. Jack Logan was on Marina's other side. Perfidia took the head of the table, with the young bald-headed Italian she had mentioned at her left. Wade French, red-faced and tired-eyed, was next to George.

"Well now," Perfidia said, after everyone had settled, and she had flattened them all with beady-eyed recognition, "what about a nice little drink? I asked you to come because I've *missed* you."

"Since last night?" Sally asked pointedly.

"Yes, dear." Perfidia blasted off a look in Sally's direction. "Since *I* wasn't invited to the Sackses' tonight, what chance do I have? And, you know," she reminded them, "we won't be here all that long. You're going to Hawaii and then I'll be gone. Please . . ." She motioned at the waiter who was standing at her elbow.

Hamilton ordered a double vodka on the rocks, with two twists. He'd need it, he thought, looking them over. A strange collection, or selection, of people. Perfidia, of course, was in perfect command. But he wondered what on earth had happened to French. For one thing, French seemed inordinately familiar with the bald-headed kid, George. George exuded infant innocence, like a child of paradise. His blue eyes were guileless and friendly. A constant smile made him look foolish. While the others chattered nervously, George put his mouth close to French's ear and whispered something that caused French to blink and shake with laughter.

But Hamilton had his own problems. Sally kept staring at him, across Logan and Marina, and even as she talked to Felix across the table, she kept her eye on him. Why?

Matching George's intimate gesture, Virginia whispered in his ear, "Peter, you are a terrible swine."

"Thank you very much," he said.

Virginia slid her hand along the banquette to the tendon behind his knee and gently pinched it. God, he thought, she knew how to destroy a person. It was his tender spot, and she had always known that. Virginia turned and deliberately began talking to Wade French. But Wade was not interested. He grunted and huffed in his usual style of communication. Hamilton smiled at Marina. "Well," he said, "how do you like California, Marina?"

"Yes, California," she replied, returning his smile a little vacantly. Her real answer was a caress. She lifted her hand and traced a finger along his jaw to his earlobe, tickling him vaguely, then back to the corner of his mouth. She parted her lips and put the tip of her tongue against her teeth. Hell, he thought, it was getting very warm. Sally's eyes widened; her mouth tightened. To hell with it, Hamilton decided. It was none of his doing. He tried to remember if Naomi had looked at all like Marina. Not much. There was a far greater Mediterranean look about Marina, and she was closer to Perfidia in coloration. Whatever, Perfidia's daughters had sexuality in common.

Marina shifted on the seat, squirmed really, and then dropped her hands under the tablecloth. With a start, he felt one hand on his knee, then his thigh, and a second later scrabbling at his fly. Jesus Christ, he thought desperately, she *was* bananas. How in the hell was he going to escape? He stared at her solemnly, but she merely grinned at him. Sally was watching, consternation on her face. He winked at her, casting his eyes heavenward.

Unfortunately, Perfidia caught that private exchange. "Well, Peter," she said frigidly, "is it *so* bad, being here?"

"No, I'm having a fine time, Perfidia."

"You needn't look so put-upon," she sneered.

"Perfidia . . ."

Marina yanked her hand away and stuck her tongue out at him. "Bad man," she said.

"Never mind, Marina," Perfidia said wearily, "it doesn't matter."

Perfidia claimed their attention now to listen again to her argument for saving Capri. While she expounded, a waiter arrived with the drinks and then another with a seafood platter, which he lowered onto the center of the table.

"I thought," Perfidia said, smiling patronizingly, "just a few little hors d'oeuvres."

"Goodie," Marina cried. She took a shrimp in her chubby fingers and tore at it with her small teeth. "Yummy."

"Yes, darling," Perfidia said. "Heavens," she went on, "I so wish we were all at the Villa Putzi at this very moment."

"It would be such fun," French agreed ponderously.

"Oh yes," Perfidia said and smiled at him. Some sort of secret exchange?

"Why don't we all just up and come to visit you, Perfidia, darling?"

"Do, Virginia, do!"

"I'll be in China," Hamilton said. "*We* will, if all goes well."

Sally nodded gravely.

"Peter! *You're* not invited anyway," Perfidia said. She was not joking, either.

"I wouldn't go, even if you did invite me!"

"Easy, sport," French said, frowning. "We're all friends, remember that!"

"Are we?" Hamilton asked, just as unpleasantly as Perfidia.

"Oh, let's do talk about something else," Perfidia growled. "Leave aside your vendetta . . ."

"I don't have any vendetta!"

"You do. Against me. I can tell you . . ."

Felix interrupted. "We're seeing you tomorrow night, aren't we, Perfidia?"

"Yes, at *his* party."

"*Our* party," Virginia corrected her. "That'll be nice, Perfidia."

Hamilton felt like leaving. He twisted his drink on the tablecloth. Fuck 'em, he thought. Now Logan was staring at him. His eyes revealed amazement, round and horrified—not horrified exactly, more glazed than anything else. Logan glanced at Marina. Now she was smiling at Logan, questioningly. Hamilton almost laughed. Logan's face had taken on a benign expression.

While all this was going on, Perfidia very frankly made her pitch to Virginia and Felix. "I certainly think you two cosmopolites should think seriously of contributing to Save Capri."

Felix reacted in a flash, not even blinking, "Perfidia, I'm already so deeply committed to saving Venice . . ."

"No reason not to save both places," Perfidia responded. "And Virginia?"

Virginia was quick about it too. "Oh, Perfidia, you know my favorite charity is an American one. I don't believe in sending my money overseas. A group of us in New York are working very hard to rebuild Valley Forge to be just as it was when Washington's army wintered there."

Perfidia's eyes narrowed. "Valley Forge? What could that possibly matter? I don't think I've ever heard of that cause."

"Well," Virginia declared brightly, "this is the first I've heard about saving Capri."

"We're just getting started, Virginia!" Then Perfidia smiled, her black eyes snapping. "After all, you're both going to be *so* rich from this book you've written about *me*."

Felix was stern with her, unrelenting. "Perfidia, it is not about *you*. It is a book about a fictional cosmetics tycoon."

French barked, "Nathan Sinclair, old sport!" He lowered his bullish eyes at Felix and Virginia at the same time. "I think it would behoove you to look into this matter of Capri."

"Yes," Perfidia said. "After all, I'm accepting the book at face value. So why shouldn't you believe in the worthiness of my cause?"

Virginia smiled very cynically. "And what sort of contribution would you think proper, dear?"

Perfidia tossed her hair. "Oh, not much. Fifty or a hundred thousand dollars would be much appreciated."

Virginia paled. She understood as well as Hamilton or Felix what Perfidia was saying. Pay up, or else.

"We'd have to think that over very carefully, Perfidia," Felix said, something close to disgust in his voice.

Perfidia nodded agreeably. "I wish you would. I *really* wish you would."

Logan, smiling erratically, his voice uneven, took some of the heat off by asking, "How is it Capri can sink, Perfidia? I thought it was like a volcanic island, all rock."

"That's just it," Perfidia replied calmly. "The volcanic substance begins to decay after a millenium or two."

Logan nodded nervously. "What's the best guess on how long it's going to be before everything *pops*?"

"It could happen in the next five years, Jack."

"Jesus! You don't say! In my lifetime." He drummed his fingers on the table and leaned forward. Hamilton could see sweat on his forehead, and there was a perplexed, dreamy look on his face. "You know, that could be a hell of a flick. *The Last Days of Capri.* Remember *The Last Days of Pompeii?*"

"Of course," Perfidia said passionately. "If you like, Jack, I'll sell you the rights to the story. It'll be yours—exclusively."

Logan's eyes swam. "How much?"

Carelessly, Perfidia said, "Oh, another hundred thousand would do, I should think."

The amount did not register on Logan's brain. "God, I can see it now," he exploded. "The final baccanale as the Villa Putzi disappears. Lots of girls and beaucoup orgy. Violins playing and then—gurgle-gurgle."

"Gurgle-gurgle?" Sally repeated. "Jesus . . ."

Perfidia laughed heartily. "No, no, dear, by then we'll be in the boats. Ha! How ironic! I arrive in Capri by boat, and I catch the last boat out of Capri. Gurgle-gurgle!" She continued to chuckle as if this were the funniest thing she'd ever heard. Then she hit the table with her fist. "But we're not going to allow that to happen, are we?" She glared at Logan. "I'll be expecting your check."

"Sure, sure," Logan said breezily. At that moment, Hamilton knew, Logan would have agreed to anything.

Despite the animation of the conversation, Wade French's head began to droop. He was falling asleep. Hamilton noticed it first, and then Perfidia. Playfully, she threw an empty crab leg at him. "Wade!" she cried. "Sleeping at the table! Heavens! Are we so boring?"

French's head jerked up. "What! Oh, sorry, Perfidia, so sorry." He rubbed his face. "It must be jet lag."

"What about another drink?" Perfidia called out jovially. "I *am* a good hostess."

Felix looked at his watch. "We've got to be going in just a few minutes, Perfidia."

French took a long swallow of his Scotch. He was having a bad time of it tonight. He choked and began coughing. George smacked him on the back. When French recovered enough to speak, he said, "I'd better go upstairs. I don't feel at all well."

"Poor Wade," Perfidia said, "not well. It must be those strawberries and cream you had at lunch. Maybe they don't agree with you."

Marina diverted her attention from Logan's pants long enough to laugh mockingly. What a tiresome little bitch she was, Hamilton thought.

"Excuse me," French said miserably. "I'll just slide out."

George moved so French could get out of the banquette.

"Should George go up with you, Wade, dear?" Perfidia asked.

"No," French said shortly. "I'll be all right. . . . I'll see you all tomorrow."

French's departure put Virginia next to George. Virginia patted the bald-headed kid's cheek. "Is this cute thing really from Italy?" Virginia asked.

"Yes," Perfidia grunted.

"George, say something in Italian for us," Virginia said.

George stared at her irritably. He was not basically a very friendly kid.

"Spaghetti!" George spit out, his face angry.

Virginia chuckled provocatively. "I don't think he's Italian at all!"

Perfidia was immediately insulted. "I tell you he's Italian. He just doesn't speak very well. He had a terrible shock."

"Oh, I am sorry," Virginia apologized.

Marina squealed indistinctly and in a jarring motion kissed Logan under the chin. It was very obvious now that she was playing with him under the tablecloth. Logan did his best to look casual, but it didn't come off. A heavy slick of sweat covered his forehead and cheeks. Marina made little *oh*ing and *ah*ing sounds, her eyes unfocused and a vapid smile on her lips.

"I'm quite looking forward to the party tomorrow night," Perfidia murmured. Her voice trailed away, and then she said abruptly, "Marina! Get up! It's time for you to go upstairs. Go with her, George."

Sullenly, Marina pushed herself away from the table and gulped down the rest of her Coke. George jumped up and took Marina's fat little arm. As they turned to leave, he muttered, *"Bona sera."*

"There! You see!" Perfidia cried. "He is Italian."

In a few moments, they all stood up to leave, thanking Perfidia for the delightful little party. Logan lagged behind, holding a napkin over his crotch.

"What's the trouble, Jack?" Hamilton asked.

Logan growled angrily, "That little shit! She had shrimp juice all over her hand. My pants are stained. How in the hell am I going to get out of here?"

299

"Walk right behind me."

"Okay, good."

They walked, the two of them, in close tandem, until they reached the porte cochere.

"Thanks, Pete," Logan said, sighing. "Jesus, what a little number that one is."

Virginia's remarks were more to the point. "What a charming little family! A blackmailer and a crooked lawyer and two wanton children. Heavens, that girl, Marina! It seems what she does best is lick her chops. Poor Jack!"

"You said it," Logan said. His face was red. "I couldn't make her stop." He was trying to convince them he was insulted by Marina's attention. Maybe he was. She might very well be too much, even for Jack Logan. "You know what I mean, Virginia." He glanced at her guiltily.

"Yes, I know what you mean," Virginia said quietly. But she was still thinking about Perfidia. "I can't think," she snorted, "whether I actually admire or hate that goddamn woman." She put her arm in Felix's. "Dear, Felix, I wish we were in Hawaii already. I don't know if I'm going to *survive* the rest of this week."

Twenty-Five

For a second, as Orville Jones sat waiting to see Jack Logan, he thought about Emily. Surprisingly, maybe not so surprisingly, the memory had receded. Already, thinking about her was like considering a whale swimming in the South Pacific, somewhere down around the continent of Antarctica. Orville wondered if her flipper was getting better.

Sally had driven him over to the studio and said she'd be back in a couple of hours to pick him up. If the interview with Logan was shorter than they expected, Orville could sort of wander around Twentieth Century, and, when it was time, walk out to Pico and wait there by the light.

Orville didn't know what to make of the arrangement Sally had with Peter Hamilton. But there was nothing he could say. He'd made the mistake, once, of criticizing Virginia too freely, and look what that had gotten him—she'd taken off for New York City.

Hamilton was a nice enough guy. He wasn't smart-alecky, a condition Orville had decided was pretty much the norm for Los Angeles and that pismire place called Hollywood. Besides, Hamilton and Sally got on well. Maybe they were even in love. If so, Orville was pleased for Sally; she was his daughter *and*, if the truth be known, a big cut above those two little shitheels who were his children by Emily.

Orville looked furtively around the outer office of Logan Productions. Legs crossed at the ankles, a secretary sat typing. She didn't have one of those secretary shields on the front of her desk—the invention someone had finally come up with to prevent horny visitors from looking up secretaries' dresses. So, scooting down just a little in his chair, covering the movement by lighting a Camel and reaching for the ashtray, Orville had a fair sight of her legs, but only as far as mid-thigh. The imperfect sighting, however, was enough to start a jingle-jangle-jingle in his pecker.

He had to admit he was a little nervous about meeting Jack Logan. Logan had been Virginia's second husband, the man who had followed Orville round and about her private spots. He could not hate Logan for that, naturally. Why would he? By then, Virginia had been out of Orville's orbit and Logan had, so to speak, filled the void. Who wouldn't have?

The main thing was that Logan was prepared to offer him a job, and Orville was not going to do or say anything to screw that up. He most emphatically was not going back to Ohio.

He finished his cigarette and put it out. The secretary shifted her legs, and all at once Orville had a longer view of the inside of her thigh. Jes-us! Her pantyhose were ripped right at the crotch, and he spotted a triangle of white skin—he thought. He couldn't be sure. She glanced at him and Orville smiled innocently. She returned the smile absently. She was not bad-looking, but her face was peaked and she was a little bit too thin, not that Orville was yearning for overstuffed skin.

Shyly, he smoothed the sleeve of the blue blazer Hamilton had lent him for the occasion. It was a bit too big, but they were close to the same size. The trousers, slightly rumpled white ducks, he had also borrowed from Pete. Pete had advised Orville that the trick was to look half and half. Dressy, but casual at the same time—that was the ticket—because Logan would probably be put together like a big white hunter in one of those African adventure movies. Underneath the blazer, Orville was wearing an open-necked white sports shirt with an Everglades alligator over the breast pocket.

He studied his fingernails until the telephone rang and the secretary said, "Yes, Mr. Logan. All right, Mr. Logan." She stood up. "Do you know the way?" she asked Orville.

He didn't, but it wasn't that far. She opened one door into a hallway and, two steps later, another door and Orville was in Logan's office. It stretched down the length of the bungalow. Logan got to his feet and put out his hand.

"Orville? Hi . . ." he said.

Logan motioned at a leather chair. Orville sat down, and Logan resumed his place in a big swivel chair on the other side of the desk. He twirled it around and threw his feet up between himself and Orville's face.

"Cigar?" Logan picked up a leather box at his elbow. Orville had to stand up to reach it. But that was okay too. He took a loose cigar out of the end of the box closest to him, sat down again, removed the cellophane, and lit it as casually as he could, as if he always started the day with a fat Havana. Logan did not take his eyes off him. Orville inhaled and exhaled a cloud of smoke. "Only the best," Logan said. His eyes were black and steady. Orville realized Logan was trying to drill into his mind, and he also suddenly realized he was sitting in a hole. He had to lift his head to look Logan in the eye. The rotten bastard! He was pure Hollywood. As Pete had predicted, Logan was dressed in khaki pants, white socks, and tennis shoes. A khaki top was unbuttoned to his navel, and a gold chain trickled down his neck to a medallion shelved on his paunch. "Well," Logan muttered, in a near sneer, "it's good to know you, Orville. We're almost relatives in a way, you know?"

Orville nodded and grinned modestly. "Sort of husbands-in-law."

"Yeah," Logan drawled. "Related by marriage. Virginia. Jeese, somebody oughta write a song about Virginia, you know." He began humming a little tune. "Our Virginia, 'tis of thee, sweet lay of the centur-y . . ."

"Ha!" Orville chuckled. "That's good. I always wondered what you were like. You're a *card*."

"Hey!" Logan laughed. "Maybe you are too. They tell me you're one hell of an accountant. What kind of accounting do you do?"

"Done it all," Orville said broadly. "Lots of corporate work, and right down to personal estate counseling. My specialty lately has been investment financing."

"What the hell is that?" Logan asked. "I'm not too clued up on all the terminology." He rolled his eyes. "I'm more on the creative side."

"It's finding investors with money to invest in investment projects," Orville said.

Logan's eyes hopped again. "Right. I get it. You *are* good though?"

"I've been doing it for thirty years or more, Jack." He tried out Logan's first name. Logan did not seem to mind.

"Okay," he said slowly, "let's give it a try. But listen, I'm telling you right now I don't have the time or tolerance to fuck around. If you don't fill the bill, then, *zzzt!*" He made the farewell sound along with a flyaway motion with his hand.

"Of course," Orville agreed, "that's the way of the world. I'm not scared of that. Accounting is accounting."

"All right, you're on. Let's see, start-up time, next Monday. Okay? Salary, for starters, thirty grand a year. How's that sound?"

Orville could easily have taken the cigar smoke too hard and fallen over in a faint. He had never made that much in Ohio. "Sounds good," he said smoothly, holding his eyeballs in balance.

Logan stared at him calculatingly, tapping his thumb on his front teeth. "Just one thing, Orville. Remember that this is very complicated bookkeeping. Sometimes things don't seem to measure up. That's because we're constantly running costs and profits through here, backing new projects with old profit money and financing others with profits to come, that kind of thing. You see what I mean?"

What Orville thought was that Logan was very confused. But he played along. "Like the building industry," he said. "Nothing to it."

Logan's eyes clicked. "You got it. It *is* like the building industry, except that we're building an art form. Am I right?"

"Right!" Orville agreed. "You're financing an art form. That's something I can respect. Buildings are only bricks. Art is art and a hell of a lot more interesting than goddamn bricks."

"Hey! I like that. Exactly, Orville! How's the cigar?"

"Beautiful."

Just as he said it, the end of the goddamn thing exploded. Orville nearly came. As it was, he leaped from his chair, grabbing what was left of the cigar out of his mouth. Jesus Christ!

Logan's feet fell off his desk and he bent over, choking with laughter.

"Son of a bitch!" Orville yelled. Then he remembered himself and grinned. "Goddamn trick cigar. Jack, if you weren't my husband-in-law, I'd belt you right in the mouth."

"Hey, hey, hey!" Logan squealed. He shoved his hand across the desk. "That seals our deal, old buddy."

Tears of joy streamed down his face. "Sorry, Orville, I couldn't resist. Come on, now, no hard feelings." He came around the desk. "Let's have a look at my pictures." Logan began pointing out his publicity shots. "Look, old buddy, here's me with Hank Fonda. You know him."

"Not personally," Orville said.

"You will. You will. Here's me and Mona Prissian. You know her?" Orville shook his head. He had never heard of a woman named Mona Prissian, as an actress or otherwise. But one thing was for sure: she had great whammers. "And here's me and Virginia, Orville. She looks good in that shot, doesn't she?"

Virginia smiled at Orville from out of the picture. Her face was radiant, beautiful, tiny. Her eyes glowed. The lilting lift of her chest was pressed against Logan's arm. Yeah, and down below, Orville assumed cynically, she probably had her hand around his pecker. Virginia had been that way, even in Ohio. But she looked very happy in the picture.

"When was that?" he asked Logan.

Logan shrugged. "About ten years ago, I guess."

The sight of her caused Orville to choke up a little. "She was always a beautiful woman," he murmured.

"Sit down," Logan said, "and tell me about Virginia back in Ohio. What was she like then?"

Orville didn't know how he could describe her. Beautiful. Vibrant. Fun. Other things, too, that had driven him crazy. He wanted to be nice about her. "Virginia . . ." he said softly, "she was my high school buddy, though I was older than her, maybe eight or nine years. . . ."

But Logan wasn't interested in that kind of background. "Was she still a virgin when you two got married?"

"Ah . . . well . . ." Orville was confused by the

306

question. The answer was no—but he was not forced to lie about it.

At that moment, Logan's phone rang. Irritably, he picked it up and said, "Yeah, what is it, Beverly?" The secretary said something that caught his attention. "Oh, shit! I forgot about that. Bring them in, Beverly."

Logan hopped up and opened his office door. He was in time to greet a very unlikely group.

Leading the way was a tall, black-haired woman with a long, severe nose and heavy, hooded eyes. She was beautiful, but formidable. "Good morning, Jack," she said in a low, hoarse voice. "Here we are—I've brought along beautiful Marina, my son-to-be George Minelli . . . and of course you know Wade French."

"We were all together last night, Perfidia," Logan said haltingly. His eyes swerved to the younger woman, a kid really, with hair black as a raven's wing. "Welcome, welcome," Logan exclaimed. "Come on, come in." He turned. Orville had stood up. "Say, folks," Logan said, "I'd like you to meet a very new friend of mine." He announced Orville's name with something like a flourish of trumpets. "Orville Jones, who just happens to be none other than Virginia Preston's first husband from Ohio. Now, ain't that something!"

The tall woman smiled loosely at Orville, her eyes sweeping him like a metal detector, and the little girl, in fact almost as big as her mother, beamed, mouth open and red tongue lolling out. The other kid was very strange looking. He was nearly bald, with only a bit of blond hair, like peach fuzz, on the top of his head. He grinned at Orville.

The big man stepped forward, so heavily you might have expected him to go through the floor. "A pleasure to know you, Mr. Jones. My name is Wade French. I've known Virginia for some years."

"Orville," Logan whooped. "This handsome lady is

307

Baroness Perfidia von Thurnsteil. The beautiful little tyke is Marina von Thurnsteil and, as you heard, the young man is George Minelli!"

"You have it right, Jack," the tall woman congratulated him.

"Good morning. How do you do? It's a pleasure to know you," Orville murmured timidly. Christ, he asked himself, a baroness? Royalty? Did Virginia know royalty too?

The baroness stepped straight up to him and thrust out her hand, its long fingers tipped with nails that could have sliced through his jacket. "Orville Jones, I am utterly fascinated," she cried resoundingly. "Any husband of Virginia's is a friend of mine!"

Wade French chuckled from far away, as if he were in a barrel. But it was not a particularly friendly laugh. "My, my," he said, "another of our heroes from *Powerhouse*."

"No," Orville disagreed quietly, "I read it. I'm nowhere in there."

"So the purpose of your visit to Hollywood is *not* to sue?" French asked.

"Uh uh," Orville muttered.

"Nor will I, Jack," the baroness declared, "rest assured. Only tiresome old Nathan."

"Is that so?" Logan asked anxiously. "I can't get it straight what's going on with that book. You're his lawyer, aren't you?" he said to French.

"I always have been," French said. "But if I were you, I wouldn't worry about it. Nathan will cool off. He never carries through on his lawsuits."

Logan beamed. "That's a relief. So we got the go-ahead? That's better news than Tums."

French nodded somberly. Orville decided then that one thing he could teach Jack Logan right away was never to trust a lawyer.

Benevolently, Logan surveyed the group, his eyes lighting again on the girl called Marina. "What I've got lined up for you good people is a little tour, a look at our set for the new epic, *Blood in the Surf*. It's about sharks," he cried, making his voice ominous for Marina. To Perfidia, he explained, "it's a sci-fi version of *Jaws*."

"Oh, *mutti, wie schön*," the little/big girl screamed.

"Yes, honey," Logan said excitedly, "it is a beautiful picture, no doubt about it. You see," he said to Perfidia, "I understand a little of the German lingo."

Perfidia merely smiled glacially. It was plain enough to Orville that she considered his new boss an idiot. Disregarding Jack, she turned back to Orville. "Mr. Jones," she said, her voice rising like steam off a mountain lake, "has anyone ever told you that you look just like Chip Douglas? You remember, the old movie star?"

Orville shook his head modestly. "I'm not familiar . . ."

Logan exclaimed, "By God, he does, you're right! He has the very same goddamn face structure. Orville, you could be his double! The high cheekbones, those blue eyes, the hollow cheeks, defiant chin. Either Chip Douglas or Leslie Howard, Perfidia."

"Either one would do," the baroness said warmly, her voice a stroke. "I *knew* Chip Douglas once."

As Orville was wondering how well she had *known* this Chip Douglas, Logan said, "Orville, would you like to go on the tour too?"

"Oh, thanks," Orville said, smiling as graciously as he could at the baroness. After all, it was not every day he was compared to a Hollywood great. He didn't know about Chip Douglas, but he did remember Leslie Howard, and *he* had really been a great, before going down, the poor bastard, in a plane crash during the war. Orville's war, that is. "I'd love it, Jack, but I have a luncheon appointment. Business, you know."

"Hey, I understand," Logan said, "no sweat. You'll have plenty of time for tours later." Again directing himself to the baroness, he went on, "I finally talked Orville into leaving godforsaken Ohio. Orville was a V-P for financing at one of the big rubber companies." Logan chuckled to himself, then aloud. " 'Course," he chortled, "rubber companies come into bad times lately, since they invented the pill. Right, Orville, old buddy?"

Orville nodded and smiled distantly, raising his eyebrows for the baroness to see he was not such a slob as Jack Logan.

The bad joke fell into dead silence. "Anyway," Logan said, undeterred, "I'm having my secretary, Beverly, take you on the tour. Then you'll come back here and we'll go over to the commissary for lunch."

"Mutti," Marina stammered, "the two men . . ." She looked first at Orville, then hotly at Logan.

"Yes, Marina," Perfidia said patiently. "You see, Jack, Marina hasn't forgotten you."

Logan blustered. "Well, I can tell you, I haven't forgotten her either. Marina is one hell of a little tyke, Perfidia."

"Yes," Perfidia said, "isn't she?"

Logan was agitated. "And *George,* Perfidia. George is a handsome lad. George, are you interested in sci-fi movies?"

George made an equivocal motion with his hand. *"Comme-çi, comme-ça,"* he said disagreeably.

"Of *course* you are, George!" Perfidia cried lightly.

Logan began speculating rapidly. "Jeese, we might have use for a bald-headed kid in *Blood in the Surf.* You know something? Bald-headed computer operators are in demand now in the picture business. Remember that space picture with the bald-headed girl? George, can you act?" he demanded.

"*Possiblemente*," George said, grunting the Italian.

"Hey!" Logan cried. "I'm going to try to set something up. Now, you guys get going. I'd come with you myself, 'cept I'm waiting for a phone call from London."

Twenty-Six

The boys' California mission had begun. They arrived at Los Angeles International Airport at five P.M. and immediately went downstairs to the car rental desk. Paul had booked them a nondescript green Ford. Simon and Shuster did not speak. They didn't need to. The reservation number was written down on a piece of paper. They flashed this at the clerk, and she confirmed that the car would be brought around in a few minutes.

"Do you require a hotel room, or rooms?" she asked.

Shuster was doing the not-talking. He shook his head, wobbling the straw boater atop his hairpiece. For this trip, Paul had bought them lightweight summer suits, Shuster's tan and Simon's light blue. They looked like brothers, except that Simon's hairpiece was black and Shuster's brown. But they certainly had been to the same barber, one would have said.

The girl tried to be friendly. "You're both named Sinclair," she commented. "Brothers, aren't you?"

Shuster nodded and pointed to his lips to let her know they were mutes.

She understood. "Oh." She blinked rapidly. "Well, *have a nice day.*" She mouthed the words vigorously.

They smiled and went outside to wait for the car. Their orders were explicit. They were to discover the whereabouts of all the enemies and then proceed with their assignment forthwith. Sometimes, in his generalship, Paul could be a little tiring, Shuster thought. Paul had everything but a war map in his office. But he was the general, or at least aide-de-camp to Boss Man. Care and caution were essential, Paul had told them. It was to be done quickly, cleanly, and without a trace. On the plane, disobeying orders, Simon and Shuster had each had a bloody mary, then in whispers discussed what they had to do. The big trouble was that there were *so* many enemies, they might become confused. Paul could not leave headquarters—thus, Simon and Shuster would have to cover a lot of ground.

When they were in the Ford, Simon pointed it toward the city. Paul had booked them a room at the Beverly Hills Hotel because Perfidia Sinclair and her daughter would be there. They were not sure, however, whether Virginia Preston and Felix James would be at the same hotel. They had figured out a partial itinerary for Preston and James by the simple stratagem of phoning Jack Logan's office and talking to a secretary named Beverly. The salient information was that there was to be a party for the two authors at the home of Peter Hamilton. They knew *all* about Peter Hamilton.

Their disguise was perfect, Paul had assured them, because none of these people had ever seen them before.

In Beverly Hills, before going on to the hotel, Simon cruised until he found a hardware store and then a parking lot where they could leave the Ford. What they needed were knives. Paul had decided it was too risky, as well as unnecessary, for them to carry knives with them in their baggage.

The store, Shuster thought, was a beauty. It had everything a culinary devotee might desire. And there were knives! There were German-made carving knives, serrated bread knives, paring knives, and the little curved knives one used to cut the heart out of a grapefruit.

Taking their time, they chose a bread knife and

carving knife apiece and presented them at the counter to another pleasant-looking California girl.

"Hello, boys," she said cheerily.

See, she had even gotten their name right. Smiling, Shuster put the knives in front of her.

"Cash or charge?"

In reply, Shuster took a wad of bills out of his right pants pocket. Again he pointed to his lips.

"What?"

The dummy didn't understand, so Shuster took one of their cards out of his jacket pocket.

SCHOOL FOR THE HANDICAPPED
Meat Cutting for the Blind
Simon Sinclair
Shuster Sinclair
New York, NY

"Uh huh," the girl murmured, "I see. Meat cutting for the blind? Isn't that kind of a risky trade?"

Shuster grunted laughter and shook his head. He placed his finger on his lips once more.

"Oh, I understand. You can't talk."

They nodded strenuously.

"Oh, sorry." She placed the knives in a long box. "Gift wrapped?"

Shuster compressed his lips and shook his head, letting her know that any old wrapped would do. When she'd finished, she placed the box in a plastic shopping bag with the name of the store prominently advertised on its side.

"Have a nice day," she said.

That was the second time they'd been told to have a nice day. This was hardly possible, Shuster told himself disparagingly, since they had been ordered not to go

315

swimming in the Beverly Hills Hotel pool. They didn't need to be told. Taking a swim would have meant doffing their hairpieces, and that was impossible. Thus, after they'd checked in, continuing their mute act, Simon and Shuster surveyed their double room, had a shower together, donned their saffron robes, and sat down to talk strategy.

They didn't get far. The only thing to do was play it by ear. Shuster considered for a moment putting in a call to New York to speak to Paul. It was clear to them that Paul wanted everybody dead, but what about Boss Man? Which of them was Nathan Sinclair's first preference?

Twenty-Seven

In what he considered a brilliant stroke of creative producing, before lunch Jack Logan had already arranged for George Minelli to play a "cameo" role in *Blood in the Surf*. It was only a bit part, but it would require at least three days' work during Perfidia and company's stay in California. The script did, in fact, call for a bald-headed youth to run a computer at a shark-tracking station in the Azores. Mozzletop, as the character was named, didn't last more than five or six scenes before being strangled by a mad scientist who, in the story, had conceived the fiendish scheme of terrorizing vacation beaches around the world with remote-controlled killer sharks, offering naturally to call off his death-fish in return for a huge ransom. Logan himself had named the villain Doctor Finn, another stroke, everyone said, of pure genius.

George, if he agreed, would be tried out and put to work that very afternoon. The way Logan had it figured out, Perfidia would insist that he agree. She did.

Logan, clever, clever man, next persuaded them that it would be best to leave George here on his own. With everybody watching, he might be too embarrassed to make his acting debut. That seemed fair enough.

Out of the blue, Logan made his next proposal. "Hey! What about if I take Marina on a little drive? Marina, baby, how about the zoo? Do you like zoos?"

"Yes, yes," she spouted, playing right into his hands, beautiful, fat little lips pouting with enthusiasm. *"Die Affen."*

Apes, monkeys, Marina liked them.

317

Perfidia could not decide whether it was a good idea. But then, after Logan had pointed out that Marina couldn't sit around the hotel bothering everybody while George became a movie star, she said yes.

"You will take good care of her, won't you, Jack?"

"As if she were my own," Logan promised.

Later, he was not so sure it had been a good idea. But, he told himself glumly, he was that way. He could not resist luscious little girls. They were like plump chicken legs.

Marina dragged him straight to the cages. Logan had never had much use for simian creatures. They reminded him too much of humans, the way they sat around scratching their asses, picking lice, and goosing each other, completely oblivious to and often disrespectful of their cousins on the other side of the bars.

"Ooh, ooh," Marina squealed. *"Schau! Die sind so schön."*

Beautiful? Not particularly, Logan thought dismally. He preferred penguins, the little mites strutting around in dinner jackets like short men at a classy stag party.

As they watched, a couple of baboons began to go at it, right before their eyes. "Jesus!" Logan snorted disgustedly. He tried to drag Marina away before people noticed how she was laughing. But she wouldn't leave. Her eyes danced lasciviously, and she was practically drooling.

"Ficken," she announced. *"Die Affen ficken."*

"Yes, dear," Logan muttered, "the little apes are fucking. Aren't they cute?"

Marina grabbed his hand. Hers was perspiring. With a shock, he felt her tickling his palm with her little finger. He knew what that meant in any language. Her chubby chest heaved under her nicely flowered Austrian dirndl.

Pressure began to build in Logan's stomach. Jesus,

what the hell was he doing? He shouldn't have minded; indeed, this was what had been in his head when he'd so carefully set up the afternoon. But she wasn't eighteen, and that kept nagging him. This had happened once before, and there was probably still a record of it in New York.

"Come on, honey," he said nervously, "I'll buy you some ice cream." What did they call it in German? *"Eis . . ."*

"Oh, yes," Marina said, *"chocolat eis."*

He wondered why on earth the girl didn't speak more English. Had they always jabbered German back on Capri?

"Marina, baby, can't you speak English?"

"Yes," she said tonelessly, "but I do not like it."

"Well, try it on me. It's not a bad language, you know."

She shrugged sullenly. But she was happier with an ice cream cone in her hand. Logan suggested they have a look at the giraffe and the brightly colored jungle birds, but she wasn't interested.

"Marina, did you ever hear the joke about the Warsaw zoo?" he asked her.

She shook her head. *"Nein."*

Logan guffawed. There wasn't any reason *he* shouldn't have a good time. "It closed," he said. "The duck died."

She stared at him for what seemed to be five minutes. Then, startling him, she began to laugh. She honked like the duck he had mentioned and continued to laugh until he shook her arm.

"Funny man," she exclaimed, her mouth open, "funny, funny man."

"Christ," he grumbled, "it's not that funny, Marina."

She took his hand again, leading him in the direction of the car as she finished mouthing the ice cream cone. Marina was a spoiled brat, he knew, a pampered little pain in the ass. But she frightened him. She was licking her fingers now, making solemn smacking sounds. Logan fished in his back pocket for a handkerchief.

"Thank you," she said. Her diction was perfect.

They got back in the car. By now she was smiling at him defiantly. No, challengingly. No, probingly. He couldn't decide what kind of smile it was. She continued to run her tongue around her lips, removing the last vestige of the chocolate flavor. Responding to his curious look, she let off a trilling laugh. What with the dirndl and her charming, childlike face, she reminded him of something out of *The Sound of Music*. "Mr. Logan," she said softly, "you are a very nice man. So nice."

Logan smiled tremulously. "Just moderately," he said.

He started the car, pleased with himself now. The crisis had passed. Mentally, he patted himself on the back. Soon she would be back at the hotel, safe and sound.

But he was wrong. As he pulled out of the parking lot, Marina slid across the seat and snuggled up to him. She lifted her angelic little face and kissed him on the underside of the chin. Immediately, he was nervous again. He remembered the night before and began to perspire. Then, damned if she didn't put her hand on his leg, as she had in the Polo Lounge. He was very frightened and more so, horrified, when she shoved her hand under his belt and felt around for his cock.

He drove carefully, seeing the road, but blind at the same time. He could not help himself. He did not stop her as she unzipped his pants, pulling his jockey shorts. Her eyes sparkled as she looked at it, then at him.

"Oh," she gasped, as if she'd just seen Santa Claus, *"ein kleines würstchen."*

"Hey! Take it easy!" But he didn't mean it. "I'm taking *you* back to the hotel."

He was on the long avenue that led away from the zoo and toward Los Feliz. He was breathing hard, but he did his best to keep his eyes on the road.

Marina jerked him a couple of times and then put her head into his lap. Dizzily, he understood she was going to do him now, right now. The touch made him reckless. After all, he told himself crazily, a guy could never get enough of this. She'd said he had a little thing, like a cocktail sausage. "Hey," Logan yelled boisterously, "just put a little mustard on there, baby!"

She didn't need to be told. She fastened her chubby lips on him and puffed, her cheeks swelling out. God, he wanted to scream, don't exhale! But she was only fooling with him. From the corner of her eye, she flashed him a mocking look, a testing look. Jesus, Logan tortured himself, I think I'm in love. She drew on him mightily, as he might have on a five-cent cigar. Her mouth was like a pump. She was pulling his gonads out of their sockets. Holy shit! Her devotion was excruciating. She was pulling him off the seat. His body sagged and shuddered, his eyes faltered.

And, goddamn it, it was about then that he sideswiped the jogger, this moron trotting along the side of the road with musical earmuffs insulating him from every other sound, most specifically that of Logan's Mercedes. The stupid bastard lurched to the side to dodge a dogturd, and Logan could not miss him. The front fender of the car caught the jogger under the ass and tumbled him in the ditch, heels flying.

Logan had sense enough to speed up and get around the next curve before the asshole had time to get his head out of the mud. The most he would see would be a metallic silver rear end puffing smoke at him.

"Jesus, Marina," Logan shouted, "you're marvelous but . . ."

"Bitte?"

She paid no attention, and she *was* marvelous. As

321

far as Marina was concerned, he had the biggest cock in the world. "Jesus," he screeched, "there I go!"

Whappo! She'd pulled it off without skipping a beat.

"Oh-la-la!" She gargled.

Carefully, she zipped him up, then returned to her side of the front seat, humming happily and looking out the window. Logan turned on the radio. The first station he found was one of those religious ones, some goof going on about the saving grace of giving.

"You betcha!" he cried.

Nevertheless, Logan was not without anxiety when they got back to the hotel. Suppose the little tyke squealed on him to Perfidia? On the bright side, Marina's attention span was not much longer than ten minutes.

He had agreed to deliver her to the Polo Lounge at about five.

As they waltzed through the hotel, he thought they didn't make a bad-looking couple. Naturally, she was a lot younger than he was but an older movie producer with a young chick on his arm was nothing new at the Beverly Hills Hotel. Marina hung on him possessively. No, he reassured himself, she was not such an idiot that she was going to tell Perfidia that she'd just blown "Uncle" Jack.

Perfidia and Wade French were sitting in a booth on the other side of the room from the bar, and there was George, already back from Twentieth.

"Hi," Logan cried jovially, "here we are. We had a good time, didn't we, baby?"

George was staring at him. He had yet to realize with how much intensity.

"Hello, darling," Perfidia said. "Was it fun, darling?"

"Mutti," Marina gasped, hideously, *"der Mann, er hat nur ein kleines."*

322

Jesus, the two-timing little bitch! Logan halted. His smile wilted. He understood enough German to know he was in trouble. French did not, evidently, nor did George. But Perfidia got it. Her face froze. Then Marina translated what she'd said in German into sign language. She measured a tiny space between her thumb and forefinger, as if to describe the size of an insect. *Him!*

"Yes, darling," Perfidia snarled. "I see you had a lot of fun and so did you, Jack! I might have known, goddamn it!"

"Aber mutti," Marina protested, *"es war . . ."*

"Shut up, darling," Perfidia said, not taking her inflamed eyes off Logan. "I'm sure it was tiny and juicy. Jesus, you *blackguard*, Jack!"

"But," he stuttered, his face red, "I . . . we . . . you . . . she . . ."

French's face turned purple. "Do I understand this? Logan, don't you realize this girl is . . . underage? You *pervert*! I'm going . . ."

Until Logan bawled his unconvincing denial, no one had raised his voice. "What?" he cried out. "She's nuts. I didn't do . . ."

Heads turned curiously. Very carefully George slid out of the booth. Logan stood rooted to his spot, amazed.

"Jesus," he muttered, beaten, "it was *her* idea. Christ, she made me hit a . . ."

George's fist crashed into his gut like a heavy piece of furniture. Logan doubled over and went down on his ass, gasping for help, air, anything that might be available in the way of succor.

"Goddamn it," he heard French mutter, "in here? Sit down, George. Get up, Logan!"

"All shut up," Perfidia grated. "Get on your feet, Jack, you louse."

It was Marina who helped him to his feet. Making

323

soothing sounds, Marina patted his arm, pushed him into the booth, and pressed close. She cast an angry look at George.

"Armer Mann," she whimpered for him. *"Du—* George—*Ungeheuer . . ."*

Beast, she had said. Yes, goddamn it, the bald-headed son of a bitch was a beast. Logan's insides hurt, ached. Everybody in the place was staring at him, and they all knew who he was. Son of a bitch!

He glared at George. "You're fired off the picture, you prick!"

George tensed, ready to scramble again, like a fighter squadron. He was doubly enraged now, seeing that Marina took Logan's side.

"George! Sit still!" Perfidia commanded, in a voice that would have stopped the Eighth Air Force. Furious, George folded back into his seat. Marina seemed to be trying to make things as bad as she could. She cooed in Logan's ear. "Marina, stop that at once!" Perfidia said. "Thank God, we're going back to Italy. This place is . . ."

George said it for her, rudely, nastily, while staring hatefully at Logan. "California sucks," he sneered.

Twenty-Eight

Evelyn James was drunk. She was alone in New York, sitting with a big Scotch and soda and the telephone, talking to Felix James in California. Naturally, she would be here alone while *everybody* she knew was in California.

"Yes, Felix," she slurred, taking a pull on the Scotch. "Get to the point."

"Did I call you? You called me, Evelyn," he said bitterly.

"What I want to know, is did you get the papers?"

"Yes," he said slowly from the long distance. "The point, I guess, is that Wade French delivered them to me at a party. Really *nice*."

She laughed harshly. "Well, so what? Too bad! You knew they were coming."

"Evelyn!"

"Shaddup! Why he had to deliver them to you himself I don't know. I was having such a good time with him here in New York."

"Evelyn!" He paused, drawing an audible breath. "It was at a party at the Mildbitterses. It could have been very embarrassing."

" 'Stoo bad," she muttered. "You and your *grand* parties."

"It was a *good* party," he said. Then, thoughtfully, he added, "It might interest you to know that your *good* friend Wade French brought Perfidia Sinclair."

Evelyn felt the pain of a neurological headache begin between her eyebrows. She set the Scotch down and held the phone so tightly that her fingers cramped.

"I see," she said. She was not drunk anymore. "Wade was with Perfidia. That's an . . . interesting combination."

"Why?"

"Well . . ." Spite and anger roiled up in her stomach. "Wade is Nathan Sinclair's lawyer, and Perfidia is in trouble with Nathan."

Coolly, Felix said, "Somebody pointed that out to Wade. He said legality has nothing to do with close friendship."

"*Close* friendship?"

"I gather he came to California with Perfidia and her daughter."

"I see."

Felix obviously did not understand that he was giving her news of the dimension of a death sentence. Felix had no more than the inkling she'd just given him of her relationship with . . . that dirty son of a bitch, Wade French.

Felix was moving along. "All right, Evelyn," he said, his voice strong, "I've got the papers now, and it may interest you to know that I'm not going to fight you. In fact, I want this over with as soon as possible. I want you to file for the divorce right away."

Evelyn picked up the Scotch and had a long swallow. "What's the big rush?"

"I want to remarry," he said flatly.

"Goddamn it," she cried, her control snapping, "Virginia Preston!"

"No, somebody else."

"Who?" she yelled.

"Evelyn, that's none of your business. What I'm saying is that I want this finalized."

A large tear trickled down Evelyn's nose and splashed into her drink. "Felix . . ." Should she say that she was sorry? That she was suddenly in the mood to take the whole thing back? No, she could never ad-

mit she was sorry. What she could say was that she
didn't want to be alone. "On what grounds?" she
asked, trying to sound tragic.

"Anything you want! We'll split everything. I won't
fight you."

"You dog!"

"Evelyn, what the hell do you want? You had
French draw up those papers. Ergo . . ."

She screamed angrily, "Ergo, my ass!"

"Evelyn!" She had never talked like this to Felix.

She vented a soppy sob. "Maybe I wasn't serious.
All I wanted was to teach you a lesson," she wailed.

"Well, you did! You opened my eyes, Evelyn!"

"Jesus Christ! Goddamn it! I'm coming to California. I want you back, Felix!"

"No!" He was determined. "I've made up my mind,
Evelyn, and nothing is going to change it."

She drained the Scotch. "I see. All right, then, Felix," she said coldly, "I'm going to take everything."

"You can't get everything. Even Wade French can't
pull that off, that crooked son of a bitch. You'll get
enough."

Evelyn drew an agonized breath. "We'll see," she
said. "Don't forget I've given you the best years of my
life, you bastard!"

"Not at all, Evelyn," he said, undismayed by the
threat. "You've kept the best years of your life for
yourself. I never had any of them."

Evelyn began to cry frantically, in frustration and
fury. "Felix, you can just go fuck yourself!"

He was so stunned, he did not answer. He hung up.

Evelyn put the phone down. She stood up and staggered. She made herself another long drink, then
turned on the TV set. She half expected to see Felix's
face loom up at her, his implacable expression of dis-
missal.

Should she call Wade French and tell him she knew everything? And that meant *everything*. He had gone to the Coast with Perfidia Sinclair—did that mean he was playing some sort of game with her and Nathan? It was just not possible that the old man had told French to go with Perfidia. Had it something to do with the book? Evelyn hazily recalled the circumstances of Perfidia's divorce from Nathan. French had handled everything. Had he, even then, been on Perfidia's side? It seemed impossible, but . . . If so, then Wade French was in a mess. If he wasn't in a mess, she would put him there. Revenge. Of course, it was revenge.

It was late, going on nine o'clock in the evening in New York, but nonetheless Evelyn dialed the number she knew would connect her with Nathan's Park Avenue home. The phone rang and rang and she let it go on. Finally, a hollow male voice said, "Yes?"

"Do I have the Sinclair residence?" she demanded.

"Which Sinclair residence?"

"Mr. Nathan Sinclair."

The voice at the other end was hostile. "I can take a message."

"My name is Evelyn James, and I want to talk to Mr. Nathan Sinclair."

"Mrs. Evelyn James?" There was curiosity, if nothing else, at the other end of the line.

"Yes, Mrs. Evelyn James. I am an old friend of Mr. Sinclair's."

"You are Mr. Felix James's wife, aren't you?"

"Obviously," she said impatiently.

"Mr. Sinclair sometimes . . . mentions your name," the man acknowledged reluctantly.

"And what is your name?"

"My name is Paul."

"And you are?"

"Mr. Sinclair's private secretary."

She had him on the run, Evelyn knew. "Well then

328

. . . Paul . . . let me tell you this. I want to visit Mr. Nathan Sinclair. I understand he is not well."

Paul was very cautious. "He is well. He is as well as . . ."

"Yes, as can be expected of a man of his age," she said irately. "I know. Will you please ask *him* if I can come to visit him tomorrow?"

"Ah, I don't know . . ."

"Never mind about what you don't know. I have important information for him."

"Information?" Paul was dismayed. "You can, uh, tell me."

"No, I am not going to tell *you*. Go now, wake him up, and ask him if I can come and visit him tomorrow afternoon."

He hesitated. Obviously he was afraid of her. Some private secretary, Evelyn thought scornfully. "All right, wait. I'll ask him," Paul said.

Evelyn waited. She was *so* angry. A wave of vindictiveness washed through her body. She would get them all. Felix, Virginia, French, Perfidia. She would even take revenge on Nathan Sinclair, who had always treated her like a slut. He would pay, too, like the others.

She came to attention when she heard the phone picked up and Paul's unsteady voice.

"Mrs. James. Come here tomorrow afternoon at two o'clock."

"I'll be there," she said.

"You know where?"

"Of course I do," she snarled.

Twenty-Nine

At least the weather was going to be all right for the party. Hamilton was not so sure about the guests. There had been a morning mist in the hills, but it had cleared in the afternoon, and the evening promised to be warm enough for the terrace to take an overbooking of people. Logan's favorite caterer had set up a bar next to the sliding doors in the living room, and two women had been busy in the kitchen since four-thirty, making hors d'oeuvres. There was plenty of ice and glasses and trays and ashtrays. Sally—bless her, he thought—had arranged the flowers inside the house and rearranged the potted plants and trees and so on around the Jacuzzi so no one stupidly, or drunkenly, would fall in.

He thought momentarily about insurance. Was he covered in case somebody did break his neck? The hell with it. Hamilton whistled happily in the shower.

When he came downstairs, Sally was in the kitchen, in the living room, and then back in the kitchen. She was wearing the dress he'd bought for her at Giorgio's. He stopped her in mid-flight. "You look terrific," he said, then added worriedly, "Trouble is, Mrs. Mildbitters is going to remember the dress," he said. "Maybe I should have bought you another one."

She put her hands on her hips. "You must be kidding," she said. "Screw her—she won't remember."

"These women have photographic memories when it comes to clothes," Hamilton said. "I'm worried—really worried. She'll say to herself, '*Mama mia*, that girl is

331

wearing the same dress she had on the other night when she was so sick.' "

Sally glared. "You know what, Hamilton, you're full of crap."

"A new dress for every party," he said, smirking.

"You're also an ass," Sally said. "Come on, don't bother me. I'm busy."

Orville was standing on the edge of the terrace, gazing through the eucalyptus toward the lights of Century City.

"How's it going, Orville?"

Orville looked worried. "Should I be here, Pete?"

"Goddamn right," Hamilton said. "You're the house guest, so you come to the party."

"Well . . . how do I look?"

Hamilton sighed. Was he fashion consultant to the Jones family? "You look fine." Orville was wearing a shimmering polyester suit.

"I haven't seen Virginia in a long time, you know," Orville said.

"So what? She hasn't seen you in a long time either. Besides, Orville, we're very civilized out here. Most of the people at the party will have been married to one another at one time or another. It's all very confused—and confusing." He laid a fatherly hand on Orville's shoulder. "You know, they're right. You *do* look like Leslie Howard. What do you say to a drink, my friend? Somebody's got to be first. There's something I want to tell you—or ask you."

"Oh?" Orville looked more concerned.

They walked around the Jacuzzi, an oasis in the deck, and gave the bartender their orders. Hamilton ordered a double vodka and Orville, sighing, took a bourbon and soda.

"Flowers look good, don't they?" Hamilton remarked. "Sally did all that."

"Yeah," Orville said, "she's a clever little demon,

332

isn't she?" He glanced at Hamilton. "What was that you were going to tell me, Pete?"

"Orville, you know—I guess you realize Sally and I are living together here. Well, hell, of course you know."

"Yeah," Orville said, "but I'm not saying anything, am I?"

"No, no."

"I mean, Pete, shit, I know it's modern times. I recognize that."

"Well, Orville, I don't want you to get any wrong ideas. I'm planning to marry her."

"Marry her?" Orville seemed to think this was a very unusual suggestion, even more unusual than living with her. "Why would you want to marry her?"

A little too impatiently, Hamilton said, "Well . . . why *do* people get married, Orville?"

Orville's eyes were puzzled. He smiled cynically. "I'm not one to recommend it," he muttered. "I'm never going to get married again myself." He glanced around cautiously. "I think, speaking for myself, Pete, it makes a lot more sense to live in sin, like you and Sally." He chuckled, laughed shortly. "Sally must take me for a complete asshole, telling me about the two rooms upstairs and all that." Orville backed off to stare at him. "You're a little older than she is."

"Yes. Ten or twelve years."

Orville smiled sardonically, a man of the world. "Well, Christ, if you want to jump off a cliff, I'm not one to try and stop you. Not if you really want to do it." He screwed up his face, trying to grin. "I guess it'd make me happy enough."

"Jesus, Orville, don't go overboard."

"She's a *very* headstrong girl, Pete."

"I know that. You know I was married before?"

Orville nodded uneasily. He did not want to embarrass Hamilton. "I heard about that. A fucking tragedy, wasn't it? You were married to the . . . baroness's other daughter. This one I met today is a fruitcake, isn't she?"

"She sure acts like it. Well . . ."

"Well what?"

"I've got the okay then?" Orville nodded easily. "Thanks," Hamilton said, "although it doesn't sound like much of a blessing, I must say. Anyway—you don't have to say anything to Sally. She doesn't know yet."

Only then did Orville break down and laugh. "What if she says no?"

"She won't say no."

"Congratulations," Orville said. "I think you're crazy, but who am I to say anything? She's just like her mother. You better hang on to your hat." Orville shook his head and chuckled waggishly. "I never told you much about the one I'm still married to. Two-Ton Toni. Jesus! That's been some life. And, Christ, what a waste of time with all this young stuff running around California. I should've come out here a long time ago."

Hamilton merely nodded. Orville amazed him, as Sally amazed him. Orville was showing the same classic signs of marginal kookiness. Perhaps she was more of a chip off the old block than she imagined.

"You know what they say," Orville murmured slyly. "There's more horse's asses in the world than there are horses."

Hamilton laughed appreciatively. He felt like hugging the man. "That's what we call the equine para-dox."

"Is that what we call it?"

The deep discussion was interrupted by a loud and jovial exclamation. "Hall-oh!"

That was Felix. "Out here, Felix," Hamilton called. Felix came ahead. "Where's Virginia?" Hamilton asked him.

334

"In the kitchen with Sally." He bounced down the steps to the terrace and across to them. "I know," he cried. "You're Orville Jones. I'm Felix James."

"A pleasure to meet you," Orville said breezily. "I enjoyed the book."

"Did you?" That pleased Felix.

He was already in riotous good humor. He draped one arm around Hamilton's shoulders and shook Orville's hand vigorously.

"And *here* is Virginia," Hamilton advised Orville.

She appeared at the sliding doors. Holding a glass, she came slowly down the steps. Orville met her more than halfway.

"Virginia!" he exclaimed. "Tell me, are you surprised to see me?"

She shook her head, unsmiling. "No, I knew you were in California. How are you feeling, Orville?"

"I couldn't be better, Virginia," he said warmly. "I want to thank you for what you did for me—with Logan."

She frowned. "It was nothing, Orville."

Hamilton took note of the fact that Sally had remained in the kitchen. Understandably, she did not want to witness this first encounter.

"Well, Virginia," Orville said, "can I kiss you?"

She held out her cheek awkwardly, and Orville carefully put his lips to it. Felix nudged Hamilton with his elbow, laughing softly.

Hamilton thought Virginia was very much off balance. He did not know what she'd expected, but clearly this was not exactly it. Perhaps she had expected some kind of old hayseed.

Looking at her first husband, she spoke again, nervously. "It's been . . . a long time, hasn't it? But, Orville, you look marvelous. You haven't put on a pound. You're as handsome as a youth."

"And you're as beautiful as ever," Orville said.

335

"I'm heavier."

"No!" Orville stepped away from her. "Well, just a little, maybe."

"Oh?" Virginia's mouth drooped petulantly. But she managed a smile. "How have you been, Orville?"

He shrugged elaborately. "I've had a humdrum life, Virginia, not like yours."

Rather too sincerely, she said, "My life hasn't been all that sensational, Orville." She glanced past him toward Felix James. Hamilton noticed how Felix shifted his feet. Then, almost with resignation, Virginia said, "Orville, let's go inside and sit for a while, before the others come. We have a few things to talk about—Sally, for one thing."

"Yeah, a good idea," Orville agreed. Holding her arm, he escorted her back into the house.

Felix tightened his grip on Hamilton's shoulder. "Virginia," he confided. "She's so pissed-off at me, she can't see straight, Peter."

"Now, why should she be?" Why, indeed? Hadn't Felix toured with her, carried her typewriter and listened when Virginia felt like talking?

Felix shook his head. Although he had loosened up to a surprising extent, he was still shy talking about some things. "Peter, she's jealous, I think. You know, after all these years, I think Virginia has fallen in love with me?"

"No!"

"Yes."

"So what's so bad about that, Felix? I've always figured you were in love with her."

Felix looked stricken. "Do you think I was? I never knew it, Peter, maybe that's the trouble. Now, Evelyn . . ."

"You're split," Hamilton reminded him. "So it ought to be clear sailing."

Felix nodded miserably. "There's only one problem,

Peter. I'm almost afraid to admit this—but *I've* fallen in love with Mona Prissian."

Hamilton began to speak, then stopped and muttered, "Now I really am surprised."

"I don't know how to explain it," Felix said. "Maybe it's not love. But, absolutely, it *is* infatuation."

"She's a very attractive woman, Felix. All woman!"

Felix nodded. "And that's why Virginia is so angry, Peter. What the hell am I going to do? I think—I'd almost bet Virginia isn't going to go on to Hawaii. She's talking about going back to New York—cancelling the rest of the tour."

"But she can't do *that*," Hamilton surmised. "You've got an obligation, don't you? Jesus, Felix, I had no idea—she's really jealous?"

Felix nodded soberly, but with a certain smugness. Hamilton wanted to say it was about time Virginia was on the receiving end of passion gone awry, but perhaps that would be too much under the circumstances.

Suddenly, Felix gasped and shivered. "God! Here she is! Mona! With that despicable man."

Within the brightly lit house, Hamilton watched Jack Logan go straight to the couch where Virginia was sitting with Orville. He cried, "Hi-yer, pal!" and bent to kiss Virginia.

Mona Prissian, on the other hand, did not even pause in the living room. She pranced and strutted across the terrace and, without noticing Hamilton, threw her arms around Felix, hugging him close, her hands tight on his back.

"Felix, my dear love!" she panted.

Felix forgot Hamilton too. He kissed Mona hungrily, voraciously, and pulled her even closer. Mona was wearing another of her form-hugging dresses, bright red again, with an ermine wrap thrown across her milky white bosom. As they grappled, Hamilton could

337

almost hear air hissing out of her pneumatic upper story.

Finally then, she saw Peter Hamilton and grinned conspiratorially. "Peter, *dear!*" She whirled away from Felix and smacked Hamilton's cheek with her red lips. "Now, Peter, before I forget, I want you and Sally to join Felix and *I* for brunch tomorrow. You know where my house is, you naughty man."

"All right," he said numbly, "that'd be nice."

It would be nice, he thought, nice to see more of Mona and Felix together. Felix was due for a highly sexed and loving relationship. Evelyn had treated him like dirt for years, and during those same years Virginia had always played with him cruelly. Mona was different. She was as infatuated with Felix as he was with her.

Clusters of people were arriving, like birds coming to light on a chosen tree. Among the first was Rita Mildbitters, who'd warned she'd be coming and going almost immediately—she had three cocktail parties to make that night. Mrs. Mildbitters stopped at the bar and, with her drink wobbling in her hand, joined them on the terrace.

"Hello, Peter," she clucked. "Marvelous view."

"It's okay . . ."

"Mrs. Mildbitters!" Mona exclaimed. "I so enjoyed your party for Felix!"

"Yes . . . hello, dear." Chances were, Hamilton thought, Mrs. Mildbitters didn't remember Mona. Nonetheless, she tilted her face so Mona could bend over and kiss it, leaving a red mark on her covering of white powder. "Is Sally feeling better tonight?" Mrs. Mildbitters asked Hamilton.

"She's fine. I don't know what it was with her the other night."

Mrs. Mildbitters chuckled tolerantly. "Probably party-itis." She didn't care. Whether people stayed or left, it was all the same to her. She was past worrying about small things. "I'm happy you got to see Perfidia again, Peter," she said, much more pointedly. "Watching you two together—I was reminded of . . ."

"Sure." He nodded hastily. "Excuse me—I'd better get by the door. I see Mark Mastoid coming in. *And* Morris Scarlatti, Felix. When is it you're going on his show?"

"Monday morning before we leave . . . for Hawaii," Felix said, obviously more convinced than ever that they were not going to leave for Hawaii. As Hamilton turned away, Felix cooed, "Rita, darling. I can't thank you enough for that gorgeous evening."

Morris Scarlatti was dressed in a gray flannel suit with a white silk cravat, the latter decorated with a diamond stick pin. His face was long, rather sad and weary, but very alert. He looked around critically, obviously not very impressed with what he saw, and walked toward the bar.

Several of the more social Beverly Hills set had come in. There were the Punjabbers, the Palm Springs insurance couple who entertained royalty and presidents, as well as Virginia whenever she journeyed to the desert; Cyrus Persopolis, banking tycoon with his popsy girlfriend; the Landowners, Betty and Bob, real estate developers, and many others. Hamilton recognized two big guns from the studios, with whom he'd done some unsatisfactory business in the past. The writer Victor Staines, darling of the social-cultural set, stood next to the kitchen door, a study in poised introversion, waiting to be approached. And . . . shit! He recognized Gladys Goldsmith of the *National Enquirer*—how had that intolerable bitch gotten in the door?

Hamilton eased up to Morris Scarlatti and ordered another big vodka martini. "Morris," he said. "How are you? Peter Hamilton."

339

"Where's Peter Hamilton?" Scarlatti demanded archly, then smiled. "Oh, hello, Peter. Where are Virginia Preston and Felix James? That's why I'm here."

Hamilton said, "Virginia is sitting there on the couch, and Felix is out on the terrace necking." He looked around, in time to see Sally scoot out of the kitchen. "And here's Sally Jones, Virginia's daughter." He grabbed Sally by the arm. "Come here, sweetie. I want you to meet this giant of the media, Morris Scarlatti."

Scarlatti smiled. "My dear," he said musingly, "you are a lovely young thing. Not like the rest of the bags in the room."

He bent and kissed her hand. Sally gushed comically, "Oh, sir, you are too kind."

Scarlatti scowled fiercely. "Don't knock it, darling."

"Come on, Morris," Hamilton laughed. "I'll introduce you to Virginia. I think," he mentioned to Sally, "that it's about time we broke up the reunion."

When Sally saw Virginia and Orville still huddled together on the couch, she laughed nervously. "What the hell do they have to talk about?"

"You, most likely." He noticed that Scarlatti was becoming restive. "Virginia is talking to her first husband, Sally's father," he explained.

"Frankly," Scarlatti muttered, "I'm totally confused."

"My mother and father," Sally stated. "Don't you get it—that's her ex-husband."

"Her other ex-husband," Hamilton said, "just walked outside."

Scarlatti ignored the information as he observed acidly, "I see the Twirdson woman. She's always on Mr. Blackwell's worst-dressed list—and deserves to be. What a cow! She looks like a drag queen in heat. Who's she with? I know—Percy Vostock."

"And Frank Orchid right behind them," Hamilton said. "Very, very big at Tintoretto Galleries."

"I'll say. All that lard should be packaged," Scarlatti said scathingly.

Hamilton led him through a knot of people, toward the couch. "Virginia . . ." He interrupted whatever it was she was saying to Orville. "Virginia, I'd like you to meet my friend Morris Scarlatti."

"Oh, yes," she cried, smiling. She glanced up and held out her hand.

"Dear lady," Scarlatti murmured. Again he kissed the hand. "Virginia Preston, yes, I read your columns as often as I can, *and*," he announced, "I've read your book, *Powerhouse*. It was delightfully scurrilous. Marvelous. And the love scenes, yes, very touching, if I may say so."

Gripping his hand, Virginia lifted herself from the couch. "I must mingle," she sighed. "Orville," she said, brushing him off, "we'll talk later." Before turning her full attention to Scarlatti, she hissed in Hamilton's ear, "Rotten bastard. Orville told me! I won't have it!"

Hamilton pulled his arm away and turned on his heel.

He could not decide at precisely which point the party began to spin out of control.

The living room had filled and, as they had planned, the overflow of guests began to spill outside. He did his best to keep track of the main players. Jack Logan was positioned close to Felix and Mona Prissian on the terrace. Virginia had drawn Morris Scarlatti into an empty spot by the fireplace and was talking to him earnestly. Orville, having been dismissed by Virginia and not really knowing anybody else well enough for inconsequential chitchat, was propped on one end of the bar, drinking bourbon. Hamilton joined Sally at the front door just as a TV crew arrived unexpectedly. He hadn't

341

known Channel 14 was invited—that was probably Felix's doing, or maybe someone at Logan Productions. It hardly mattered and there was no way to keep them out anyway. The roving reporter, Cecile Armstrong, a tall, chisel-faced Miss America blonde, had a way about her.

"Where's Felix James?" she demanded.

"Out on the terrace."

"Which one?"

"The man with the black hair who's standing next to the *zaftig* redhead. Not redhead, more brownish red. Not the porky guy. The other guy."

Cecile, like an infantry sergeant, made the traditional gesture for "Forward!" Her crew followed her, practically bowling people over as they made for the terrace. Well, he thought tiredly, TV coverage was valuable for the book, as it might be even for him at some later date if Cecile Armstrong ever found out, by accident, that he was *the* Peter Hamilton, the intellectual man who made documentaries.

"She'd grind you into the pavement," Sally sputtered.

"She'd walk on your face," Hamilton agreed. "You want to be a career girl, Sally? A media star?"

"Who says I want to be a goddamn career girl?"

Now, he thought, was the time to say something, before Virginia got to her. "Your mother is sore at me. You know why?" She shook her head indifferently. "Because I told your father that I was probably going to marry you."

She looked at him coolly. "What are you saying, sweet nuts?"

"I just said it, didn't I?" Maybe she was going to say no after all. Lamely, he went on, "I thought it might be more convenient if we make this Chinese trip."

"Hamilton," she muttered, "don't play around."

"I'm not playing around," he said. "I know you

342

don't believe in marriage," he went on, "only in having babies out of wedlock and all that. But it would be more convenient."

Sally stared at him incredulously. "A marriage of convenience? That's disgusting, Hamilton!"

"Oh, yeah? Oh, yeah?" More people were coming in. He drew her to the side. "Listen, sweetie, when we get to China, you know they're very puritanical over there."

"I thought the Commies believed in free love."

"In theory only. They get very nervous about hotel rooms. What I'm saying is I don't want to be running up and down some hotel corridor in my jockstrap hiding from a commissar."

"Hamilton, you know something? You are a very romantic person." She smiled at him infuriatingly. "You could always jerk off."

"Sally, I'm warning you. Goddamn it, go upstairs and look at that sign."

"Hamilton," she said, "you're a dope. I'll put the matter under advisement. Now get out of here." Her eyes glistened, from something. "I've got to check some coats."

It was about this time, as she was recovering from his proposal, that the two screwballs arrived. At least, Hamilton thought worriedly, they had all the vital signs of screwballs. They were dressed in identical suits and looked like twins. They had the same haircuts, neatly trimmed and with identical sideburns. They might both have just been discharged from the Marine Corps.

One of the young men, grinning ingratiatingly, presented Hamilton with a card.

ENTERTAINMENT FOR THE HANDICAPPED
NEW YORK, NY
SIMON AND SHUSTER BROTHERS

"Yes," Hamilton said slowly. He could not imagine how these two had gotten wind of the party. "Are you—you guys on the guest list?"

One young man nodded; the other shook his head no. But their mutual expression was one of humbleness, then entreaty. The one with the brown hair put his finger to his lips and wobbled his head.

"Hamilton," Sally said, "you dope—they can't speak."

They nodded. Yes, that was it. "Entertainment for the handicapped?" Hamilton asked, reading from the card. They bobbed their heads again. Yes, yes, that was it.

"Come on in, for Christ's sake," Sally exclaimed, making the decision for him. "Have a drink, Simon and Shuster."

"Wait a minute," Hamilton said irritably. "I want to get the name straight here. Are you brothers, or is Brothers your last name?"

Again one nodded and the other shook his head. Both looked extremely anxious.

"Christ, Hamilton," Sally said impatiently. "What does it matter? You can see they're in a hell of an important kind of business. . . . Are you Shuster?" She pointed at the one with black hair. He smiled at her lovingly and shook his head. "Oh, so you're Simon then. And this is Shuster."

"I think you got it, Sally," Hamilton said sarcastically.

"My name is Sally Jones," she spouted, "and this is your host, Peter Hamilton."

At mention of his name, their eyes grew serious. They bowed from the waist and shook his hand. Their fingers were soft and wet. "I've never heard of your organization," he commented. "But I guess that doesn't mean anything, does it?"

The two boys were staring at him. Shuster, brown-

344

haired Shuster, seemed to be in command. He was about twenty-five, Hamilton would have guessed. Simon was a little older, maybe, and the quieter of the two, if that was the proper description. Even if he'd been able to talk, he probably wouldn't have had much to say.

"Well," he said, "have a drink, boys, then I'll introduce you to Virginia Preston and Felix James." They nodded thankfully and headed for the bar. Simon pointed at the vodka bottle, and Simon put his hand on the Scotch. The bartender poured two drinks. "They may be mutes," Hamilton said to Sally, "but they're also a pair of creeps."

"Don't be cruel," she said. "You know, I think they're wearing hairpieces."

That would explain the perfect coiffures. "That makes them even more weird."

"What's so weird?"

"Never mind. Forget it. I'll introduce them."

Hamilton took the two boys by the arm and transported them to Virginia. Felix and she were together now, standing in front of the fireplace in the hot television lights while Cecile Armstrong asked them inane questions. In a moment, Cecile told the crew to cut the lights and started talking to Morris Scarlatti.

"Virginia, Felix," Hamilton said, "I'd like you to meet Simon and Shuster Brothers. They're with a group in New York called Entertainment for the Handicapped. They, uh, crashed but what the hell. They'd like to . . . well, not speak to you. They can't speak. I guess they'd like to look at you for a while. You do the talking. Right?" he asked Shuster.

Shuster nodded. Quickly, Virginia grabbed Shuster's hand. "Lovely," she said, "isn't that lovely, Felix, that these two boys have come to our party?"

"It certainly is," Felix said absently. "It's lovely." His eyes were out on the terrace, where Jack Logan

345

was talking to Mona Prissian. Mona was trying to get away, but Logan clung to her arm. "A very worthy cause," Felix mumbled.

"Have you read our book, boys?" Virginia demanded. "You know, it's going to be made into a movie. It *could* be captioned for the deaf, couldn't it, Peter?"

"Sure, sure," he said, "but I don't think that's very common yet in the movies."

Shuster pulled a pad out of his jacket and wrote something. He handed the message to Hamilton. "There's always a first time," it said.

"Yeah, that's true," Hamilton agreed. "Let's see— do you know anybody else here?" Obviously, they didn't. "I guess I could introduce you to Mona Prissian," he suggested, glancing at Felix. "She's a world-famous actress." But what he really should do, he thought, was turn them loose. They had their calling cards. Let them introduce themselves. He was not in a very kindly mood. He was still, as a matter of fact, smarting over what Virginia had said to him. Then he had something of an inspiration. He wanted to see how Cecile Armstrong would handle the unexpected. He dragged them over to where she was talking to Morris Scarlatti. "Excuse me, Miss Armstrong, I've got something that might interest you for 'Fourteen.' Meet Simon and Shuster Brothers. They're from a group in New York called Entertainment for the Handicapped—movies for the deaf, *Playboy* magazine in Braille, that kind of thing," he said recklessly. "Could be a hell of an interview for you."

"Where's my camera crew?" she asked.

"At the bar."

"Samson!" Cecile called. "Set up again!" She placed the two boys at the terrace door. They looked confused, not knowing what was happening. Within seconds, Cecile was talking into a camera. "Tonight, we have two people here in Hollywood that we're, well, just very proud to present to you. They represent Entertainment for the Handicapped and they've come to *our* party for Virginia and Felix Preston. . . ." She muffed the names. "Virginia," Cecile said, "just come here for a minute and greet our two New York guests, will you?"

Virginia pushed herself between Simon and Shuster.

"Now, Virginia," Cecile said with intent interest, "just what *is* Entertainment for the Handicapped?"

The camera whirred busily. Simon and Shuster were stunned. Talk about camera-shy!

"I'll explain," Virginia said enthusiastically, a look of sad concern on her face. "You see, these two boys are mutes but, even with that handicap, they're out here to convince the whole Hollywood community to make allowance for people who are physically disadvantaged. The deaf can't hear movies, one of our precious commodities, and the blind can't see them. We lucky people forget that. . . ."

"Too true, too true," Cecile seconded, her face almost tearful. "Simon . . . Shuster," she asked them directly, "are you having any success?"

The attention was too much for the boys. Shuster clapped his hand over his face and Simon ducked into his suit coat.

"Ah, ah," Cecile cried, "you see, viewers, handicapped people are so shy! And why? Who can explain that?" She stepped into the camera for a close-up, her voice shaking. "So, there you have it, darling viewers. Entertainment for the Handicapped! A new dimension for this wonderful town called . . . *Hollywood*." The smile trickled away as the camera ground down. "Cut it!" she said curtly. "That's it. Thanks," she told Hamilton. "That'll make a good little insert. It'll go network."

"Network! My, how marvelous."

Scarlatti frowned at him. "Don't knock it, Peter," he said.

Simon and Shuster had not recovered from their exposure. Simon was shaking, and Shuster's lip quivered.

"Come on, boys," Hamilton said, "it didn't hurt, did it?"

They looked very thoughtful, very sorrowful. Hamilton patted their backs and took them down on the terrace, making for Logan and Mona Prissian.

"*I* didn't get on camera," Mona sniffed. But when she understood about Simon and Shuster, she forgot about being upstaged. "You mean these two good-looking lads are actually *mute*?"

"That's it," Hamilton said.

"God!" she cried. "See, Jack, count your blessings."

Logan sneered. "I do—every day. One, two. One, two. Yeah, okay, they're both there."

"Jack," Mona said angrily, "try to show a bit more *politesse*. Don't be such a *churl*!"

Logan's mouth curled scornfully. Then he moaned. "Oh, Christ. My God, I should have brought Duke with me!"

"What's ailing you?" Hamilton asked. He turned. Logan's swift change of expression must have been due, at least partly, to Perfidia Sinclair von Thurnsteil. For Perfidia had made her entrance.

She stood, statuesque and motionless, at the terrace door. She was encased—there was no other word for it—in a clinging black dress, full-length and cut down the front nearly to the navel. Perfidia was without jewelry except for a single and light-shattering ruby, which hung on a chain between her breasts. Over her shoulders was a flowing black cape with a crimson lining. Her short hair shone like black night. Even from the terrace, Hamilton could see the lethal flash of her eyes.

"Holy mackerel," Hamilton said.

"Cross yourself," Logan muttered. "It's the devil."

348

Beside them, Shuster gaped at the vision, then turned his head away.

Perfidia spotted them and descended the two steps to the terrace. She lifted her right arm and pointed at Mona Prissian. "Perfidia!" she howled. "It is Perfidia Sinclair von Thurnsteil!"

Mona reeled back. "What do you mean?" she cried.

Perfidia thundered, "What do I mean? Are *you* to be *me*?"

Mona recovered quickly. "My dear lady," she said coldly, "I am to play a part in a movie. That is all I know."

"Yes," Perfidia said. Her eyes bulged. "You are to play *me* in this movie." Hamilton could not decide if she were really so outraged or merely acting. Such anger surely could not be so readily on tap. Perfidia pointed at Logan. "You! You have arranged this debacle."

Logan was trembling. "Perfidia," he chattered, "you know all about it. You said you didn't give a damn." He tried to get behind Hamilton.

"I did not know that this *creature* was to play *me*!"

"Oh?" Mona echoed her furiously. "And what, pray tell, objection could *you* have to that?"

Perfidia whirled her cape. Maybe she was possessed, Hamilton considered—but he didn't think so. There had to be a method to this madness. Perfidia next threw her arms high, as if to denounce them all.

"Perfidia . . ." Logan whimpered. "Perfidia, please calm down. Mona's signed to play the part of Pauline Power, not of Perfidia Sinclair von . . ."

"I am beautiful," Perfidia screamed. She aimed her finger at Mona again. "This is trash!"

Mona snorted, her chest heaving. "You're out of your flipping mind, dragon lady! Tell her, Jack!"

"Perfidia . . ." Logan was not in a state to form words.

349

"Tell her, Jack!"

Weakly, Logan tried. "Perfidia, we're making a movie of a novel. . . . It's got nothing to do . . ."

"Silence!" Perfidia decreed. The eyes descended from the height of insanity toward slyness. "I will tell you. In the interests of saving Capri, I will play the part of Pauline Power!"

"What!" Despite his fear, Logan was incensed. "What! Perfidia, you're not a fucking actress."

"Silence," she bellowed again. "Yes, I will play the part, or there will be no movie."

Ah, Hamilton thought he had it now. Quietly, he told Logan, "I think you're going to have to make your donation to Save Capri. . . ."

"I care for *nothing* else!" Perfidia exclaimed. If her eyes had been spikes, Logan would have been nailed to the deck.

"You fucking blackmailer!"

"You," she snarled viciously, "pervert!"

Logan seemed about to pass out. "Perfidia, I don't . . ." He looked around wildly. "Orville! Orville Jones!" He shouted.

Orville was not far away. He had been watching the unlikely demonstration from close by the Jacuzzi. "What seems to be the problem?" he asked, very quietly.

"Orville, baby," Logan gasped. "Monday morning, bright and early. A check for Perfidia Sinclair von . . . Thurnsteil, for rights to . . . *The Last Days of Capri.* Fifty grand?" He looked abjectly at Perfidia.

"One hundred," she said softly, "and script approval."

Logan nodded, looking at his shoes.

"Okay," Orville said. "Why all the histrionics? It's a straight business deal, isn't it?"

Perfidia whirled at his voice. "You! The man who looks like Chip Douglas."

"That's what they tell me," Orville said.

Perfidia smiled thoughtfully, as if bathing her hysteria in baby oil. The cape finally settled around her shoulders. She approached Orville, placed her hands on his arms and then, in a gesture that did not logically follow her previous performance, kissed him gently on both cheeks.

Orville, self-possessed as he was, was taken aback. "Baroness . . ."

"Chip!"

"No, not Chip," he stammered. "Just plain Orville Jones."

"Of Logan Productions."

Orville glanced at Jack Logan. "Yeah," he said, "I guess so."

"We must talk," Perfidia said. She turned for a second to Mona. "I apologize. You *are* a beautiful woman."

"So are you, duckie," Mona muttered. "What do you mean by calling my friend Jack a pervert?"

Perfidia smiled. "Nothing. Pay no attention."

Orville stared at Perfidia. "You should cool down, little lady," he advised. "All that screaming is not good for the blood pressure."

Perfidia nodded, gazing into his face. "Yes, *tell* me. You are the man who should tell me how to behave." She sighed for all to hear. "I was in love once with a man called Chip Douglas."

Orville reminded her again. "I'm Orville Jones."

"Orville," Perfidia moaned. "Orfeo . . . I shall call you Orfeo."

Hamilton remembered Simon and Shuster. Shoulder to shoulder, they stood mesmerized by Perfidia.

Mona was perplexed. "What the hell is this all about?"

She might well ask, Hamilton thought, but the answer was simple. It was about money. As if to emphasize the point, Wade French came out on the terrace. One could practically see one hundred-dollar bills sticking out of his pockets. But French walked with dignity; the deck seemed to creak under his feet.

"Hello, everybody," he said in his low, rumbling voice.

Then he stopped. He was staring at Simon and Shuster. A shadow of recognition crossed his face. Hamilton heard a small exclamation at his side. Shuster had made a noise, something between a grunt and a squeal. French's eyes cleared quickly. He turned to Perfidia.

"What's all the excitement?"

"Nothing," she said. "I have been whooping with joy over Jack's generous contribution to Save Capri."

"Good," French said, "very good."

"Yeah," Logan said spitefully, "just great."

"Wade, do you know everybody?" Hamilton asked. He was beginning to feel idiotic, playing host like this.

"I think so." French belched lightly. "Stomach again."

"Try an antacid," Orville suggested.

"Yes," French said, "yes, I will."

"I don't think you've met these two gentlemen," Hamilton said, clearing the way for Simon and Shuster. "They're from an organization in New York called Entertainment for the Handicapped. This is Simon and this is Shuster, Brothers."

French's eyes were steady. "How do you do?" he said.

Hamilton was sure now that French had met them before. "Mr. French," he said casually, "is a lawyer from New York." Again, he heard the intimation of a whimper develop in Shuster's numb voicebox.

Perfidia cried, "And don't forget me! Hello, Simon and Shuster. I'm Perfidia Sinclair von Thurnsteil of Capri." Perfidia was happy now; yes, she was so happy.

352

The boys' heads drooped. They were so shy, Hamilton thought.

Perfidia gathered the bottom of her cape for another twirl. This time, she did it quite gaily. "Goodness, I must say hello to Virginia and Felix. Come with me, Orfeo."

She attached herself to Orville's arm and made for the inside of the house.

"Well," Hamilton said.

"Yeah," Logan exploded, "well is right! The bitch. She nailed me for one hundred thousand dollars."

"Did she?" French said. "Why should you object to that? Look what you were able to buy for it." There was threat in his heavy voice.

"Fuck you," Logan said bitterly. "I think you're in cahoots with her."

For a second, Hamilton thought for sure French was going to haul off and punch Logan. But he controlled himself. "Logan," he said blackly, "what you just said is grounds for a lawsuit!"

"Fuck you! Sue!"

French sneered and turned around. His heels pounded on the deck.

"I've been done," Logan groaned. "I've been fucking done."

Mona gathered her ermine closely around her bosom as if taken by sudden chill. Anxiously, she said, "Only because she called you a pervert, Jack. You wouldn't have paid one hundred thousand dollars to protect *my* movie."

"Just shut up!" Logan exclaimed. "I'm getting the hell out of here. Jesus, some party I'm paying for! Everybody insulting me and blackmailing me. So long, Peter! You've done it again!"

"Well," Mona said, "I'm not leaving with you."

Logan's brown face was a crosscross of worry and wrinkles. "I don't give a shit," he said. "Get Felix to take you home. And that means I'm leaving Duke at your house, Mona. I'm not going back there now to pick him up."

Mona said stridently, "I don't want that goddamn monster around."

"Too bad," Logan sneered. "*Goo-bye*. Don't get smart-assed with me, Mona. Remember," he smiled, "I can always get Perfidia to take your place on the picture."

Mona was not frightened. "Pay me off then, you pervert," she shouted.

Logan shook his head angrily and whipped away. Hamilton saw him grunt at Sally when he got near the front door. And then he was gone.

Mona looked dismal. "Peter, what do you think?"

"Mona, I don't know what the hell to think. I don't believe any of this."

"Peter," she whispered, "take me to Felix. *Where* is Felix?"

Inside, after a quick word with Virginia and Felix, Perfidia had cornered Morris Scarlatti. Still holding tightly to Orville's arm, she said, "My dear Mr. Scarlatti, such a Florentine name. Completely beautiful. You *must* interview me. I *must* tell you about Capri and its sad prognosis."

Scarlatti nodded. He was completely thrown by this lady from Capri. He rolled his eyes at Hamilton, asking for a way of escape.

"Besides which, dear sir," Perfidia kept on, "are you aware that I am the protagonist of Virginia and Felix's book. *I* am Pauline Power. I am Perfidia Sinclair von Thurnsteil. Miss Prissian," she appealed, turning to Hamilton and Mona, "am I not telling the truth?"

"I wouldn't have any idea," Mona said evasively. "I didn't write the book, and I haven't finished reading it."

"Nonetheless . . . nonetheless," Perfidia murmured.

354

"Dear lady . . ." Scarlatti murmured.

"We *must* save Capri," Perfidia cried.

Orville pulled at her arm. "Cool it, little lady," he counseled. "Don't worry about Capri. It'll take care of itself."

"Oh, dear man!" Perfidia turned to him, hung her head on his shoulder, and began to cry. It was all, obviously, too much for her.

At last, then, Sally—thank God for Sally—jostled up to Hamilton. "What's cooking?" she demanded.

Hamilton shrugged. "Not an awful lot," he said.

Sally stared in disbelief at Orville and Perfidia. Orville smiled at her, rather smugly, a little proudly.

Wade French ploughed back into the group. He was white and drawn. "Perfidia, darling, I must . . . go. I'm feeling terrible."

Perfidia didn't move her face from Orville's lapel. "Strawberries and cream again, Wade?"

Painfully, his hand over his heart, French mumbled, "Yes, I think so, Fido."

Fido? Everybody caught that. Perfidia started. "Go then, Wade," she said harshly. "Orville Jones will bring me back to the hotel."

"What?" French said. "I thought you'd leave with me."

"Farewell, Wade," Perfidia said, "good night, sweet prince."

French's face became troubled. He looked at Orville, uncomprehending, then at Perfidia. "Perfidia?"

"Good night, Wade," Perfidia said firmly, "and farewell! I have finally found my knight in shining armor. Orfeo!" She put her cheek next to Orville's. Orville Jones, Hamilton asked himself, a knight in shining armor? This seemed an unlikely role for the gaunt Ohioan, in his sparkling polyester suit.

Hamilton surveyed the group. Virginia was grinning. She was standing next to Felix, Mona was huddled close to him on the other side and, as it happened, Felix had one arm around each of them, as if to shield them from this madness.

"Perfidia," French stammered with embarrassment, "what do you mean?"

"It is simple." Perfidia shrugged. "Orfeo and I—together _we_ shall Save Capri. Orfeo is a financial genius."

Orville's eyes widened. "Genius, little lady, I don't know . . ."

Morris Scarlatti tapped Hamilton on the shoulder, then whispered in his ear, "This woman is insane. That island is no more sinking than I am. I couldn't put her on the show. She'd make a fool of me."

"Morris, if I were you, I _wouldn't_ put her on your show."

In seconds, French had turned from impressive to ruined. But there was something dogged about him. "Perfidia, I think you'd better come with me now."

"No! Someone bring me a drink! A brandy and soda!"

"Perfidia," French said sullenly, "I think you've had enough."

She ignored him. "Orfeo, may I have a drink?"

French had the temerity to put his hand on her arm. Perfidia shook it off angrily. French grabbed her by the shoulder.

"Hey, there," Orville exclaimed, "not so rough, big man!"

A look of fury transformed Shuster's face. Gallantly, he leaped forward. His block knocked French off balance.

Furiously, French said, "You, you little son of a bitch. I know I've seen you before . . . somewhere."

Intently, cruelly, Shuster hit French again with both elbows. French released Perfidia and swiped at Shuster with the flat of his hand. Shuster ducked but not far enough. The hairpiece—Sally was right—flew off Shuster's head like a bird and sailed through the terrace door.

"Say," Orville shouted, "knock off the rough stuff, you guys!"

Orville pulled French away from Shuster, who was grunting and squalling with rage.

"Rotten little son of a bitch," French panted. "Let me go, you!"

Perfidia began to scream. She tossed her hands in the air. "Wade, just get out of here! Get *out*!"

Gasping, French began to back away. "You'll be sorry, you stupid fool!"

"Why should I be sorry?" she taunted him.

"I'll cancel everything," he yelled. "I'll cut the ground out from under your feet. You won't get *any* money!"

Perfidia laughed gleefully, then stepped forward. She slapped him. The sound of her palm hitting his face splattered like the impact of a body hitting against cement. The other guests were mindful that something slightly untoward was happening. Now they stopped their small talk and focused on French and Perfidia.

French put his hand to his face. "Fido . . ."

"Don't Fido me!" Perfidia screamed. "You've wounded me—physically and mentally. You are a lout!"

French flinched before her words. Stubbornly, he tried to make the best of it. "Lout?" he repeated, laughing disbelievingly. "*You* can call me a lout?"

"Yes, I can," Perfidia declared for all to hear. "I can call you a lout—and I do. You lout!"

French drew himself up to full height and sucked in his stomach. He looked around, smoothing the front of his vest and toying with its open bottom button as if to ask generally, *Do I, Wade French, look like a lout?* "I think I will be going now," he said grimly. "Good

357

night, Peter . . . Felix . . . Virginia. Good night, all. It has been a perfectly splendid evening, yes, *stellar*."

Then, amid the dead silence, he made for the front door.

"And stay away from me," Perfidia screeched after him. "You . . . lecherous . . . abomination."

Virginia, to give her credit, announced dryly, "Perfidia, that's what I call having the last word."

Perfidia turned and glared. She seemed about to unleash more fury on Virginia. Then she moaned desperately and threw herself in Orville's arms. Placidly, he petted her. "Nothing to get your balls in an uproar about, Baroness," he said soothingly.

Virginia noticed then that Felix's arm was around her waist. She broke free, staring at him angrily, and crossed the room to Hamilton and Sally. "I want you to take me back to the hotel," she said. "As far as I am concerned, the party is over, and I'm going into total seclusion."

Morris Scarlatti stepped forward. "Dear lady," he said, "allow me to drive you to your hotel." He frowned distastefully. "I think I've been here long enough—and *seen* enough. Dear boy," he said to Hamilton, "such delightful people."

Behind them, Perfidia murmured, "Orfeo, sweet Orfeo."

"You bet, Baroness," Orville said.

Thirty

When he got back to the hotel, Wade French locked the door of his room securely. He did not want to be disturbed. He loosened his tie and sat down and tried, calmly, to assess the damage. The sight of this strange man-child Shuster, the person he'd seen that day in the outer office of the Nathan Sinclair Park Avenue apartment, had unnerved him completely. Then the quarrel with Perfidia . . . and the vicious attack. He was frightened. One thing was certain—within hours, Nathan Sinclair would know that he, Wade French, was in California in the company of his archenemy, Perfidia Sinclair.

Good God! It could not be worse. And everything else that had happened was as nothing compared to the fact that Perfidia had cast him adrift. She had lived up to her name once again. Perfidious Perfidia. They'd joked about it before. But it was not a laughing matter now. French was very depressed.

He undressed. Dinner? He'd forget that. He wasn't hungry now. He carefully hung his suit on a hanger. He removed his shirt and tie and then went into the bathroom. He saw in the mirror that his face was still red where Perfidia had slapped him.

And now? The future was bleak. Capri was lost. He hoped the goddamn island *would* sink into the sea and take her along with it, and her crazy daughter and the ruffian George, whom Perfidia in the blink of an eye had turned into a fatherless Italian nobleman. George. He thought of dear, hairless little George and smiled. He was surprised but not completely astounded when an erection began to develop within his boxer shorts. Yes, he could admit it now, since everything was crumbling. French grasped himself happily, a full-blown erection. Should he try to get George down here before Perfidia returned? Or should he forget it and maintain the image of proper attorney? Better to stay proper, he thought regretfully. It would not do to cave in too soon. He smiled and, holding his stiffened member, returned to the bedroom.

It was past midnight in New York, but what did that matter? Evelyn would be glad to hear from him.

"Evelyn, darling," he said, "it's Wade."

"Whom?"

Something icy pierced his brain. "Me. Wade."

"I don't know any Wade," she said. "I once knew a Wade, but he died of treachery."

The icy lance drove down his backbone. "What? I don't understand you."

"In California on business? Delivering Felix the papers? When all the time, you're there with Perfidia Sinclair? Oh, yes, I know everything."

Her voice was singsong. He thought desperately that she might be drunk. "Not so! Not so, Evelyn! Perfidia just happened to be out here, by accident."

"Wade," she said, her voice as cold as the sharp object that had now reached his heart, "I am not a fool. But never mind. Tomorrow I'm going to see Nathan Sinclair. Perhaps he'll be able to tell me you're in California on a hush-hush confidential matter."

"I don't think," French said slowly, "that it would do to mention it to him. There are some things that it's better for him not to know. Evelyn . . ." He tried it on her. "There's something I have in mind that'll definitely come out in your favor."

"Of course," she said bitterly, "I understand completely, Wade."

Yes, he thought helplessly, she did understand. That was the trouble.

"Evelyn," he muttered, "you know that I love only you."

She laughed scornfully. "Good-bye, Wade," she said.

The phone went dead, and French sat there dumbly, the receiver dangling in his hand. His erection had wilted in his shorts. Now, he realized, he was truly done for. Perfidia . . . Evelyn. What could he do?

Retreat, that was the only thing left. He must get back to New York, to make Evelyn see reason. But he could not make it before tomorrow. He tried again for an assessment. When Sinclair discovered from Evelyn that he was keeping company with Perfidia, that would be the end of his profitable association with the House of Sinclair. But, hell, he had other clients. All his eggs were not in the Sinclair basket. He was respected, a pillar of the legal establishment. He was a member in good standing of the University Club. He had an apartment in New York, property in New Jersey, a Swiss bank account he never talked about. Yes, he was all right. He was not done for yet. It was not as bad as all that. But he *was* angry. He gripped the arms of the chair. Power! He still possessed that.

He pulled the phone up by its cord and dialed Perfidia's suite.

"Huh?" George answered. He was cautious on the phone, wasn't he?

"George," French said, "could you come down to my room for a minute, please? There's a message for Perfidia."

"Okay." Monosyllabic George.

French stood up and flexed his muscles, then stretched toward the ceiling. He had played football once. He smiled. To hell with them, he thought. He walked to the door and waited. In a second, there was a light tap. French unlocked the door and opened it.

George was there, barefoot, smiling his idiot's smile, his light blue eyes trusting. A T-shirt was pulled tightly across his chest, and a light pair of cotton pants gripped him across the buttocks like the universal embrace.

"Come in," French said.

Unconcerned, George stepped into the room. French closed the door and locked it again. George tensed. He knew.

"No," he said.

"Yes," French replied.

George tried to get around him to the door, but he didn't make it. French grabbed him around the waist and lifted him off the floor, pressing the lithe body against his own. He squeezed George until his eyes dimmed. Then he walked across the room and tossed George down on the bed. French took the neck of the T-shirt in his fingers and, marveling again at his power, ripped it down the front with a single tug. He slapped George soundly across the face to keep him from struggling, then undid the white pants and pulled them from the body. Underneath, George was naked. His eyes pleaded for . . . what? French stood over him for a moment, glaring down at the body. It was young and smooth, like a newborn colt's.

"Now, George," French said thoughtfully, "now then . . ."

Thirty-One

Orville Jones did not know what to make of this thing called Fate, or happenstance. It seemed a lifetime since he had shuffled into that kitchen in Ohio and announced he was going to California.

And now, wonder of wonders, here he was. More to the point, he was walking into the Beverly Hills Hotel with this striking woman, and heads did turn.

"Orfeo," Perfidia said, "you must bring me to the suite. I'm afraid of . . ."

"Of course, Baroness."

They swept across the lobby and into the elevator. Upstairs, she put her finger to her lips as they went down the corridor. She stopped to take the key out of her jeweled handbag and opened the door.

"Enter," she said softly, looking ravishingly at him over her shoulder.

Orville stepped inside. He was not too pleased to see her crazy kid sitting there on a couch, staring at the television set. Marina, that was her name. She was dressed in a very short baby-doll nightgown, and Orville realized with a start that he could see the hair on her snatch between her crossed legs.

"Darling," Perfidia asked, "where's George?"

Marina snorted, *"Weg,"* not taking her eyes off the TV.

"Gone? Gone where, Marina?"

The child shook her head.

Orville knew what he would have done. He would have let her have one in the chops. But Perfidia only exhaled disgustedly. "God, how do I put up with all this?" she demanded rhetorically. "Marina, you remember Mr. Jones."

Briefly, the childlike eyes flicked at Orville. *"Der Mann."*

"Yes, darling, the man." Perfidia looked helplessly at Orville, indicating again that she didn't know what to do. "Come, Orfeo."

Orville, not caring by now what she called him, followed her into the next room, which obviously was the bedroom. Perfidia slammed the door.

"Help me, please, remove my cape," she said. She turned her back so Orville could reach to undo the buttons over her bosom. As he fiddled with them, she took his hands in her own and squeezed them, then lifted them to her mouth to kiss them thankfully. "Dear man," she sighed, "so uncomplicated and simple."

Orville laughed. "Not so simple as all that, little lady."

"I mean uncomplicated in the larger sense, a man of straightforward and simple desires. Isn't that so?"

"I guess so," he agreed willingly enough. It didn't interest him much either way.

When she had finished smothering his hands in moist kisses and caresses, she placed one hand over each of her breasts. Jesus! Now, Orville could be sure something was up. And one thing was him.

"Aah," Perfidia sighed.

"Just a minute, little lady," Orville reminded her, "let's just get this cape off you. What say?"

Carefully, he removed the garment from her shoulders and put it over a chair. Perfidia patted her hair, her eyes alight and her bosom heaving. She pressed her body against the length of him.

"Aah, ha!" she gasped greedily. "Finally, I have found the man to measure up to my dear, dead Putzi."

"He was your husband? He died?" Orville asked.

"Yes." Orville didn't know about measuring up to a dead German baron. "We will have wine," Perfidia went on, getting off the subject of Putzi soon enough. "Open the bottle of Chateau Latour there on the cabinet while I make myself fresh."

She hurried across the room to what had to be the bath and closed the door behind her. Orville, still not understanding very much, attended to the wine. He removed the foil from the top of the bottle and then corkscrewed. The cork came out with a pop. He put his nose to the bottle. It was French, and to him it smelled just fine. He poured a little in a glass and tasted. It tasted okay too.

Then, without warning, her arms were around him from behind. The arms were bare, and Orville knew instinctively that the rest of her was too.

"Dear Orfeo," she whispered into the short hair on his neck. Without turning, he took in her scent. She smelled a little like the wine, fresh and tart. Hers was a strong and pungent body odor, and blended into it he recognized the waft of female desire, slightly sour, but so very distinctive to the male nostril. Perfidia ran her hands over his chest, then down his belly to his thighs and crotch, to grab his stuff.

"Jesus, little lady!"

She turned him and stepped away. Her nude body gleamed, making a statement as strong as her eyes. Perfidia was slim and firm. The tits stood out stiffly, the belly was round, and between her thighs a heavy patch of pure black hair glittered moistly.

"Whew! That's a hell of a figure, little lady." Truly, he had never seen anything like it.

"Take off your clothes, Orfeo," she said.

"Right!" Orville slid out of his jacket and tossed it on top of her cape. He loosened his blue tie and pulled it over his head. Next, he kicked off his shoes and, more quickly, noting her steamy expression, got out of his pants. Perfidia nodded. His jockey shorts were bulging, he noted proudly, and Perfidia's eyes fell and remained on that apex of his physique. He fooled with her a little, taking so much care to fold his pants along the creases and place them neatly on another chair. Orville was not especially bashful, but it always caused him some concern to reveal the full stature of his pecker. Shyly, he pulled down his jockeys. It sprang at her like a tiger.

"Yes." Perfidia breathed in slowly. "Yes." Without another word and with no shyness of her own, she approached and took it in her two hands. Orville had always been told he was well hung, and she seemed to agree. *"Dio,"* she murmured, lapsing into what he guessed was Italian. "A stallion, Orfeo."

"Well, not exactly, little lady," he said modestly.

Softly, she squeezed and rubbed, her eyes on him as she fondled. Orville touched his hands to her upright breasts, stroking the tiny black nipples. Perfidia's eyes closed, and she groaned heavily when he ran one hand along her side to her hip and between her legs. He felt the smooth, full-lipped thing. It was awash in a fluid stickiness.

"Orfeo," she said softly, "we have a custom in Capri . . ."

"Shall I call you Fido?" he asked, remembering French's use of the endearment.

"Good God, no, Orfeo." Her eyes blinked open. "Are you mad? That is a thing of the distant past."

"What about *Perf*, short for Perfidia?" he suggested. "I can't keep calling you Baroness. Perf . . . the perfect little body."

"Yes, fine, fine," she agreed impatiently. "But first, the custom of ancient Capri. It deals with wine and sacrifice."

Wine and sacrifice? That sounded a bit weird. Curiously, Orville remarked, "You are really hung up on Capri, aren't you, Perf?"

"Capri? My roots are in the rocky soil of Capri, Orfeo. Capri is my heaven."

She was a knock-out, Orville appreciated, but he could not quite escape the suspicion that she was a little bit off center. "Well, whatever is important to you personally is *very* important," he muttered.

"It is essential to me," Perfidia growled. "Come. It is painless but vital to me. I am one who lives by tradition."

"Tradition is very . . ."

"Yes, yes, Orfeo."

She led him to the cabinet, on which stood the bottle of French wine. Perfidia chose a wine glass with care and, surprisingly enough, placed it under his scrotum, pressing it upward so that his nuts dangled inside. Then after solemnly eyeing him, she poured red wine over his pecker and nuts until the glass was full. He felt the smarting of the tannic acid. Still, he didn't say anything. Jesus! This was one tradition he had never heard of.

"Don't move," Perfidia whispered. "Your organs must drink. Drink."

"It sure is cooling, Perf," he murmured, thinking that this sort of thing must date way back to the time the old Roman emperors carried on so badly on the Isle of Capri.

The wine was staining him, that had to be for sure. He hoped it was not bad for the skin.

Finally, after what seemed about five or ten minutes, Perfidia removed the glass and slowly lifted it to her mouth. Now he *was* surprised. "Perf . . . what're you doing that for?"

She did not answer. Her body shook massively as she sipped. "It is now goat's blood," she told him. "I drink of the goat's blood."

367

Jesus, it seemed to him this was vaguely blasphemous, maybe more than just vaguely. Perfidia's eyes widened as she drank, gulping and swallowing. She ran her tongue over her lips, which were stained red. She drank more deeply.

"What's it taste like?"

"It tastes of virility," she said. She threw her head back, drained the glass, and put it down.

"Well, that does it, I guess," Orville said.

"Yes." She smiled with satisfaction. "The tradition is unbroken. We can proceed."

Again she put her hands on him, then knelt and took him with her lips. "Dear, blessed, anointed being," she whispered. She turned her head to the side so she could take his nuts in her mouth. She gobbled on them as if they were not nuts but fruit. Orville's pecker jerked from the deliciousness of it. This was the sort of thing that had never interested Emily very much. Obviously, she knew naught of tradition.

"Hold it now, Perf. Now's the time . . ."

"Time? We have time."

"I mean, otherwise I'm going to squirt right across the room."

She let him go, dropped on her hands and knees in the middle of the carpet, and waggled her bottom at him. Jesus, Orville told himself, and now this?

"Is this the way you . . ." he started to ask.

"Yes," she grunted, "like this."

Well, if that was what she wanted, who was he to object? Orville knelt behind her, placing his hands on her hips. Perfidia reached up under him and placed his pecker at the entrance of her porthole. Slowly, he eased into the dark, viscous channel, another place where, as they said, the sun never shone. Perfidia loosed a restrained scream and, as he poled forward, she began to shake. Perspiration broke out on her back, and she butted against him. Orville began to sweat too. He hit bottom, and she grunted resoundingly. The wine, despite her mouth, still stung on his nuts and drove him on. He urged himself forward and, not a second later, a shrill animal sound burst from her throat and seemed to echo from the walls. She wailed incessantly now at each of his thrusts, sure to wake the neighbors. But he could not stop.

Nor did he pay any attention when the bedroom door opened. The kid was coming in? So what? Orville wasn't going to stop because of her.

"Mutti?" There was a big question mark in Marina's voice.

"Ugh, darling," Perfidia rasped. *"Mutti's* busy."

"Aber mutti . . ."

"Be quiet, darling," Perfidia cried hoarsely, angrily, "can't you see . . ."

The child was crouching behind him now but Orville was undeterred. Then he felt the little hand. It had seized him by the nuts and was dragging him down, trying to pull him out. He resisted, and in fact the frantic fingers accentuated his one last blast of energy. He rammed her, like an icebreaker, and exploded with a bang. His voice came to him simultaneously. "Hey! Let go of those goddamn things, goddamn it!"

But Marina held on fiercely. Perfidia collapsed under him into the carpet, panting and crying out.

"Tell her to let go of my balls!"

"Marina, Marina," Perfidia roared. *"Lass los!"*

At that, the grip relaxed. Orville turned around to look at her. The kid was glowering at him. What kind of crazy thing was this? Orville had always believed that screwing should be a private sort of thing.

"Jesus, kid, why don't you go in the other room and leave us alone?"

Perfidia rolled over on her back, her chest still rising

and falling. "Darling," she muttered, "go watch TV. *Geh, Geh,* Marina."

Marina then did something that Orville would not forgive. She spit in his face. He lashed out at her but missed. She hopped up and began calling him names in German. She *was* crazy. Finally, however, she marched to the door and slammed it.

"Oh, Orfeo," Perfidia said, "darling Orfeo. Soon we leave for Capri. You'll do the check Monday morning?"

"Sure I will," he said, then added bitterly, "Is that why we went through this *tradition*? So I'd be sure to do the check?"

"No, no," she cried. "When we have the check, we will leave, you and I."

"I've never been to Capri," Orville said dreamily. "I've never been to Europe except when I was in the Big Red One."

"And now you will become the Baron of Capri," Perfidia sighed.

"And her?" Orville demanded, pointing toward the other room.

"My little girl, of course. My little girl must come with us."

"And that bald-headed kid?"

"No," she said waspishly, "we will lose him at the airport."

Orville shook his head. "Better lose her too."

"What, darling?" She raised her head and stared at him sadly. "I could not."

"No dice," Orville said determinedly. "I don't want her around yanking on my balls every time we have a little . . ."

Perfidia was bewildered by his hardness. "But what would I do with her?"

Orville shook his head. "I don't know. But if it's going to be you and me, Perf, then it's *only* you and me."

He slid toward her and put his hands on her tits. With one finger, he traced the fine line of them, the curve, along her ribs. He leaned over and put his mouth on the left one, over the small black nipple that puckered, no bigger than a mole. Perfidia trembled at his touch, and tears came to her eyes. "Listen, Perf," Orville said, "you'll think of something."

"Orfeo," she groaned, "you are my master."

Thirty-Two

Sunday broke earlier in New York, and it was a rainy day. Evelyn made herself a pot of coffee and went back to bed with the *New York Times*. She read until noon and then got up, showered, and dressed carefully. She put on sheer black stockings and fastened them onto a garter belt. Nathan had always liked stockings and a garter belt. Then she chose a tweedy dress and pearls for her neck. By the time she was ready to leave, the rain had slackened. For the stroll up Park Avenue, she donned a raincoat and selected an umbrella. She was ready to leave at one-thirty.

Evelyn sat down for a moment to check the contents of her pocketbook. The most important thing was the long blank legal document that across the top and in impressive script announced it was a Last Will and Testament.

The air outside was damp and fresh from the rain. Evelyn walked slowly, for she did not have far to go. She studied the buildings, the taxicabs and their passengers, other pedestrians. Everything seemed to register on her brain as vividly as she could see, up ahead, the apartment buildings squatted around Central Park. This was a very important day. No one recognized her, and little did they know that the Sinclair fortune was about to change hands.

She arrived at his apartment house at ten minutes before two.

"Mr. Sinclair's suite," she told the elevator operator.

Evelyn was not at all surprised to be greeted at the elevator door by a roly-poly young man in a yellow-colored robe. He was bald and his lips were chubby. Evelyn had surmised from things Wade French had said that Nathan had gotten into some mighty deep water.

"Mrs. James?"

She nodded gravely. "Yes."

"Come in," the young man said. "I'm Paul. Mr. Sinclair is expecting you."

"Good."

Paul ushered her into an outer office and told her to wait one minute. He opened another door, then another. In these silent rooms, the noise was precise, distinct. In a little while, she heard him coming back.

"All right," Paul said. "Follow me."

Evelyn was nervous despite her resolve. Who wouldn't be? Not many people got to see the great Nathan Sinclair. But when she did see him, she would not have recognized the old man if she hadn't known she was in his apartment. Nathan was not merely old but ancient. His face had disintegrated into loose skin, which hung off the bones like wilted lettuce; a jutting nose, all bone; a sharp point of chin; and eyes that were weak and rheumy. Evelyn was shaken and ashamed, somehow, to be looking at him. Her eyes followed the line of his body, scarcely discernible under a light wool blanket.

"Nathan," Evelyn murmured, as if her heart would break.

His voice was a mere rustle of tissue in his throat. She could hardly hear him. "Evelyn, is it you? Evelyn, you've come to see me—at last."

His eyes became a bit more alert. They widened and seemed to take up most of his face. They were the only thing about him that still seemed alive. That and possibly his hair. The hair—what was left of it—was white verging on yellow. It was wispy and too long in the back.

"I've come to see you, Nathan," she said, as vitally as she could, for now she was frightened as well as nervous. "I've come because there are some important things . . ."

Paul tried to intervene. "Now is not the time for important things, Mrs. James. You can see that Mr. Sinclair is very tired."

Evelyn turned. She took Paul's arm in her fingers and led him away from the bed. "What have you done to him, you son of a bitch?" she demanded fiercely. "Does he have a doctor?"

Paul returned her look with blazing eyes. "I see to him. Mr. Sinclair does not like doctors," he said hostilely.

"He should see a doctor," she said flatly. "You are going to answer for this."

Behind them, Nathan commenced to sputter. "What? What are you saying, you two?"

Loudly, Evelyn said, "I want him to leave the room."

Paul began to protest, but Nathan waved his frail hand. "Leave."

Casting her a hateful look, Paul went to the door.

"Close it behind you," Evelyn ordered.

She sat down on a straight-backed chair by Nathan's bed, then leaned forward to do her duty. She kissed his repulsive cheek. His eyes twitched, and she saw a tear in the corner of his eye. But it was a permanent fixture. Strange fluid rimmed his eyelids. God, he was old. He was close to the end, she thought. To think that once . . . she shuddered and put her lips close to his wrinkled ear. "Wade French is in California with Perfidia," she told him, gauging her voice to the threshold of his deafness.

His body jerked. "What?"

"Yes. Wade and Perfidia. Wade is a traitor, Nathan. He has always been against you."

375

"Oh, Christ," he muttered. He tried to roar but couldn't. "Christ. A traitor. All of them are traitors. I should have known, Evelyn. This is *so*?"

"Yes, all of them are. Except for one person, Nathan."

He knew whom she meant. "Yes, Evelyn. You!" he groaned. "You're my friend. My last . . . my only friend."

"And this boy? Who is he?"

"Nobody," he whispered. "Paul. He takes care of me. The others that took care of me are gone—Simon and Shuster and Babylon."

The names. Insane, she told herself. "Where are the others?"

"Away, I think. They had to go away."

"Nathan," Evelyn said urgently, "you must let *me* take care of you now. You look so weak."

"Yes, I am weak," he admitted, a strange thing for Nathan Sinclair to acknowledge. But she noted that his eyes were still crafty. There was slyness in there; he judged that she could still be used. But he was wrong. "Will you help me, Evelyn?" he asked. "Will you . . . help me?"

She nodded. She was trying to decide when she might spring the legal document on him. It would be a terrible mistake to miscalculate now. Surreptitiously, she opened her pocketbook and slid the paper out. She slipped it onto the table beside his bed. She had reason to be careful. Her thoughts had transferred. Nathan was thinking money. Not so very odd, though, she thought. Money was the closest thing even to his fading heart.

"Evelyn," he whispered, "you're going to be taken care of . . . in my will."

"Oh, Nathan," she said, as if grief-stricken. "You shouldn't . . ."

"No, no, I have to tell you," he said eagerly. "I

know now that I'm going to die. For a while, I was sure I wouldn't . . . ever . . . die. But now I know. Seeing you again, I know. You're still so young. But you'll be old too, Evelyn."

"I know," she murmured.

"Will you stay with me until the end?" he asked. "Will you help me?"

"Yes." A tear trickled down her nose as she remembered some of the good things about him. There were *some*. But he had never been a man to deserve sorrow. "But what about the young man?"

"Send him away, Evelyn, send him away. I don't want him here anymore. Evelyn . . ." His voice became haunted. "He scares me. I think he hates me."

"All right, Nathan, I'll send him away." She had something else to tell him. "I'm divorcing Felix, Nathan. The book . . ."

He groaned again, shaking his head from side to side. "The book, Evelyn, the goddamned book. It is vicious about me, and hateful."

"Yes, Nathan." He was possessed by his hate and the fear of being hated.

"Will you be . . . kind to me, Evelyn?"

Evelyn blanched. This was *his* expression. It was an expression he'd always used, whenever she'd visited him in the lonely, empty hours at Sinclair Towers. She looked at the blanket. It was impossible, but his thighs were shuddering.

"Evelyn," he said softly, "I'm watching your face. Evelyn, if you're kind to me, you'll get everything. You promise?"

"Yes, Nathan," she said, her lips shaking, sickness in her soul, "I'll be kind to you. Wasn't I always?"

She moved from the chair and sat down beside the vanishing body. She placed one hand on his cheek, gently stroking. With the other, she reached for the legal paper.

Thirty-Three

"I've been thinking about what you said," Sally commented thoughtfully as they drove across the hills toward Mona Prissian's.

"What I said about what?" Peter had not mentioned his half-assed proposal again, having decided it was best for her to get back to it herself.

She stared soberly out the window of the Pinto. "You know, about the name change."

"Oh?"

Not looking at him, her hands crossed in her lap, she muttered, "I'll do it, if that's what you want. You're right. It would be convenient."

"Hey! Good! I'm glad you agree."

Sally tried to sound just as casual. A business arrangement? Sure. "When would you . . . uh, like to fit it in your schedule?"

"Well, there's a little preliminary paperwork. It might take a week or ten days. No use rushing ourselves." He glanced at her, his hands jumping on the steering wheel.

"All right," Sally said. "I'll write it in my book."

Hamilton nodded. "Nice day, isn't it? Our party, of course, bombed. I'm sure that'll be well reported in the *National Enquirer*."

"Yeah," she said laconically. She pursed her lips, trying to keep a straight face. But in a second she broke up. She yelled, "You bastard, Hamilton. You are a real ding-a-ling!"

"So are you, Silly Sally."

Sally thrust her hand across his stomach and hugged him.

"Hey, watch it! I'm driving!"

"I love you, Hamilton," she cried.

"Good," he said. "That makes it even more convenient, doesn't it?"

Mona's manservant, the redoubtable Wang, let them in the house and pointed them in the direction of poolside. Outside, in the warm sunshine, Mona and Felix were sitting side by side in deck chairs. Their hair was wet—so they'd been in the water. *Sans* what? . . . Probably everything, Hamilton decided.

"Dear people," Mona said, "I'm glad you're here."

"Hi, Peter, Sally," Felix called. He smiled toward them. Hamilton had never seen him so happy. He hadn't known Felix could smile so broadly. Obviously, he had overnighted chez Prissian.

"Wang is making brunch at this very moment," Mona chirped. Mona's renowned knockers, which filled her bra top, were outlined to final detail in the clinging wetness, as she jumped out of her deck chair and kissed Sally on the lips. She did the same for Hamilton, leaving his shirt damp.

"Hello," Sally said. She was still embarrassed by the fullness of the woman.

Hamilton made them bloody marys and sat down on a stool next to Sally's feet.

"Well," Felix drawled, "how are you feeling after your party? It was quite a night, wasn't it? I don't think I've ever witnessed such fireworks all at one time."

Hamilton grinned. "I was telling Sally we bombed in Hollywood."

"And after *we* left?" Mona asked.

"That was more or less it," Sally grumped. "Orville drove Madame P home and hasn't been seen since."

"My God," Felix exclaimed. "Do you think Orville can handle her?" he asked Hamilton.

Hamilton nodded nonchalantly. "I think Orville could handle anything. Cool as a cucumber—just like his little daughter."

"Cool? I'm not cool," Sally said.

"What about Jack?" Hamilton asked. "Any word from Jack?"

Mona looked around uneasily. "I hope not. No, I hope he comes and gets his hairless hound. There." She pointed. Duke had again chosen the bush on the other side of the pool for his resting place.

"Hello, there, Duke," Hamilton said. "Woof-woof."

The dog opened one mournful eye. That strenuous movement seemed enough to make the doorbell ring.

"I wonder who it could be," Mona said lazily. "Maybe your master, ugly beast!"

Felix looked worried. Hamilton read his mind—Felix feared it might be Virginia come to pull him out of the clutches of La Prissian.

"Sally," Felix said emotionally, giving word to his thought, "Virginia is very angry with me."

"I know," she said. "Don't feel bad, Felix. Peter told me all about it."

"You see," Mona said, very seriously for her, "Felix and I are enormously in love. *Enormously.* We are *servs* of love."

Servants of love? In servitude to love? Why couldn't Mona just say it?

"Virginia doesn't have any claim on you, Felix," Sally said anxiously.

"I know, Sally. But Virginia is so . . ."

"What?"

"I don't know, Sally. But lately, she seems so vulnerable."

Mona stood up. "I'd better see who that is," she said.

381

At that moment, Wang appeared. He gestured into the shadow of the doorway, behind him. The next thing they saw was a shining bald head. Christ, Hamilton thought angrily, it was one of those screwballs from the night before. What the hell did he mean coming here on a Sunday morning? Mona surely hadn't invited him to brunch.

"Oh," she said, just as put out but trying to be nice about it, "it's the young man from Peter's party."

In retrospect, it should have been a warning when Logan's dog, Duke, growled and came to with a burst of energy. Duke's legs were stiff under him, runty tail curled and ears bristling. Then Duke barked, a long yowl. Hadn't Logan said the hairless wonder didn't ever bark? The dog began to move menacingly around the pool.

"Duke!" Mona yelled, telling him to shut up.

Simon moved before the dog, so fast that no one had time to react. The action was like a single pulse of electricity. Simon slid around Wang, his eyes fixed furiously on Felix. Simon's hand came away from the inside of his jacket, and in the hand was a long knife. It flashed in the sun. Mona cried out and rushed forward, understanding before Hamilton that Felix was the target.

Duke launched himself from the side of the pool, but the knife had already come down, like a bolt. It entered Mona's body just above the left breast and with such fierceness that it must have cut straight to her heart. Simon wrenched it away, and the knife reappeared as if riding on gushing blood. Sally shrieked and Hamilton started to his feet.

But Simon was finished. Duke grabbed the knife arm in his wide mouth, and Hamilton heard the crunch of bone. Simon screamed but only for a split second. From behind him, Wang's hand descended and caught Simon at the side of the neck. Now there was an even more definitive cracking. Simon's head lurched forward, then back. He dropped to the concrete, and the knife slipped out of his hand and clattered into the pool, leaving a red trail behind it as it sank.

Felix screamed. "Oh, my God! Mona! Mona!" He fell out of his deck chair and crawled toward her body to kneel beside it in the widening pool of her blood, rubbing her hands and kissing her.

Duke yowled again and stared sorrowfully at Simon's dead face.

Thirty-Four

Wade French stood beside George, now so cold and unloving on the bed. George was angry with him; his body was so icy, the lips colorless and stiff.

"Wake up," French said curtly, "stop pretending. I know you're fooling me, George. Wake up, sport."

But George did not move. There was a musty froth at the corners of his mouth, and his neck was bruised. Why would that be, French asked himself.

He walked to the window. Through the slats in the blind, he could see the midday sun bright on Sunset Boulevard and, from the distance of the courts, he could hear the *whack* of tennis balls. He turned back to the bed.

"George?"

The eyes were wide open, staring vacantly at the ceiling.

French began to cry. Silently, he wept. He could not remember what had happened, that was the trouble. All he knew was that George had resisted, then given in and then defied him again.

The thing to do, French told himself, making an assessment, was to get dressed and very quietly go downstairs, pay his bill, and get back to New York. That was his judgment—get away from here.

He went into the bathroom and dried his tears. He turned on the shower and stepped inside. He washed himself very carefully, toweled down vigorously, and walked into the other room again. George had not moved a muscle.

French got a fresh pair of boxer shorts out of a

drawer and slipped into them. Yes, that was the ticket, get away from here. By the time he'd reached New York, no one would be the wiser. Was he to answer for what happened in his hotel room after he'd checked out? It was no more than circumstantial, at best—or worse. Prints? He retrieved the wet towel and put it around George's neck, scrubbing the skin, scrubbing it free of prints. He paused and thought about getting George out of the room. Was that possible on a busy Sunday without somebody seeing him? It *was* possible. What he needed was a broom closet, something like that.

Then, he told himself, what he'd do would be to take a vacation. Switzerland, yes, he smiled. He would go visit his money, as they'd said in those radio commercials.

He was putting his clothes carefully in his suitcase when the knock came at the door. If he hadn't been frightened, he told himself, he would have been inhuman. First things first. He rolled George off the bed. Then put his head next to the crack of the door and gruffly said, "Yes?"

A voice grunted. Probably Perfidia. He could get rid of her easily enough. He opened the door an inch and then, goddamn it, it was too late. There was a violent shove, and in an instant there was somebody else in the room with him.

He recognized the man immediately. It was the bald-headed one who called himself Shuster. Shuster was glaring at him, bug-eyed and, as he did so, he also pulled a long knife out of the inside of his jacket. French retreated across the room, and Shuster followed, wagging the knife at French's stomach.

"No," French said, "please . . . no!"

Shuster hissed, "Yes."

Then he saw the body.

"Bab-y-lon," he cried out, horrified.

386

Babylon, French thought wildly, Babylon?

Shuster's knife hand dropped and, French told himself, now was the time to jump him. Shuster would serve as his alibi. He had come back to the room, yes, after a night out, and what had he found? Yes, yes.

But then the phone rang. Shuster turned, whimpering noises choking his throat, tragic tears in his eyes. The phone rang. Shuster lifted the knife again, pointing it straight at French's midriff.

"Answer," he commanded, pointing at the phone.

Thank God, the phone, French thought. Help! But he knew Shuster would kill him before he could shout.

His hand was shaking so much, he could hardly hold the phone. "Yes?" His voice quavered.

The voice. Evelyn. "Wade," she said, "I have to tell you that Nathan Sinclair is dead. He died not more than five minutes ago."

In a dull voice, French repeated what she'd said. "Nathan Sinclair is dead. How?"

"Quietly," she said sardonically, "at home. He signed a new will. Isn't that ironic, Wade?"

"Evelyn, I love you!" French exclaimed. "You know that."

"Oh, yes," she said bitingly.

She hung up and French stood, transfixed, the phone hanging from his hand. Tears swept across his vision, and he became aware of the heavy thumping in his chest. The man, Shuster was his name, reached for the phone and put it back in its rest.

"I . . . please," French begged. "Sinclair is dead. It doesn't matter now. Sinclair is dead, I tell you."

Shuster waved the knife toward this dead creature called Babylon, or George. French knew that now, right now, was his only chance. He must overpower Shuster. French was a man of stature. They would believe him when he told them what happened.

But the pounding in his chest was heavier, deeper. It was like a man shouting inside him to get out.

"No," he pleaded, "please, no. Stop it!"

But then, too late, it was all pain and finality. The thumping, the sensation of hot, slashing pain. French's eyes were forced shut by the agony, and then he understood it all—everything converged in infinity.

Thirty-Five

Evelyn covered Nathan's face with the wool blanket and told Paul to call a doctor and the police. There was nothing unusual about such a death. Nathan had simply expired of old age. But God, as she'd just told French, it was ironic. At one moment, he was there, quivering under her hands, then the next moment, he was gone.

But, she thought philosophically, perhaps this was the way he would have chosen. It had always been so important to him in earlier years. And so she had fulfilled his last request for "kindness," this delivered after his signature on the bottom of the Last Will and Testament. Evelyn glanced at her hand. It had been the coup de grace.

Paul was sweating heavily, stinking of sour sweat, just as Nathan did, or had. They'd never even washed him. Under the blanket, the sight of his body had been almost more than she could stand, filthy, streaked with excrement, and covered with bedsores.

"You," she said disgustedly, "I want you to sign your name here, as a witness to this document."

"No," he said, snarling.

"Yes, sign."

"You can't make me."

"But I can pay you. Sign, and I'll pay you."

"How much?"

"We'll work that out later, after you've had a bath. It's all mine now. Sign or you'll get nothing."

"There's another will," he said stubbornly, resisting her. "It was to us."

"It won't hold up. They'd say you terrorized him. As it is, you mistreated him. I'll say so . . . that you killed him. *Sign!*"

He tried to get away from her, but she caught his saffron robe and yanked him around. She slapped him sharply across one cheek, then backhanded the other. "Sign, you miserable creature and I'll protect you!"

She put the paper down on his desk in the anteroom and the pen in his hand.

"It needs two signatures," Paul said.

"I'll get the other one, don't worry." She'd force French to sign it when he got back to New York and to carry it off. Whatever else he was, he was a respected legal person. "Sign it, you bastard!"

Paul scrawled a name at the bottom of the paper. Then he sat down and cried, his fat body trembling inside his robe.

Thirty-Six

Jack Logan was not displeased by Perfidia's Sunday morning proposition. It sounded hardhearted, even medieval, to negotiate about selling a human being, but Perfidia *was* hardhearted. She told him on the phone that she'd throw in Marina, along with the rights to the story about the end of Capri, for the hundred thousand dollars.

Yes, Perfidia said, Marina had her own passport. As she spoke, Logan was pondering something else. Namely, getting across the Mexican border by nightfall Monday. The idea was almost a godsend.

"All right, Perfidia," he murmured, as she talked, thinking she had to convince him. "All right . . ."

He'd found out from Beverly, his secretary, that the police had called Saturday morning. She was a beaver, Beverly, working Saturday morning. They'd wanted to know where he lived. Naturally, being loyal, she'd said she didn't know.

Logan thought it could only be one thing—the hit and run outside the zoo. Somebody had gotten his license plate number. Well, hell, he'd been at the office all day, hadn't he—hadn't he, Beverly? And somebody had obviously swiped his car, or borrowed it. He had a habit of leaving his keys in the thing in case somebody wanted to move it.

A little trip to Mexico was indicated, and it would be a joy to have the little girl with him. Logan loved her in a certain way. It was not every little girl that could do to Logan what Marina could and enjoy it so much. He thought she did enjoy it and she liked him. She'd sided with him when George had belted him.

"Perfidia, I agree, I agree." But why put it off? "I'll tell you what. I'll do the check today—you'll accept a personal check?"

She paused. "How do I know it's good?"

"It's a bank in the . . . Bahamas." Shit, he hated to tell people about that.

"All right," she said. "Bring it over tonight."

"Yes, I will," he promised.

Yes, yes, he thought, after they'd hung up, a little trip to Mexico was indicated. He wasn't sure he had enough in that account to cover the check, but what the hell? By then, he'd be long gone.

Orville was lying on the bed in his skivvies, smoking a Camel. It was just about high noon. Perfidia put the phone down and reached for the cigarette. She took a drag.

"He bought it," she said. "Aren't you proud of me, Orfeo?"

"Yeah, man," Orville said.

Perfidia started again about Capri, the villa there and the marvelous balmy weather, the Italian wine. "Orfeo," she mused, "you will be my baron and I will be your Perfidia Sinclair von Thurnsteil Jones."

"Yeah, Perf." He shifted his head on the pillow and looked at her. Her dusky skin moved him. It was almost as if Perfidia had had a light slap from the old tar brush. Outside, the California sun beamed down on his good fortune. He hadn't yet mentioned that he had still to get loose of Emily but, hell, Perfidia hadn't mentioned marriage, only sex and lots of it. "It's good," he said, "that you thought of marrying her to Logan. I think that's a very logical way out of this. He'll make a star out of her."

Perfidia laughed cleverly. "If he hadn't taken her,

Orfeo, he knew I'd turn him in for doing nasty things to a minor. . . . But I will miss my little girl." She frowned introspectively. "I wonder where my little boy has gotten to?"

"Fuck him," Orville said expansively. "Let's just hope he doesn't show up in Capri. I'm sure Logan will, sooner or later."

"We'll cross that bridge when we come to it, Orfeo," Perfidia said. "The main thing is that you will be with me, my great stud of a man."

But speaking of the little girl, there was an ear-splitting scream from the living room of the suite.

"Shit," Perfidia said, "George must be back."

Not exactly, Orville quickly understood. Marina burst through the door, a crouching figure close behind her. Orville sat up. He recognized the bald-headed kid who'd been at Pete's party.

"What the hell do you want?" Orville bawled. "Get out of here!"

The kid started screaming. "Her!" He pointed at Perfidia.

Perfidia exclaimed, "I thought he was a mute!"

"Bab-y-lon!" the bald-headed kid screamed again.

"Orfeo—this man is calling me the whore of Babylon!"

"*Mutti!*" Marina was terrified. Who wouldn't be? This kid was even crazier than she was. His eyes bucked and rolled in their sockets. From beneath his coat, he pulled out a long butcher knife. The blade was dripping.

"Blood!" Perfidia screeched.

Blood? Holy shit! This was a crisis and Orville, in a flash, remembered he had not met a crisis since the Battle of the Bulge. He jumped off the bed, putting himself heroically between the knife and Perfidia. Naturally, Orville was defenseless. The kid, his eyes frenzied, crept toward him, motioning him to get out of the way of danger. Small chance of that.

"Orfeo!" Perfidia shrieked.

Orville looked around for some form of weapon, anything. A chair would do, but he hadn't time to reach it and still stand between the knife and Perfidia.

Instinctively, he grabbed her heavy cape off the chair where he'd dropped it the night before. He whirled it at the kid's face, scraping him across the staring eyeballs. It was enough, thank God, to turn him. He thrust the knife at Orville, and Orville whipped the cape again. It wrapped around the kid's face, and he pulled hard, spinning him off balance. Next Orville flung the cape around the knife hand and jumped him. It was a dangerous thing to do, but it had to be done. He grabbed the wool-swathed hump of fist and knife and turned it back on the kid. He felt the point of the knife slice through the wool and then, as he pushed harder, he felt flesh give. The kid screamed and his eyes focused on Orville in disbelief. Orville's hand was wet as the blood leaped into the fabric. The kid began to go down, screaming like a stuck pig. Which, indeed, he was. For good measure, Orville clumped him in the balls with his knee.

He looked down. The kid had had it, or at least he was badly damaged. Orville extracted the knife from the soggy black cape, careful to leave the prints where they should be.

Then he stepped back. He looked at his shorts. He was drenched in warm blood, which already was turning rusty brown. Perfidia was sitting up in bed, her arms crossed over her bare bosom, rocking and moaning hysterically.

Orville folded his own arms over his chest and then put his bare foot on the kid's throat as he'd watched the gladiators do in Ben Hur.

"Vincit," he announced sternly. Naturally, he wasn't as calm and cool as he tried to sound. "Perfidia! Perfidia! Stop screeching and call the house dick, and tell him to get his ass up here—on the double!"

Thirty-Seven

Virginia decided that morning that, no matter what Felix said about it, she was canceling the Hawaiian part of their tour. Here, in California, she had reached the end of her patience. She was fed up with Felix and, more than that, she was fed up with *Powerhouse*. The thought—though it had not yet come to any more than that—of another book disgusted her. It had been her idea to do *Powerhouse* in the first place. Felix had been only lukewarm for the idea; then, politely, as Felix used to be, he had gone along with her. They'd begun working on it in the evenings, Felix's motive, Virginia now understood, to get away from Evelyn. Was it then, she wondered, when she'd first begun seriously to toy with him? She remembered the writing of the first sex scene. Felix had been terribly embarrassed. He sure as hell wasn't embarrassed anymore. It was uncomfortably clear to Virginia that Mona Prissian didn't make him shy.

"And so," Pauline Power told her husband Marcel, aging tycoon, "you see, my dear, it's over between us. I have found true love at last. He is a Corsican, a descendant of bandit chieftains. You must understand, he causes my blood to boil."

"You whore," Marcel stated darkly.

"Whore, no," Pauline replied calmly. "A woman in love, yes."

But Marcel Power was not to be thwarted. Enraged, menacingly, he approached her and, with one quick gesture, wrapped his hand in her thick blonde hair. "Whore!" he repeated, his voice louder and more threatening than she had ever heard it, "whore! We'll see about that." Cruelly, he twisted Pauline to the teak floor. She cried out in pain and suddenly became aware of a high wind blowing through the sails of the yacht.

Power stood over her, his legs bare under his Gucci dressing gown. He was like a defied Titan, Zeus of old. Reaching down, he seized the soft chenille of her Balmain evening gown and ripped it away from her body, revealing her pure white breasts, then her belly quaking in fright. And finally, the perfection of her loins—they were no longer *his*!

"Why is it," Power shouted, a froth on his lips, "that you never wear underwear anymore? Is it because of *him*, your Corsican bandit?"

Her eyes grew cold. He might think she was defeated, but she would never surrender. Nor would she mention Raoul's name before him. "Do your worst," she murmured.

Without another word, Marcel ripped off the sash of his gown and kicked aside his monogrammed velvet slippers. He knelt, roughly parting her stiffened legs. His manhood was engorged, as much with fury as with lust. Pauline covered her eyes with her hands, for she could not bear to look at it, not after Raoul's gentle love.

"And now, Marcel," she said, and it would be the last word she would ever speak to him, even if she lived forever, "and now I will hate you, Marcel, not merely despise you for the beast you are!"

"You've said it before, whore! What do I care about that?" Power screamed.

And then he was upon her. Pauline bit her lips and did not give him satisfaction by crying out. . . .

Virginia tossed the book on the floor. She would never look at it again. No more. She had to get back to New York. Brooding angrily, she propped pillows behind her head and stared at the wall. Felix had not even bothered to put in a token early-morning appearance at the hotel. He was gone, lost to her now. He was in love with Mona Prissian. And she, Virginia? Cruelly, she owned up. No one. She had no one. It had come to a pretty pass, hadn't it? Formerly so sought after and so elusive, the object of lust and desire in a hundred male hearts, and now not a murmur of an improper advance. No one had made a pass at her since Dallas. Had she suddenly become so unapproachable? What had happened? Had she changed? She couldn't think how. She was the same Virginia—available and, God knows, willing. Somehow, in some way, she felt diminished. She ran her hand down her chest, fondled her perfect breasts for a moment, and then put the palm flat on her belly. Nothing. Not a single answering throb or suggestion of passion requited. She had had it. Of desire, there was no more. The thought of a man, any man, turned her cold. She was not interested. She was finished. That was the word for it—finished.

Virginia closed her eyes and pressed her head against the pillows. Then a second wave of self-loathing burst on her. She had had it all, and now she had nothing. She was not even very good friends with her own daughter. She was nothing, as trashy as their book.

But, Christ, what would she do now? She didn't want to see Felix anymore. Did she hate him? No, she could not blame him. He hadn't done anything to her. Finally, after decades of friendship, they had made love, and it had led nowhere, at least for her. It had served to set *him* loose. Through her, he had apparently found himself. Helping him find himself, she had lost.

The inevitable question plagued her with maddening insistence. Did she *love* Felix now? Was that the problem, as simple as that? It had never seemed likely or possible that Virginia Preston could ever love Felix

James. Yet, it was logical, given her forlorn state of mind, that she did. There was no point in floundering around, trying to hide the truth. She loved Felix—and he loved Mona Prissian.

The next question was whether she should fight Mona Prissian for his affections. Perhaps she should go to Hawaii. She could get him back in Hawaii, under the bamboo trees—boom-boom.

Virginia threw the pillows aside and went into the bathroom. She threw cold water in her face, then studied herself in the mirror. Yes, she was the same Virginia Preston, femme fatale. She smiled and winked at herself drolly. No good to get so depressed. Before, she had pursued love as a form of sport, but now she would have to be less amateur and more professional about it. Virginia recognized that Mona Prissian was a formidable sex goddess. She, on the other hand, was finely tuned, like a musical instrument, a violin compared to Mona's bass drum. And there was the difference, the winning point. She was like a whip. Prissian was a piece of rope.

Virginia marched back into the living room of the suite and sat down to wait for him. He had to come back sometime. She turned on the TV set; it was six o'clock, time for the news. There was something about Washington, then Moscow, then Ulan Bator, where a revolution was in progress. The Russians were in trouble again. Virginia listened vaguely, her mind occupied by what she had decided would be the coming battle for Felix James. Then she sat up straight.

The announcer had begun a report on the death that day, in New York, of Nathan Sinclair, founder of the huge cosmetics conglomerate, House of Sinclair. At the age of eighty-eight, Sinclair's death had ended a story of American achievement, a Horatio Alger tale of the rise of a poor East Side lad to one of the Fortune Five Hundred. Sinclair had been thrice married, the last time to a fabled beauty and former model, Perfidia Strangel. The former Mrs. Sinclair now divided her time between her home in Capri and New York City. . . .

Perfidia Strangel—Virginia had forgotten about Perfidia's maiden name. Good heavens! So it had finally happened, she thought. Thoughtfully, Virginia stood up and turned off the TV set, then sat again to contemplate the news. Nathan—she remembered *Moisturizer II,* the night off Capri, the storm, the violence of the man, his towering arrogance but also his cleverness, business acumen, financial daring. Yes, Nathan, long of face, heavily muscled, a terrible man. Horatio Alger? No, a cruel rake, unprincipled, a man of no conscience.

And now he was dead. Virginia wondered if she should say a little prayer for him. No. Wherever he had gotten to, Nathan would be grinning and cursing still, despising anyone who had the nerve to feel sorry for him or regret his passing.

Virginia shivered. For a second, she could almost feel him there in the room with her. She gathered her dressing gown around her. He would be there, prying her legs apart, as he'd done to Pauline Power, whipping out his greasy thing. A wave of disgust swept her—appropriately, for she had toyed with Nathan too.

Fortunately, the phone rang to interrupt her thoughts.

"Yes."

"Virginia." The voice was Peter Hamilton's.

"Peter," she said shakily, "I just heard on the news—Nathan Sinclair is dead."

Hamilton's voice was very somber. "Virginia, never mind about that. Something *terrible* has happened. You've got to come over to my house right away."

"What! Not . . . Sally . . . Felix?" she whispered, terror-stricken.

"No, no, not them. Mona Prissian—she's dead. She

401

was stabbed—we were there for brunch. One of those guys from last night. He came in with a knife, Mona got in the way, protecting Felix. Be careful! The other one . . . come over right away. Felix is . . . I don't know. I think he needs you. . . ."

"Peter, Peter," Virginia cried.

But he'd hung up.

Thirty-Eight

Sally wrapped Felix in a blanket and sat him out on the terrace, and Peter brought him a large brandy.

"Peter . . ." Felix stared out at the trees, the gulch which ran down toward the city. "Peter, my God, did you ever see anything so terrible?"

"No, Felix, never," Hamilton said. "Look—I called Virginia."

Felix nodded slowly. He didn't care. He drank some brandy and turned his head toward Hamilton. His eyes were red from crying. There was dried blood on the back of his hand. "Peter, you know, I really did love that woman."

"I know, Felix . . . I'm sorry. It's the worst . . . Jesus, we don't even know who that guy was. Why?"

"Wang killed him," Felix muttered. "Maybe we'll never know now."

Wang, the karate chopper supreme. He was as much or more distraught than Felix. They'd brought him back here too, and he was now stretched out numbly in the study, with Logan's dog, Duke, slumbering at his side.

After the bloody half-second, before the police and paramedics had arrived at Mona's house, they'd done their best with her. But it had been no use. Fortunately, Hamilton remembered, she had already been gone, unconscious from the shock of the knife wound.

The police took down all the information and then they had waited and waited with the two dead bodies until the county coroner arrived.

The police weren't exactly callous, but over the

months of increasing Los Angeles mayhem, they had become fairly realistic about murder. One of them took Hamilton aside and asked him about Wang. Of course, there was nothing Hamilton could tell him except that he'd been brought here from the Far East by the dead woman, Mona Prissian. The detective had nodded and said, "One thing, he's pretty deadly. He must have broken that guy's neck in fourteen places."

And still they had no idea who he was. Simon, that's all they knew. Simon Brothers? From where?

Sally came out on the terrace. Her face was still white.

"The cop is here."

"What cop?"

"That detective named Brady. He wants to talk to you. Go on."

Sally sat down beside Felix, took his hand, and stroked it. Then she began crying again. She put her head down on the blanket, and Felix stroked her hair.

The detective beckoned for Hamilton to come outside with him. "You said there were two of these bald-headed guys at your party last night?"

"Yes, they had a card. It said Simon and Shuster Brothers, from New York."

"That's all?" Detective Brady shook his head. "It's very funny. We had another incident this afternoon. Another bald-headed guy—at the Beverly Hills Hotel."

"Jesus! What happened?"

Brady scratched his head. "Weird," he muttered, "very weird. Another bald-headed guy with a butcher knife. He knifed a man named . . ." He consulted his notebook. "A man named Wade French and evidently strangled another kid—who also happens to be bald-headed—then went down to a suite on the same floor and attacked a woman named Perfidia Sinclair, her daughter, and a man named Orville Jones."

404

"Oh, my God," Hamilton exclaimed. "What happened? Are they . . ."

"Well, they're okay and goddamn lucky, thanks to this Jones character. Somehow he fought him off and managed to stick the knife in this baldy's gut. He's dead." Brady stopped and stared at Hamilton, as if he might have the answer. Hamilton could only shake his head. "Well, so what we've got," he said, "is two bald-headed, no, three bald-headed guys, all dead, one actress, dead. And one man named Wade French, dead."

"French too?"

"All of them," Brady repeated. "Quite a little epidemic for a Sunday afternoon in Beverly Hills, wouldn't you say?"

"Son of a bitch," Hamilton breathed.

"We don't know who any of them are."

"We know Mona Prissian," Hamilton said. "She's an actress, was an actress. Wade French was an attorney from New York."

"Doing what out here?"

Hamilton shook his head. "Beats me. Business, I guess. He worked for a man named Nathan Sinclair. . . ." He remembered Virginia's news. "Christ, you're not going to believe this, but Sinclair died this afternoon in New York. But that must have been old age. He was old as the goddamn hills."

Brady's eyes were steady. "Do you see any connection?"

Hamilton chuckled glumly. "Not unless there's another bald-headed guy roaming around." Then he began to tremble as his intuition swept him. Maybe it was too wild, but slowly he said, "I don't want to complicate this, but I should tell you anyway. I don't know if you remember, but there was a case about a year ago. In Malibu. I had a wife . . . named Naomi." He lowered his eyes; it was still painful to relate. "She was, uh, shacked up with an actor named Scanlon. Anyway, to make a rotten story short, she and this man Scanlon were cut up. You people never were able to find out who did it. *But* . . ." He looked up. "It was knives. . . ."

Detective Brady wrote in his notebook again. "Unsolved, was it? We could check all the prints against what we'll have from today."

"The thing about it is," Hamilton said slowly, "Naomi was the daughter of Perfidia Sinclair, the woman one of the guys went after this afternoon. Perfidia is Nathan Sinclair's ex-wife, the guy who died in New York."

Brady became a little gruff. "Just a minute," he said, "this is getting kind of complicated. You're saying what happened last year to your wife might have some connection with today?"

"I'm not *saying*. I'm speculating . . ."

It was then that a cab, with Virginia inside, pulled up outside his house. She climbed out swiftly, gave the driver a bill, and told him to keep the change. "Peter, Peter!" she exclaimed.

"Easy, Virginia," Hamilton said. "This is Detective Brady. Virginia Preston."

"Where's Felix?"

"Inside, Virginia. Wait a second, Virginia—Wade French got killed today too."

That stopped her. Her face peaked anxiously. "Why? How?" she cried.

"A guy knifed him at the Beverly Hills Hotel. He was going to get Perfidia too. Orville stopped him!"

"Orville?"

"Yes," Brady said, "not only stopped him. He killed him."

"Orville?" Virginia repeated slowly.

"Yes, Virginia. Orville is a hero, isn't he?" he asked Brady.

"I suppose," Brady agreed. "Him and the China-man. And that dog."

"Heroes?" Virginia said sharply.

"Yeah," Brady said uncomfortably, "modern-day heroes."

"Good God!" Virginia shook her head and walked slowly into the house.

"Who's she?"

"Virginia Preston. She used to be married to one of the heroes."

"Not the Chinaman?"

"No, no, Orville Jones."

"Oh, yes," Brady said, "I've got his name written down already. Virginia Preston, you say . . ."

Thirty-Nine

Jack Logan had spent the afternoon getting his things together. He didn't want to travel heavy, but on the other hand, he needed enough clothes for an extended stay in Mexico, so he selected his wardrobe with care. Beach clothes were important, for he expected to be spending a lot of time lolling in the sand with delectable little Marina at his side. He would need several pairs of more formal slacks, a blazer or two, and four or five safari suits. Then underwear, socks, and shoes. Altogether, he had enough to fill two suitcases, and with whatever the little sexpot brought with her, there'd still be enough space left in the trunk of the Mercedes for the sack of cement. Logan chuckled to himself. The cement idea was a pretty good one, and it had always been in the back of his mind as an escape plan—if he ever needed one.

When it was dark enough, Logan went into his garden with a shovel and began digging beside a rosebush next to the orange tree. About a foot down, he hit the metal box. It was here that he had hidden his Krugerrands, the one-ounce coins of pure gold, each now worth at least five hundred and likely any day to jump toward a thousand. All it needed was another Middle East oil crisis.

Over the last, lush years, Logan had buried something like 800 of them, that is 800 ounces of gold, carefully paid for out of Logan Productions cost overruns and bonuses. At sixteen ounces to the pound, that would come to about fifty pounds in weight. When he had the box out of the ground, Logan next went into the garage for the bag of cement. Very carefully, he opened the top of the bag and began to stir in the coins with his hands. When he had completed that task as well as he could manage, he resealed the bag, using a big stapler and gaffer's tape from the studio. The hard part was lifting the bag now and getting it into the back of the Mercedes. Grunting, straining, bringing himself to the edge of hernia, he hoisted it to his knee and then heaved it into the trunk, all one hundred pounds or so. He spread burlap over the sack and then went inside for his suitcases.

It was a perfect idea. If anybody said anything, the reason for the cement was to hold down the ass end of the car, which had a tendency to ride high.

When he was ready he made himself a quick hamburger and had a bracing glass of Scotch. He caught the end of the seven o'clock news. Shit! From New York, it was reported that cosmetics czar Nathan Sinclair had died at the age of eighty-eight. Old bastard. Well, there wouldn't be any trouble now about the movie, would there? Not that it mattered. He chuckled to himself. Maybe he'd make the movie when he got to Capri. Yeah, that would be the perfect spot. It wouldn't be any great trick to combine the story of Nathan Sinclair with the last days of Capri. For a second, he wondered if Perfidia would get any more of the old fucker's money.

Then came the next news item, of great interest in Hollywood, the announcer said. Mona Prissian, English-born actress and star of many great hits, had been murdered during the afternoon, victim of a vicious knife assault.

Logan dropped his Scotch on the floor. His breath caught in his throat, and he choked. He cried out. Tears jumped to his eyes. Mona! Dead! But it was true because it was on the news. It was impossible for him to picture her as dead. He thought of the tits first. Yes,

410

those great, beautiful tits. It was not within reason that those tits could be dead.

He sat there dumbly for a good ten minutes before it occurred to him that this could be used to advantage. He called his answering service.

Brokenly, he asked, "Janie? Is it Janie? Yes. Janie, I've just had word of the death of Mona Prissian." He sobbed. "Janie, anybody calls me tonight or tomorrow, tell 'em I'm just grief-stricken over the loss of my most important star, and my dear friend. I'm going into seclusion, Janie. I'm going to the beach to sit and stare at the waves. . . ."

"Yes, Mr. Logan," she said. "I'm sorry. I truly am sorry."

Logan wrote the check for Perfidia and then drove straight to the Beverly Hills Hotel. The attendant took the Mercedes, and Logan went inside to the house phones and asked for Perfidia.

Her voice was strained. "Come up, Jack."

Logan found them in front of the television set, an open bottle of Dom Perignon on the coffee table. Perfidia and Orville were both in dressing gowns, but Marina was dressed in a white sailor suit with blue trim. Logan saw one suitcase parked by the door.

Logan made his face sorrowful. "I can't believe it about Mona."

"Jack," Perfidia said, "did you bring the check?"

"Yes." He eyed her owlishly, trying to tell her it was in really poor taste to be talking about money right now. "Here it is. My personal account. You'll have to trust me."

"I trust you, Jack," she said, as Orville nodded. "The police said it'd be all right if Marina goes away for a few days with her Uncle Jack. Anything to get her away from this city of terrible tragedy!"

"Why?" he demanded. "Not because of Mona.

411

You couldn't care less. Not because of Sinclair, that old shitheel!"

Perfidia's eyes rounded. "Jack, you don't know? Tragedy, here! Wade French was killed, and the man was going to kill me too. But Orville killed him first."

"Is this true?" Logan asked Orville.

Orville nodded. "True as blue. I killed the son of a bitch when he came after this little lady here."

"Mutti," Marina said gleefully. *"Das ist der Mann!"*

"Yes, darling, it's the man," Perfidia said. Her face darkened. "I'm giving this little girl into your personal care, Jack. Here is her passport. You pledge her safety and well-being?"

"Naturally," he grinned.

"Yeah," Orville said. "I hope so." He was not smiling so nonchalantly.

"So what?" Logan said. "You've got yours. What the hell do you care?"

"Jack—just go," Perfidia said wearily. She tightened her dressing gown. "We, Orfeo and I, must stay here a few more days. There are police formalities. But Marina can leave—now."

"Okay, let's get going then, honey. Are you all ready?"

"Fertig und loswartig," Marina chirped.

"Which means?"

"Ready and willing," Perfidia translated.

Perfidia watched sadly as Logan escorted Marina through the door, holding her affectionately by the arm, the suitcase in his other hand. Then she sighed and smiled tremulously. "Orfeo," she murmured, "alone at last."

"Yep, alone at last. Ready and willing."

With an eager shrug, Perfidia dropped her silken dressing gown from her shoulders. Orville stood up and gathered her body in his arms. "Orfeo." She sagged sideways and wet her lips.

Without another word, she dropped to her hands and knees. Jesus, Orville thought, she was so hot, she couldn't even wait to get into the bedroom. He smiled. The events of the afternoon had inspired in him a new and confident view of himself.

"Hey, there, Perf! Let's try something else here. He whapped her across the ass with the palm of his hand.

"Orfeo!"

"Roll over, honey," Orville said boisterously. "I want to try a new position. It's called the missionary one because all the missionaries used it whilst screwing all those native girls in the South Seas."

"But, Orfeo," Perfidia wailed.

"Come on, now, Perf, you're going to like it. Say— what'd you do with that check from Logan?"

"There." She pointed to it on the coffee table.

"Right on," Orville said. "Now, let's see."

Perfidia was on her back, staring at him moistly. Orville got down between her legs and grinned at her. She tried to smile. Her eyes were hopeful, and her lips quivered when he put his hands on her bare shoulders.

"Orfeo, aren't you going to take off your shirt?"

"Nope."

"Socks?"

"Nope," he said.

"Orfeo," she said, trying again to elude his dominance, "did I ever tell you about the strawberries and cream? It's another of our Capri traditions."

"Perf, if it is, it'll wait till we get there, won't it? Right now, I feel like a classical, traditional American-style grind. What about you?"

He knew she would say the right thing.

"God bless America," Perfidia said.

Forty

Time, the sweet hours of quiet and solitude, possessed a healing quality of their own. Felix, although drawn and sad, still shaken by the memory of Mona's death, had recovered enough by morning to dress himself and then to make some new arrangements for himself and Virginia. First, they cancelled their appearance on the Morris Scarlatti show. Then they were going to drive back to the hotel and check out. From there they would go out to Malibu for a few therapeutic days at the beachhouse of Felix's friends, Herbert and Nora Sacks. A few days by the sea would put him right again, Felix said.

But what about Wang? It seemed they had inherited him from Mona Prissian. After Virginia and Felix left, Hamilton and Sally drove to the Prissian house and, with the permission of the watchman on the scene, collected Wang's few belongings. Wang made it known that henceforth he would spread his sleeping mat in the Hamilton kitchen or downstairs study.

Hamilton had tried to get in touch with Logan but both his answering service and his secretary reported Jack was in such deep shock about Mona that he wasn't taking any calls. Well, Hamilton thought, there was nothing more they could do.

And they were well out of it. For the first time in over a year, Hamilton felt undefined black dread removed from his subconscious. For, later Monday, the police had reported to him that the fingerprints matched: the two men who had killed Naomi and Jeff

Scanlon were, no doubt, the same two dispatched so abruptly Sunday afternoon by Orville Jones and Wang.

Hamilton was happy to pass on this bit of information to Perfidia Sinclair von Thurnsteil. She took it with her usual grace. "Peter, dear boy, I never believed you did it anyway," she said.

"That's what I told her," Orville said. "I told her you wouldn't do a thing like that, Pete."

Perfidia chided him, "Orfeo, you were never familiar with the case."

Orfeo? Sally glanced quickly at Hamilton. They were sitting, the four of them, in the Polo Lounge having what amounted, it seemed, to a farewell drink. Perfidia and Orville were leaving for Capri.

Perfidia went on affectionately, "Orfeo has been the instrument of my revenge. He killed one of the men who killed my daughter. I shall never forget that."

Orville shrugged uncomfortably and Sally put her hand nervously to her face. "I hate to think about it."

"That your father can be a violent man, darling?" Perfidia asked. She smiled inwardly. "Sally, it was purely self-defense. My, you should have seen him. He was beautiful!"

"Perf," Orville objected. "I was saving my ass."

"Whatever," she said. "It was awful about Wade, wasn't it?"

Orville shook his head hopelessly. "Who would have thought a guy like that, with his three-piece suits, would be a queer?"

"Orfeo," Perfidia said in a kindly voice. "It is not our job to judge or our task to condemn."

Hamilton stared at her. He didn't believe it. Such soppy tolerance out of Perfidia rang like a cracked bell. What game was she playing now? Her next statement was positively awesome.

Solemnly, she said, "I have, you know, an unerring instinct for the doomed. I avoid them like anathema."

416

"Meaning Wade French?" Hamilton asked sharply.

She shrugged. "If you will."

Hamilton thought that this was perhaps the most terrible thing he had ever heard her say. She stared back at him calmly, her face set.

"Wade French *was* doomed," Perfidia stated, "from the very beginning."

Sally chuckled nervously. "But aren't we all?"

"Not that way," Hamilton muttered. Didn't she see? Perfidia embraced them, then kissed them good-bye without a second thought.

Orville interrupted, "Hey! *We're* alive—even if we are doomed. That comes later."

Sally nodded, then anxiously quipped, "Life is but death postponed." She wasn't smiling as she usually did when she launched a "saying."

"You put it so well," Hamilton said grimly.

"You don't get it, do you?" she cried. "You're so dense."

Orville cleared his throat. "Sally, I don't understand why you keep calling this man names."

"Because I love him," Sally murmured. "Can *you* understand that?"

Orville blinked and nodded.

Perfidia seized the moment. "Isn't that marvelous, Orfeo?" She smiled beatifically. "You see, Orfeo and I have likewise discovered love. Isn't that so, Orfeo?"

"Seems so, Perf," Orville acknowledged, with touching bashfulness.

"So . . ." Hamilton tried to think of acceptable words of approval. "You'll be leaving soon then?"

Orville nodded. "Perf knows a guy at the State Department to help me get a passport pronto. Then, yes, Pete," he said, "we're off to little old Capri, like the little old swallows."

"The swallows get back to Capistrano, not Capri,"

Sally corrected him sharply. "And what are *you* going to do over there, *Father*?"

"Live happily ever after, *Daughter*," Orville muttered.

"Whatever!" Perfidia said warmly. "Dear, we're almost related again," she told Hamilton. "This time I'll be your stepmother-in-law."

"Does that worry you?"

Perfidia, for a second, looked concerned. She realized what they were thinking but she did not respond in kind. Meekly—for Perfidia—she said, "No, no, of course not. I want you to be very happy, dear Peter."

"Jesus," Sally said, "don't be too sure! We're not married yet, you know. Who knows? Maybe we'll never get married."

"I see, darling," Perfidia said coolly. Then she sneered. "Whatever you may think, we *do* want you to be happy. Don't we, Orfeo?"

"Of course," Orville said. "And Sally wants us to be happy too. *Don't* you, Sally?"

Haltingly, Sally nodded. "Oh, yes—why not?"

Casually, Hamilton kept his eye on Perfidia and Orville. Their relationship had to be the most remarkable outcome of this remarkable mess. Was it possible for a woman like Perfidia to change? Did the leopard change its spots? How was Orville going to survive this strange woman?

Orville said thoughtfully, "Perfidia's got to stop in New York to pick up a check from the estate of this man Nathan Sinclair. *True*, Perfidia?" She nodded, her eyes like melting ice. "Yes, something Wade French arranged before his . . ."

"Untimely departure?" Sally said. "That was nice of him."

"Yes," Perfidia said, brushing aside the sarcasm, "he was a helpful man."

"Though doomed," Hamilton said softly.

"Yes," Perfidia continued, without a skipped beat. "Tragic for the world to lose such a clever lawyer."

"Don't you find it ironic that Evelyn James was with Sinclair when he died?" Hamilton asked.

"*Very* ironic," Perfidia said acidly. "Of course, they had always been very close. Not many people knew it, but I did—Evelyn was one of Nathan's long-time mistresses. Not that *I* cared," she drawled. "And, no, I don't think it would make any sense to tell Felix about it now, do you?"

"I doubt if he'd give a damn."

Orville advised heavily, "Let sleeping logs lie."

"Sleeping *dogs,* Father," Sally corrected him. "Speaking of which, what are we going to do with Jack's dog?"

"He came with Wang," Hamilton said. "We've got to keep him. He was one of the heroes of the afternoon."

"Yes," she grunted, "he's not the kind of dog I had in mind."

"Don't say anything about Duke," Hamilton warned her.

"Right, Sally," her father said. "Sometimes, Sally, you can be full of crap."

"Really? I wonder where I get that from?"

"From Virginia," Orville growled. "I'm as steady as the North Star and my course is set on automatic pilot."

Hamilton wondered how much it would take to jar him off that course.

But Perfidia laughed gleefully, exaggerating her good will. "Dear Sally, dear Orfeo," she cried, "you are two of a kind. You and Sally are nature's own comedians." Perfidia laid her long hand on Sally's arm. Sally started. "Darling, I want you to be my friend," Perfidia said ingratiatingly.

Sally regarded her frankly, staring at Perfidia's hand. "We'll see," she said.

Forty-One

Evelyn James watched Paul crouch by the seashore, cleaning sea bass. His arms moved energetically as he wielded his Swiss army knife. The top of his bare head shone in the hard coastal light.

Paul was not a bad sort, she had come to discover in the couple of days they'd been up in Maine. He was more cheerful now that he had been removed from the ghoulish surroundings of Nathan's life and death. He was letting his hair grow, and although he was too pudgy, the excess would disappear soon enough in the northern clime.

Evelyn gathered her saffron robe about her own skinny frame and paced down the steps outside the kitchen. She walked slowly toward Paul along the path that led to the Atlantic Ocean. Seeing her approach, he smiled. His facial expressions were reserved, and he tended to be secretive. There were things he obviously preferred not to discuss.

All he knew, and all he needed to know, was that Nathan Sinclair was dead and that Nathan's final will and testament was in the works. It was not going to be so easy now that Wade French was dead, vilely murdered in Los Angeles. The witnessing signatures, Evelyn knew, might not stand up in court. But, on the other hand, who was to say they wouldn't? She had slipped the Latino elevator operator in the Park Avenue building a fifty-dollar bill to add his name and address to the document. He would swear in court that he had been present during those final, hectic moments and had witnessed Nathan Sinclair signing his name for the very last time. If he didn't so swear in court, Evelyn had warned him, she would have him bumped off. Being from New York, he knew that such a hit was the easiest thing in the world to arrange.

Therefore, Evelyn was optimistic.

But there was something else—the dreams. Evelyn had dreamed of Nathan every night since his death. He came to her in her dreams in scorchingly realistic fashion, screaming, his eyes yellowish and fevered, and calling her a cunt. It must be, Evelyn thought, a function of the soul. Nathan's soul was restless, drifting between Heaven and Hell. But it would pass, she thought. He would finally take his place in hell, and his spirit would be exorcized from her dreams. She hoped so, anyway, for her nights had not been peaceful.

"I've finished," Paul said. He folded his knife and put it into the shallow pan along with the headless and gutted fish.

"You've done well," Evelyn said. "Come, let's go back to the house."

"Yes," he said. He looked at her meekly. "I like your robe."

"It's comfortable. It flows around me when I walk."

"Yes."

She walked beside him up the path to the house. Paul put the tray of cleaned fish down by the sink and said, "Now I will do the potatoes." He opened the drawer where she kept all the kitchen hardware and chose a small paring knife. He tested the blade with his thumb. "Sharp," he said.

"Yes." Fascinated, Evelyn watched as Paul unfurled long peels of potato skin and dropped them in the sink. When he'd finished, she said, "Fine. These are Maine potatoes, you know, the best. We'll just put them in a pot and let them cook."

"Yes," Paul said. He washed off the knife, dried it, and dropped it back in the drawer.

422

Evelyn looked at the clock on the wall over the refrigerator. It was three in the afternoon. "What shall we do now?" she asked. "We won't eat until five."

Paul smiled gently. His eyes were so warm. "I will worship you again," he said simply.

Evelyn nodded. Yes, that was fine. It would help put the shade of Nathan Sinclair out of her mind. She had braided her hair in the morning and wrapped it around her head, holding it fast, like a pastry roll, with hair pins. Standing there now, she removed the hair pins and allowed the hair to fall around her head.

"It is gorgeous," Paul observed.

"Yes."

She took his hand and led him away from the kitchen and up the staircase to the second floor. From the bedroom, there was a marvelous view of the sea. Evelyn was a water person and, as a water person, she was one who controlled other people, as she now controlled Paul.

Paul pulled off his robe and placed it carefully across the bed. Then he helped her out of her robe and meticulously laid it on top of his, matching the two garments perfectly.

"Yes," Paul sighed, "this is a oneness."

"Uh huh," she muttered.

Paul then assumed his worshipful position face down on the floor. He rested his head on his clasped hands while his substantial rump arched at the sky. Evelyn sat down on it, feeling his warm skin under her thighs.

"Ooom," Paul muttered, "ooom."

Whatever that meant, Evelyn did not know. But he always insisted on saying it as he faced east toward Greenwich, England, Calcutta, and Katmandu.

"Yes," Evelyn said, "ooom, kazoom."

Sitting astride him, she could see through the window to the shimmering sea.

Finally, having ooomed several more times, Paul took his hands from beneath his face and pressed his forehead to the floor. He reached for her feet and wiggled his fingers between her toes. He worked them gently, then more excitedly, rubbing the tips of her big toes with his thumbnails. Evelyn began to shake. Never, before meeting Paul, had she realized how sensitive toes were, and, luckily for her, he appeared to have an acute case of foot fetishism. He groaned as he caressed her toes.

Hell, Evelyn thought, what would Felix have said? And did she give a damn what he thought? No. It didn't matter anymore. Felix was past. Through half-closed eyes, Evelyn gazed out the window. Far away, it seemed to her, she could see Nathan's face. It rolled on the shining ocean like a tiny beach ball. Away, she thought, vile spirit!

Paul produced a long-drawn sigh of submission. "Mea culpa," he moaned, "mea culpa . . ."

Mea culpa of what? That didn't matter either, she told herself. Let him think he was guilty. Let him keep his guilt complex. It might be good for him. Now was her moment to get up. Evelyn stood and Paul rolled over on his back. His stalk was rigid. Carefully, Evelyn extended her right foot and put her toes under his testicles. He gasped and ejaculated all over the arch of her foot.

Well, she thought wearily, if that's what he liked, she didn't have any great objection to it. And, God, he really did worship her feet—her right foot probably more than the left one.

It seemed to her then, as she glanced outside again, that Nathan had come closer. Paul was licking her right foot. And suddenly, Nathan's face was at the window. His mouth, loose-lipped and gaping, formed the word: *Cunt!*

Evelyn laughed loudly and waved a finger at him.

Cunt, maybe so, but she was still alive, she shouted back at him.

Paul licked her ankle. His tongue was long and rough. Then her kneecaps. If he did this much longer, she told herself, he was going to lick the skin right off her bones.

Then, from outside, probably far out at sea, she heard the explosion of a cannon being fired. Maneuvers, she told herself, naval maneuvers. The next sound was a shrill, whistling one and, from the other side of the house, there was a resounding *clump*!

Impossible. But it *was* possible. There was a second explosion at sea and, again, the whistling approach of a projectile . . . and another *thump*! Christ, she thought, they were being shelled. The world had gone to war with a house in Maine.

Nathan, the son of a bitch. He had worked his magic. He was going to destroy them. His face was at the window, leering. The distant shot echoed, and this time she never heard the screech of the approaching shell.

Forty-Two

Strangely enough, Jack Logan was not having any great success with Marina von Thurnsteil. After safely clearing the border late Sunday night, he had made first for Ensenada, and they'd put up in a motel overlooking the fishing harbor. But now Logan was worried—it was too risky leaving the bag of cement in the car overnight. After all, what if somebody stole the car? That wouldn't be any big news in Mexico.

He worried all night and spent most of the dark hours sitting at the window of the room, keeping his eye on the Mercedes.

And Marina. So hot to get in his pants before and thereby running him into trouble on the way back from the zoo, now she wouldn't cooperate at all.

"No," she said repeatedly, *"nein."* She wouldn't sit with him at the window. *"Nein, ich will nicht."* She didn't want to.

"But, baby, here we are in old Mecc-ic-co, on the lam. Come on, baby, give us a little head."

"Nein!"

Sleepy and frustrated the next morning, he tried to decide what to do about the gold. Marina wanted to go swimming, so they continued on the road south. The going was slower now; the road detoured through muddy bypasses because of rain washouts during the winter. They made it to the beach near a little town called San Quentin, not to be confused with the prison, but still it gave Logan a squeamish feeling. And Marina was no more cooperative.

On the third day out, she brought up the subject of

marriage, and he was stunned. He hadn't figured the dopey kid knew there was such a thing.

"Okay, baby, okay, I'll marry you. Now what about a little . . ."

"Nein, nein!" Her black eyes were fiery but shrewd. There was nothing crazy about her now. *"Ich will das nicht tun."*

Which seemed to signify, he groaned to himself, that he wasn't getting any more until he'd married her. Christ, he thought disgustedly, this was a dramatic turn of events.

"All right, baby, all right." Logan thought maybe he could get some dumbo of a Mexican priest to perform the ceremony. But even that wouldn't be simple. First of all, he couldn't explain in Spanish what he wanted and, even if he lucked out, what about all the papers?

On the fourth day, advised by the suspicious owner of their motel of a good swimming beach a few miles to the south, Logan loaded the car and set off. The beach was miles from the main road, and the sand was worse than snow. But he made it.

"All right, baby," Logan said, "so go swimming."

Marina leaped out of the car and threw her clothes off. Logan sat down, his heels in the sand, and lit a cigar. There was not a soul in sight, and the beach must have been four miles long. Marina dashed into the light surf.

"Hey, baby," Logan shouted. "Be careful. There's sharks in these here waters."

But she didn't listen. She ran, naked, back and forth across the sand and in and out of the sparkling water, her perfect little ass flashing in the sun, her masterful little tits flopping, mad laughter in her throat.

Logan gulped. He admitted it—Marina grabbed at his heart strings.

Wet, her hair plastered to her head, she ran back up to him and flopped down in the sand beside him.

"Honey, you're beautiful," he murmured, "but you're going to get sand in your snatch."

Logan reached for one of her tits but, giggling, she slapped away his hand. He tried to grab her legs; she rolled away. She was some kind of nymphet. She jumped up and danced in the sand in front of him, bumping her juicy little twat in his face.

"You marry me—yes?"

"Yes," he said, "yes, yes."

"You are a nice man, Jack Logan," she said calmly then. Again, he was stunned. Where had that voice come from? "But I will need much money."

"Money? Money I've got, honey," he said, his eyes glued to her.

"Will you love me?"

"Yes, yes, I will."

"And I will be in the films?"

"Of course. I'm going to make you a star."

"Gut!" she cried, back in the German. "And when we are married, I will let you make love to me."

"Baby," Logan asked plaintively, "why didn't you ever talk before? Why did you always act like an idiot?"

Her eyes were amused. She brushed water off her face. "It was easier. People expect nothing and get nothing."

"And George?"

Marina snapped her fingers and laughed merrily. "You will come swimming, Jack Logan?"

"No. Yes. Maybe later. I've got to do something first. You can help me."

She walked back to the car with him, her bare body warm beside him. But now he was thinking about something else—the gold. He opened the trunk of the car and pointed at the bag of cement.

"We've got to get that out of there."

"Why?"

429

"Because. And it's heavy."

Together, straining for purchase, they lifted the heavy bag out and dropped it on the sand. Logan ripped the top open.

"Now we'll need something to put all the stuff in."

He didn't know what he was doing exactly, or why here. Marina was intensely curious. There was a pail in the back of the car. He set it in the sand beside the bag and then thrust his hand into the powdery cement. One by one, he drew out the coins and threw them in the pail.

"Gold," he said.

Marina's eyes flickered. "You are a pirate, finding gold in the sand. A buried treasure."

"Yeah," he said. He turned his head and kissed her. She gave him her mouth. Maybe he could buy it, he thought. "Kind of like . . . Bluebeard."

When Logan had found as many of the coins as he could with his hands, he got a blanket out of the car and spread it in the sand. He began pouring portions of the cement and gold mixture on the blanket. The loose coins gleamed in the sun. Marina knelt beside him, sweating and grunting, and helped. Soon the pail began to fill.

"What will we do with it?" she asked.

He shook his head. "I dunno. That's a problem."

"A bank," she suggested.

"Yeah, something."

In the end, they tossed the blanket to find the last of them. Then Logan put the pail back in the trunk and closed it.

"Now I'll have a swim," he said. "I need it. Christ, it's hot."

"Yes, come," she said seriously.

Logan unbuttoned his shirt, and Marina ran her hand through his chest hair. Admiringly, eagerly, she lipped his left nipple, over his heart. He took off his

430

shoes and socks, pulled down his pants, and then removed his shorts. Marina hefted him fondly. Evidently, the sight of all his riches made her more amenable.

Then she ran ahead of him toward the ocean. He caught up with her in knee-deep water and grabbed her in his arms. She laughed and giggled and drove him crazy. She drew him down in the water, wrapped her legs around him. On his knees and against her she let him inside.

"Ah," she cried, her head back, face laughing, hair dipping into the surf, "we are rich and famous."

"Yes, baby, yes, yes!" Logan yelled. Christ, he thought wonderously, he did love her. She gripped him warmly, moving and jerking against him, bringing the best out in him. And God, the tits! The red nipples rippled in the surf. And he was going to come, gloriously.

But then they were bumped. At first, Logan thought it was a log, that debris from the sea had hit him from behind. Then he saw the goddamned thing and screamed. It came right at them in the shallow water, hungrily, the fucking monster, and hit them again, ripping. He saw the blood in the surf and heard Marina scream. And then they were swept away.

Forty-Three

Orville watched Perfidia's ass and muscular legs as she strode ahead of him down the long white corridor toward the TWA departure lounge. She was wearing a light white dress that swayed with her body, for, on Orville's very strongly stated advice, she had laid aside her black widow's garb. Her shoes were white, too, and high-heeled, and upon her sleek black hair she wore a white, wide-brimmed felt hat. She was the most elegant woman in the airport, bar none, Orville thought, his self-satisfaction almost itchy enough to scratch. She belonged to him. For a moment there, what with her asinine Capri traditions and two-by-four preening, you might have thought that Orville had been sucked without a sound into her bloodstream. But, no way. Perfidia was his thing and, from now on, whatever traditions were practiced would be strictly of the cornbelt variety. Selfishly, Orville undressed her while she marched so regally in front of him, seeing the marbled flanks, the cleavage, the dimpled belly and slick thighs, the scintillating catchall of his delight. Perfidia was a hell of a woman, he thought, chuckling to himself, but *he* was hell on wheels.

Though they were up to nothing more serious than boarding a plane, Perfidia walked as though she had a far more serious purpose, some sort of rendezvous with destiny. And she did. Him. Now and then, she turned and smiled cunningly, to make sure he was close behind. Orville winked, showing his teeth in casual assurance. Maybe he'd be there, maybe he wouldn't. You never knew. But why shouldn't he be with her? He

433

knew what Sally thought—that Perfidia was going to eat him alive and spit him out like watermelon seeds, as she had that poor simp Wade French. But not bloody likely.

Orville didn't look too bad himself, if he did say so. He had, in a lightning stroke, stripped his Ohio bank account of its most exposed liquidity and now, of course, had made Perfidia put him on salary as her financial advisor. She hadn't liked the idea of paying for him and his extraordinary favors, but it had been a case of either-or. Either she did or he went to work for what was left of Logan Productions, the indication being that he would immediately stop payment on Logan's Bahamas check. Shit, Orville thought, it was probably going to bounce anyway—but Perfidia didn't know that.

Orville had also taken himself to Pete Hamilton's favorite men's store and bought a couple of new double-breasted blazers, which looked good on his spare frame, gray flannel pants and a few shirts and ties. He'd get the rest of his wardrobe in Italy. Perfidia had a tailor and, besides, there was probably a room full of Baron Putzi's classy gear.

Fortunately for him, he realized with a deadening jolt of the eyeballs, he was wearing what they called "shades" and would not be readily recognizable to anyone who'd known him in his previous life—anyone such as Emily.

And here, bearing down on him, though she didn't know it, was *Emily*!

She was being pushed along in a wheelchair by a sweaty black man and sweaty no wonder with that mass wedged into the contraption. Emily was very angry—so what else was new? There was a surly, belligerent look on her face that meant only one thing—if she ever found him, it would be curtains. No, he told himself, Emily was a far more fearsome woman than the hellion of Capri could ever be.

Orville averted his face as he neared her. Between her knees, she was gripping a pair of metal crutches, the perfect murder weapon. Over her shoulder, she bawled, "Hurry up!"

"Lady," said the man pushing the wheelchair, "I'm going as fast as I can. What's the big rush?"

"Rush? I'm looking for a man and I don't want him to get away!"

Jesus Christ, she sounded like some kind of a bounty hunter. Then he was abreast of her. Emily's cheeks were the color of putty and puffy with unsuppressed rage. Evidently, some slightly faulty intuition told her she was on the track, closing in on him like an overfed hound dog. She never knew how close she was.

Orville passed her and their lives began to diverge, hardly poignantly, with each of his steps. Safe now, he turned and watched as she disappeared into the terminal. He smiled: Close one door and another opens, he advised himself sardonically. This was probably the last he'd ever see of Emily Jones, neé Hackenbush, formerly svelte Bushwhacker Airlines stewardess.

"Orfeo!" Perfidia was waiting for him to catch up. "Orfeo, my love, why did you stop and leave me alone?" She put her hand on his arm and squeezed possessively. Perfidia didn't want to lose him either.

"I . . . I thought I saw somebody I knew once a long time ago."

"Darling, *caro,* Orfeo, we're always seeing people we think we knew once upon a time. But it's never them. It's not important even if it is them."

"Nope, Perf," Orville said, "not so. Once in a while it is them and that could be very important."

Hamilton hired the same limousine to pick up Virginia and Felix in Malibu and then to take them on to the airport. They were heading back to New York. It was a beautiful day for a drive to the beach. He and Sally huddled in the back seat.

"Let's neck," she said.

Hamilton studied her face. "If you remember, little miss," he reminded her, "you shocked the hell out of this man not much more than a week ago. Now . . . again?" He called up front. "Do you remember us?"

"Could I forget?" the driver asked.

Sally giggled and flicked her eyelashes on Hamilton's cheek. "Give us a kiss, handsome."

Hamilton gave up. He kissed her carefully, tasting the freshness, staring into her deep, clear eyes. "Minx," he said.

She whispered in his ear. "You were sensational this morning. I'm still warm thinking about it. Kiss me again, handsome."

"Go ahead," the driver said. "I don't care."

Virginia and Felix were packed and ready when they got to the Sacks' house, although Felix had reason again to be much preoccupied with the tragic ways of the world. They'd heard only a couple of days before about Evelyn's sudden death, blown away with her house in Maine, something freaky about a furnace valve. There had been another shattered body in the debris, whether man or woman it was not possible to say, although the guess was that it had been a man. Felix, according to Virginia's whispered report, was less affected by the end of Evelyn that he had been about Mona. It had been Act of God versus Act of Man.

They took the same places in the limousine they'd occupied that other day. The difference was that Virginia sat close to Felix and held his hand.

"Well, here we are," Virginia said, "the survivors. I'm surprised we've lived through this."

Felix didn't seem upset by the realistic tone of the

436

assessment. "We would have to say it's been an eventful time, wouldn't we? But I suppose it's all part of the learning process."

"What do you mean by that, Felix?" Virginia asked teasingly. "I suppose you're saying that I've finally matured."

"Virginia . . ."

"All's well that ends well," Sally said in a sing-song voice.

Virginia frowned. "It didn't end too well for some of us, dear."

"No," Felix said quietly, "it certainly didn't." He glanced at Hamilton as if he'd understand. "I still can't believe any of it actually happened. Evelyn . . ." For Evelyn, read Mona, Hamilton thought. "Evelyn . . . well, she got what she wanted. To die in Maine in her beloved house."

"Yes . . ." Virginia considered Evelyn for a moment, then said, "I'm surely glad we're going back to New York. Aren't you, Felix? The column will be like a nursery rhyme compared to all this."

Felix nodded. His thin face was as somber and serious as the old Felix's face had always been. Very softly, he said, "I'd say we've had enough excitement for a while." He looked at Hamilton again. "You may as well know—Virginia and I, we're going to share digs in New York."

Hamilton smiled. "Very subtle, Felix." He thought it would be best then to say something a bit unsentimental. "It took you two long enough to find each other."

"Only twenty years or so," Virginia said calmly. "But, you know, we've always been so busy. And there were always *other* attachments."

That was for him. Hamilton nodded. There, now, he saw it, the phenomenon—Virginia was departing his neighborhood. "Yes, always busy, busy, busy," he murmured.

Sally interrupted with a forced exclamation. "*Mother,* you're blushing! Well! But remember, the blush is the first bud on the rosebush of happiness."

Virginia seemed very flustered. "Sally, stop saying those God-awful things. Peter, I'm warning you, she is a terrible girl. She always was and she's going to drive you absolutely crazy."

Hamilton nodded. "I don't doubt it at all."

"Mother," Sally said, ominously, "try to be serious."

"Sally, I am serious. But with you around, that's very difficult."

"Mother, I have something very important to tell you. I hope you're not going to be shocked."

Virginia's eyes narrowed. "If this is another of those *aphorisms* of yours . . ."

"Mother," Sally said sternly, "you know an aphorism is God's way of slapping you on the back."

"Sally, blast it . . ."

"Mother, what I have to tell you is, you're going to be a grandmother. What do you think of that?"

Virginia's face froze. Her light blue eyes snapped. "What do you mean? You're trying to make me feel old again. How dare you! *When* did this happen?"

Sally grinned. "About two hours ago."

Virginia's face flushed. "You horrible girl! That is not amusing. I want to advise you of one thing. I'm far too young to be a grandmother. Aren't I, Felix?"

"No," Felix said. He patted her hand. "You're young and headstrong, irresponsible, but not too young to be a grandmother."

"Felix!" Virginia pouted. "I hate all of you."

But she didn't mean it, that was clear enough. She smiled sardonically at Sally, her eyes puzzled. Finally, perhaps, Virginia had realized her daughter was a kook.

Idly, Hamilton asked, "When do you start work on your next book?"

Virginia was shocked he would even mention such a thing. "No more books! That's it with the books, isn't it, Felix? It's too . . . dangerous."

"I don't know," Felix said, shaking his head, "I have a plot."

"Well, just forget it," Virginia said. Then she asked, "About what? Not about all this out here, I hope. Nobody would believe it."

"They're not supposed to, Virginia," Felix said.

Hamilton looked at the kook. "Why don't you write a book about Sally? She's a character."

Sally stared at him icily, then began to laugh. "Good idea, old cock," she exclaimed, then glanced at her mother. She was thinking hard. "Remember what Confucius said . . ." Virginia's face widened in horror. Sally told them, defenseless as they were, "Confucius said the last chapter is but the first in life's unravelling tale."

ALSO BY BARNEY LEASON

Over 1.5 million copies in print!

☐ 41-031-X   416 pages $2.95

Welcome to the land of silk and money, where the world's most glamorous — and amorous — come to spend their endless nights dancing chic-to-chic under dazzling lights.

Here, against the outrageously decadent background of Beverly Hills — its hopscotch bedrooms and grand estates, posh restaurants and luxurious hotels — is the shocking story of society dame Belle Cooper and her passionate struggle to become a woman of integrity and independent means.

Not since *Scruples* has a novel laid bare the lives — and loves — of people who have everything...and will pay any price for *more*!

More Bestselling Fiction from Pinnacle